EARTH SCREAM

BOOK 6 IN THE EARTH SONG SERIES

NICK COOK

VOICE FROM THE CLOUDS

ABOUT THE AUTHOR

Somewhere back in the mists of time, Nick was born in the great
sprawling metropolis of London. He grew up in a family where
art was always a huge influence. Tapping into this, Nick finished
college with a fine art degree tucked into his back pocket. Faced
with the prospect of actually trying to make a living from his
talents, he plunged into the emerging video game industry back
in the eighties. It was the start of a long career and he produced
graphics for many of the top-selling games on the early home
computers, including *Aliens* and *Enduro Racer*. Those
pioneering games may look crude now, but back then they were
considered to be cutting edge. As the industry exploded into the
one we know today, Nick's career went supernova. He worked on
titles such as *X-Com*, and set up two studios, which produced

Warzone 2100 and the *Conflict: Desert Storm* series. He has around forty published titles to his name.

As great as the video game industry is, a little voice kept nagging inside Nick's head, and at the end of 2006 he was finally ready to pursue his other passion as a full-time career: writing. Many years later, he completed his first trilogy, *Cloud Riders*. And the rest, as they say, is history.

Nick has many interests, from space exploration and astronomy to travelling the world. He has flown light aircraft and microlights, an experience he used as research for *Cloud Riders*. He's always loved to cook, but then you'd expect it with his surname. His writing in many ways reflects his own curiosity about the world around him. He loves to let his imagination run riot to pose the question: *What if?*

For everyone who has ever dreamed of becoming an astronaut and experiencing the overview effect for themselves.

CHAPTER ONE

I, Lauren Stelleck, gazed out across the silver grey landscape painted with a dark palette of shadows. Small to huge boulders the size of a car stretched away within the endless crater field, where meteorites had bombarded the surface over countless millennia. And over all of it, enhancing the sheer ethereal beauty of what I was witnessing, was a perfect, pitch black sky. Within it hung a tapestry of pinprick stars not enlarged by the effect of our own atmosphere. Certainly the brilliance of the ribbon of the Milky Way through it, the hub of our own galaxy, was clearer than any view I'd ever seen back on Earth, and it was beyond breathtaking.

This was the stuff of my dreams and it filled me with an utter sense of awe, because here I was on our very own moon.

But for all the stark grandeur of this lunar landscape, I was also under no illusions about just how hostile this wasteland expanse of rocks and craters really was. And that made me exceedingly grateful for the trickle of warmth through my suit's heating and the cooling capillary system designed to cope with vast changes in temperature. One moment you could be standing in freezing minus 173 Celsius in the shade on our moon and the next being baked alive when the sun came up in 127 Celsius heat. If the suit's temperature control system failed for any reason I would either be boiled or frozen alive within moments. A cheery thought about the stark reality of just how hazardous life in space really was for humans, a life which rarely looked that way in the movies.

I had the clearest ever memory of gazing at the moon through my first refractor as a child. In that moment, that glowing object in the sky that nightly changed from a crescent to a disc and back again, had been transformed into a very real place for me now. And like many, I'd watched the original moon landing recordings online, watched every film and documentary ever made about them, not to mention reading the crew's autobiographies. We were talking here about someone truly obsessed with all things space, who even had a signed autobiography of Buzz Aldrin sitting in their storage locker back at Eden. That was thanks to Aunt Lucy snagging it for me when Buzz had come to Oxford to do a talk. How I had dreamed about becoming an astronaut myself one day until the usual reality of adult life had swept those fantasies away. But in my former life, I had done the next best thing. I'd chosen a job where I could journey into the cosmos, courtesy of the Lovell telescope where I worked as a radio astronomer.

If you had told me now where I would be standing today, as I approached the fifth anniversary of leaving my old job, I would have laughed in your face.

So here, impossibly, I was, peering through the faceplate of my space helmet, standing on the surface of the moon. As always, the tech of the Sky Dreamer corp, who funded and supplied everything that made this mission possible, was once again over-delivering. The image intensifier built into my helmet was doing a great job of turning the tapestry of darkness into a landscape of boulders and sloping angles — the surface around me. The summit of the ridge was just above me, so temptingly close now. This formation at my current location marked the terminus that separated day from night and was rimmed with the light of our sun.

Strictly speaking, I should have had Pink Floyd's *Dark Side of the Moon* thumping out of my helmet speakers about now, because that's exactly where I was standing in the shadows. But rather than choosing the classic rock song that Steve, my old boss from Jodrell Bank, would have totally approved of, I had a very specific soundtrack in mind ready for the big moment when I reached the top.

I glanced back down the slope towards the temporary moon outpost that we'd established around the dig site, picked out by the spotlights mounted on tripods around it. Plumes of dirt were being kicked up in slow motion thanks to the low-G environment. This flurry of activity was down to our six Tin Head robots that had been fitted with excavation shovels for this mission. They had continued the digging that they'd started the previous day without so much as a five-second break and had already more than proved themselves adept at the task. Beyond the cloud of dirt being thrown up by their tireless work, our spaceships *Ariel*, an $X103$, and the much bigger *Thor*, an $X104$, stood on their landing legs. Both looked like something straight out of the pages of an old sci-fi B-movie, sitting there on the lunar surface with the stars stretching away behind them. I'd once referred to them as craft, but now I'd ridden *Ariel* out into space as far as our moon, they would now and always be known to me as *ships* capable of voyaging out into the unknown, just like our ancient ancestors had once done in sailing ships.

But of the sheer romance of space exploration there was a brutal reality also in play. Having learnt lessons from our previous encounters with the Overseers, standing guard in a constellation above the dig site were a dozen WASPs that had been adapted for space work with manoeuvring thrusters. Ruby was on the case, keeping an eye out in case — like on so many occasions before — the Overseers attempted to steam in and destroy the micro mind before we'd had a chance to retrieve it. Not that this was our only line of defence — above them, about three klicks up, was the shining pill-shaped Tic Tac craft of the Greys, also standing guard. The enigmatic aliens who rarely ever directly communicated with us had taken up guard positions just like this one over every micro mind that had been activated by the Resonancy Generator broadcast, which we'd discovered hidden beneath the ocean bed off the shores of Cuba.

Yes, it had been quite the year of activity since then.

Niki was visible outside *Thor* with a couple of his crew, keeping a close eye on the excavation's progress as well as keeping half an eye on me.

Part of me — even though I'd insisted on doing this trip solo for all sorts of reasons — really wished that Jack and Mike were here right now. I knew both of them would have so got a kick out of this, but they were back on Earth preparing for a final dig at Angkor Wat in Cambodia, where we'd dropped them off with another team. Even a trip to the moon hadn't been enough to tempt Jack away from the chance to excavate that famous archaeological location, and it turned out that Mike had been desperate to visit the place too. But just as I had always dreamed of travelling to the moon as a child, for Jack it had been the siren call of discovering ancient sites inspired by museum exhibitions with his uncle. So this mission had been as easy a choice for me as Angkor Wat had been for Jack. We both marched to slightly different beats but we so got each other's madness.

As I continued my ascent up through the darkness, I returned my attention to the slope ahead of me.

The low-G environment of the moon had taken some getting

used to, especially emerging from the new airlock that had been fitted inside *Ariel's* ramp. Within the ship the REV drive had been tweaked to keep gravity to one G. But the moment I'd first moved out through the gravity bubble surrounding *Ariel*, I'd felt my weight drop away significantly as I'd taken my first step on the surface of the moon. I'd been so caught out by the sudden change in gravity that it had almost sent me sprawling to faceplant the surface. At least, I would have if Niki hadn't caught me, grinning and wagging his finger.

After that I quickly confirmed the presence of the micro mind beneath the surface with the Empyrean Key. Once the excavation had started in earnest there wasn't exactly a lot for me to do, so rather than just mooch around in the cockpit, here I was heading out on a little excursion from the excavation site that lay on the dark side of the moon.

Apart from my own breathing and the sounds of my space suit's motors and compressors whirring away in the background, there was distinct, dare I say otherworldly silence all around me. Although our moon had the thinnest of thin atmospheres, it was still basically considered to be a vacuum. And as Niki had already lectured me on multiple occasions before I went off on this jaunt, one mishap could end up ripping my suit and I would be as good as dead.

'*No one in space can hear you scream,*' he'd said. Quite the motivational speaker was our Niki, when he wanted to be. He was also able to talk pure geek when he wanted to make a point to me.

Of course I'd taken his advice seriously and had run at least three suit diagnostics during the thousand-metre slow motion hike to the top of this ridge. In reality, if I did have a problem Erin would have *Ariel* here in seconds if she needed to. But the small risk that was left was all worth it, just to see Earth with my mark one eyeball, like those early *Apollo* astronauts had, rather than just seeing it displayed on a virtual cockpit. Yes, this imminent experience was going to be at a whole other level to anything I'd experienced so far.

'Hey, Lauren, are you doing okay up there?' Erin's voice said over the comm channel. 'I'm reading an elevated heart rate and your oxygen consumption is up.'

'Sorry, that's just me getting excited about what I'm about to see,' I replied.

'Oh, you mean the live view of the dawn on Earth as seen from space.'

'That's the one.'

'Then I'll leave you in peace to enjoy it. You should have about twenty minutes to yourself until it's time for Lucy to merge with this latest micro mind discovery.'

'Then I intend to make the most of every glorious moment of it,' I replied. 'Just call me if Niki needs me back down at the dig site for any reason.'

'Will do,' Erin replied. 'Over and out for now.'

Erin, our not so new pilot, had fitted right into the team. But that was still tinged with sadness for me as it was difficult not to still think of it as Tom's seat, one that she had taken over after he died during the Cuba mission. Even a year's passing hadn't softened the loss of someone who'd become like a mentor to me.

But what would he say if he could see me now?

The darkness was starting to thin as the penumbra glowing around the edges of the rock began to grow stronger along the ridge above me. A quick check of the clock on my HUD confirmed I had about thirty seconds until the dawn rose over the moon as it emerged from Earth's shadow.

I quickened my pace, painfully aware now that my heart rate was climbing rapidly, but thankfully the comm channel remained quiet — although Erin would be watching my EVA like a hawk. For now she was obviously just putting it down to sheer excitement rather than any thought that I was about to have a cardiac emergency.

I stepped round a boulder sticking out of the regolith surface to see the summit just a few metres in front of me up a final steep slope. Leaning into them to keep my balance, I took several steps, my boots burrowing into the loose surface. Then at last I crested the top and my heart squeezed at the sheer, jaw dropping beauty of what I was witnessing.

Stretched out before me was Oceanus Procellarum, also more poetically known as the Ocean of Storms, a hopelessly romantic name for the expanse of moon dust that was just beginning to be illuminated with the faint browns of the building dawn. More impressive in the foreground was the huge Grimaldi Crater. The chunk of space rock that had carved that particular hole out of the moon's surface must have been enormous. But all that paled into significance compared to the beauty of our very own Earth hanging in space in the distance. And that incredible view was everything that I'd ever dreamed of.

Our homeworld's dark side was currently facing me, the lights of our major cities from Sidney to Tokyo flaming like fireflies in the night. The eastern rim of our planet was already glowing with the light of the sun beyond, the rays of which were now beginning to hit the moon. Yes, I'd timed my ascent perfectly.

My helmet's visor was already automatically responding to the rapidly growing brightness, electronically dimming the view so my retinas wouldn't get burned out by what was coming any moment now.

Then like the classic diamond ring shot of a solar eclipse, the sun began to emerge around the right side of Earth, illuminating its edge with a beautiful crescent of golds and blues.

I let out a gasp as I took in the breathtaking sight. As the full intensity of the sunlight reached the moon it was suddenly lit with bright whites and greys in a narrow band of brilliance, starting at the foot of the ridge that I was standing on. The band of luminance across the face of the moon began to widen rapidly, shadows rushing away from it like a pack of black wolves pursued by the light.

Tears had already filled my eyes at the beauty of the spectacle that I was witnessing.

'Wow, that's quite the sight,' Erin said over my comm link. 'I hope you don't mind but I was keeping an eye on it via your helmet's camera feed.'

'Not at all — something like this needs to be shared,' I replied.

I blinked away my tears, desperate now to scratch my eyes, but which so wasn't going to happen until I could get back to *Ariel* to take my helmet off.

I stood there for a moment, soaking that extraordinary view in, breathing it into the depths of my very soul.

That's what this was all about, protecting our extraordinary world at any cost from the extinction event that was heading our way in the form of the Kimprak invasion force, an invasion force that was now less than a year away. In preparation for that alien invasion day, we'd thankfully made great progress with our defence *plan b*, namely the increased production of the X-craft fleet tenfold.

That was mainly thanks to Serenity Base's automated production plant all the way out on 16 Psyche, a giant metallic asteroid between the orbits of Mars and Jupiter. The combined fleet of craft had grown to just over eight hundred in number. With all the railguns built into the *Pangolin* contingent of Troy's Sol fleet, as it had now been named, Jodie was sure that that alone would be enough to inflict serious damage on the Kimprak's asteroid ship, possibly even destroy it if the bombardment was sustained for long enough. The final line of defence would be two hundred ships of the Earth wing, which would fall under my command — and it really *was* our last line of defence if those damn invaders got past Troy.

This was our *plan b*, although it had taken a significant step forward since we'd activated the Resonancy Generator signal in the sea off Cuba. Since then, over the last year, it had been like an all you can eat buffet for Lucy, who'd had merged with micro mind after micro mind as we'd recovered them. Now, after this latest micro mind recovery mission on the moon and the handful of others that Troy and his team had already recovered from across the solar system, we were finally down to our last one. And that was the mission that Jack and Mike were executing in the dead of night at Angkor Wat.

This was a moments day for all sorts of reasons because after four years of constant effort we were hopefully going to unlock the plan that the Angelus had so carefully locked away in the depths of the micro minds' combined psyches. Certainly, based on what we'd already seen of the Angelus tech — and if the incredible megastructure of the Resonancy Generator was anything to go by — it promised to be truly mind-blowing, whatever it was.

The sun had cleared the limb of the earth and the crescent was growing into the new day.

I gazed out at the Earth, lost in wonder at just how fragile it looked under that thin blue atmosphere. And on that ball of rock that we called home were countless billions of souls who, whether they realised it or not, were relying on us to defend them from the nightmare that was coming for each and every one of them.

I lingered a moment longer, gazing at that exquisite planet of ours just hanging there in the darkness of space. She was truly beautiful.

But as amazing as the view was, it wasn't the only reason I was here.

I cleared my throat. 'Delphi, please play the live radio broadcast of "Earth Song".'

'Relaying NASA satellite feed,' she said.

The particular satellite that I was about to be patched into was part of a network that had been launched by the space agency to secretly listen to the eerie electric and magnetic radio signals that our world had been sending into space.

As Delphi responded to my request, the familiar crackles and flutters of the song's radio signature filled my headphones. At once my synaesthesia, the gift that allowed my brain to see certain sounds as images, began to kick in. If I thought the view was breathtaking before, it was nothing compared to what I could see now and certainly something that no other human had ever seen before.

The whole globe was now covered with a mesmerising display of pulsating geometric symbols flowing into each other, constantly changing in a bewildering pattern. Colours ranged from blues to greens with occasional flashes of red, which rippled out from the poles in a cascade of light. It was like a mathematician had dreamed up a geometric version of the Aurora Borealis and had painted our whole world with dancing patterns of light.

This was what Earth Song was for me, a tangible manifestation of what others heard as a random series of the radio moans and warbles of our world. But to my synaesthesia, that same sound revealed its hidden structure, the visual language of a race who'd once visited our planet and left their footprints permanently there.

As I watched, mesmerised by the light show, Niki's voice came over the comm, breaking my reverie.

'Hi, Lauren, we've just finished unearthing the micro mind. You need to get yourself back down here to do the honours,' he said.

I reluctantly dragged my eyes away from the magnificent view. 'On my way,' I replied.

'As always, take it slowly and very, very carefully.'

'Will do.'

I took one last mental snapshot of that incredible spectacle — a moment I knew I'd remember for the rest of my life, however long that would be — and then headed back towards the excavation site and the unearthed micro mind that was waiting for me to activate it with my Empyrean Key.

CHAPTER TWO

I STARTED to head back down the slope, being careful not to pick up too much speed that would end up with me tumbling end over end and damaging my suit. If that happened I might be tempted to embrace the option of rapid death rather than face the look of disappointment on Niki's face whilst he lectured me about how he'd trusted me to be careful on my excursion.

Below me, the Tin Heads had dug the wide trench deeper to expose the micro mind in the short time that I'd been away. The robots being impervious to a lack of an atmosphere — not to mention the fact that they were tireless workers — made them ideal for an operation like this, one which would have been a lot more dangerous and challenging for humans to carry out in this hostile environment.

The Tin Heads had become something of a fixture on most missions these days, with a handful normally kept stored in the large cargo bay of the X104s. Niki had even been testing the robots in training exercises with heavy machine guns and the results had apparently been promising. He'd kept threatening to try them out on an actual combat mission, controlled from the

CIC of our X-craft by our weapons officers. At the rate we were going with the WASP swarms already an active part of our missions, just a single one of our ships was slowly turning into a formidable war machine in its own right.

The dozen robots had all backed away from the site, their hydraulic shovels raised. Right in the middle of the trench they had just finished digging sat a freshly excavated blue micro mind, glowing like a gem in the darkness. If it hadn't been a tetrahedron shape — and the fact it was also lit up — the scene before me would have been a dead ringer from that moment in the film 2001 *Space Odyssey* where they uncovered the monolith on the moon.

I managed to reach the bottom of the ridge without any major mishaps apart from a few brief, heartbeat-skipping slides. But then at last safely back on the plateau, I immediately began to break into the lolloping sort of skipping run as perfected by the *Apollo* astronauts, which I'd practised back in a vast, deep water training pool at Eden. Thankfully, since stepping out of *Ariel's* artificial gravity field onto the surface and since my first stumble, I'd found myself adapting quickly to the low-G environment.

With hopping steps I made my way towards Niki, who was standing on the edge of the site waiting for me. As I neared, I couldn't make his face out behind his gold faceplate, just a fisheye reflection of me in my white suit with its blue arm flashes, bouncing over the lunar surface towards him.

As I neared, Niki turned towards me.

'Good, you're here at last. No problems on your little field trip?' he said over my helmet's speakers.

I beamed at him then realised a micro second afterwards that it was entirely wasted behind my tinted visor.

'Not a misstep anywhere and thank you for letting me indulge a childhood dream,' I said.

I might not have been able to see him smile either, but I could still hear his chuckle. 'No problem, anyway we're all set here for you to do your party piece and activate the micro mind.'

'Then I'd better get to it onboard *Ariel* to do the honours. You'd better do the same before the electronic pulse happens when they merge.'

'Yes, I don't much fancy being out here in the open if our space suits suddenly go offline as a result,' Niki replied.

We separated and I headed towards *Ariel* as Niki made his way back to *Thor,* the massive hundred-metres-wide *Pangolin* X104 ship that was easily twice the size of our own X103.

'What about the Tin Heads?' I asked over the comm as I started heading up the ramp.

'Nothing to worry about there,' Niki replied. 'Along with all our X-craft, their systems have recently been hardened by Jodie's Forge team to cope with even a nuclear EM pulse, so they can easily cope with this.'

'Good to know,' I said, entering the new internal airlock that had been fitted to *Ariel*, another recent upgrade to all the fleet to allow space flight manoeuvres if needed without depressurising the whole cabin to make EVAs.

I pressed my palm on the control and the door slid sideways to reveal an airlock room large enough to hold four people in a squeeze. As I entered it, full Earth gravity grabbed onto me again. Even though I knew it had been coming, it still managed to take me by surprise as my normal body returned with a vengeance. It was certainly hard not to feel like a baby elephant after the low gravity environment beyond *Ariel's* hull that I'd been so enjoying just a moment ago. As I entered the artificial gravity field generated by *Ariel's* antigravity REV drive, I felt the full Earth gravity grabbing onto me again.

I waited until the light above the door into the cockpit cycled green before unclipping my helmet. A moment later I was entering the cockpit to see Erin and Ruby watching the three-sixty virtual cockpit display showing the dig site, together with an enhanced view of the night sky rendered with nebulas glowing like multicoloured jewels, just like the best astrophotography thanks to the video frame stacking system, another recent upgrade by the Forge team back at Eden. The effect made the view even more stunning than the one I'd just seen with my mark one eyeballs.

'So we're almost ready for the grand finale, Commander,' Ruby said as she glanced over towards me, her hand in a bucket of popcorn that she'd smuggled onboard.

Her in-flight snack was partly down to Alice, the president of Sky Dreamer. The previous night, in homage to our journey to the moon mission, she'd arranged a showing of *First Man* on Eden's giant IMAX screen. It had been very well attended, especially by the X-craft flight crews, including ourselves, who all fancied ourselves as astronauts.

'Yes, all set,' I replied as I took out the Empyrean Key, a carved stone ball smaller than a baseball, from my bag and headed over to the flight deck railing to look down at the site.

The sloped trench that the Tin Heads had dug was glowing a dull blue light just faintly visible in the heart of the crystal tetrahedron-shaped micro mind. That indicated the AI was currently in a dormant, low-power state.

I held up the Empyrean Key. 'Delphi, please initiate carrier tone,' I said.

At once Eden's AI system, which was baked into all of our systems from ships to even our spacesuits, responded. 'Broadcasting carrier tone now,' she said with her usual *nothing's going to flap me* tone.

A crystal clear note rang out in the cockpit and with a flicker of light a single shape flickered into existence over the stone orb. It was a single dot icon with radiating circular lines around it. What I was about to do was almost down to muscle memory now as I had done this for all the other micro minds we'd recovered over the last year where I'd attended the excavations in person. The ones that I hadn't, on the moons discovered around our solar system, had been brought back to Eden for me to activate. But of course with our moon being so relatively close to Earth, I'd insisted on training up as an astronaut and doing this mission in person.

With a tilt of my wrist I rotated into the selection window and then rolled my hand forwards like I was twisting a motorcycle accelerator. The icon turned green as it was activated. Immediately the micro mind outside flared with intense blue light, casting shadows from the Tin Heads gathered around the tetrahedron crystal and adding to the already surreal, almost religious nature of the experience as they stood witness to what was about to happen.

Erin shook her head. 'To think that micro mind has remained hidden here on the moon for countless thousands of years and just like that, it starts up the first time.'

'Only because the Resonancy Generator was able to remotely activate the self-repair function,' I replied. 'Thanks to that they had plenty of time to sort themselves out after that Kimprak virus wreaked so much havoc in their systems. Anyway, we'd better give Lucy a call to say that we're ready for her.'

'Did someone mention my name?' Lucy's voice said over the comm channel. 'I arrived ages ago and have been mooching around up here in a geostationary orbit getting seriously bored.'

'Yes, sorry about that, but like always we need to keep you away from any potential danger in case of any Overseer attacks,' I replied.

'Yes, I know, the same old. Anyway, I'm on my way down to you now.'

Despite the logistical headache of recovering a micro mind from the moon, this had all gone remarkably smoothly so far. But the problem was that not every recovery had gone to plan like this. On way too many occasions the Overseers had still managed to crash the party with sneak attacks that had got past our defences, and even the Tic Tacs. So far we'd lost a total of seven micro minds thanks to heavy missile bombardments that had overwhelmed our attempts to protect the micro minds that had been destroyed. We knew the total number of the micro minds woken up by the Resonancy Generator broadcast had been a hundred. That was thanks to some sub-space carrier witchcraft using quantum entanglement and them pinging Lucy to say that they were awake.

The consequences of those seven losses even Lucy didn't know, but now we were down to just the last two micro minds that we'd discover, one way or another by the end of today, and we'd learn if we'd finally retrieved enough of them to achieve critical mass. I was keeping everything crossed that hopefully, after all these years of searching and putting our lives on the line, that it would finally unlock whatever secret was buried so deep in the AI's matrix structure. Whatever it was, everyone's instincts were that it was going to be off the scale compared to anything we'd witnessed so far.

We all looked up to the heavens on the virtual cockpit to see a bright blue star separate itself from the constellations overhead and start to speed directly down towards us. The point of light quickly zipped between the three gleaming white pill-shaped craft of the Greys, who were standing guard over the site. Then it grew larger fast until it resolved itself into Lucy's merged micro mind ship as she hurtled to an absolute stop directly over our heads. Her star-shaped crystal had merged with so many other micro minds that from a distance she now resembled a sphere rather than a star-shaped craft.

'Okay, time for the grand finale,' Lucy said over the comm channel.

Her merged micro mind ship pulsed with several bursts of staccato light and the micro mind in the excavated trench did the same far below her. The lights sequence grew even faster in both craft, a choreographed dance of patterns as the ground around the dig site started to vibrate slightly beneath our feet. Then with a slight shudder, the freshly recovered micro mind started to slowly rise from the surface, freeing itself of the last remains of the moon regolith with a shower of glittering moon dust.

Lucy and the other AI, now both shining like blue suns, started to close upon each other.

This was a dance that I'd personally watched over ninety-three times in the last year, but it would always be endlessly fascinating to me. To witness the way that two separate Angelus AIs fused together to become one, was to glimpse the astonishing Angelus multi-dimensional technology of E8 that race was able to so effortlessly utilise.

Rather than take the good five minutes of solid effort to get out of my suit and not wanting to miss a beat of what was about to happen, I just rested my arms on the railing as I looked out at the virtual cockpit around the flight deck.

Outside, Lucy and the moon micro mind closed the distance between each other to less than thirty metres. As they closed to less than touching distance, bursts of lightning started to flicker between the two craft as a bright blue aura enveloped both of them. Then with a cascade of blinding sparks, the two entities started to slide into each as though their crystal structures had turned from a solid into a clay-like malleable structure.

'I'm seeing the usual build of electromagnetic energy on our sensors,' Ruby said. 'Get ready for that EM pulse.'

Sure enough a pulse of blinding light erupted from both Angelus AIs and our virtual cockpit turned white as *Ariel's* cameras were briefly overwhelmed. But then the view faded quickly back to normal to reveal Lucy's merged micro minds hanging above us against the canopy of stars. Not that I could see them but I knew an extra three points were now incorporated into Lucy's star-shaped craft from the freshly absorbed micro mind.

I mentally held my breath. Would this micro mind be enough to finally trigger the big reveal of the Angelus secret buried within their collective AI consciousnesses?

'Oh come on already,' Erin said as she sat forward in her seat and drummed her fingers on the arms.

Ruby grabbed another handful of popcorn as she looked at her readouts. 'Energy signature is returning to normal, so any minute now...'

'And I'm back,' Lucy said. 'Yep, everything checks out here.' Her face appeared in a video window overlaid on the virtual cockpit. 'But I'm afraid, before you all ask, that once again this micro mind isn't the magic key that we were hoping for.'

I slumped back into my seat. 'Oh bloody hell, this means that everything is coming down to the wire and is down to Jack and Mike recovering that final micro mind at Angkor Wat.'

'And if that still isn't enough to finally unlock whatever this secret Angelus defence for our world is, what then?' Erin asked.

'We'll cross that bridge as and when we get to it, but let's try to stay positive everyone,' I said. Those might have been my actual words, but inside I was desperately worried about exactly that outcome myself.

'Okay, it looks like it's a wrap,' Niki's voice said over the comm. 'I'm going to start loading the Tin Heads back onboard.'

'We're going to head back to Earth now to join Jack and Mike on their final dig,' I replied.

'Let's just hope micro mind one hundred is the magic number,' Niki replied. 'Anyway, we'll see you there.'

'Okay, over and out for now,' I replied.

I glanced back up towards our homeworld that was just

peeking above the moon ridge. The sooner we got back there the sooner we could wrap up over four and half years of effort. And if this went as we all hoped it would, I for one intended to party with the best of them. Maybe I'd even give Ruby a run for her money at the Rock Garden in Eden to mark what could well be one of the most important moments for our species in its entire history.

CHAPTER THREE

THE EARTH WAS GROWING LARGER by the second as *Ariel* raced towards it. Lucy had already made her own way back as we'd departed the moon's orbit. Despite the esoteric nature of our own REV drive, we still relied on a far more conventional propulsion system. So as we'd left the moon, Erin had rotated our ship until our homeworld was sitting directly overhead in our cockpit as a small disc. Then she'd engaged our multimode rocket thrusters to push us through space.

As usual, the Tic Tacs had simply vanished without a word; once again the enigmatic Greys piloting them — true to form — hadn't once attempted to communicate with us. One moment they were there and the next they simply weren't. Lucy had once told us that she strongly suspected they used some form of multi-dimensional drive to power their ships. Mike, our very own cutting edge physicist, had agreed, saying it would explain how that allowed them to pull their disappearing acts as they jumped between parallel realities. It was another example of how these days, I just accepted as fact the extraordinary things that would have once well and truly blown my mind.

The journey back had been uneventful and as always our X103 was more nimble than Niki's X104. We'd quickly outpaced Niki and his flight crew onboard *Thor*, which was about forty minutes between us as Erin had accelerated to around fifty thousand miles per hour. For a real world comparison that was easily twice the speed the old *Apollo* missions travelled between the Earth and the moon. Of course, both our X-craft were capable of even greater speeds, thanks to the new helical drives that had been fitted to the whole fleet. Ultimately, the system was capable of approaching eighty percent the speed of light, but only after a week of steady acceleration, which ruled it out when you were talking about relatively short hops like this to our own moon. The plan was they would hopefully come into their own as and when we had to head out to meet the Kimprak asteroid ship in just over six months to engage and hopefully destroy it.

Erin adjusted our flight path to the right hand side of our world, towards the night side of where our destination was.

'How far out are we, Erin?' I asked.

'ETA to Angkor Wat is around twelve minutes,' she replied.

I nodded. 'And any update from Jack and Mike, Ruby?'

'Nothing so far, but you know what Jack is like.'

'Yes, he's probably up to his neck in mud right about now and having the time of his life on the dig,' I replied. 'He was telling me that Angkor Wat is yet another site on his archaeological bucket list.'

Ruby chuckled. 'Yeah, the guy practically elbowed all the other flight crews out of the way to make sure that he was the one who got to excavate the site. And remind me who authorised that again?' She smirked at me.

'Hey, what can I say? It seems that dating the Commander has its upsides.'

'You can say that again,' Erin replied. But then she caught the look I cast her way and she immediately held up her hands. 'Sorry, Lauren, I didn't mean to say actually say that out loud.'

Ruby laughed. 'Hey, don't you worry, you're fitting right in with the team. After all it's our job to keep it real for our very own esteemed Earth Fleet Commander.'

'Yeah, yeah, yeah,' I replied, shaking my head at her.

But to be honest that was exactly how I liked things to be, just the right side of informal when we weren't in a life or death situation. I certainly viewed every single one of our team as close friends and that now included Erin, who it felt like had been with us from the start.

Of course, that didn't stop me thinking of Tom, who I found myself missing each and every day. I'd even sometimes found myself gazing at his name on the memorial wall in Eden. His death had hit me far harder than I expected and had also dramatically underlined how none of us were invulnerable. Often, when I was certain I was alone, I asked his advice at the memorial wall when something had come up; in many ways it had become my very own version of a church. Of course, Tom never answered me, which would have so freaked me out if he had. So, forever practical, instead I'd just tried to put myself in his shoes and approach things as he would have if he'd still been with us.

When he'd been buried and because he had no other living relatives, Alice had asked me if there was anything from his belongings that I'd like to keep. Most things had been too painful to even look at, but one thing that I'd hung onto was a book. Although I'd half expected his shelves to be crammed with classic spy novels, the lone book that I'd found was a hardback copy of Shakespeare's *The Tempest*. I'd never had Tom pegged as a Shakespeare fan, but the pages of that book had been well-thumbed and it was obviously a much loved copy. Partly out of intrigue about why it had obviously meant a lot to him, I'd helped myself to that book, but had left everything else. So far it had sat on the shelf in the bedroom that I shared with Jack in Alice's house. But as soon as I had a moment I was going to dive in and read it, maybe hopefully gaining an insight as to why it had meant so much to Tom.

Ruby glanced across at me. 'We have an incoming radio transmission from Troy, who is running some fleet manoeuvre drills.'

'Put him up on the main screen, number one.'

Ruby just rolled her eyes at my lame Trekkie joke and a moment later, Troy's face was looking out at us from the deck of *Falcon One*, his X104.

'So I hear congratulations are in order from Niki and your moon mission went without a hitch,' he said in his smooth Texan accent.

'Yes, everything went as smoothy as we hoped and the micro mind has already merged with Lucy.'

'So ninety-nine recovered and just one to go?'

'Exactly, and as we haven't heard otherwise, Jack and Mike are hopefully on track too with the final micro mind.'

'Good to hear. So how does it feel to take your first steps on another world, Lauren?'

I smiled to myself. Yes, Troy so got why this had been such a big moment for me.

'Pretty mind-blowing actually,' I replied. 'Talk about all my childhood fantasies of becoming an astronaut coming true all at once. Anyway, how have your manoeuvres been going with the new ships that you've been building out there?'

'Very well and you should see what I'm seeing right now because it's quite the sight. Actually, why don't we do exactly that? I'm relaying our virtual cockpit view so you can see it for yourselves.'

'Okay, got it,' Ruby said. 'Transferring data feed now.'

The view of Earth on our virtual cockpit vanished and was replaced by what Troy and his crew were currently witnessing from the bridge of *Falcon*.

Over two hundred X-craft, a mixture of X103s and X104s were stretched out ahead of us on the virtual view, all labelled with metadata tags listing armaments and current velocity. They were arranged into a diamond pattern and were making a perfectly coordinated roll, training fire onto a distant asteroid that was being chiselled down to size by the impacts from minigun and railgun rounds.

Under Troy's command — who had been building from raw materials mined directly from Psyche 16 — the Serenity Base fleet had grown considerably over the last year. And that push towards hitting increased production numbers of building six ships a day had been supported by the expansion. The base had grown significantly to a compliment of over a thousand people. Troy's larger Sol fleet, as it had become known, would be our first line of defence against the alien mechanised invasion force called the Kimprak. The latest computer simulation estimated that their giant asteroid ship — propelled by a massive, laser-powered solar sail — was starting to get uncomfortably close at just over six months out. The second line of defence would be our much smaller Earth fleet, under my command, and was projected to be just three hundred ships by the time the Kimprak arrived. The hope was that if everything went to plan they wouldn't be needed. *If*...

'Wow, when did your fleet get that big, Troy?' Erin asked.

'Yeah, I know, but it's hardly a surprise after we started hitting our production targets out of the park,' Troy replied. 'And as you can see right now, I've been starting to intensify the training program for the fleet so they can work as one coherent battle unit. We've even started sending out small squadrons of three ships on regular patrols to help everyone get into the right mindset for what's to come. Talking of which, have you started training with Earth fleet yet, Lauren?'

'As much as I hate to say it, no. But our priority has been to track down the last of the micro minds. Hopefully, after today we can start to turn our minds to training, like you guys.'

Troy nodded. 'Tracking down those micro minds absolutely has to take number one priority. After all, if you do manage to activate the Angelus plan, Eden's plan b can be put on ice and we can bring all these crews and their ships home.'

'That would be the best outcome,' I replied. 'But even so, I'm so still coming out to see you guys when we have a chance.'

'Good, now you've earned your space wings, I'll keep you to that. Especially if you bring another bottle of that Highland Park you sent out on the last supply mission to Serenity.'

'Oh, don't you worry, I will.'

Erin looked up from her flight console. 'Lauren, we're starting to detect the outer reaches of Earth's gravity well and we need to get ready to enter the atmosphere,' she said.

'Sounds like you're about to get busy, so let's sign off for now,' Troy said.

'Okay, we'll be in contact afterwards. Take care and hope your manoeuvres go well.'

'Oh they will,' Troy replied with a smile.

The video window closed and once again we were treated to an uninterrupted view of the Earth, which now filled up most of the forward section of our spherical cockpit screen.

Over the months I'd found myself comparing notes more and more with Troy, whose experience I was increasingly leaning on for guidance. If he'd picked up on the impostor syndrome that I was severely suffering from in my role as Commander, so far at least he'd been too much of a gentleman to say anything. And then, of course, was Niki, whose considerable military experience had been a real asset. He'd also taken on the role of mentor to me, maybe because — as I suspected privately — Troy had had a quiet word with him. Whatever the reason, one day Niki had just announced he was going to put me through an intensive period of strategic training. It had included wargaming, recreating classic military conflicts with something I'd once made the mistake of calling *toy soldiers* to his face when we'd been playing the historical battle of Waterloo. It hadn't gone down well. But he'd still lent me his not exactly small collection of military text books, which I was slowly but surely churning my way through.

'Okay, adjusting *Ariel* for terrestrial flight as we approach the atmosphere,' Erin said. 'ETA is twenty minutes until landing at Angkor Wat.'

With a slight hum from the REV drive beneath the cockpit, she rotated our ship until Earth was centred directly before us. In the dead centre was Asia, with India, China and Australia radiating around it, all helpfully labelled and outlined on the virtual cockpit like some sort of giant desk globe version of our world.

As we started to decelerate towards the upper atmosphere, a new label popped up for Cambodia. Then a green destination marker with Angkor Wat popped up right in the middle.

'Hang on, I'm picking up a transmission on the emergency frequency,' Ruby said, looking at a pulsing red warning triangle on one of her screens.

My blood immediately ran cold. Apart from us, there was only one other current live mission that would use that — Jack and Mike's mission at Angkor Wat.

'Let's hear it,' I said.

Ruby pressed the icon and at once the speakers in the cockpit burst into life with the rattle of machine gun fire.

'This is Viking mission calling, we need urgent assist,' Jack said. 'We've just come under a sustained Overseer attack and need additional support.'

My mouth went dry and I flicked on the comm channel. '*Ariel* here, Jack.' Despite the surge of fear within me, it was also countered by a hardened battle calmness and ability to think clearly in life or death situations; I was already marshalling my thoughts. 'We're heading down to your position right now, but have you got any more intel you can give us?'

'It's a combined Overseer land and air attack, Lauren. We have a significant number of enemy troops, probably two hundred at least and a squadron of at least ten TR-3Bs engaging our ships, *Archimedes*, *Da Vinci* and *Galileo*, along with the three Tic Tacs that were already here on guard duty. The crews have just contacted Eden and the only good news is that reinforcements are on the way.'

'And the bad news is?'

'They're at least forty minutes out, but I don't think we can hold out that long hunkered down in the ruins. Any chance you guys can get here first?'

I cast Erin a look. 'Can we cut down that ETA of yours? Our team's lives and that last micro mind are on the line.'

Erin, who'd already begun toggling screens and examining the settings for our fusion reactor, nodded. 'If I max out the REV drive we can probably cut it down to six minutes.'

'Then do it,' I replied. I opened up a second channel on my comm. 'Niki, have you been listening into this?'

His voice came over the radio. 'Yes and I've already instructed our pilot to push our ship to its maximum speed too. We should reach Angkor Wat about thirty minutes behind you.'

'Okay, then that will have to do.' But already my mind was racing ahead, thinking about possible tactical approaches. I had an idea to help deal with the ground assault.

'Is there any chance you could prep your Tin Heads for

combat, Niki? Something tells me we are going to have to throw everything we have into this fight.'

'Yes and it will be as good a test as any for them for military use. Anyway, leave it to us and they'll be ready to be deployed the moment we get there.'

A coughing sound cut in over the frequency.

'I could always beat you to it and lend a helping hand until you get there,' Lucy said.

I was immediately tempted by her offer. Even with our upgraded drive, Lucy's micro mind craft could still seriously outpace us when she put her mind to it. But as appealing as that option was, I also knew I couldn't let her do it, because even with Jack, Mike and the rest of their team's lives on the line it was still too big a risk to lose her.

'Sorry, Lucy, you know that isn't an option as much as I want it to be,' I replied. 'If we lost you now it would be an absolute disaster.'

A long sigh came over the radio link. 'Okay, but if you change your mind I'll be there.'

'I know you will,' I replied.

A loud *whumping* sound echoed over the radio.

'What the hell was that?' Ruby asked.

'A damned incoming mortar round,' Jack replied. 'Looks like this crap day is just going from bad to worse.'

'Oh bloody hell, Jack,' I replied. 'Just hang in there; we're going to get to you as fast as possible, even if it means melting *Ariel's* drive.'

'Do whatever you can,' he replied, just as another explosion filled the background.

Erin shot me a tense look as she pushed the throttle to the max and *Ariel* began to speed down towards Angkor Wat. But whether we could actually get there in time I had no idea. And if I lost Mike and especially Jack...

Even as the sense of despair threatened to rise up through me I was already pushing it back down. That wasn't what any of them needed from me right now. I had to be the cool, calm-headed commander that they needed me to be, and somehow I'd become good at it over the years. I was going to be the very defini-tion of laser focus and I already knew I would do whatever it took to keep them all alive down there.

CHAPTER FOUR

THE VIRTUAL COCKPIT display was glowing with red plasma fire around *Ariel's* hull as Erin sped us down towards Angkor Wat. Normally the powerful gravity bubble shield enveloping our ship would have protected us from the re-entry manoeuvre heating up our hull, but thanks to the sheer nosebleed speed that we were diving down through the atmosphere at, even that was starting to get overwhelmed. And just to really add the finishing touch to the drama, below us the tops of towering cumulus nimbus clouds were crackling with fierce bursts of lightning in the darkness.

'Oh great, as if this isn't going to be a tricky enough fight as it is, it looks like we're flying straight into a thunderstorm,' Erin said.

'But that's nothing you can't deal with, is it?' I asked.

'Normally I wouldn't advise flying any aircraft by choice into a thunderstorm, but then our ride to the stars isn't just any old aircraft, are you, girl?' Erin tapped the arm of her flight seat.

'Isn't that the truth. Ruby, are you reading any enemy craft on our sensors yet?'

'No, but that's hardly surprising with the level of electrical interference being generated by that storm,' our Weapons Officer replied.

'In that case, let's see if Jack can supply us with any more intel.' I toggled on the comm channel. 'Jack, how are you holding out down there?'

Only the crackle of static filled our speakers.

The knot of anxiety that had been growing since I last spoke to him grew tighter. 'Jack, are you reading us, over?'

Once again I was only answered with the crackle of static. I was just starting to have nightmare thoughts when a man's voice suddenly came through over the channel.

'*Archimedes* here, Commander. We lost contact with the ground site about three minutes ago, but we have had our hands too full up here in a full-blown dogfight with those TR-3Bs. We're hoping it's just this electrical storm interrupting our comms, but we haven't had a chance to go and check for ourselves, yet. Our Tactical Officer is relaying our tactical data via the QEC radio link, which — thankfully — hasn't been affected.'

Lost contact... My mouth became bone dry as my mind rushed to Jack and Mike lying in a ditch, their bodies peppered with bullets. I forced myself to focus.

'Understood, but what's your current tactical situation, *Archimedes?*'

'To be honest, we're doing badly up here even with the Tic Tacs' help. Our WASP swarm has already been depleted and we could do with that backup.'

'Don't worry, we're going to do what we can,' I replied.

Ruby gave me a thumbs up. 'Receiving the data now over the QEC link.'

At least that was one small blessing — our comms were still working along with everything to with the QEC system that all our ships had. QEC was an acronym for quantum entangled radio communication. The physics explanation was that it used an effect famously known as *spooky action* at a distance. It was this that enabled our craft to instantly communicate with each other, no matter how far apart they were. It was one of the tech toys that Lucy had been able to share with us after she managed to sidestep the Angelus equivalent of a prime directive.

As Ruby transferred the data to our virtual cockpit it lit up with a tactical display that was also available on a screen mounted to one side of my flight seat. This was another of the upgrades to X-fleet, where every flight seat now had its own information and control panel that could be called upon when needed.

The enhanced display instantly transformed the opaque thunderstorms to a semi-transparent view, the low pressure boundaries even picked out as it processed the weather data being live streamed from each of our ships. Of even more tactical significance were the fifteen ships or more that were now being rendered on our cockpit. The majority of the craft, highlighted with red boxes, were TR-3Bs, the homegrown US military triangular-shaped ships that had fallen under Overseer command. The remainder were lit green, one for *Archimedes*, *Da Vinci* and *Galileo*. The remaining three were tagged as Tic Tac Grey ships, our unofficial allies in this war who had very much proved themselves as such in countless firefights with the Overseers.

The markers appeared to be buzzing through the heart of the thunderstorm cell at impossible speeds, with streams of railgun, minigun and missile shots filling the air between the swarm of ships.

'Darn it, talk about diving into a hornet's nest,' Erin said.

But already my mind was rushing ahead to consider our tactical options.

As I saw it we had two high priority situations. One was obviously the current air battle, but just as important – if not more so

– was the situation on the ground. Apart from the highly personal aspect of people I cared about that could be dead, or at the very least in serious danger, there was also the even bigger question of what had happened to the micro mind that Jack and Mike had been trying to recover. If we didn't get our hands on it, it could be game over for the Angelus secret plan. I needed to make major tactical decisions and fast. Once again a calmness settled over me.

I toggled the channel. 'Niki, exactly how far behind us are you?'

'Twenty-nine minutes and eight seconds to be exact, although we are in danger of melting our fusion reactor.'

'Okay, looks like your wish to try out the Tin Heads in active combat is about to come true. Your first priority will be to drop them off at the dig site to help deal with any enemy soldiers down there. Once you've done that you'll need to get *Thor* into that firefight.'

'Understood. What about our WASP swarm? We could deploy it at the site.'

'That's where the second part of my plan will come into play. Ruby, I want you to slave both our own WASPs to my combat helmet.'

She narrowed her gaze at me. 'And why wouldn't I be controlling them?'

'Because I'll be on the ground commanding them as I try to locate Jack and Mike's team. I'll also doing my best to protect that micro mind if it hasn't already fallen into enemy hands. Then, whilst I'm busy with that, you and Erin can join in with the air battle up here.'

Ruby gave me a straight look. 'As kick-arse as that plan sounds, Commander, to be absolutely blunt there's something I need to voice here. There's a very real possibility that we've lost contact with Jack and Mike because they could both be dead.'

Erin winced, but remained mute even as her mouth thinned.

Even my Teflon-plated, Commander emotional armour trembled under that assault, because there it was, my nightmare scenario laid bare for us all to pick over. It took a huge act of willpower not to scream at Ruby for even daring to suggest it.

Instead I just shook my head, doing my best to ignore the churn of emotions spinning up inside me. 'Even if that's true, Ruby, our number one priority is to protect that micro mind, whatever the cost. And this isn't a discussion, this is a direct order.' The moment the words had left my mouth I felt awful pulling rank on Ruby like this, but there simply wasn't time to debate the pros and cons of the situation.

Erin glanced between us, frowning at seeing the grown-ups square off against each like this.

But thankfully Ruby just shrugged. 'Okay, you're the boss. Just try not to lose too many of my WASPs, okay?'

Despite the tension between us I felt a smile curl the corner of my lips. 'I'll do my best.' We exchanged the barest of nods, but I knew it meant that we both understood where the other was coming from, and respected that position.

'Niki, I'm handing over effective command of the squadron to you to coordinate the attack, especially when our own reinforcements get here.'

'Understood, Lauren,' he replied with the verbal equivalent of not batting an eyelid. But of course Niki was someone who absolutely believed in the chain of command. Whatever he thought of my hare-brained plan to go charging in by myself, for now at least he was going to keep it to himself. But even if I pulled this off, I already knew that the ticking off I would receive from him afterwards was going to be epic.

'Okay, Erin, you need to plot a flight path for us and Niki to avoid that firefight and to come in hot. I'll have the ramp open, just get low enough that I can jump down from it for a quick exit. At the same time, Ruby, you can launch your WASPs.'

Both women nodded and set to work making my seat-of-the-pants plan a reality. Meanwhile, I headed over to the equipment locker to get ready to cope with whatever it was I was heading into on a solo mission yet again.

———

I stood at the exit of *Ariel's* airlock facing the closed ramp, suited, booted and wearing a black combat uniform with a shell of layered Kevlar built into it to protect my vital organs. As usual my Mossad .22 LRS was in its holster, but for this mission I was also bringing a series assault rifle in the form of a Heckler and Koch 416 fitted with a Starbright scope. Ruby had kitted it out for me with a clip-on AGM Wolverine night vision extension. If that hadn't been enough it had also been adapted by the Forge team back at Eden to pipe a live feed straight to my HUD, complete with a targeting reticle. As Ruby often said, we always got the best toys to play with on our missions.

But every bit as important as all the weapons I was loaded up with — and that included as many fragmentation grenades as I could carry — I also had the all-important Empyrean Key stowed in my bag. When it came down to my mission, rescuing the others — if they were still alive — was secondary to activating the micro mind.

'Okay, Commander, we're coming in to land, get ready,' Erin said through my helmet's speakers.

The ramp started to lower and for the first time I had a direct eyeball view of the ancient towers of the Angkor Wat in the distance as we sped towards it. The numerous stone towers of the ancient temple complex were illuminated every so often by the lightning flashes, almost giving it the skyline of a city.

In a conventional transport craft with its rear ramp lowered, the air would have been roaring in my ears by now. But thanks to the gravity bubble that surrounded *Ariel* and reduced the air friction to almost zero, instead it was eerily quiet beyond the door as the jungle rushed past beneath us, Erin bringing us in so low to avoid being detected that we were partially skimming the treetops. The only sounds were the distant rumble of thunder and the branches whipping around in the strong storm wind.

I glanced up to see the odd streak of tracer fire and in one instance, the trail of a missile arcing up into the storm clouds above us. That — and the occasional orange flash in the clouds rather than the white of sheet lightning — suggested that something had just been taken out by all the weapons fire that was being traded up there. I desperately hoped that it wasn't one of our ships.

Down here it was almost tranquil by comparison. There wasn't even so much as a muzzle flash to give away the presence of any Overseer soldiers on the ground. But my spideysenses were already tingling. I might not be able to see them, but every instinct told me that they were somewhere out there in the darkness.

With mind-bending speed we reached Angkor Wat. This was the site that Jack, with considerable enthusiasm it might be said, had insisted on giving me a PowerPoint presentation on the previous week. It had even included numerous slides about how it had been built back in the twelfth century by King Suryavarman II and how he had dedicated the temple to the god Vishnu. Jack had been positively raving about how important Angkor Wat was from a historical perspective and to say he was excited about the prospect of seeing it would have been a serious understatement. I may have nodded off once or twice, having already finished an exhausting day of training using a spacesuit in the deep water tank, but thankfully there hadn't been a test at the end of Jack's presentation. But the potential tragedy of all of this was that having now visited one of his bucket list archaeological sites, there could be a very real chance that the love of my life was dead, along with Mike and the security squad Niki had sent to guard them.

But once again that almost unsettling calm was taking hold and pushing the lid back down on my emotions before they could continue their spiral down into despair. So when Ruby's voice came over the comm it was something of a welcome distraction.

'Okay, WASP swarm is all set with armour-piercing rounds loaded into their magazines,' she said. 'The moment they launch, their camera views will be available in your helmet's HUD. But to stop you being overwhelmed with too much information flooding in at once, I've programmed Delphi to only contact you if she needs you to initiate any specific orders. But if you just want to kick off a serious firefight, and to hell with stealth, just tell her to initiate the Omega attack pattern and she'll take care of the rest. She obviously isn't me, but she should do almost as good a job.'

'Thanks, Ruby, and good luck with whatever is waiting for you and Erin upstairs.'

'Don't you worry about us — we're taking our A-game to that fight.'

I smiled in the darkness. 'You always do.'

'You better believe it, Commander. Okay, touch down in ten, so get ready.'

I took a centering breath as the last of the surrounding jungle zipped past and we began to slow rapidly. As already planned with Erin, she was flying us towards a flat area of lawn in the south east corner of the complex. *Ariel* flew over a black moat reflecting the storm clouds that surrounded the temple site as we came in to land. I flicked down my helmet's HUD, which was immediately filled with a large green marker for the excavation site. Worryingly, there were still no other markers for any of our guys, including Jack and Mike.

'I'm not seeing anyone's transponders,' I said into my helmet's mic.

'That's because the Overseers are up to their old tricks and swamping this entire area, jamming frequencies across the radio frequency,' Ruby said. 'I'm boosting the WASP's swarm transmitter power to cut through it to your suit's standard radio antenna, but it's only just managing it and it won't be a very stable link as we can't use a QEC link. I'm afraid it also looks like we'll lose radio contact with you when we get any real distance away.'

'Understood, just relay to Niki to deposit his Tin Head forces at the dig site when he arrives and I'll rendezvous with them when I get there,' I replied.

'Will do, Commander, and good hunting...' Ruby paused. 'Look, for what it's worth this isn't exactly Jack and Mike's first rodeo with the Overseers. If anyone could survive this, it's those two.'

I blinked at the sudden gentleness in her voice. 'I just hope you're right, Ruby,' I replied as I tightened my grip on the HK416 assault rifle.

The ground came rushing up to meet *Ariel* before Erin levelled the ship off just a couple of metres over it. Without hesitating, I jumped and landed in a squat position to absorb the impact.

As I started to take in my surroundings, the rich smell of the surrounding jungle was already filling my nostrils. Even this scent, which hinted at a rich and diverse biosystem, was in stark contrast to the moon I'd just been on six hours previously. But I was already scanning the terrain around me for any potential life as *Ariel's* miniguns arced left and right above to give me covering fire if necessary. Then our ship's bottom hatch opened and just like the insects they were named after, our twelve WASP drones dropped out of *Ariel* like their namesakes leaving the nest. With whisper-quiet props, they all sped up and away, half of them heading over the temple site and the rest heading out to take up a perimeter-guarding pattern beyond the moat over the jungle.

The ramp was already closing behind me as *Ariel* fully cloaked again. Then, like a sigh on the wind, she rushed straight up into the storm clouds overhead and disappeared from view.

That was it. Apart from my robotic helpers, I was on my own.

I activated my HK416's night vision scope with an eye blink that was monitored by my helmet's systems. Immediately a small video window appeared to the top right of my HUD, displaying a live video that I could enlarge if I needed to. I broke into a run, heading straight for the cover of the low stone wall ahead of me and already praying that I wasn't too late.

CHAPTER FIVE

I'D DUCKED down behind the cover of the wall and was taking a moment to orientate myself. The one thing that was for certain was that the temple complex was suspiciously quiet in front of me, and the ominous lack of cicada sound was telling. But if Jack and Mike's position had been overrun I would have expected to hear some sort of chatter from the Overseer soldiers as they got ready to blow the micro mind — that was, if they hadn't already.

Keep thinking happy thoughts, Lauren...

I so badly needed a situation report from the guys and I cursed internally that our comms were still being jammed. It was a tactic straight out of the Overseers' handbook. Our QEC radios, which were pretty bulky bits of equipment, might be fine for ship to ship comms, but were far too big to be carried.

Unfortunately the only way around the communications blackout was for a support X-craft to be in reasonably close proximity to boost the signal enough for me to be able to hear it. And that so wasn't going to happen whilst there was a massive air battle happening that needed every single ship we could throw into that fight.

Thankfully, there was a green circle in the corner of my HUD, which meant that I had a steady connection to my WASP drones. They would stay that way as long I kept them to less than a couple of klicks out. Any further than that and the Overseer jamming would overwhelm the connection. But Ruby had prepared for even that eventuality. In the event of a communication loss, Delphi was ordered to return the WASPs to their launch point to try and reacquire the signal.

Okay, time to find out what my eyes in the sky are seeing...

I flicked my gaze towards the green icon and blinked, activating the HUD's eye-tracking control menu system. Immediately a dozen tiny video windows appeared, each showing a green box to indicate that their Delphi AIs hadn't detected anything so far. The feeds themselves were utilising the WASPs' infrared cameras because it was far easier to spot the heat signatures of people in the pitch darkness, even beneath the jungle canopy.

The swarm was moving in a pre-programmed search sequence. Half were now patrolling the perimeter along the outer moat. The rest were still heading inwards, cautiously using different routes towards where the micro mind was being excavated in the dead centre of the main temple. This was also where we'd dropped Jack and Mike off into the protection of Niki's security team that had already been on site. As the drones began to pass over Angkor Wat, I could see that the entire area was a labyrinth of buildings and courtyards, which also meant there were plenty of places for someone to hide in, including the enemy.

With eye-controlled HUD selections, I narrowed down the video feeds to just those six for now. My priority remained discovering what had happened here. I was hoping against hope that I would simply find Jack, Mike and the others clustered around the dig site having successfully repelled the attack.

As the minutes stretched out it was doing nothing for my

nerves as I scanned each and every live feed coming in, looking for anything out of the ordinary, something which was already pushing my powers of perception to its limits. Thankfully Delphi was on the case, analysing all the data that was coming in, and it was the AI that spotted something out of the ordinary before I did. One of the feeds flashed red a split second before I registered the body lying face down on the ground. My heart was pounding so hard in my chest that I thought it might be about to burst. I increased the video window to maximum until it took over most of my HUD.

'Delphi, take WASP seven in for a closer look at that body,' I said as quietly as I could, relying on my throat mic to pick it up.

'Affirmative, Commander,' Delphi replied through my helmet speakers, which were so sensitive that even someone standing a foot away wouldn't be able to overhear the words.

The view began to close in on the sprawled body, the back half of the man's head missing and a carbine still clutched in his clawed hand. The guy was wearing a black uniform, which absolutely didn't help as all of our people, including Jack, Mike and the rest of Niki's security team were too. And with our comms being jammed the usual electronic tags that would normally tell me if he'd been one of ours wasn't working, which was odd as the WASP was almost on top of the guy now. It could mean that either the transmitter had been damaged or better still, this was actually one of the enemy soldiers.

Delphi brought the WASP in to hover just over the body. There were no other bullet wounds visible on the man's corpse. This had been a clean kill shot, which could possibly indicate a sniper or even a round of one of our own WASPs. That was another thing that worried me. Apart from my drones, no other WASP transponders were being picked up by our systems, which could mean they were just out of range, but instinct told me had to be a very bad sign. This body was the first real clue to what had happened here — I needed to find out answers and fast.

'Okay, Delphi, position WASP to crosscheck that casualty against personnel deployed for Angkor Wat mission.'

'Repositioning WASP unit seven for a biometric check now,' Delphi replied.

The drone slowly lowered itself until it had a clear view of the man's profile and his very broken nose where it had smashed into the cobbled stone floor when he'd collapsed. But although relief surged through me when I saw it wasn't either Jack or Mike, that feeling was followed immediately by a sense of guilt because it could still be another member of our team.

However, Delphi was already on the case. Plotted points linked by lines appeared over the man's cheeks and eyes, a few flicking around the broken nose, but unable to get a lock on the radically altered profile. The other markers blinked green as they locked into place.

'Subject unidentified,' Delphi finally announced.

I leant my head back against the wall and let out a long breath — that meant it had to be one of the Overseer soldiers. But that was also bad news as it meant at least one of their people had reached the Angkor Wat temple inner complex. The question was, had the rest of the Overseer attack force too and if so, had they reached the actual excavation site within it where our team had been?

'Delphi return WASP seven to search pattern Delta.'

'WASP unit seven returning to search pattern Delta,' the AI replied.

The video view shifted away from the grisly sight of the dead man's face as the drone rose back up into the sky.

I switched back to the feeds from the rest of the drones converging on the dig site to find there were multiple alerts of dead bodies being found. I repeated the actions that I'd just done, with Delphi running more running biometric checks on the other corpses. But thankfully each and every one of them turned out to be Overseer soldiers. Then the drones finally started to find the destroyed WASPs that the security team had brought with them to help defend the area, which had obviously put up a stiff fight defending Jack, Mike and the others. Whether they'd survived or not, I was almost certainly about to find out.

The first of my WASPs had almost reached the courtyard area at the top of a steep temple. This was where our TREENO CubeSat network had first detected a neutron burst when the Resonancy Generator in Cuba had sent out its *time to wake up* alarm call to the remaining dormant micro minds hidden around our world.

For somewhere that was obviously a major tourist destination during the day, the recovery of the micro mind had been deliberately set up as a night mission. The few security guards who should have been on site had been bribed to stay home that night whilst Jack removed the necessary flagstones from the floor at the top of the temple. Then once the micro mind had been recovered the idea was that they would simply put everything back as it was, so that by morning no one would know that anyone had been there. That had been the plan, but the numerous dead bodies — not to mention bullet holes in the stonework — were going to raise a lot of difficult questions when the sun rose above the horizon the following day.

A green destination marker had appeared overlaid in the WASP's video feed inside a central room in the middle of the courtyard. Within it were the edges of a deep excavated hole, with flagstones that had been removed from the floor piled up carefully around its edges. One of Mike's deep-ground-scanning radar systems was lying abandoned to one side. There was absolutely no question that this was Jack's dig site.

The drone moved into the room, its sensors revealing absolutely no movement as it headed towards the edge of the hole, then its camera pivoted down to look into it. Relief surged through me as I saw a strong blue glow coming from beneath the camo net that had been used to cover the bottom of the hole. The team must have placed it there to hide the presence of the micro mind when they'd been forced to retreat. The great news for the sake of our world's survival was that as the micro mind was still glowing, it was obviously still intact. But where was everyone else, especially Jack and Mike?

Tactically speaking, I knew the sensible thing would be to wait until Niki's Tin Heads got here for some serious backup, which could only be less than twenty-five minutes away by now. But with everything apparently so quiet, and especially as I had my guardian angels in the form of a swarm of WASPs, I needed to know sooner rather than later what had happened, if only so we could get the micro mind away from here as quickly as possible. Also, despite the aerial views I had of the site, sometimes there was no substitute for boots on the ground and instinct, and this was so one of those moments.

'Delphi, put WASP units ten, eleven and twelve into guard mode over the target site. Drones seven, eight and nine are to rendezvous back with me and escort me in.'

'Understood. Orders relayed,' Delphi replied.

I closed up the video feed and minimised the information in my HUD to an overlaid transparent map showing my current position and the target and the sniper scope view from the Starbright. It was time to move.

With my head down, I approached the end of the low wall and extended my HK416 round the edge of it, using its scope view in my HUD to see what was happening. There wasn't a sign of anyone between me and the temple. About two hundred metres above me the reassuring sight of the three dark silhouettes of the WASP drones against the flickering storm clouds overhead, slid silently into position to form a triangular formation.

I slipped my assault rifle into full auto-mode, because if experience had taught me anything it was that if I did run into any trouble it would be sudden and violent.

In a crouching position I headed along the wall towards a square-columned stone gatehouse, flanked by a couple of palm trees, the walls decorated with numerous stone relief carvings of women. According to the map, each cardinal point had an entrance like this to enter the walled city temple through.

As I approached it was obvious Delphi was now running the WASPs in full AI mode and was really looking out for me. As soon as I'd begun my approach towards the bottom of the steps, one of the WASPs, unit seven according to the data tag my HUD had assigned to it, dropped down from the sky. Immediately it began to head through into the passageway at the top of the steps to scout ahead. As the drone disappeared from view, its short-barrelled weapon was already sweeping left to right. Hopefully if there was anyone waiting to ambush me, seven would take the brunt of the attack as the drone flushed my would-be attackers out.

Not taking any chances, I moved between the pillars to the right hand side, using them as cover as I darted between them.

Seven had reached a junction and did an automatic three-sixty rotation to check out each passageway. I held my breath, waiting for the spark of sniper round to take the drone out, but when none came I breathed a sigh of relief. The passageways on either side appeared to be very long and running the length of the boundary wall inside. About twenty metres down stood the statue of a figure with cloth wrapped round it like a toga. Absolutely perfect cover for someone to pop out from behind and take me out. It seemed Delphi was aware of the threat too, because Seven was already speeding towards it.

I quickly headed to the junction and sighted my HK416 on the statue, daring anybody to make a sudden appearance. But once again Seven reached it without incident and performed a circling manoeuvre around it. Not finding any bogeymen crouching behind the cover of the statue, Seven sped back towards me and headed past to follow the same procedure round the statue on the opposite side of me. That completed, the drone returned to me like an obedient dog. Then with a ninety degree turn, it headed out through the passageway dead ahead into the wide open space beyond. With the faintest whir of its props, Seven headed back up into the sky to rejoin the rest of the formation that was already in position, waiting for me to reappear.

So far so good, but the longer I went without running into anyone, the more my nerves were being stretched piano-wire tight.

Despite my eyes in the sky, just to reassure myself, I used my assault rifle's night vision scope to check that I couldn't see anyone. But once again, nothing seemed out of place, just the moaning of the wind through the structure, nothing else.

Sweat beginning to trickle down my back, I crept out from the passageway, sweeping my HK416. Still nothing.

Ahead of me was a wide stone boulevard leading directly to the Angkor Wat temple itself. More significantly, it was also where the location marker for the dig site was now tagged with a large green HUD marker, showing the position of the micro mind.

X marks the spot, I thought to myself.

Dotted along the walkway I could see at least three of the Overseer soldiers lying dead on the floor, no doubt taken out by either one of the security team or their WASPs. Tactically speaking, I would be in a similarly exposed position if I stepped out into that boulevard for an Overseer sniper hidden somewhere to take me out.

I scanned the terrain, having made a tactical decision. This was the direct approach so I needed to do the equivalent of going *off piste* in the hope of not walking straight into an ambush. I leapt over the balustrade and landed on the dry, grassy ground just beneath it. Following the shadow line I crept towards the temple, tracking the route of the boulevard above.

As I neared the silhouetted outline of the temple, I could see it was dominated by a cluster of towers in the middle that reminded me somewhat of a stone version of a head of wheat in the way that it tapered towards the top surrounded by upward-facing spikes. Squat, flat-roofed stone buildings linked them together. As I crept over the grass towards the temple, the six reassuring blue blips on my HUD indicated that the WASP swarm was keeping pace with me.

The itch in my chest, where I felt convinced that a sniper round with my name on it was going to penetrate my body armour at any moment, only relaxed when I finally reached the front of the temple steps without incident.

Just ahead, a series of steps running between statues of what might have been stylised lions, stood guard. Again, too open a target to just head straight up those steps. Instead I headed along the side of the terrace until I drew alongside a second gatehouse style structure. According to my map, which had automatically changed to a schematic view of the temple as I neared it, the gatehouse led directly into the outer gallery of the main temple. I began to scale the wall up to the side of the gatehouse, thankful for plenty of footholds and handholds.

Talk about making life difficult for yourself, Lauren.

But deep down I knew that an abundance of caution in a situation like this was always a good idea when you didn't know exactly what sort of tactical situation you were getting into.

With a final heave I pulled myself up onto a ledge. The problem was that I could see no way onto the roofs of the buildings ahead of me, so I was going to head in through the entrance to gain access to the temple. In that case, it was time to send the troops in.

'Delphi, order WASPs seven through to twelve to begin a room-clearing sweep of the structure directly ahead of me.

'Affirmative, Commander,' the AI replied.

Six dark shapes dropped quickly out of the sky and disappeared into the building through the entrance nearest to me, plus two entrances further out. I pulled up the WASPs' video feeds to see them quickly zipping through the building, scanning each room and courtyard thoroughly, before moving on.

Apart from a few more dead bodies, once again there was no sign of anyone living. But something still made no sense to me — if the assault had failed, and presumably it had because the micro mind was still there, then where the hell were Jack, Mike and the rest of the team? Could they have been captured, but for some reason the Overseers had decided to leave the micro mind behind? No, that didn't make any sense either.

'Sweep complete, returning WASPs to overwatch delta pattern,' Delphi announced.

At once the videos showed all six craft zipping back up into the sky.

I quickly grabbed the opportunity to check in with the drones that I'd posted on guard duty on the outer perimeter. Again, apart from some reported sightings of monkeys in the surrounding jungle, there was absolutely no sign of any human activity out there.

So, the only way I was going to find out what had happened would be to head towards the excavation site. At least there I could activate the micro mind and send it on its way to rendezvous with Lucy.

Based on the continuing orange flashes in the clouds, the air battle was still raging above. No doubt Ruby and Erin were helping to give the TR-3Bs hell up there. Just for a moment a hole appeared in the cloud to reveal a half moon...that same moon that I'd been standing on less than six hours ago. My mission there already seemed like a dream experience, certainly not something that could really have happened. The moon disappeared again behind a rolling mass of cloud, darkening the landscape back to a cobweb of shadows.

Time to do this.

My HK416 at the ready and once again using the pillars as cover, I moved swiftly between them through the gatehouse into a raised open passageway that ran between two smaller courtyards surrounded by viewing galleries. Normally I would have been extremely careful moving through them, but knowing they had already been scouted by my WASPs I ran along the corridor towards another set of steps at the far end. A few moments later, I reached the inner courtyard in front of the main temple, which was adorned with towers in the middle and presented me with a steep flight of steps leading up to the top. I could just see the three WASPs hovering around its summit where the green HUD marker was still hovering, indicating the presence of the micro mind.

It's now or never, Lauren...

I jogged silently across the courtyard towards the steep steps, feeling very exposed. The tension had grown so tight in every muscle of my body that I was almost willing to hear a gunshot to alleviate the tension a bit. A firefight I could cope with, but this drawn-out waiting game was seriously starting to fray my nerves.

I grabbed one last chance to try and make contact with Jack, toggling on the comm channel in case I was close enough now to cut through the Overseers' jamming. 'Jack, are you there?'

Only the hiss of static came back.

Bloody hell...

I slung my HK416 over my shoulder and unholstered my

LRS pistol — easier to use if needed on the steep ascent up the temple. I began to climb, my ears straining to hear even the smallest sound to give away the hint of someone hiding.

The ancient temple steps were definitely not health and safety standard because they were at least a forty-five degree angle, if not more. I'd probably have to make the return trip down on my bum to avoid slipping and cracking my skull open.

As I neared the top I spotted a bulky, four-rotored armoured drone crumpled on the steps, with a twisted gun barrel sticking out of it. This was new. It looked like the Overseers must have followed our lead using drones in the battlefield, and that was anything but a good development.

I reached the top, where the central seven towers of the inner temple towered over me. I took a sip of water, trying to ease the tightness in my throat. With a deep breath, I headed through a short passageway into the final small courtyard at the top. It was surrounded on each side by a tall, elongated, pineapple-shaped tower. Ahead of me, in a central stone wall room that had the tallest of the towers, a distinct blue glow was coming from a hole dug in the middle of the floor — this was the room that had been covered by the camo net.

As tempting as it was to rush in there and activate the micro mind with my Empyrean Key, I hung back in the doorway, scanning the surrounding passageways that opened onto the courtyard.

Still no sign of anyone. My mind was made up — it was time to head for the micro mind.

As I started to step towards the inner room, I spotted blood splatters across the floor and spent bullet casings everywhere glinting in the storm light. There had obviously been an intense firefight up here, which meant Jack, Mike and the others had come under a sustained attack in this very place. My stomach scrunched into a tight ball, but before I could even begin to emotionally process what that fully meant, the tranquility of the night was transformed in a split-second.

Alerts erupted in my HUD from the six WASPs I'd left guarding the outer perimeter. I rushed back through the passageway to look out from the temple towards the distant boundary wall, and immediately saw flashes of gunfire erupting above it. I pulled up the WASP feeds to see the drones I'd left in position there were swooping around, firing at dozen of contacts, but none on the ground. Whatever these things were they were swooping around the sky every bit as fast as my own WASPs.

'Multiple enemy drone contacts detected and engaging,' Delphi calmly announced.

Damn it. The Overseers were using our own tactic against us — they had their own bloody drones!

Two of the video feeds blinked out and in the distance I saw a couple of WASPs spinning towards the ground, blue flames streaming from their battery packs.

I glanced back towards the micro mind, still glowing under the cameo net. I needed to get it activated and out of here as fast as possible, so that Lucy could rendezvous with it high up in orbit if necessary.

I raced back to the hole, pulling the Empyrean key out, ready to activate the icon the moment it appeared. I was just about to issue the command to Delphi to activate the carrier tone when suddenly I heard the footfall of people approaching my position fast.

I pulled my LRS out and aimed it towards the doorway as a figure from outside rushed towards it. But seeing me, the figure skidded to a stop, arms already up as I aimed my pistol straight towards the guy's head.

'For god's sake, don't shoot! It's me, Lauren!' the figure shouted — it was Jack's voice.

As recognition kicked in, I stared at him, the gun suddenly trembling in my hand as I lowered it.

More people were emerging from behind Jack including Mike, moving effortlessly on his prosthetic leg, all of them taking up defensive positions inside the room, in the courtyard and on top of the temple. Then despite my so-called battle calm, all I wanted to do was throw my arms around Jack and never let him go.

CHAPTER SIX

At last I pulled away from Jack and briefly hugged Mike, before staring at both of them. 'Thank god you guys are okay, but where the hell did you just come from?'

'We'd already repelled a smaller attack, where they were obviously testing out our defences,' Jack replied. 'So we'd been lying in wait for the next assault; we knew one had to be coming. The problem was, we'd already taken casualties and it was a tough call, but with our people stretched thin we were forced to briefly abandon this site. That allowed me to set up a triage dealing with them in one of the lower rooms in the temple. That's also where we transported the micro mind to using an Agie anti-grav plate, in order to protect it.'

I widened my eyes and glanced back towards the covered hole with the blue light glowing from beneath it.

'Oh that,' Mike said. 'That's just my Sky Wire with its screen set to blue. You didn't think we'd just abandon the micro mind so that the Overseer mercs could capture it, did you, Lauren?'

'Now I think about it, of course you wouldn't — I should have known that.' I shook my head and then glanced at the blood stains on his sleeves, grimacing. 'Abandoning this position was definitely the right call by the look of it.'

Jack grimaced and nodded. 'We really didn't have any other choice but to fall back. That was just before the Overseers managed to kill all comms, so I couldn't let you know what was happening here. But we did have a couple of snipers keeping an eye on this location to take out any Overseers who showed their faces. It was one of them who spotted you climbing the steps of this temple.'

'Okay, but the thing I still don't understand is that I scanned the whole site and couldn't see anyone alive down here, even with my WASPs?'

'That's because I got everyone to use the old foil-lined camo blanket trick to hide our body's heat signatures,' Mike said. 'It also seems the Overseers have been learning through their previous encounters with us and were using their own version of battlefield drones fitted with thermal cameras. They sent about twenty in, which managed to take out our WASPs.'

'Then they set to work on us along with a ground troop assault that was also attempting to storm our position,' Jack added.

'Okay, there'll be time to debrief later, but we need to get into position because it looks like another major assault is about to kick off,' I said.

'Then let's get ready to give them a reception they won't forget in a hurry,' Jack replied.

The three of us joined the rest of the security team as they headed out to the upper level of the stepped temple, granting us a clear view of the ancient site beneath us. I'd studied enough under Niki to know that at least holding the high ground like this would give us an advantage tactically. It would make our lives slightly easier defending this position, while things would be more difficult for the parachutists about to attempt to storm it.

I hunkered down next to Mike and Jack, resting my HK416 and pulling up the Starbright's image-intensified view on my HUD.

Mike peered at my rifle. 'Bloody hell, Lauren, talk about being ready to hunt bear. You've obviously been hanging out with Ruby way too much on the weapons range.'

'You need the right tools for the job,' I replied as I checked over the current status of my WASPs. 'Oh shit. They managed to take out the six drones I left guarding the outer perimeter and my others are already heading out to reinforce them. To be honest, I'm surprised that the Overseers didn't simply try lobbing lots of missiles at this place to take the micro mind out.'

But Jack was already shaking his head. 'The Overseers are obviously desperate to get their hands on it at any cost, rather than just take it out like they have with the others.'

Mike nodded. 'Yeah, they would have had the same intel we did about where all those neutrino bursts came from that were triggered by the Resonancy Generator. By now they would have worked out that this micro mind is the last one left that they can run their bloody experiments on.'

'So you reckon we're facing an all-out assault to capture it?' I asked.

'Based on what we've already had to deal with, it's certainly looking that way,' Jack replied.

I grimaced and then glanced at my watch. 'Okay, but the one good bit of news is that Niki should be arriving with some rein-forcements in about ten minutes, so we need to just hold out until then.'

'Defend the hill at all costs, in other words,' Jack replied.

I shrugged. 'Pretty much.'

'Right, but what are those bastards up to now then? It's gone suspiciously quiet out there,' Mike said.

He was right — the sound of distant gunfire had fallen away and there weren't any sightings from my last four WASPs either.

Jack began laying out spare magazines for his Steyr AUG. The weapon was a gas-operated selective fire rifle — his latest choice for combat, mainly because of its reliability and weight. He also had his Benelli tactical shotgun slung over his back. My boyfriend might be a former field surgeon, but he took his choice of weapons on a mission very seriously. And the fact that I even knew anything about his weapons were testament to just how much my life had changed since my former civilian role as a radio telescope operator at the Jodrell Bank in England. Life had been so simple back then.

I flipped my HUD up and placed my eye directly to the Wolverine night vision extension on my Starbright, settling my body into a sniping position around the HK416 and turning the selector to single shot mode.

I used night vision scope view on my HUD to scan the distant jungle line, looking for any hint of movement, but saw absolutely nothing.

We all settled into the wait and a minute became two, then became ten, the waiting ratcheting up the tension with every moment.

'What the hell are the Overseers waiting for, a personal invite to attack us?' Mike finally said, his tone strained as an eleventh minute threatened to pass.

The question had barely left his mouth when I heard a warning bleep in my helmet's speakers.

'Multiple incoming enemy targets detected by WASPs, Commander,' Delphi said. 'What are your orders?'

I pulled up the video feeds in my HUD to see most of the windows breaking up with lots of static. That was almost certainly everything to do with the Overseer jamming and how far away from me the remaining WASPs were currently located. But between the crackles of interference, I saw multiple lock boxes on each drone's feed of what appeared to be fast moving military helicopters flying towards the temple complex.

'Shit, we have at least six helicopters heading in at low altitude,' I said.

'Damn it, we'll need to break open those Stinger missiles that we brought with us,' Jack said.

'Do it, because we're going to have a very small window to repel them,' I replied.

Jack nodded and slid himself back off the ledge and headed into the temple, gathering up several of the security guards to go with him.

'So much for having the high ground — we're going to be sitting ducks up here,' Mike said, sweeping the horizon with his binoculars.

'Then let's see what we can do about slowing them down until the cavalry gets here in the form of *Thor* in...' I glanced at my smartwatch, 'in about three minutes time.'

'How are we going to do that exactly?' Mike asked.

'Like this,' I said. 'Delphi, intercept approaching helicopters and take them down.'

'Understood and engaging now.'

Through the crackles of static I could see the four remaining WASPs beginning to sweep forward straight towards the approaching targets.

A stream of tracer fire lanced out from the distant silhouettes of helicopters as Jack arrived back with a Stinger missile, a weapon that consisted of a long cylindrical black tube with a large grip attached to it. The other security guards he'd taken with him were appearing left and right of us, armed with more Stingers and taking up firing positions.

Jack sighted along the Stinger as tracer fire lit up the far landscape and my WASPs traded fire with the attacking helicopters with a distant crackle of bullets.

'Those look like UH-60 Black Hawks,' Mike said as he watched the firefight.

'Since when could you identify military aircraft, buddy?' Jack said.

'Since Niki sat me down and made me study up on anything military so I would be able to identify them in the field.'

One of my last three video windows blinked out. It was followed by a blossom of fire that lit up the jungle for a moment as one of the helicopters went gyrating down in trailing smoke.

'Scrub one Black Hawk taken out by a WASP,' Jack said, shaking his head.

I watched the video feeds as the door gunners in the Black Hawks fired machine guns at the WASPs as they ducked and weaved through the sky around the helicopters, harrying them as they swept in towards us. Then two of the video windows went blank within seconds of each other as the gunners finally swatted my drones out of the sky.

And then there was one...

'Delphi, order the last WASP unit to directly ram the rotors of one of those Black Hawks,' I said.

'Confirming order, WASP unit is on its way in,' Delphi replied.

Mike cast me a grim look. 'But it will almost certainly be filled with ground troops, Lauren.'

Once again my battle-hardened emotional armour slid back into place. 'Look, I know, but if we can trim down that Overseer attack force as much as we can before they reach us, it's going to increase our odds of survival.'

He held my gaze for a moment and then gave me the faintest nod. He might not like it but at least he understood the *why*.

I watched my last WASP swoop in a spiralling dive straight

down from above the Black Hawk towards its rotors, where its door gunners couldn't target it. The spinning hub of the blades grew large fast and then the video blinked out. At the same time a loud bang echoed from one of the helicopters in the distance and a moment later it suddenly veered sideways and crashed into the ground.

'Time to light them up, team,' Jack called out.

He and the other security guards aimed their Stingers and pulled the triggers on the grip stocks. With a popping sound, five missiles burst from the ends of the launch tubes and a moment later their rockets ignited to speed the missiles away towards the gunships.

Chaff clouds were already bursting from the Black Hawks as the Stingers streaked towards them. All the pilots pulled hard turn manoeuvres and two of our missiles hurtled past them on the left. But the fourth Black Hawk wasn't so lucky — the Stinger struck it squarely in the cockpit and it lit up in an explosion. The remains of the shattered helicopter went tumbling into the far wall of the temple, its rotors shattering as it struck the ground.

Jack cast me a grim *we had to do this* look as the last three Black Hawks came in to land and Overseer troops began to leap from them.

The last of my WASPs lost connection when the soldiers fired up at it as they raced towards the temple.

I sighted on one of the many doorways with my HK416. 'Okay, get ready everyone,' I called out.

Everyone took up firing positions as we prepared for what was bound to be an all-out assault.

I had just taken a centering breath, ready for what was about to happen, when suddenly the young female security guard that I didn't even know the name of, toppled forward, blood spraying from the back of her chest as a bullet passed straight through her.

Soldiers clad in black were appearing from everywhere at the same time in a coordinated assault, firing as they closed in on the base of the temple.

Cold sweat running down my back, I sighted my HK416 on the man who'd just appeared from behind a Buddha statue and pulled the trigger. The carbine spun away from his head as a spark flew from it.

I aimed again, breathing out as I took the second shot. This time, he clutched his chest as he collapsed to his knees and toppled forward.

Red searing lines of bullets burst from the machine gunner in the lead Black Hawk as it took off, driving us down to lie flat on our faces as it scythed through the walls behind us.

'Fucking hell!' Mike yelled, clasping his hands behind his head as the other two Black Hawks took off too.

I glanced across to see Jack desperately trying to launch a fresh missile tube to the Stinger grip stock even as the large calibre attack rounds whizzed within centimetres of him. Beyond brave didn't even get close to describing his coolness in the heat of battle.

And then I saw it — something appearing in the sky right in front of the stream of the machine gunners' tracer fire. The helicopter rounds ricocheted off it with a stream of sparks, outlining a huge, invisible disc a hundred metres wide.

'Oh thank god, the calvary just got here,' Jack said.

Suddenly, dropping straight away from what had to be *Thor* in full cloaking mode, twelve Tin Head robots appeared. They plummeted down the thirty metres to the ground and landed with a large metallic clang as they absorbed the manoeuvre by going into a crouch in front of the Overseer soldiers, a fall that would certainly have broken every bone in a human's body.

Immediately the enemy troops concentrated their fire on what they obviously perceived as a new, even bigger threat.

But the Tin Heads were already splitting apart as a group of bullets pinged off them while they wielded the massive Barrett M82 rifles that Ruby also favoured for sniping. And as she had delighted in telling me many times, that piece of hardware could put a round straight through a lightly armoured vehicle without even pausing for breath.

Like a scene straight out of the *Terminator* movies, the tracked robots sped towards the paratroopers, firing as they closed in on the enemy.

Meanwhile, Niki and his crew onboard *Thor* weren't hanging around either. They headed straight towards the Black Hawks, which in a last, desperate manoeuvre fired their missiles straight towards the X104. But like always, the gravity shield did its job, deflecting the missile and making them veer away into corkscrewing flights into the sky.

Then it was *Thor's* turn.

With the distinctive whine of its miniguns spooling up, with a fearsome gun rattle, four streams of bullets converged on the helicopters one by one, slicing through them. Moments later huge explosions ripped the Black Hawks apart and shrapnel tumbled across the outer lawns of Angkor Wat.

The Overseer soldiers left on the ground didn't stand a chance. Within a matter of minutes the ground fighting was all over and bodies were littered everywhere. Then like some sort of gun salute, with a massive *boom*, *Thor* discharged its railgun. A trail of vapour sped up from it, high in the sky towards the west. A moment later there was a pinprick of a fireball flash just visible through the break in the clouds.

'Can you hear me now, Lauren?' Niki's voice suddenly said over my radio.

'Loud and clear. You managed to cut through the jamming then?'

'Yeah, we just took out an EA-6B Prowler aircraft, high over the battlefield, which was responsible for that jamming. Anyway, according to our sensors you are completely in the clear now. We're just going to help finish off the TR-3Bs in the aerial battle, although *Ariel* in particular has been giving them a bloody nose. But the enemy forces won't be able to last much longer because our reinforcements will be here in five minutes. See you on the other side.'

'Good hunting, Niki,' I replied.

'Oh it will be,' he said with a chuckle. There was the barest stir in the wind as the invisible craft departed and a split second later a neat hole appeared in the storm clouds directly overhead as *Thor* joined the battle.

The security team were slowly beginning to stand around us as *Thor's* WASP swept into a defensive pattern overhead. The Tin Heads were also taking up guard positions at the base of the stepped pyramid.

The bitter hum of adrenaline tanging my mouth, I holstered my LRS and withdrew the Empyrean Key. 'Time to get this mission wrapped up, guys.'

Jack blew his cheeks out and nodded as Mike wiped the sweat from his brow and got shakily back to his feet. Then together we headed back through the doorway towards the central tower where the micro mind was waiting for me to do my thing.

CHAPTER SEVEN

THE STORM CLOUDS had passed and now a starry night filled the heavens above us. Jack, Mike and the security team had gathered around me at the summit of Angkor Wat in the small courtyard at the top of the temple. With an Agie anti-gravity plate we'd manoeuvred the micro mind out from its hiding place in one of the temple rooms and had brought it back to the courtyard, so it now had a clear view of the sky to lift up into.

Incredibly, in the firefight we'd suffered only one casualty, namely the woman I'd seen shot and I now knew was called Megan. But the six injured, having been prepped by Jack with emergency field dressings, drugs and drips, were already on their way back to Eden onboard a Pangolin.

Above us, six of the Eden squadron including *Ariel* and *Thor*, having defeated the last of the TR-3Bs, sat in a hovering guard formation. After having fought so hard for this moment — where we were about to retrieve the last part of the micro mind puzzle — there was no way that any of us was taking any chances.

'Ruby, any sign of enemy activity on *Ariel's* sensors?'

'Completely clear and that also goes for the outer defence ring of X103s and X104s that you ordered to create that perimeter fifty miles out.'

Jack gave me a nod. 'You really are a natural when it comes to taking on this Commander role, aren't you?'

'I'm certainly trying my best to be,' I replied.

And I was. I wanted desperately to justify Tom's confidence in me before he'd died and so I had thrown myself into all the tactical training that Niki set up for me. But I wasn't a one-woman island either and I knew that I lacked practical experience in larger scale battlefield tactics, especially when utilising dozens of X-craft in the air. So I'd quickly learned to pick the brains of others, especially Niki, Troy and even Jack to challenge my own strategies for fleet combat scenarios to see if they could spot any holes.

'So just remind me where being Commander means throwing yourself constantly into frontline combat?' Mike asked, giving me a pointed look.

I held up my hands. 'Hey, if you want me to retire to the relative safety of a bunker issuing orders to others to risk their lives whilst I'm safe, I can tell you now, that so isn't going to ever happen.'

Mike smiled. 'Knowing you like we do, no it probably isn't going to be anytime soon.'

'You know me so well,' I replied as the corners of my mouth curled up. 'Besides I couldn't live with myself if something happened to you guys because I wasn't out in the field to be there for you.'

'Nothing wrong with leading from the front, but maybe next time wait for your backup to turn up first before charging into an unknown tactical situation,' Jack said.

This time I grimaced because I knew my partner was right.

'Okay, that's a fair enough criticism, Jack, and maybe it was a bit of a heart over head decision, but hey, it was you guys and...' I spread my hands wide.

Jack's face broke into a smile. 'Yeah, I would have done absolutely the same if the situation had been reversed.'

I snorted. 'I so know that you would. So maybe enough with the lectures to each other and let's call Lucy in for the big finale.' I adjusted my helmet's mic. 'Lucy, are you there?'

'Of course, my little sunflower. I'm in geostationary orbit and I've been listening in the whole time. Although goodness, I was tempted to charge in to help you.'

'Well thank you for not doing that and endangering yourself,' I replied. 'Anyway, it's looking safe from our end for you to head down when you're ready.'

'Then I'll be with you in the shake of a lamb's tail,' Lucy replied.

We all gazed up to see a distant point of light heading down towards us at an impossible speed. In less than a couple of seconds, Lucy's micro mind ship came to an absolute stop about a klick up and directly over Angkor Wat like an alien version of the star of Bethlehem.

I selected the fleet channel in my HUD. 'Attention all X-craft, you are to retreat to a safe distance from the upcoming electronic pulse.' Using the eye-controlled selection menu in the HUD I pulled up a fleet tactical map and watched the green pulsing dots for each craft head outwards in an expanding circular formation. I pivoted my HUD up as I knew it would crash the moment the micro minds merged.

'I can't believe this moment is finally about to happen after all these years,' Mike said.

'You better believe it, buddy,' Jack said. 'We've certainly all worked hard enough to make this day a reality.'

I nodded. 'Isn't that the truth.'

A fluttering feeling growing inside me, I positioned myself next to the micro mind glowing faintly before us and took the Empyrean Key out of my bag. And then it hit me that this was probably the last time I'd ever had to do this to activate an ancient Angelus AI. It seemed that everyone around me recognised the significance of this moment, because conversation had stopped and all eyes were on me.

'Delphi, initiate carrier tone,' I whispered, painfully aware that I was the centre of everyone's attention.

'Initiating carrier tone,' she replied.

With a tingle of anticipation itching over my skin I watched the single dot and radiating lines icon appear pulsing in green over the Empyrean Key. I rotated it into the selection window and flicked my wrist forward; at once the icon turned solid green.

A pulse of intense blue light blazed through the micro mind before us. Then in utter silence it began to rise into the sky away from Angkor Wat, the site where it had laid undisturbed for thousands of years until this very night.

It was Jack who started the clapping first, but then he was quickly joined by Mike and then all the others as the shining crystal craft rose majestically up towards Lucy, who was already descending towards her AI twin.

Suddenly I was blinking back tears as a dozen emotions surged through me...the tears of someone who had been on a very long journey that had tested them to the depths of their very soul yet had somehow survived everything to arrive at this moment.

'Hey you,' Jack said, reaching over and squeezing my shoulder.

'Sorry, getting all the emotions right now,' I replied, flapping my hands in front of my face.

'Yeah, a big moment if ever there was one. Any thoughts on what might happen when they merge though, Mike?'

'We literally have no way of knowing,' Mike replied. His gaze had been fixed on the micro mind as it ascended to meet Lucy.

This was also something I'd discussed at length with Lucy and she was as much in the dark as anyone. My own hunch was that it was some sort of switch. But if that were true, what exactly would it turn on?

Lucy was descending towards the last micro mind, the usual plasma bursts flickering between the pair as they closed the distance. Then came the finale of starburst sparks as the Angelus AIs merged their crystal matrix structures into each other and became one. I was already raising my hand to shield my eyes in anticipation of the blinding white light that burst from the two craft, briefly turning night to day over the ancient temple. Then the light was fading away and it was just Lucy hanging there with the other micro mind absorbed into her matrix.

I held my breath, I suspected along with every other person witnessing that event for the big reveal that had to be coming. But Lucy just hung there in the sky being her usual glowing self.

With a hum I heard my helmet's systems rebooting. At the same moment the Tin Heads gimbal eyes started glowing with soft blue again after having briefly dimmed during the pulse, as they scanned for any possible threat that might threaten their humans.

And as we waited, the eyes of everyone gathered there turned towards me expectantly.

'Um, Lucy, I don't want to rush you, but is anything happening up there?' I asked.

Only silence came back over the radio.

Then without any warning an ear-splitting bass tone rang out so deep that it made the whole temple vibrate beneath us. My helmet's active noise cancellation was already trying to do its best to try and suppress the deafening sound, but Mike, who'd taken his combat helmet off, had his hands clamped to his ears as he sagged to his knees, gritting his teeth.

I grabbed his helmet and toggled its systems on as I shoved it hard down onto his head. Mike shot me a grateful look as the bass note continued to shake the world around us. Then as suddenly as it had it started, it stopped dead, but my ears were still ringing as I looked up to see Lucy glowing a brilliant orange. She briefly pulsed white before zipping sideways, straight towards the horizon. She was gone in the blink of an eye.

'Lucy, where the hell are you going?' I asked.

Once again there was no response, which only helped throw fuel on the fire of the dread growing inside me.

Jack peered at the distant patch of sky that Lucy had just vanished into. 'Is this all part of the Angelus plan to take off like that?'

'It could be, but going where exactly?' I replied.

Mike sucked his cheeks in. 'It was interesting that she headed off horizontally rather than going into space. That suggests she might be making her way to some location here on Earth.'

'Okay, if so then I don't need to point out that wherever she's going, she's unprotected,' I replied. 'Niki, can you send some craft after her?' I spoke into the comm channel.

'Already done, Lauren,' Niki replied. 'I issued the order the moment she headed off. I've dispatched two X103s and X104s. Unfortunately, she has already left them far behind and they have lost contact with her.'

'Oh bloody hell, so what are we going to do now?' I asked the others.

'Well working on the assumption that this is all part of the big plan, and knowing Lucy, she will be in touch as soon as she is able to,' Mike said.

'So what are we going to do in the meantime?' Jack asked.

'I don't think we've any other choice but to head back to Eden and keep everything crossed that Lucy phones home before the Overseers get to her first,' I replied.

Jack and Mike both gave me grim looks, but nodded.

I gazed out at the distant horizon where Lucy had disappeared, as a knot of worry began to tighten in my stomach. Just like that, we were no longer able to protect Lucy and she was out there by herself.

CHAPTER EIGHT

THE FOLLOWING morning in the briefing room back at Eden, according to the clock on the wall it had just crawled past 5am. I felt distinctly groggy as I cradled my empty coffee mug, sadly not because of any all-night celebration party. Instead, the stark reality and anxiety of losing contact with Lucy had left me unable to sleep. I'd dragged myself to the meeting room, where I'd set up camp as I waited for news to roll in. But so far, there'd been absolutely nothing.

Of course it was difficult for my mind not to jump to nightmare scenarios in which Lucy had been captured or destroyed, or even gone rogue on us just as Red had done, and simply abandoned us to our fate with the Kimprak. But I knew deep down — the thought that I kept hanging onto — was that if Lucy had anything to do with it, there was no way on Earth that she'd let that scenario happen... *if* being the operative word here.

To kill some time and in an attempt to try to distract myself, I'd been browsing the BBC news from the UK, something that I hadn't done in forever. It was strange to see all the same old stuff being reported, from jobs being lost thanks to a car plant being shut down, to a piece about how some actor had been caught in a scandal with a member of the royal family who'd just checked into a drug rehab clinic.

One piece of news that had jumped out and made my astronomer's heart beat faster was the discovery of two asteroids that had been nicknamed Pollux and Castor, that had passed near the Earth. They had been discovered by the La Silla Observatory in Chile, far out beyond the orbit of our moon. If I'd realised when we'd been out there, I might have suggested a quick fly by on the way back, just for the thrill of being the first people to witness it.

But the news that had really caught my eye for all the wrong reasons was an item about a politician called Alexander Langton who'd managed to organise something of a coup within his own political party and then somehow seized the top job to become the UK's new unelected prime minister.

I distinctly remembered Langton because of all the bad press that had followed him round like a swarm of flies following a bad smell. He'd been our local MP, and had been parachuted by his party into Macclesfield ward then had somehow won a parliamentary seat by promising the moon to anyone gullible enough to believe his particular brand of spin. It soon became clear that he was one of those politicians who excelled in the ability to lie through his teeth to people's faces but never to be held to account over anything that he had said. Langton scoring the top job wasn't good news in any way or form for my country and learning about it did nothing to lighten the sense of despair that I was currently feeling.

The door opened and a very bleary-eyed Jack appeared with two Thermos coffee cups in his hand.

'When I realised you were missing from the bed I figured you might be here,' he said.

I placed my tablet down on the table. 'You know me way too

well. And yes, I've been like a cat on a hot tin roof waiting to hear what's happened to Lucy.'

'So, no report of any sightings from all the X-craft that Niki sent out then?' Jack asked as he sat down next to me.

'Nothing at all and before you ask, I've had Delphi trailing through social media for any sightings of a blazing blue fireball.'

'That's hardly surprising is it? The last fix one of our X103s had on her was that she was heading south over the Indian Ocean before the crew lost her. Unless someone onboard a boat spotted Lucy flying overhead, it's not surprising that no one has reported seeing anything odd, that region is so remote. Anyway, one of these is for you.' He pushed one of the mugs towards me along the table.'

'Mind reader,' I said, opening the lid and taking a much needed mouthful of fresh black coffee.

'I try my best to be, although it's not always easy with you,' Jack replied with a smile.

The door opened again and this time Mike and Alice — the president of the Sky Dreamer Corp, which had made our efforts to recover the micro minds possible — entered the room.

'See, I told you they'd be here,' Alice said to Mike. 'But please tell me you haven't been here all night?'

Jack shook his head. 'I just arrived, but I reckon that Lauren's been here since the small hours.'

'You do know that Delphi would have sent you an alert if she found out anything, Lauren,' Alice said, manoeuvring her wheelchair towards the head of the oval meeting table.

'Yes, I know, but I keep wracking my brains that we're missing something obvious,' I replied. 'It's been looping through my head. So I thought I might as well wait it out here rather than stare at the ceiling in our bedroom all night.'

'Yeah, tell me about it,' Mike said. 'We're this close to a breakthrough and then this happens.'

Alice looked around the table at us and shook her head. 'Will you look at all the long faces in here? It's like I've just wandered into a stable.'

We all gave her a blank look before I realised what she meant. 'Oh — like horses?'

'Exactly,' she replied. 'And before you give up, it's not even been eight hours since Lucy went missing and you're all imagining the worst-case scenario. Maybe it's because I was born an optimist, but I can't help but feel that everything is going to work out fine. You just wait and see. Anyway, my suggestion is this: I've always found that exercise can really help at times like these, it takes your mind off things.'

'Yes, I could probably do with a run just to burn off my nervous energy,' I replied, turning towards Jack. 'Fancy joining me to do exactly that, topside?'

'As long as you promise to slow down a bit. Not all of us are built to run marathons like you are.'

I smiled at him as I warmed to the idea of a run in the fresh air. 'I promise not to embarrass you.'

'Always a good thing,' he said, shaking his head with an amused look.

I'd settled into my usual running rhythm as I jogged beneath the jungle canopy, which was providing some welcome shelter from the strength of the sun overhead. Of course I was running at nowhere near my usual speed, purely for the benefit of my running partner, who despite being fit was barely keeping up with my leisurely pace.

But Alice had been right, the exercise proved to be a welcome distraction. The flow of my run was almost like moving mediation. The churn of my thoughts had already been muted by the drum beat of my feet on the ground and the rocking of my arms back and forth as I settled into my running rhythm. It was certainly in the middle of exercise that I often found my greatest sense of stillness and that was something I needed on this day more than most. Yes, cool Commander on the surface, but frantically paddling like crazy to stay afloat.

A chorus of whoops came from a troop of monkeys in the trees, sounding the alarm call as we passed beneath them. The branches began to shake as they started to move away, followed by a flutter of leaves swirling down towards the jungle floor.

'Once, on a trip in the Amazon rainforest, a guide had told me that was called monkey rain,' I said, glancing back at Jack.

'Just as long as it's just leaves and not monkey crap, then I'm fine with it.'

I laughed as he accelerated a bit to pull up alongside me.

'So how are we doing now, Lauren?' he asked.

'Certainly much better for having some fresh air in my lungs and a break from tying myself in a knot of worry waiting for news. How about you?'

'Personally, I'm not as worried as you are, although not as relaxed as Alice seems to be. After all, this isn't the first time that Lucy's gone dark on us. And it has always worked out okay in the past.'

'I appreciate your semi-optimism, but I know I won't be able to relax until we hear that she's okay and this disappearing act is all part of the big Angelus plan.'

'Yeah, I so know where you're coming from,' Jack replied. 'Anyway, are we done yet because I could do with getting back for a shower after exercising in this heat.'

'I've already got that covered. There's a stretch of river that we're about to reach and I'd love to take a dip. A great way to cool off from the heat midway through a run.'

'But I didn't bring any swimming trunks with me,' Jack said.

I cast a grin in his direction. 'Who said anything about swimsuits?'

'Oh...' Jack's grin was so wide that it practically reached his ears. Then suddenly he put on a burst of speed and overtook me. 'Come on, slow coach.'

'So that's what it takes to motivate you on a run,' I said, laughing as I sped up to catch up with my very own Viking.

After all the usual things that you'd expect to happen between two consenting adults who were crazy about each other and found themselves naked in a river with no one to see them had happened, at last I'd discovered a brief sense of contentment and stillness inside me. We were stretched out together on a rock on the embankment, both of us soaking up the dappled foliage sunlight under the jungle canopy that overhung the river as we dried off *au naturel*.

I turned my head and smiled at Jack. 'Now that's what I call a way to take my mind off something.'

'It seemed like the only decent thing to do,' Jack said, returning my smile.

'You, sir, are a complete gentleman.'

'I aim to please, mam,' he said, tipping his imaginary hat.

I laughed. 'Oh and you do it so well.'

Jack snorted, but then looked at me in a way that actually made me go weak at the knees.

'There was something I wanted to ask you, Lauren,' he said, with more than an earnest hint to his voice.

Immediately my mind jumped to the obvious conclusion. If this wasn't the perfect place for a marriage proposal, I didn't know what would be. It would certainly be a very romantic memory to tell our grandchildren.

I sat up and scooped my wet hair over my shoulder, throwing him my best wide-eyed naked water nymph expression. 'What is it, Jack?'

'I don't know about you, but I was wondering what will happen next for us if everything ends up going to plan and we do actually end up defeating the Kimprak?'

Okay, this wasn't the marriage proposal I'd been expecting a moment ago, but in many ways it was just as poignant a question. What was the next part of *our* story going to look like?

I shook my head. 'Do you know I haven't even stopped to think about that. But it sounds like you've given it some thought?'

'Yes, I have actually. Obviously archaeology is in my DNA and you know I'm never happier than when I'm on a dig. So I was thinking I could get back to that, maybe even return to Orkney because even though that bastard Colonel Alvarez destroyed Skara Brae, there are plenty of other sites across that island that I'd love to explore.'

And I could immediately picture it. Jack back doing what he loved on those windswept, beautiful islands. But if radio telescope had been my passion, where exactly did that leave *us* as a couple?

'So what about you, what's your dream?' he asked.

'I don't know really.' I took a breath. 'To be absolutely honest as long as we're together, I really don't care.' And as I said it, I actually meant it. Jack was my anchor in life and as long as we were an item, we could make it work.

But Jack was giving me a thoughtful look. 'Which was exactly what I was about to say to you. Yes, archaeology might be the thing that makes me tick, but I would sacrifice that all to be by your side, Lauren. And if that means mowing the yard whilst you're off having fun doing your astronomy thing, so be it.'

'You'd really sacrifice your career for mine?'

'If that's what it takes for you to be happy, then I'm all in.'

Okay, so this might not have been a marriage proposal, but this was something just as romantic.

I held his hands in mine. 'Let's get one thing clear, if we do actually pull off this whole saving the world gig, then we're going to make it work for both of us, even if it's a six month time share between Orkney and Jodrell Bank.'

' Yeah, that could so work. No wonder that I love you so damned much, Lauren Stelleck.'

'And I you, Jack Harper.' I wrapped myself around him for some serious kissing, leading to where it might, when I heard a background hum growing louder.

I glanced up to see a WASP drone descending directly over the river and rotating towards us.

'Clothes!' Jack said.

We both grabbed our running kit and started pulling it on. The drone seemed to deliberately turn its back on us as it waited for us to get dressed. I was pulling my top on when it eventually spun back around until its camera was facing us again.

Jodie's voice said from the drone's speaker. 'Um, sorry for crashing your party, guys, but, Lauren, I've just fitted the new Battle Command centre hardware to *Ariel*. I could really do with you here to put it through its paces in simulation mode to iron out any kinks.'

'You could have called me on my watch,' I said, hoping my face wasn't as bright red as the burning sensation running through me felt like it was.

'Actually I tried to but you didn't pick up,' Jodie's voice replied.

I glanced at my wrist to see that I didn't actually have my smartwatch on. It was then that I remembered that in my bleary, sleep deprived state that I'd left it on the bedside cabinet.

'Sorry, my mistake,' I said.

'No problem, but that's why I sent a WASP unit to find you.

All I can say is that you two make a very beautiful couple. You could almost be Swedish, cavorting naked in nature like that.'

'I think that's a compliment,' Jack said, shaking his head at me.

I laughed. 'Okay, thanks — I think — we'll see you back at the ranch in a moment, Jodie.'

'Good and sorry again about interrupting your fun,' she replied.

The WASP zipped back up into the air as quickly as it had appeared.

'Do we have to rush straight back?' Jack asked with an innocent expression.

I laughed, jumping back to my feet and dancing away from him before he could grab hold of me. 'Catch me if you can,' I said, setting off at my proper running speed back along the path into the jungle, feeling a lot lighter in myself than I had even an hour ago.

CHAPTER NINE

Erin, Ruby and I sat inside *Ariel* in hangar bay one. Outside on the virtual cockpit we could see Jack, Alice, Jodie and Mike all gazing at the screens of a control station that was connected by an umbilical electrical cord to one of the data outlets in our ship's hull.

'We're ready to run the new Battle Command centre simulation when you're ready, Lauren,' Alice said over the cockpit speakers.

I turned to Erin and Ruby. 'Are you guys ready to give this a whirl?'

'I say bring it on,' Ruby said, cracking her knuckles and then, very disconcertingly, her neck by stretching it from side to side.

'Oh I'm looking forward to this, it should be a real test of my flying skills,' Erin said.

'It will be,' Alice said over the link. 'Your job, Erin and Ruby, is to keep the Commander alive. Lauren, your role will be to issue orders that don't end up costing the lives of most of the crews in your simulated fleet.'

'Wow, no pressure or anything,' I replied.

'You wouldn't be in the command role if we didn't think you could handle it,' Alice said. 'Besides, no one expects you to do all the heavy lifting by yourself. That's what the Battle Command Centre is there for. It will be constantly running its own tactical simulations in the background, suggesting different strategies that you might want to use, with percentage scores against each one for successful outcomes. It uses a fuzzy logic system that has studied nearly every human battle that has ever happened in history.'

'Then with all due respect, why not let the battle computer run the entire thing?' I replied. 'Reading a few books and playing war games with Niki hardly makes me qualified for this role. Surely there must be no end of retired generals that you could recruit for this?'

'But none with your instincts, Lauren,' Jack said, cutting in. 'You are a natural commander whether you realise it or not. You have made the right calls time and time again, making the tough choices of balancing lives against what needed to happen. I certainly don't know a single person here who wouldn't trust their life in your hands. However smart a computer is, it is still a computer and doesn't have your instincts.'

'Absolutely,' Mike added. 'There is no substitute for a seat of your pants, Lauren Stelleck, plan when the shit is hitting the proverbial fan.'

I laughed. 'Okay, but at least this way you get to test out all your belief in me with this simulation. I just hope it isn't misplaced.'

'With all due respect, Lauren, a little more self-belief please,' Alice said. 'You should have heard the way that Tom used to speak about you. He told me all the time that he'd rarely come across anyone with half of your talent for thinking on your feet during a mission.'

'You mean, as in blowing stuff up and making the Overseers' life as difficult as possible?'

'That's the one,' Alice said. 'So let's put that theory to the test. Begin the simulation please, Jodie.'

Eden's Chief Scientist nodded. 'Just a quick heads up before we kick off, Lauren. You'll be facing a superior force of TR-3Bs in this combat simulation, their three hundred craft to your hundred. And as we're talking about you here, Lauren, I probably need to remind you to not throw *Ariel* into the frontline of the combat unless you absolutely have to. If the fleet loses you, they lose their commander and the simulation will continue to run and show what that outcome looks like. And none of us want to see that, do we?'

'Okay, got it, no charging in like a hooligan during a football pitch invasion,' I replied.

'That's the one,' she replied, grinning at me. 'Starting sim in three, two, one...'

Suddenly the view on the virtual cockpit changed from that of the hangar to one of space. The large disc of the Earth was behind us and the moon a crescent in the distance. In front of us, in a random pattern, was a large fleet of X103s and Pangolins with sunlight glinting off their rendered hulls.

'Woah, that's quite the head rush — it feels so damned real,' Ruby said.

'You'll find it even more real when things kick off,' Jodie said. 'We've programmed your REV drive to simulate the gravitational shifts that you would experience during combat flight.'

'So we can pull some Gs during serious manoeuvres?' Erin asked.

'If it overwhelms the gravity dampeners in real life flight, then yes,' Jodie replied.

'Then let's give this bird a shakedown.'

Before I could stop our pilot, Erin slammed the throttle hard forward and rushed headlong towards our own fleet. As promised the extreme acceleration and the resultant G-forces quickly overwhelmed our REV drive. Suddenly we were all pressed back into our seats by the simulated nosebleed-fast acceleration. Then just to put the icing on the cake, our hotshot pilot began slaloming between our other ships, throwing us from left to right in our seats in the high speed manoeuvre.

'Enough already, Erin!' I said as my breakfast of a bacon bagel threatened to make a reappearance.

'Sorry,' she replied with a wide grin that suggested she was anything but.

'Guys, this is meant to be a battle simulation, remember?' Jack said over the comm.

I shook my head at Erin. 'Exactly, so less playing and please get us back to our starting position to try that again.'

'Would it be okay to just try out this one new manoeuvre that I've been practising?' Erin said.

I narrowed my eyes at her. 'Yes, but please don't let me regret that decision.'

'Got it,' she replied, eyes sparkling.

We raced towards one of our Pangolins horizontally and as we passed it, Erin pivoted *Ariel* so that she was angled towards the other ship throughout the manoeuvre. Then she raised the control stick and immediately our ship raced straight upwards, this time pressing my bum hard into my flight seat. Then with her grin growing ever wider, Erin switched direction again in a right-angled flight path and then we were flying back over the Pangolin. I was absolutely certain that if the simulated craft had a human crew onboard they would have been wondering what the hell was going on with our X103 by now.

But Erin still wasn't done. Suddenly we were plummeting straight down before we came to a dead stop at the place where we had started her crazy manoeuvre.

'What the hell do you call that?' I said, glaring at her as I gulped in some air.

'Square dancing,' Erin replied. 'It was something I learned in the theory classes with the other pilots and have been itching to try out. Throw a bit of random movement into it and it will be almost impossible for the enemy to hit us. Also, if you noticed, I was able to keep *Ariel* orientated throughout that manoeuvre for maximum lock on the Pangolin.'

'You go girl,' Ruby said, leaning across from her CIC station and high-fiving her.

'Bloody hell, all I know is that we're going to have to start supplying all our X-craft with sick bags if everyone is going to start pulling that particular move during combat,' I said.

'Actually, as a former stunt pilot, I rather approve, but let's keep focused on the task in hand,' Alice said over the comm. 'So, let's restart the sim and go around again.'

Our fleet disappeared round us on the virtual cockpit and suddenly we were hanging in space back at the position where we'd first entered the sim.

'Okay, this time, Lauren, can you ask Delphi to initiate the Battle Command mode?'

I nodded. As my stomach began to settle again I grabbed a drink of water from my bottle in the newly installed cup holder, one upgrade I so approved of.

I took a deep breath. 'Delphi, please initiate Battle Command mode.'

The view on the virtual cockpit showed our fleet waiting patiently for whatever I was about to put them through, although it was reduced from a three-sixty view to a large central panel on the cockpit ahead of us. The right panel was currently blank, but the one to the left was displaying a geometrical isometric grid. Lines rose up from it to a cluster of triangular green markers. Next to those were metadata tags for each of our ships including our own, which was ringed by a pulsing green marker labelled *Ariel*.

'That left hand screen looks a lot like one of Niki's tabletop wargame setups, but in 3D,' I said.

'Exactly,' Jack said over the link. 'It will give you a clear bird's eye view of what's happening, to help you make tactical decisions.'

'It's certainly a lot less confusing than it is seeing the battle from the perspective of just our own ship.'

'That's the whole point of this Battle Command centre,' Jodie said. 'It's meant to give you an overview of engagement with the enemy.'

'That will hopefully help you when making fleet-wide tactical decisions,' Alice said. 'Obviously, in any battle the one-to-one fighting will come down to the skills of individual pilots, but as a commander, Lauren, you should always be looking at the bigger picture of which units need to be where.'

'I understand, but as I keep saying, I still feel seriously out of my depth here,' I said.

'And that's why Delphi will help you with the heavy lifting,' Jack replied. 'She'll offer up tactical suggestions that you can choose between. But that's the key, *you* choose them not her. Trust your instincts, Lauren, like you have during combat missions — I think you'll surprise yourself.'

'We'll see about that...' I replied, not feeling the least bit confident by his pep talk.

'Okay, to see if the Battle Command Centre is as intuitive as I hope it is to control, we're going to keep quiet during this simulation run and just let you see if you can work out the control interface,' Jodie said. 'But if it gets too much, just say pause to Delphi and I'll brief you on any aspect of the system that isn't clear.'

'Sounds good, so let's give this thing a try then,' I replied.

'Good luck, but you're not going to need it — you're so going to nail it,' Jack said.

Before I could think of a suitably self-derisory comment, the left-hand map panel in the virtual cockpit lit up with a distant cluster of tight red triangles.

'Enemy contact, according to our sensors,' Ruby said, looking at her CIC screen. 'Three hundred TR-3Bs by the look of it, equipped with an armament railgun and at least a third of the units with laser turrets. And true to form they've launched a wave of railgun salvos straight at our fleet.'

Immediately, a swarm of blips started to move at a relative crawl across the map towards the target from the enemy ships. But the metadata tags tracking the hypersonic rounds told a different story and showed that they were actually moving at an equivalent of Mach 10.

'Wow, we have ages to get out of the way before the rounds get anywhere near us,' Erin said, shaking her head.

'Welcome to the world of space combat,' Ruby said. 'It's all on a whole other scale and those projectiles won't reach our fleet for five minutes yet according to our sensors.'

'Good, that means more time to consider our countermove,' I said.

For the first time, the right-hand panel lit up with multiple options, listed phonetically, followed by a short bit of text describing what they did. The first option listed, *Alpha*, had a diagram of green triangles scattered randomly beneath it. There was also a probability score of ten percent ship casualties on our side with five percent for the attacking ships. The next option, *Beta*, showed a square, evenly arranged formation. That increased our casualty projection to twelve percent, but raised the enemy's to around thirty.

There were other options, all clearly listed, but the one that immediately caught my eye was the *Delta* option. In the diagram for that one our fleet had been into phalanx formations.

That absolutely reminded me of one of the Roman tabletop gaming sessions that I'd played with Niki, a recreation of Battle of Cynoscephalae in 197 BC. That had been the real life battle where the Romans had used phalanx formations to totally decimate the Macedon army using the traditional warfare tactic of pretty much charging in.

The stats for the *Delta* option were even more striking, two percent casualty for us to the seventy-five of the attacking force. If those figures were right we'd decimate the approaching formation of ships and then could pick off the survivors in a melee.

'Delphi, initiate Battle Command option *Delta*,' I said.

'Initiating Command *Delta*,' our AI repeated.

At once our ships began to gracefully rearrange themselves into neat phalanxes that would have made a Centurion Commander very proud.

'Very cool,' Erin said.

'And just as straightforward to control as Jodie hoped it would be,' I replied, realising she, along with the others, would almost certainly be listening into our cockpit chatter.

A new list of attack patterns had now opened up. Option *Echo* was listed as a firing solution using wide field railgun rounds targeting that had a five percent chance of hitting anything. Option *Foxtrot* was individual ship targeting, which only had a one percent target of our railgun rounds finding their marks. The option for using our miniguns was greyed out with *range exceeded* messages next to it.

'Those don't look like great odds to me,' I said.

'That's because of the distances involved,' Ruby replied. 'Even with the speed those railgun rounds are moving at, there's still plenty of time to get out of the way, hence the low likelihood of hitting anything.'

'Hang on, look — those hit statistic numbers are starting to tick up,' Erin said.

She was right. Both options had increased a couple of percent.

'That's not surprising because the enemy ships are getting closer, so increasing the odds of a direct hit,' Ruby replied. 'So which option are you going to go with, Commander?'

'Actually, neither of them for now. Firing at these sorts of ranges is simply throwing ordnance away, so we need to wait.'

'Until we see the white of their eyes,' Ruby replied with an amused expression. 'But that's a good call and probably about to be underlined by the hypersonic round fire by the TR-3B fleet.'

My gaze flicked over to the battle map to see the blinking dots for the incoming rounds sail past below our fleet's position, passing through where it had been before I'd issued the *Delta* manoeuvre.

'Amateurs,' Ruby said in a scoffing tone as the hypersonic rounds sailed away into empty space.

Option *Alpha* for a wide-field random firing pattern had now ticked up to ten percent.

'Delphi, initiate option *Alpha* firing solution.'

'Initiating option *Alpha*,' our AI replied.

At once the large Pangolin X104s in our fleet opened fire with their railguns and it was less than three minutes, according to the displayed ETA, for the swarm of green dots rushing out from our fleet to reach the TR-3Bs.

Ruby glanced over her CIC screen. 'Enemy fleet will be in range of our miniguns in two minutes, Commander. Just a shame that we can't use our AIM missiles as they can't manoeuvre in space.'

Jodie's voice cut in. 'Sorry to interrupt, but actually, I've got the Forge team working on exactly that — space torpedoes. We're aiming to have them ready long before the Kimprak arrive here.

Anyway, carry on, Lauren, because I can tell you that you're already doing brilliantly.'

'It's a bit soon to be planning a victory lap, but we'll see...' I replied.

The cockpit fell silent again as we all watched the rounds hurtle towards the fleet. The TR-3Bs were beginning to move into a very random formation and it looked like whatever military playbook the sim was using for the enemy fleet had just been thrown out of the window. It was probably an attempt by Delphi to simulate the Captains on those opposing ships panicking, which meant that we were playing this game in easy mode.

At last and after what seemed like forever, multiple explosions lit up the enemy fleet and a total of twenty-eight of their craft blinked out of existence.

A new tactical sub-option had now appeared on the formation listing for the *Delta* option that I'd previously ordered, *Advance X104s to frontline.*

'What's that about?' I said, gesturing towards it.

'Probably because those current laser variants of the TR-3Bs are about to come into weapon range.'

'And Delphi wants me to use the X104's heavier armour to soak up the laser blasts?'

'I think that's exactly it,' Ruby replied.

I nodded. 'Delphi, initiate *Delta* sub-option one, advance X104s.'

'Advancing X104s,' the AI replied.

Our heavy craft started to move forward through the lines to take their positions at the front of the fleet.

A new option for continual railgun firing came up, but even though the chance of a successful strike was only eleven percent, I ordered them to do it anyway. Any opportunity to thin out their ranks before they reached us for closer combat, I'd grab with both hands. But our hypersonic rounds had barely been fired when an alarm warbled.

'We're in laser weapon range,' Ruby called out.

Dozens of beams of energy lanced out all at once and travelling at the speed of light, ate up the distance in a shockingly small amount of time. Too fast to avoid, they struck dozens of our X104s, as we could see all too well in the central viewing screen as green flashes lit up. Immediately, the metadata tags on the battle display started to show ablative shield damage as the Pangolins soaked up the punishment, just like they were designed to do.

But now for the first time we could see the distant TR-3Bs visually speeding towards us on the main central screen. At that same moment the greyed-out minigun option lit up at last.

'Delphi, initiate option *India* attack pattern,' I called out, leaning forward a fraction against my harness.

'Initiating option *India*,' Delphi replied.

A barrage of minigun fire tracer lit up as the lead wing of TR-3Bs hurtled towards our ships. But as I hoped they would be, they were shredded apart by the armour-piercing rounds as they were hit. One by one, explosions lit up the leading edge of the attacking ships and the total enemy ships dropped by another fifty to two hundred and twenty.

But we were starting to take casualties on our side too. Three Pangolins and five X103s blinked out of existence as intense laser fire locked onto them. I'd barely the time to process what had happened when a new list of options appeared under the formation list, option *Juliet* to melee.

'Delphi, initiate option *Juliet* now!' I shouted, so caught up in this fight I no longer thought of it as a simulation, but a real life and death struggle.

At once every ship in our fleet broke apart and began

engaging the enemy one on one as the TR-3Bs swept into our ranks.

The firefight was shocking, ships detonating rapidly on both sides. In less than a minute there was just a single TR-3B left, which was taken out by a Pangolin's railgun.

I whooped and punched the air. 'Take that, Overseers!'

But Erin and Ruby were looking at me with strange expressions on their faces.

'What's wrong? We won, didn't we?' I said.

Erin grimaced and gestured towards the Battle Command screen map. It was only then, for the first time, that I realised only a dozen of our X-craft were left on the battlefield, including *Ariel*.

I stared at the total number of losses displayed for all to see — eighty-nine percent — as shame slammed into me.

'Oh bloody hell, that so got away from me,' I said.

Ruby shook her head at me. 'Yes, we saw, because you should never have selected the melee option. Didn't you see how low the odds were beneath it?'

I grimaced. 'To be absolutely honest, no I didn't.'

'It was ninety percent casualties projected to destroy the attacking fleet,' Ruby said. 'So it looks like Delphi nailed it with the battle projections. Just a shame that our Commander didn't.'

I winced at her harsh words, but I knew she was right — I shouldn't haven't gone for the melee option. It was exactly what Niki had shown me when we'd wargamed the Battle of Cynoscephalae, and how the Roman army discipline of holding the phalanx formation had won them such a crushing victory. It was a shame I had forgotten about that same lesson just now, when it mattered most. I winced inwardly at my usual hot-headedness costing so many virtual lives.

'This is what training is for and at the end of the day this was just a simulation,' Erin said.

'Just as damned well,' Ruby muttered under her breath.

Before I could reassure her that I was going to learn a lesson from what had just happened, the virtual cockpit went blank as the cockpit lights came up and the airlock door opened.

Mike came rushing in and gestured towards us to follow him.

'Don't tell me, Alice wants to see me about my performance just now?' I said.

'Huh?' Then he rapidly shook his head. 'Sorry, we were all distracted from your sim battle by what's just happened. We just received multiple contacts from the TREENO CubeSat network — it detected a massive neutrino spike. Not only that, but the IceCube station did too and the reading was off the scale.'

'IceCube as in the Antarctic research station?' I asked.

'That's right,' Jack said, appearing in the doorway. 'And it all kicked off a few minutes ago. The epicentre seems to be bang in the middle of the Antarctica landmass.

I stared at it, a spark of hope igniting inside me. 'Antarctica is to the south of the Indian Ocean — right where Lucy was last spotted.'

'Exactly,' Jack said, now smiling at me.

My spark of hope ignited into a flame, pushing aside my performance as a battlefield Commander for a moment. 'Then it sounds like we need to sort out some serious cold weather gear because it looks like we're going on an expedition to the South Pole.'

'We better get our thermals out then,' Mike said, grinning at me.

CHAPTER TEN

Six hours later and now joined by Mike and Jack onboard *Ariel,* the simulated view of a large fleet of our X-craft had now been replaced by a real life one. Seventy of our ships stretched away around us in formation as we flew high through the atmosphere towards Antarctica.

Erin kept glancing around at the other craft as she piloted *Ariel.* 'This is the biggest single deployment we've had of the Earth fleet. There's a lot of combined firepower around us.'

'You better believe it, it's probably enough to invade a small country if we wanted to,' Ruby replied.

'Let's just stick to the plan, shall we?' I said. 'Talking of which, once we arrive at the site the priority will be to form a protective shield around Lucy if she really is there.'

'Then let's just pray that the Overseers haven't beaten us to her,' Jack said.

'Unfortunately, we all know that is a real possibility,' Mike replied. 'They would have seen the neutrino pulse just like we did. But the main thing in our favour beating them to Lucy is that they haven't got anything like as large as our own TREENO network, so in theory will mean it will take them longer to triangulate her position. The problem for us is that there's been constant bursts of neutrino activity coming from what we have to assume is Lucy's location every thirty-three minutes.'

'Talk about a *come and get me, why don't you* invite,' Jack said.

'Exactly,' Mike replied. 'Assuming it really is Lucy, the next question is why are these pulses continuing?'

'Presumably this is all still part of the ongoing Angelus plan,' I said.

Mike nodded. 'That's my guess too and if so, this continuing activity could actually be a very good sign.'

'Yes, it could and I'm certainly intrigued about that location. I can't help wondering if there is some sort of Angelus artefact under the ice there,' Jack said.

'You mean something like the Resonancy Generator?' I asked.

Jack shrugged. 'It could be. But if the Resonancy Generator was the opening act to the grand finale, I can't wait to discover what we might be about to find there.'

'About that — here's an interesting fact for you about Antarctica: it's always had more than its fair share of magnetic anomalies,' Mike said. 'In fact, a huge one was discovered by a Russian science team, which bored three miles down through the ice to discover an underground lake with a closed-off ecosystem. The theory was that maybe the anomaly was caused by the Earth's crust being thinner at that point.'

'You're not saying that's where Lucy may have landed, are you?' Jack asked.

Mike shook his head. 'No, the neutrino burst is a hundred miles west of that location, but it's also an area where there is another magnetic anomaly that's never been investigated.'

'So you think this might be significant?' I asked.

'I'm not sure, but *Thor* is carrying a lot of scientific kit so that me, and the rest of the science team, can do a thorough survey of the site when we arrive. To be honest, I'm itching to start analysing the data — my instinct is that we're about to hit the jackpot.'

'Well, you won't have to wait much longer,' Erin said. 'We're about five minutes out and the Antarctica landmass should be coming into view any moment now.'

'That's good, because if this is Lucy, I just need to see with my own eyes that she's okay,' I said. I glanced over at Erin. 'As the *fasten your seat belt* sign isn't up, is it okay to walk the flight deck and stretch my legs for a bit?'

She chuckled. 'Knock yourself out, Lauren. And if anyone needs a comfort break, now's the time as the rest room will be locked as we come in to land.'

'And return your table to a stowed position and secure any loose bags too, right?' Jack asked.

She laughed. 'Yeah, that as well.'

I unfastened my harness and after having a good, full body Yoga stretch, I headed towards the front of the flight deck. Jack joined me.

Together, we leant on the railing like *Ariel* was a cruise ship on a voyage, looking out over the endless sea far below us, topped with rolling, white-capped waves.

'You know, I've always wanted to travel to Antarctica, partly because it's the remotest place on Earth,' Jack said.

'There aren't exactly a lot of archaeological sites there for you to get excited about though, are there?' I asked.

'Hey, a holiday destination doesn't always have to include ancient ruins, although if I'm honest it normally does. But there is something about an untouched wilderness that tugs at my explorer's soul.'

'You and me both. But have you seen the cost of cruise tickets to get there though? I researched going once and quickly gave up on the idea when I realised it was going to cost me half a year's salary.'

'Yes, that's the one. Although I have to say, we're going to arrive in quite some style this time around, onboard *Ariel*.'

I laughed. 'Aren't we just.'

He glanced across at me. 'Hey, I also just wanted to grab a quiet word about how you're doing after that simulation run?'

The shame and embarrassment I'd felt at the first real test of my abilities as a Fleet Commander, came flying back to me at full force. 'Not great if I'm honest, Jack. I got so caught up in playing it like a computer game that I acted instinctively rather than thinking things through, and taking a moment to check my options. What's really haunting me is what if I do that in a real life battle? Do that and I could end up throwing away countless hundreds of lives because I selected the wrong bloody option at the wrong bloody time.'

'Well you wouldn't be the first Commander to do exactly that in a real life battle, but I promise you that you will never be one of those leaders who carelessly sacrifices the lives of others. And that's because you care — really care — Lauren, and that's a good thing. I also promise you that when the moment comes during a large scale battle, even when you're having to think of the bigger tactical picture, you'll make the right call. A sim is one thing, but real life is completely another.'

'Thank you. Sometimes I honestly think that you're the only person who really gets me.'

'Don't be so sure about that. You're surrounded by friends who get your special brand of Lauren madness. But I warn you, there may be moments when you have to sacrifice some ships in order to win a battle.'

'You mean literally order crews into certain death situations?'

'I do, and as hard as it will be for you, sometimes that might be the only option available to save even greater losses.'

'In that case, I hope it never comes to that.'

'Well if it ever does, I'll always be here for you.'

I reached over and squeezed his hand. 'And vice versa.'

We looked out in companionable silence, arms slightly touching, towards a thin sliver of white on the horizon and the towering, billowy clouds above.

'I think that's land ahoy, Commander,' Jack said, turning towards me with a smile.

I barely had time to nod, because thanks to the Mach 9 we were currently flying at, the line of white had already expanded into a large expanse of sea ice stretching towards a snow-covered rocky coastline ahead of us.

Ruby made a *humph* sound and we turned to see her frowning at one of her screens. 'Looks like we're about to enter an intense snowstorm over the target site. According to the weather data from the Antarctica ground station, visibility will be less than a couple of klicks and the forecast is for it to get a lot worse.'

Mike rolled his eyes. 'As though the freezing temperatures aren't enough by themselves.'

'Just as well we've come prepared for anything,' I replied. 'Niki has even loaded *Thor* with snowcats and snowmobiles so there's no need to travel anywhere on foot.'

'As long as there is plenty of coffee I can cope with some nippy temperatures,' Mike said.

'I think it's a bit more than that, more like minus seventy Fahrenheit,' I replied. 'But thankfully our heated arctic gear should be more than able to cope with that.'

'Which is exactly why I brought an Accuracy International Arctic Warfare rifle with me,' Ruby said. 'It's highly reliable in sub-zero conditions like this.'

'I'm hoping that this doesn't end up in yet another ground

fight,' Mike replied. 'The mission at Angkor Wat was enough to last me several lifetimes.'

'We always have to assume the worst case,' I replied. 'Maybe one of these days we'll be pleasantly surprised and today will be that day.'

The others just gave me the *look*.

I held up my hands. 'Okay, who am I trying to kid? Especially with our track record. But with the amount of firepower our X-craft fleet has, I'd like to see the Overseers try.'

That statement was met with a lot more positive nods.

I returned my attention to the sea ice suddenly being replaced by land as we passed over the shoreline. Now the odd rocky peak was rising above a smooth snow field as we headed straight towards the looming stormfront. It looked majestic from within the safety of *Ariel*, but I knew that the conditions out there were so extreme that no one could last long without the right equipment.

'If you'd like to return to your seats, we'll be commencing a landing approach in a few minutes,' Erin said.

As Jack and I strapped ourselves back in, snowflakes began to whip past *Ariel* as we reached the edge of the blizzard. But as soon as we entered the bank of cloud, visibility cut right down and we could barely see the ground anymore. The other X-craft were still clearly visible though, including *Thor* to our stern, thanks to the virtual cockpit's enhanced rendering system.

'Okay, forty klicks out and beginning to decelerate,' Erin said as she pulled back on the throttle.

Immediately we began to slow and the fleet behind us matched our revised speed perfectly thanks to Delphi's ship to ship communications, which helped coordinate our fleet's movements. That was something of an essential considering the speed we were tearing through the sky at, if we didn't want to end up with X-craft piling into each other. That feature would be particularly important during any air battles when our ships were performing extreme manoeuvres.

Almost like a single organism the fleet dropped to *just* a thousand miles per hour as we closed on the coordinates of our target.

Mike was looking at a sensor screen that he'd pulled up on his flight seat console. 'If Lucy sticks to her thirty-three minute schedule there should be another neutrino pulse in three, two, one...'

A brief crackle of interference passed through the virtual cockpit.

'As regular as an atomic clock,' Mike said, shaking his head.

I gazed at the green destination marker that had now appeared dead ahead of us on the virtual cockpit with the distance indicator next to it rapidly running down. According to a mini version of the battle computer's 3D map on my console, I couldn't see any markers for enemy craft, but even so I wanted to make doubly sure.

'Ruby, any sight of enemy activity?' I asked.

'None at all,' she replied. 'If the Overseers plan on making an appearance they haven't turned up yet.'

'Probably too busy licking their wounds after what happened at Angkor Wat,' Jack said.

I hoped his optimism was right, but our enemy had always been tenacious before, so why should this time be any different?

'Okay, just five nautical miles out, but I can't get any sort of sensor lock on whatever it is,' Erin said. 'But if it is Lucy we should be able to see her any moment now.'

The sense of anticipation grew inside me as we slowed to what amounted to a relative crawl for *Ariel,* as the rest of the fleet once again matched our change in velocity.

The snow was falling more heavily now and we could barely see any distance. Then suddenly I caught the barest glint of gold through the swirling curtains of snow. The blizzard thinned in a *da-da* moment.

A feeling of sheer joy surged through me as I saw Lucy's burning yellow star half buried in the ground, sitting in the middle of a wide impact crater that had thrown snow outwards for hundreds of metres. I felt every muscle in my body relax once I realised that apart from the strange golden colour, Lucy looked to be still in one piece.

'Ruby, can you try to make contact with her?' I said, sitting forward in my seat.

'I've been pinging her for the last five minutes, but I'm receiving no voice or data packets coming back.'

'So she must be still offline then?' Mike asked.

'Maybe this is like a longer, more drawn-out version of what normally only lasts a few minutes during a micro mind merging process?' Jack said. Then his eyes widened. 'Hang on, we're missing something obvious here.'

I caught on as my mind jumped to the same conclusion that had struck him. 'Using my Empyrean Key to see if she responds?'

Mike was already nodding his agreement. 'If anything will make her take notice away from whatever it is that she's doing, I think that's as likely to work as anything.'

'Okay, but that impact crater is too sloping for us to land in, so we'll need to find a spot to set down just beyond its perimeter,' Erin said.

I nodded. 'Ruby, could you please radio Niki and ask *Thor* to join us down on the ground with a snowcat and his Tin Heads to deploy on guard duty? Then order the rest of the fleet to form a defensive wall around this site.'

'You mean I get to play with your snazzy new Battle Command Centre?' she asked.

'Yes, but just try not to launch an attack on any unsuspecting penguins or seals whilst we're gone.'

She snorted and snapped me a salute. 'Roger that, Commander. Then her fingers were flying over her keyboard and a moment later she had the Battle Command Centre on her CIC screen.

'Okay, Erin, take us in,' I said.

Our pilot dipped her chin towards me and immediately *Ariel* slowly descended towards the ground as the blizzard swirled around the gravity field bubble, enveloping us.

I glanced towards the others. 'Okay guys, let's hope that our arctic gear is as good as Jodie said it is, because we're about to seriously put it to the test.'

CHAPTER ELEVEN

THE BLIZZARD WAS HOWLING around the snowcat as Niki drove it trundling down the snowy slope on its wide rubber caterpillar tracks towards the bottom of the impact crater where Lucy was nestling like a glowing coal. We were flanked on either side by a couple of the white, camo- painted Tin Head robots that Niki had deployed to guard us. Meanwhile, the rest of the robotic squad was patrolling the perimeter.

In the howling blizzard Ruby had told us that it was a no-go launching the WASPs, so instead she had ordered three other X-craft to form a protective ceiling above us. Normally they would have been totally invisible, but in the swirling snowstorm their gravity blisters were revealed as transparent oval outlines. Meanwhile, Ruby — using one of the Battle Command Centre options — had ordered the rest of the fleet to ten klicks out to form a protective wall of craft. Any attack by the Overseers would have to go through them first to reach us.

Mike was watching the display on the cab with a hawklike gaze. 'Okay, according to the TREENO satellite parked almost directly overhead, neutrino activity is currently non-existent. The next pulse is due in twenty minutes, so it would be better if weren't standing right next to it when that happens. Much safer to be back onboard our craft, which has sufficient shielding to absorb the pulse.'

'What, you're saying that we're going to be facing dangerously high levels of radiation down in that crater?' Jack asked.

'Not from one burst, but if we are exposed to more than one it will begin to add up, so better to play it safe for the sake of everyone's long-term health.'

'You do realise that you've now made every single one of us paranoid about dying from radiation sickness?' I replied.

'Yep, that's my self-appointed role — to scare the crap out of people so they can stay safe on this mission,' Niki replied.

'In that case, our time at the actual site will be limited to around five minutes before we have to head back,' I said. 'Hopefully, that should be long enough for me to establish contact with Lucy using the Empyrean Key.'

The others nodded, meanwhile the snowcat's cabin rocked as a gust of wind howled round it.

Niki glanced at a weather station display on the dash. 'Okay, these conditions are getting much worse and very quickly. Maybe we should consider moving Lucy inside *Thor* with some Agie plates.'

'That doesn't sound like a good idea on two counts,' Mike replied. 'One, you don't want her throwing out large neutrino pulses inside any of our ships for obvious reasons. Second, the fact that she's here at all suggests she's come here for a reason, unless this really is just a random crash on her part. But I think based on the fact that this is pretty much bang on top of that magnetic anomaly that I mentioned before, my guess is that this is anything but a coincidence. I think even attempting to airlift her back to Eden could be seriously counterproductive to whatever the grand Angelus plan is.'

'Then it sounds like we're going to have to leave her where she crash landed,' I said.

Just then our snowcat bounced over some shattered chunks of permafrost ice as Niki slowed us to a stop and immediately started a countdown timer on his Sky Wire.

'That's twelve minutes and counting before we have to leave to get back safely before the next pulse,' he said. 'Everyone make sure that your suit's heating system is set to high. It's going to be a decidedly chilly minus forty when you factor in the wind chill.'

I nodded and along with everyone else I toggled down the sealed visor with its inbuilt heating element. My HUD flickered into existence, projected onto the curved visor. Also, like a pair of tinted ski goggles, the view had already automatically dimmed to a much more comfortable amber, which was a considerable help when trying to make things out in what was now the almost featureless white of the blizzard screaming past the cab's windows.

Niki grabbed a coiled rope from the back seat.

'What's that for?' I asked.

'I'm going to keep us roped with one end tethered to the snowcat. You wouldn't believe how easy it is to get disorientated in a blizzard like this.'

'Isn't that a bit of an overkill when we have a GPS map built into our helmet's HUD?' Mike asked.

'Not if your suit's system fails for any reason. So I like to keep it old school, just in case.'

Niki had to press his shoulder against the wind howling on the other side of the door. As he pushed it open the blizzard blew into the cab and the temperature display on my HUD dropped from what had been a reasonable but cosy fifty Fahrenheit down to the minus forty outside.

Jack opened the door on our side with a lot less effort as it wasn't facing into the wind. Then having checked the Empyrean Key was safely stowed in my bag, I followed him and Mike out into the raging gale.

The moment I stepped outside, apart from the glowing coal of Lucy's micro mind ship sitting at the bottom of the crater a hundred metres away from us, it was almost impossible to see anything else.

Niki loomed out of the blizzard as we huddled under cover from the wind behind the snowcat. He connected the carabiner on the rope to the front bull bars of the vehicle and then handed the other end to us.

'Okay, whatever you do, don't let go of this rope, it could literally be your lifeline in this storm.' Niki said over my helmet's speakers, without which it would have been impossible to hear over the screaming wind.

Mike and Jack nodded as I wrapped the rope around my hand.

He tied the other end of the rope around his waist and then gave us a thumbs up. He turned and headed down towards Lucy with driving steps through the snow.

The moment I stepped out of cover of the snowcat, I was buffeted hard by the wind, making me slip until I angled my body into it.

I could just make out the lip of the crater above us and the silhouettes of one of the Tin Heads, as snow blew in waves across the top. In a storm this intense it would only take a matter of hours for Lucy to become buried under a significant blanket of snow.

The blizzard closed in again. Now I could barely see the guys in front and behind me, let alone anything else. In that moment, despite the reassuring map markers in my HUD for everyone's locations, as well as Lucy and the Bobcat, I was most grateful for the tactile sense of the rope gripped in my mittened hand. It felt exactly like what it was, a reassuring anchor in the storm. Maybe Niki really did have a point after all?

With driving steps I kept pushing forward with the others. At one point Mike slipped, but Jack was immediately on the case, grabbing onto his arm to steady him before he was whipped away by the storm.

There was zero talk over the comm channel, all of us concentrating too hard on just staying upright. But gradually, with every step, a glowing ball of light began to grow stronger as we neared the marker for Lucy.

'Okay, Lauren, do whatever you have to as quickly as possible when we reach Lucy,' Niki finally said, breaking the strained silence. 'Mike, the same goes for you placing your sensors. This storm is much worse than I expected and we'll have less than five minutes at the site before we need to turn round. We need to give ourselves plenty of time to get back to our ships before the next pulse hits.'

'Don't worry, I'm not going to hang around out here any longer than I have to,' I replied.

'The same goes for me,' Mike said. 'Jack, can you give me a hand placing the sensors?'

'You've got it, buddy,' Jack replied.

The light intensified considerably like a lighthouse beacon guiding us through the snow-storm as we neared our destination. Then suddenly, like a white curtain had been pulled back, we were standing before Lucy, her micro mind glowing deep gold. The most important thing that I immediately noticed — and breathed a mental sigh of relief about — was that my initial assessment had been right, there wasn't a crack to be seen in her crystal matrix anywhere. I also noticed that there were crystal roots burrowing out from her, straight down into the bedrock beneath that her crash landing had exposed. A tangible warmth was radiating from her that was doing a lot to take the edge off the vicious windchill.

'Looks like Lucy has made herself at home here,' Mike said, gesturing towards the root system. 'And that suggests to me that there really is something significant at this location.'

'Maybe something to do with that magnetic anomaly?' I asked.

'Whatever it is, talking as the man responsible for keeping you all alive, you can debate this later when we're safely back onboard,' Niki said. 'Meanwhile, you need to keep focused and do what you came here to do.'

'Yes, sorry, I'm on it now,' I replied.

I might be the Commander, but I knew that wouldn't stop Niki, who was in charge of security, bossing me around whenever he needed to. And as far as I was concerned that was a very good thing and something that I would always encourage him to do. As Jack might say, it was all about keeping it *real*.

I unslung my small rucksack with some difficulty thanks to my heavily insulated mittens but a moment later I had the Empyrean Key clasped in my hand.

Mike was already busy driving the hardened steel spikes of the probes into the rock with Jack's assistance, using a lump hammer.

'Okay, Delphi, transmitting carrier tone,' I said.

'Transmitting carrier tone now,' she replied.

The familiar deep chime rang out through my speakers as the snow swirled around me.

Nothing happened.

'Any good?' Niki asked, peering at me through my faceplate.

'Nothing yet.' I tried turning up the volume of the carrier tone, but once again no icons appeared.

Then Niki was pointing to the external speakers on my helmet. 'Lauren, they're blocked with ice. There's no external tone being generated to bounce off that stone of yours.'

'Oh bloody hell, I didn't think about that.'

'Let me try scraping them off,' Niki said. He withdrew a small knife from a pouch on his belt. 'Okay, hold still,' he said

He started to work away at the ice that had begun crusting around the side of my helmet but after a couple of minutes of work, he shook his head.

'Sorry, it's freezing up again as quickly as I can clear it,' he said. 'Although we have all this technology at our disposal, we're easily defeated by a bit of ice.'

But an idea was already forming in my mind. 'Niki, the carrier tone is working fine within my helmet so I'm going to crack my visor open a fraction to let the sound out.'

'Are you sure? Your face will be literally frozen off with thirty seconds exposure if it's unprotected in these temperatures.'

'Understood but don't worry — I won't be exposing my face to this for any longer than I have to.'

He nodded, and positioned himself to act as some kind of human wind barrier for me.

As I cracked my mask open, my breath was literally stolen away. Cold didn't get anywhere close to describing what the temperature was like. The heated environment of my combat suit had in no way prepared me for what was coming. It was a cold so intense that could I feel the temperature draining away instantly from the surface of my skin.

Teeth chattering, I looked down at the Empyrean Key to see a single glorious icon hover there. And it was something I'd never seen before — a segmented hexagram.

Without even hesitating, I spun it into the selection window and flicked my wrist forward.

Just like that, the storm disappeared around us as we were

yanked straight out of our world and into something that couldn't have been a starker contrast if it had tried.

CHAPTER TWELVE

Niki and I were standing together, whilst nearby, both in a crouched position on the ground, were Mike — who still had one of his sensors clutched in his hand — and Jack, who'd been about to hammer into the ground. They were both staring around them, slack-jawed with good reason.

We'd materialised in a large, spherical, dome-shaped room at least fifty metres wide and were on a broad balcony that curved around the edge of it. The first thing that immediately seized our attention was along a walkway that headed out towards the middle of the domed room — a version of Lucy's micro mind identical to the one we'd just left behind in our world. She hung in mid-air, glowing with the same golden light as her twin. But this version was much more incredible compared to the one we'd left behind in Antarctica. The merged micro mind ship before us had prismatic reflected versions of itself within it, stretching away towards infinity within the multi-faceted segments that made it up. It was a bit like one of those changing rooms where two mirrors face each other, allowing you to see your own reflection repeated disconcertingly, vanishing away into the distance.

Golden light rippled through the edges of the fused crystals, adding to the totally mesmerising illusion that you could fall into it and keep falling forever. If that wasn't enough of a spectacle to steal the breath away, it was hovering in the centre of a translucent hologram of Earth wrapped around it.

I pulled off my helmet as my HUD was indicating a very comfortable room temperature; the others did the same.

'Woah, that's quite the head rush! But where the hell are we?' Jack asked.

'I'm guessing that this is some sort of construct in E8, like the other environments,' I replied.

'I think it has to be,' Mike said as we all turned to take in the rest of the room.

Around us were pillared alcoves. The domed ceiling appeared to be a sort of Buckminster Fuller construction with tessellated triangular panels that had recesses built into each of them. There were four closed doorways on opposite sides of the round room, with no sign of any control panel to open them.

As my eyes adjusted to the shadows in the alcoves, the air caught in my throat when I realised there were stationary figures here too. Most were men and women, but a few were featureless humanoid figures just like Eranos, who I'd met back at the Resonancy Generator and who hadn't taken on a human identity. It was then that I spotted Lucy among them and relief surged through me.

'Oh thank god,' Jack said, also noticing her.

I turned and gestured towards the other figures. 'These must be all the AI avatars for each of the micro minds that we've recovered that have merged with Lucy.'

The others nodded as we headed over towards Lucy. As we did so, I spotted the intricate carvings of Angel type creatures around each of the alcoves.

'Hey, have you noticed that at least seven of the alcoves are empty?' Niki said.

I glanced around and saw that he was right.

'That's also the same number missing that the Overseers managed to destroy — it can't be a coincidence,' Mike said.

'Those damned bastards have so much to answer for,' Jack said, shaking his head.

As we reached Lucy, I took in the grey, tight-fitting jumpsuit that was doing wonders for her figure.

I smiled at her. 'Hey, trouble, good to see that you're okay, but you didn't half give us all a scare there for a moment.'

Lucy didn't so much as blink in response.

Jack reached his fingers up towards her face and clicked them. 'Lucy, are you awake?'

Once again she didn't even twitch.

Concern began to rise up through me as I reached out for her hand. 'Lucy?' But instead of soft fingers brushing my fingertips, I felt something as hard as the carved walls of the alcove she was standing in.

I snatched my hand away and drew it to my mouth. 'She feels like she's been turned to stone.'

Jack crossed to Poseidon, who was standing in an alcove a few along from Lucy. He touched the avatar's shoulder and frowned.

'Same thing here, Lauren,' he said.

'This doesn't make sense, why are they like this?' Mike said.

We all stared around the room that we'd found ourselves in, looking for any clue as to what was going on. Niki and Jack went to try and open the doors with absolutely no luck. But as I continued to stare at Lucy, wondering how we could fix whatever had obviously gone wrong, a *whoop* came from behind me.

I turned to see Mike standing at the edge of the balcony, looking at the merged micro minds with his hands on top of his head.

'Bloody hell, why didn't I see this before?' he said as we all headed towards him. 'Although in fairness, it's only become more obvious because the merged micro minds are semi-transparent here in E8.'

'See what, Mike?' Niki asked.

'The shape that the merged tetrahedrons of each micro mind make up. It's actually a geometric shape that you should recognise too, Lauren and Jack.'

'We should?' Jack asked, his brow furrowing.

'Yes, think about the sketch I showed you in that caravan in Orkney,' Mike said. 'Remember I showed you it in my notebook when I was explaining the theory of E8?'

In a split second it all came rushing back. 'I remember. A multi-pointed star made from overlapping triangles, something about the mathematical representation of E8 quasicrystals.'

'Okay, I hate to feel like the slow one here, but quasi what?' Niki asked.

'The theory of E8 proposes that quasicrystals create our reality and that everything we know is just, in a sense, a shadow of a quasicrystal in the eighth dimension,' Mike replied. 'Maybe an easier way to think of it is that the quasicrystal is the source code for our reality.'

Jack was nodding. 'Yes, you drew a star shape that was formed from lots of triangular shapes rotated around a central axis.'

Mike nodded and gestured towards the merged micro minds. 'And that's exactly what we're looking at here. And not in one or two dimensions like I drew in that sketch, but in three dimensions, as we can see now. Well I say three, but look at the way the micro mind seems to be refracting reflections — I'd say we're seeing a whole lot more than three dimensions within it.'

My pulse sped up. 'Are you saying that Lucy has actually been building one of these quasicrystals all this time?'

'If not, it's one hell of a coincidence, Lauren,' Mike replied.

Niki looked between us, his forehead creasing. 'Okay, if that's true, then what will this completed quasicrystal actually do, guys?'

I turned to gaze around us at all the frozen avatars bearing silent witness to our discussion. And then the fragments of the puzzle fell into place and I knew, just knew I was on the right track to solving this.

I pointed to the empty alcoves around us. 'No, not all the micro mind crystals are here. Hence the empty alcoves. Lucy talked about there being redundancy built into the system once before, but what if there aren't enough micro minds here for the quasicrystal to be able to do whatever it was designed to do by the Angelus? And what if those neutrino pulses that have been happening every thirty-three minutes since we got here are a bit like a rocket launch sequence? But it keeps getting shut down by the safety computers because they're really not happy that everything is happening within nominal parameters?'

Jack was now nodding. 'So, running with your rocket launch analogy, Lauren — which I really love by the way — the algorithm detects an anomaly, AKA a missing micro mind, and just like that, shuts down the rocket launch when the computers detect an error.'

'That sounds an awful lot like leaping to a conclusion,' Niki said.

'No, actually I think it perfectly fits the facts that we know,' Mike said. 'Okay, maybe it is a leap, but still a very educated one.'

I beamed at him. 'Exactly.' I turned back towards Lucy. 'And maybe that's why Lucy and all the other avatars are frozen, because they're stuck in some sort of computer boot-up sequence.'

Niki sucked the air in over his teeth. 'If that's true, it's a shame we can't just ask Lucy, especially regarding what we could do about it.'

Jack glanced at my hand and then his eyes widened. 'Hang on, we may be able to do exactly that. There seems to be some sort of icon floating over your Empyrean Key, Lauren.'

I'd been so awestruck when we'd been transported here, I hadn't even thought to look at the stone orb still clutched in my hand. But now, I glanced down to see what looked like two cursors pointing towards each other. Of course, here in E8 the others didn't need synaesthesia to see what only I could on our own world.

I breathed out a huge sigh of relief. 'Okay, this is good because whatever it does, it means something is still running. Also, another new icon that I've never seen before.'

'Then what are we waiting for, turn the damned thing on already,' Niki said.

I grinned at him, totally approving of his *let's just do this* approach. With a flick of my wrist I activated the icon.

At once, all around us rectangular holographic windows appeared in front of each of the avatars in their alcoves. Within each one, dozens of mathematical symbols and sine wave graphs floated.

'Okay, this looks like a step in the right direction,' Mike said, as we all headed back to the holographic display in front of Lucy.

As we neared her, I realised that there was something instantly familiar about the sine wave patterns floating in front of her in the holographic window. And then I knew where I'd seen something similar before.

'Hey, those look exactly like the data we used to capture from radio telescope sessions at Jodrell Bank.' I reached out to point towards the graph and my fingertip just touched the hologram. Of all the things I might have expected it wasn't a slight resistance in the air as though there was a physical surface there.

The sine wave had reacted too, expanding to show a section of it in far greater detail.

Mike whistled. 'This is some sort of holographic interface.'

'And I felt a physical reaction too as I touched it,' I replied.

With a growing sense of wonder, I moved my finger left and right in the air, feeling the tickle of the graph as I scrolled through the sine wave. Then I pulled my finger back and the window stayed where it was. I tried double clicking on one of the formulas and it immediately expanded to fill the virtual screen.

'Wow, I've heard of research in haptic holograms that use high-frequency sound waves emitted by tiny speakers to create the sensation of touching a floating object, but this is at a whole other level,' Mike said, shaking his head.

'So what does that advanced Angelus interface do, exactly?' Niki asked.

'Maybe it's some sort of diagnostic system as it's in front of each figure,' Jack said, examining the holographic window in front of Poseidon, which also contained a sine wave. 'If so, I wonder if I did this...' He tapped his finger on the waveform.

At once, haunting whale song filled the room and Poseidon immediately stirred, his eyes fluttering under his lids.

'Now will you look at that?' Niki said, gesturing with his chin towards the quasicrystal.

I turned to see that one of the crystals in the merged micro mind had lit up blue.

I quickly turned back to Poseidon, whose eyes were moving under his still closed lids. 'Poseidon, can you hear me? We need you to wake up.'

But then he stilled again as the song and hologram faded away. Presumably what had to be Poseidon's individual micro mind in the quasicrystal then turned from blue back to orange.

Immediately I pressed the sine wave in the window in front of Lucy. At once, the same thing happened and whale song filled the room as another micro mind lit up within the quasicrystal. Lucy's head was moving from left to right like she was trying to wake up. I took her hand and this time rather than unyielding stone, I felt soft flesh.

'Lucy, you can do this,' I said.

But then the song was fading away and Lucy stilled again as her flesh stiffened back to stone.

'Damn it, this feels so close to waking her and the other avatars up,' Jack said.

'So what can we do about it?' Niki asked.

'I think this supports Lauren's stalled boot-up theory,' Mike said. 'If we can find a way to get past this, I'm betting that every single AI in here would be wide awake and fully functioning again.'

'Okay, that's great in theory, but how the hell do we go about making that happen?' Jack asked.

My eyes scanned the room looking for any hint of a solution. Then I noticed that the windows in front of the empty alcoves were blank, missing the sine wave data for the whale-like song.

I turned to face the others. 'Okay, I might be going out on a limb here, but maybe the problem is the missing parts of the data from those micro minds that were destroyed.'

'You think if we had them we would be able to complete this boot-up sequence?' Jack asked.

'I think it's certainly a strong possibility,' I replied. 'But the obvious issue is that that's not going to happen when those micro minds were destroyed by our bloody friends the Overseers. Their mindless violence may have cost the Earth our best chance to defend it.'

But Mike, who'd been studying one of the formulas in an empty alcove, held up his hands. 'Woah there, before you go off the deep end, Lauren, I think there might be a way, actually. These mathematical equations seem to link to the sine wave that was transmitted. Even if we don't have the sine waves themselves, it looks like we do have the formula for generating the songs for the missing micro minds.'

I stared at him. 'You're saying that by analysing them we might be able to recreate them?'

'I don't see why not, although I am going to have to do some serious number crunching and bring in the big guns in the form of Jodie and the science team to help.'

'Then let's get them down here to Antarctica as fast as possible — we've got nothing to lose,' I replied.

I faced Lucy again. Whatever it took, I was determined that we'd find a way to wake her and the others up. Then once we'd done that, maybe we'd have a real chance of discovering what this place was and how it could help us defend our world.

CHAPTER THIRTEEN

THE BLUE SKY overhead had thankfully replaced the blizzard of the previous day. But the sunlight was now so bright, intensified by the blinding snow, that it hurt my eyes. I'd had to dim my visor to its darkest level to stop me from squinting.

In the much improved conditions I drove one of the electric-powered Taiga snowmobiles that had been transported onboard *Thor* along with the snowcat towards the X103 that had just arrived. I was taking it easy on the Taiga, having earlier learned my lesson with the ridiculous amount of instant whiplash torque that its electric motors generated. After almost instantly losing control on a couple of occasions, I'd quickly learnt to take it easy with the throttle of this beast of a machine.

I flicked my gaze up to the sky, where I couldn't see even a hint of the X-craft guarding our site, thanks to their chameleon camo system that now wasn't being compromised by a blizzard. The system was so good, in fact, that I wouldn't even have known they were there if it hadn't been for the tactical display on my HUD, which showed a cluster of green overlaid blips that Ruby had ordered into a hundred-mile radius around the site.

After what we'd found in the E8 Angelus hall, Alice had insisted on sending extra reinforcements to protect the site. Thanks to her we were up to a hundred and twenty ships in our fleet now, well over half the contingent of the Earth fleet. But it was a decision that I certainly wasn't going to argue with. Too much was at stake here to take any chances from an Overseer sneak attack. We needed time to work out what we were dealing with and how best to help Lucy and the other micro minds complete what we were all increasingly convinced was some sort of stuck boot-up sequence.

I reached the X103 marker for the cloaked ship and switched off the motor of my snowmobile. Then, appearing hanging in mid-air like some sort of doorway to another world, the ramp of the X-craft began to lower. The next moment, Jodie appeared walking down it, wearing a big white parka with a large, fur-rimmed hood, goggles and a ski mask — the uniform of choice for the science team, who'd been sporting it since their arrival. Jodie was also carrying a metal briefcase containing a vital piece of equipment that Mike had specifically requested.

When Jodie spotted me, she gave me an enthusiastic wave and practically bounded towards me, her insulated boots crunching through the snow. She was the very definition of perky, boundless energy. I really needed to start eating whatever it was that she had for breakfast — probably pickled herring, knowing her Swedish roots.

'Hi Lauren, how have you been getting on here?' she said, reaching my snowmobile.

'Mike's still hitting his head against a brick wall trying to piece together the missing micro mind broadcasts — he's hoping you'll be able to help him crack it.' I replied.

Jodie patted the briefcase she was carrying. 'With some luck this portable radio spectrum analyser will serve up a few insights about what's going on.'

'Good, because it feels like we are seriously close to making a breakthrough and the answer is just staring us in the face.'

'If only Lucy was here to tell us what to do,' Jodie replied.

'Well hopefully it won't be much longer until she comes out of whatever dormant state it is that she's in and she can help us.' I glanced at the HUD countdown timer I'd set as a reminder. 'Okay, we've eight minutes until the next neutrino pulse and I'd like to try and get that spectrum analyser set up to see if we can register anything during the next burst. Hop on and I'll give you a lift.'

Jodie nodded and a moment later she was riding pillion behind me on the Taiga.

As we crested the lip of the impact crater, I could see how much the scene below had been transformed over the last twenty-four hours. A large white camo net now covered the hundred-metre wide impact crater. That was apart from a hole for the ramp, which I headed for on the snowmobile.

The camo net was an extra level of precaution to disguise the crash site. What with that and our ships heavily camouflaged in the air above us, there wouldn't be a lot for any passing military spy satellite to spot down here, although I wasn't convinced that would exactly help us when Lucy was sending out that neutrino pulse every thirty-three minutes to give away her presence. The IceCube station team monitoring neutrino activity on the other side of the Antarctica landmass certainly had to be seriously scratching their heads about what was going in their own back-yard. One way or another, word would eventually get out and someone would come to investigate.

As we dropped beneath the cover of the net on the ramp, the large inflatable dome that had been erected over Lucy's micro mind came into view. Hot air blowers were currently filling the structure to help make life more comfortable for the scientists who were busy analysing it between neutrino pulses, when they weren't having to retreat back to the safety of one of our shielded ships. That was also why the equipment they were using was in lead-lined boxes that could be closed up during the pulses.

I pulled up next to the inflatable habitat and a short while later Jodie and I were heading through the fabric version of an airlock into the toasty dome interior. Men and women in more of the white parka outfits, but with hoods down and gloves off, had connected Lucy up to a rack of monitoring equipment.

'Oh this looks like home from home,' Jodie said, as her gaze took in all the shiny equipment with numerous displays and banks of flashing lights. 'I can set up here and get started.'

I flicked my visor up. 'Actually if you don't mind, not here, Jodie. Mike wants you to join us over in E8 where the real action is happening.'

'Oh right.' Jodie eyes lit up as if she'd just discovered that she'd won an all-expenses paid luxury holiday to the Virgin Islands.

I headed over with her to stand next to Lucy, and took the Empyrean Key out in readiness. 'Okay, can everyone in here just give us a moment to clear the tent? I don't want to teleport you all over to E8 like I did by accident last time.'

I didn't need to tell them twice — every single member of the scientific team instantly pulled up their parka hoods and practically ran out of the door.

I shrugged at Jodie. 'It's all been a bit disconcerting for them; they were minding their own business, concentrating on their work and the next thing they knew they had been transported to E8, wondering what the hell had just happened.'

Jodie grinned at me. 'I can imagine.'

'Oh, you'll do better than that in a moment when you experience it for yourself. But I warn you now, it's seriously spectacular over there during a neutrino pulse.' I turned towards the glowing golden merged micro minds. 'Delphi, transmit carrier tone.'

'Transmitting carrier tone,' the AI replied through my helmet's speakers.

The segmented circular icon appeared and with a flick of my wrist, I activated it.

Our world blurred away around us and then suddenly we were standing in the spherical hall in E8. In contrast to my first visit the hall was now filled with dozens more of the scientific team running a battery of tests, including exploring the holographic interfaces in front of the stationary avatars. Multiple triangular panels were now floating around the holographic Earth, scattered across the continents.

To one side of the room a group of engineers was still attempting to open one of the four doorways that were as locked as they had been since we had first seen them. They'd tried everything, including using a thermal lance that should have been hot enough to melt rock, but even that hadn't worked. I'd already had to refuse point blank the request from one of them to try a C4 charge to try and blow them open, while I flapped my hands at all the things in the hall that could be badly damaged by the resultant blast. The only person missing was Niki, who'd I'd tasked to work with Ruby to take command of the fleet in my absence.

'What are those?' Jodie said, gesturing towards the panels as we took off our arctic gear, appreciating the very pleasant ambient temperature of the room.

'Mike's working theory is that maybe we are looking at some sort of Angelus shield system for our world.'

Jodie's mouth literally fell open. 'That's the secret Angelus plan to protect us?'

'It certainly could be and if so, it would make all the difference in a pitch battle against the Kimprak invasion force.'

'Wow, absolutely,' Jodie replied.

Mike, who'd been working on a laptop set up next to the quasicrystal, spotted Jodie, headed over and hugged her. 'Great, you've made it in time for the next neutrino pulse — it'll be any moment now.'

Jodie nodded. 'Exactly how long have we got?'

I gestured to the large red LED clock display mounted above the racks of equipment. 'Just two minutes according to the atomic clock that your team brought with them.'

Jodie gave me a puzzled look. 'Hang on, I thought time ran independently here in E8 —how come it's running at the same rate as on our world?'

Mike shrugged. 'Our best guess is that with Lucy offline it's defaulted to the same spacetime that we're crossed over from to get here.'

Jodie's eyes widened. 'Then we need to get back before the pulse fries all the kit in here like back in the tent.'

I held up my hands. 'Relax, Jodie, the neutrino pulse isn't happening here, although we have no idea why.'

She tapped her fingers on her lips and got the narrowed-eyed, hunting cat look that she did when she was trying to crack a really juicy problem. 'So it's just restricted to our world, now that's very interesting.'

'Yes, there are so many mysteries to crack here,' Mike said. He gestured to the case in her hand. 'Talking of which, is that the radio spectrum analyser?'

'It is — let's get it set up and listen to what we're dealing with, specifically those missing sine wave data patterns that you mentioned,' Jodie replied, placing the silver briefcase on a bench and opening it.

'I'll leave you crazy kids to your toys,' I said.

My eyes hunted for Jack among the science team. I spotted

him on the far side of the balcony taking photos of the circular wall that the avatar alcoves were set into. I headed over to him as he framed a shot on his Sky Wire of an angel with stylised wings carved around it. But rather than feathers, its wings seemed to be constructed from flowing lines that reached up and over the adjacent alcoves with the frozen avatars standing within them, almost in a protective stance. In this cavern, where there were so many wonders to choose from, I hadn't really taken that much notice of them. But I could see now that those same angel-type designs in variations of male and female were replicated over every alcove.

'Hey, Jack, how have you been getting on?' I asked as I reached him.

He lowered the Nikon camera he'd been using and turned to look at me with a wide grin. 'Like a kid in candy store. I could literally write a dozen papers about all the carvings in here. After this, I'm seriously tempted to get into xenoarchaeology.'

'If my sci-fi nerdism serves me correctly, that's the study of alien archaeology isn't it?'

'Exactly right. And what we have here is the first actual evidence of any Angelus art or sculpture that we've ever found, as opposed to human-created work dedicated to them. And that could tell us more about their culture than anything else we've discovered about them so far.'

I nodded, casting a fresh eye over the intricate carvings with renewed interest. 'So it looked like they believed in angels, which suggests a similar belief system to some of our own religions. That can't be a coincidence can it?'

'I think it's far more than that, Lauren. Did you know that Angelus is actually Latin for angel?'

I stared at him. 'You're not trying to say that the race who built Lucy were actually angels?'

'Not in the way you mean, as divine beings. But rather as an alien race that maybe looked like the carvings depicted here and we now know for a fact visited our world throughout human ancient history.'

A sense of awe filled me as I absorbed the revelation and I peered harder at the strange wings. 'And what about their wings? There's not a feather to be seen anywhere.'

'That's intrigued me too,' Jack replied. 'Maybe that was our far more primitive ancient culture's interpretation about their,' he made air quotes, '*wings,* being styled like our own bird wings. Maybe they were something more esoteric if these are a more literal version of how the Angelus actually looked.'

'Or this could just be,' I did my own air quotes, '*art.*'

Jack laughed. 'Yes, that too. But regardless, it would be a fascinating area of study in its own right and is certainly something I would love to do more of.'

'Once an archaeologist always an archaeologist, hey?'

'Pretty much,' Jack replied with a broad smile.

I turned, taking in all the towering figures, their wings curving over the avatars in the alcoves. 'This whole place screams significance, reverence even like it could almost be a church.'

'Easy to see why, if it's all about unleashing some sort of ultimate defence for a whole world,' Jack replied. He looked over my shoulder. 'Hey, just thirty seconds till the next neutrino burst.'

'Good, I'm keen to see how Mike and Jodie have got on with setting up the radio spectrum analyser.'

'Oh that could be interesting, I'll tag along,' Jack replied.

We headed over to find Mike and Jodie standing at a desk that had been set up in front of the Earth hologram, their heads bent together as they studied the display in the open briefcase, Jodie's hand resting lightly on Mike's arm.

'How's it looking, guys?' I asked as we reached them.

'We're all set to go, just waiting for the next neutrino pulse to happen back in my world,' Jodie said.

'Oh you're going to love the light show that goes along with it,' Jack said.

'What light show?' Jodie asked.

'One that caught us out when it first happened,' I replied. 'But although I could try to explain it, it's probably best just to witness it for yourself.'

Jack nodded. 'I've watched it dozens of times since yesterday and it still hasn't gotten old.'

An alarm chimed out and everyone stopped what they were doing to look towards the quasicrystal.

'Neutrino pulse will commence on Earth in ten seconds,' Delphi's voice announced.

Jodie gave us a questioning look as we all turned to watch the atomic clock tick down to zero. As it hit it, immediately the song of every micro mind filled the room in a symphony of voices. And as they did so, each of the avatars began to twitch within their alcoves like sleepers desperately trying to wake, Lucy most of all, whose activity had become increasingly frenetic after each successive pulse.

Since we'd been fiddling with the interfaces, one of the scientists had managed to surround the Earth hologram with the almost complete layer of blue triangles, their sides interlocked. But notably there were seven gaps in what had encouraged Mike's idea of it being an Earth shield. Each of the triangular segments that were there was pulsing with similar expanding fractal patterns to those in the quasicrystal — they were obviously somehow linked.

And then, like always, the micro mind symphony faded away as the quasicrystal became solid once more, returning to its previous golden colour. As it did so, the hologram triangles surrounding the Earth returned to a semi-transparent blue and shrank away from each other, opening up gaps between them.

'Neutrino burst completed, timer reset for next phase period,' Delphi announced.

Once again the atomic clock display was set to thirty-three minutes and the countdown began again as everyone got back to work.

'And so we go around yet again,' Jack said, shaking his head.

Jodie turned to look at us. 'Holy shit, you weren't kidding when you said it was spectacular.'

'Yeah, we know,' I said, smiling. 'But what does your spectrum analyser say?'

Mike turned the laptop hooked up to the briefcase device, towards us. 'See for yourselves.'

The bar chart on the screen was packed with lots of peaks.

'So what are looking at?' Jack asked.

'At a glance, a very dense signal,' I replied.

Jodie nodded. 'Every available frequency seems to be packed out with data. But the spectrum analyser has also turned up something rather interesting. Here, let me show you.' She zoomed in on a section of data where there was a blank section.

'A missing micro mind transmission by any chance?' I asked.

'You hit the nail on the head,' Mike said. 'There are six other gaps like this one during this failed start-up sequence.'

'So in other words, you really do need to crack those mathematic equations if whatever this is is going to progress any further?' I said.

'Exactly and that's why Jodie and me and all the science team will be pulling an all- nighter.'

'If there is any way I can help with that...' I said.

'Absolutely,' Mike replied. 'You've got a good head for maths haven't you?'

'My understanding of mathematics is pretty rudimentary compared to what you guys can do, but I'll do my best to keep up.'

Jack held up both hands. 'That isn't my area, but if you need any fresh coffee brewing whilst I get on with my archaeological work, I'm so your man.'

'Good, because I think we're going to need a lot of caffeine to help us power through tonight.' I replied, before gesturing around us. 'And the sooner we crack this, the sooner we can finally get to the bottom of what this mysterious place is all about.'

CHAPTER FOURTEEN

THE HALF DOZEN transparent whiteboards that Mike had organised were now all filled with complex formulas written with multicoloured fluorescent pens.

I'd tried to keep up, knowing a reasonable amount of mathematics from my radio telescope days, but I'd quickly been outpaced as the equations had evolved and become fiendishly complex. But Jodie and Mike had been tag wrestling the hell out of the data, along with the sharpest minds in the rest of the science team. Eventually they'd become so completely lost in their own world that the rest of us might as well not have been there.

Jack headed over with two fresh cups of coffee, totally understanding the mental rocket fuel everyone needed to try and help us crack this.

'They really should take a break, they've been at it for twelve hours straight now,' he said as he handed me one of the thermal cups.

'You try telling them that,' I said, taking a sip of the coffee. 'I've tried several times but have gotten absolutely nowhere.'

'That reminds me of a certain strong-willed woman I know that the word tenacious doesn't even get close to describing,' Jack replied, giving me a direct look.

'I know and I've done my best to help but this is so far beyond me now that it isn't funny.'

'Yeah, those squiggles on the board look like a nest of spiders has gone mad with a set of Sharpies.'

I laughed. 'Great analogy.' I took a long sip of the dark roast coffee, inhaling the smoky scent of the Brazilian beans that Jack knew I loved so much.

A whoop came from Jodie, who was now hugging Mike.

'Okay, that sounds promising,' Jack said. We both immediately headed over.

'Please tell me this is good news, guys?' I asked as we reached them.

Mike beamed at us as he broke away from Jodie. 'The best news, Lauren.' He pointed to seven formulas on a whiteboard to the right of all the others. 'By a process of mathematical extrapolation, we have more or less worked out the missing data for each of the micro minds.'

Jack rubbed the back of his neck with his hand as he peered at the formulas on the board. 'That's great, but what happens now?'

'We're going to try broadcasting when the next neutrino pulse happens, to coincide with the micro minds generating their songs,' Jodie replied.

Our gazes travelled to the countdown timer that had now reached ten minutes.

Jodie turned to me. 'Lauren, we could really do with your help transcribing this data and getting it ready for broadcast. You too, Jack.'

'Seriously?' he said.

'Honestly, all you have to do is type some numbers into a computer, although there's going to be a lot of them,' Mike said.

'Then we're both over this like a rash,' I replied.

———

My fingers were cramping as I frantically typed in the numbers that had been listed on the whiteboard.

Mike and Jodie had just finished, as had the faster of the touch-typists from among the science team. Jack had eventually opted out, saying his two-finger stepping style would be a hindrance more than any real help.

Very unhelpfully for my concentration, a small crowd had assembled around me as the timer to the next pulse counted down to the last minute. Then when I made a small typo there was a collective groan, which did absolutely nothing for my confidence. Just to add to the pressure, Jodie was practically bouncing on her feet next to me, obviously desperate to take over and get it done at twice the speed that I was managing. Maybe it was small acts of petulance on my part, but there was no way that I wasn't going to finish this by myself.

With a final flurry of my fingers across the keyboard, like a pianist reaching the crescendo at the end of a performance, I reached the last line, hit return and immediately held my hands up.

'And I'm done.'

Mike practically tore my laptop from my hands as I handed it to him. His fingers flew over the keyboard and he opened up a program.

'Transferring final data packet now,' he said.

A progress bar filled the screen as the countdown timer ticked down to the last thirty seconds.

'Come on,' I muttered under my breath. I knew if we missed

this window we could obviously try again in another thirty-three minutes, but as far as I was concerned the sooner we could crack this the happier I'd be. But whatever the outcome, at least we would know one way or another whether this hack had actually worked.

The anticipation grew white hot inside me as the progress bar reached the end.

'And we're all uploaded, over to you, Jodie,' Mike called across to her as she sat down in front of another laptop hooked up to a large set of speakers.

'On it,' she replied. 'Ready to synchronise broadcast.'

Everyone in the room turned to watched the countdown tick to the last five seconds. As soon as it hit zero, once again the familiar whale-like song filled the room and the patterns appeared within the quasicrystal.

'Broadcasting code patch now.' Jodie said, peering at the computer screen and selecting an icon.

Seven separate rising and falling tones, a bit like band members of an orchestra arriving late to a performance, suddenly joined in with the whale song chorus. Their notes rose until they matched perfectly the pitch of the micro mind symphony. Then their songs began to weave tighter around the others until they became indistinguishable from the rest.

The effect was immediate. New blue hexagonal plates appeared in the gaps around the holographic version of our world and locked into place, joining the rest to now totally encircle the planet.

'Shields up,' Jack whispered, but loud enough to make those closest to him smile, especially me.

Then I held my breath along with everyone else. Whatever else happened from here on out, this was obviously already a step forward from where we'd been even just a moment ago.

The micro mind chorus ebbed away to be replaced by radio

whistles and crackles that rose and fell in slow modulations. To most people it would have sounded just like random noise, but it was something I instantly recognised as I'd listened to it so often on headphones. And not that there was any doubt in my mind, but the entire globe was now dancing with the geometric patterns that I'd last seen back on the moon thanks to my synaesthesia.

'That's the Earth Song broadcast signal isn't it, Lauren?' Jodie asked, also staring at the patterns — over here in E8, everyone was able to see them for themselves.

'Yes, I'm sure of it,' I replied.

But Mike was peering at his laptop's display. 'You're almost right, Lauren.'

'What do you mean *almost*?'

'I mean that it's almost identical apart from a few key frequency changes. My guess is that has everything to do with the code patches for the missing AIs that we've just installed.'

'Oh my god, Lucy's woken up,' Jack said, staring over my shoulder towards her alcove.

I turned to see not just Lucy's eyes open, but also all of the other avatars too.

I was instantly running towards her with the others close behind me.

'Lucy, are you okay?' I said as I reached her.

She managed a faint nod. 'Yes, but...' Her voice faded as her eyes began to flutter again, a move replicated by every avatar around us.

I grabbed her shoulders. 'Stay with us, Lucy.'

Her eyes opened again and gazed into mine. 'New Earth Song...you must aim broadcast...towards Earth's core. Remember to trust me...' Then her eyes closed again at the same moment the crackles and whistles faded to silence around us.

'Neutrino burst completed, timer reset for next phase,' Delphi said.

Lucy's shoulders stiffened to stone within my grasp. I tried shaking her again but it was like trying to shake a statue.

I headed back to Mike and Jodie. 'What went wrong?'

Mike pointed at the spectrum analyser display. 'I'm not sure looking at this, because the broadcast obviously worked going by the sound we just heard and the fact that Lucy and the others briefly woke up.'

Jodie's eyes snapped wide and then her hands flew over her keyboard.

'What are you doing?' Mike asked, peering over her shoulder.

'Comparing the signal we just heard to the original Earth Song broadcast...and here we go.'

A second red sine wave appeared over a blue one, the two almost exactly in sync apart from a few differences that I could see across the radio spectrum.

'What you're looking at is the original Earth Song in blue, and the one that we just heard is in red. As I'm sure you can see for yourselves, they're slightly different.'

'Hang on, Lucy said something about broadcasting the new Earth Song signal, presumably just like the Resonancy Generator did?' Jack asked.

I slowly nodded. 'So in other words, we need to do the same again to change our world's radio signature.'

'You make that sound so easy,' Jodie replied. 'But even if we understood how the Resonancy Generator worked, I'm not sure we have time to build something of the scale of that Angelus transmitter.'

'No, you're taking me too literally,' I replied. 'We're talking about a signal and signals can be broadcast. And some of the biggest transmitters that I know of on the planet are radio telescopes. They can be set up to broadcast a signal, not just receive them. If we link a network of dishes together, we could beam out those frequency patches as we just did here to plug the gaps in the current Earth Song broadcast.'

A slow smile filled Jack's face. 'You mean create our very own DIY Resonancy Generator in other words?'

I nodded enthusiastically at him. 'Precisely.'

'Okay, I really like where you are going with this; I could put together a mathematical sim to model how that could actually work,' Mike said.

'Brilliant, because I know just the person to help us pull off such a crazy project, although I will also need to talk to Alice about conjuring up some serious research funding to sweeten the deal.'

I grabbed the Empyrean Key as I got ready to shift back, because suddenly there was somewhere I needed to be as quickly as possible.

'Where are you tearing off to?' Jack asked.

'*We're* heading off to Jodrell Bank to scrounge a huge favour,' I said, beaming at him.

CHAPTER FIFTEEN

THE NIGHTTIME PATCHWORK of fields and hedges that surrounded my old place of work — which I hadn't seen for years — skimmed past below us. I was already feeling a real pang of nostalgia for my old life. Things had been so much simpler back then when my life hadn't involved saving the entire world.

Jack glanced across at Erin. 'What's our ETA?'

I jumped in before she could reply. 'We're less than five minutes out.'

'Good guess, Lauren,' Erin said, looking more than a little impressed.

I shook my head. 'No, I should know because I used to drive through this area five days a week and often more, putting in overtime whenever I could.'

Jack gave me one of his *peering into my soul* looks. 'Do you miss it here?'

'Sometimes. Listening to the sounds of the universe never gets old, particularly when it ignites a light show in my synaesthesia.'

Mike, who'd been working non-stop on his laptop throughout the flight on his sim program, looked up from its screen towards me. 'But then if you hadn't left your job behind then you would never have met all of us wonderful guys.'

'You reckon that's a good thing?' Ruby said, smirking at him.

I laughed. 'For what it's worth, I wouldn't have traded my time with you all for the world, even for what was my dream job at the time.'

'What, including getting shot at?' Mike asked.

I raised my eyebrows at him. 'Okay, maybe a little bit less of that.'

On the virtual cockpit in the distance the unmistakable bowl shape of the Lovell dish came into view and Erin started to slow *Ariel* as we neared it. At seeing the large radio telescope dish again, my heart actually did a little flip. Yes, I had definitely missed this place and the people who worked here.

'So where do you want me to land? Presumably not in the car park...' Erin asked.

'Absolutely right,' I replied. 'Even fully stealthed-up, I'd rather not take the chance of someone driving their car into one of our landing legs. There's a large field just to the east of the site, so land there and we'll make our way on foot to the site.'

'Talking of which, they are expecting us, right?' Jack asked.

'Yes, I contacted my old boss, Steve Andrews. He's working the nightshift like I used to do with him back in the good old days. Of course he immediately gave me a massive lecture about being a lousy friend and not getting in contact before.'

'You have had rather a lot on your mind since you last worked here,' Jack said.

Mike nodded. 'Isn't that the truth. My friends are convinced I have deliberately ghosted all of them, especially after I closed down all my social media accounts.'

'Well hopefully one day we can all actually get to see our family and friends again, at least once we defeat the Kimprak,' Erin replied.

My insides twisted at the mention of family. Whether these guys realised it or not, along with Lucy, they were my family now.

Jack once again cast me a very knowing look that suggested he knew exactly what I was thinking — and of course he did. We'd had so many heart-to-hearts over the years that we both knew exactly how each other ticked, especially over something like this. Unfortunately he was too far away in his flight seat to reach across and squeeze my hand and me, his. So instead he just settled for a dip of the chin, which I duly returned. Yes, we so got each other.

As Lovell drew closer I could see that the control room lights were lit up. But there were also quite a lot of cars in the staff car park considering it was 2am. Apparently, Steve was there along with a fair chunk of the team — they were tracking Pollux and Castor asteroids as they made their near Earth pass. But even something like the discovery of a couple of asteroids seemed a bit prosaic compared to the fact that we were already mining the giant 16-Psyche asteroid out beyond the orbit of Mars. If only Steve knew the truth.

But my joy at seeing my old place of work was also tinged with more than a large amount of sadness. The last night I'd worked had been the one Colonel Alvarez and his mercs had attacked us. People had died in that assault, including Kiera, an MI5 field operative who'd done her best to protect us. Her name, along with so many others, had been inscribed into hangar bay one back at Eden. And seeing this place again was also bringing back the trauma of those events that had so drastically changed my life forever.

Erin steered us deftly round Lovell until she'd manoeuvred us directly over a cornfield next to the site and brought us into land. Hopefully, the control room wasn't going crazy right now with weird signals coming out of nowhere and scrambling their readings of the asteroids.

'Okay, what's the plan here, Lauren?' Jack asked. 'I'm assuming we're not going in there armed to the teeth like we do for a normal mission?'

'God no! I realise I may be a bit out of practise on the socialising front, but the last time I looked, seeing an old friend didn't involve turning up to a party carrying a firearm, even one discreetly hidden under my shirt.'

'Fair enough, but shouldn't we maybe change out of our combat gear rather than look like a bunch of paramilitaries turning up at a march?' Mike said.

'Good point,' I replied. 'So you, Jack and I need to get changed into something that looks a bit more civilian. Ruby and Erin, you can hold the fort here.'

Ruby cracked her knuckles. 'Excellent, that will give me a chance to win my money back off Erin. She's turned out to be quite the card shark.'

'Hey, I'm just a woman with skills,' Erin said, grinning at her.

———

Now dressed in a much more civilian-friendly fleece jacket, jeans and T-shirt, with Jack and Mike similarly attired, and having found a gap in the chain link fence that I knew about that still hadn't been repaired, we headed towards the control room with the giant shadow of Lovell towering over us. The radio telescope dish seemed to be aimed just past the crescent of the new moon towards the ecliptic, an imaginary line that astronomers used to denote the line of the planets in our solar system that orbited our sun. It suggested that they might be actively tracking the asteroid duo heading in that Steve had been gushing about when I'd called him on my Sky Wire. In fact, he'd practically been casual when I said I was going to pop by with some friends to discuss something important with him. And this was the same guy that also knew that I'd jumped with both feet into the crazy world of UFO hunters. Then, apart from the time I'd reached out to him from Orkney when we'd first run into Lucy, as far as he was concerned I'd disappeared off the face of the planet for the last four years. At the very least, that should have warranted a few probing questions about what I'd been up to, but he hadn't even mentioned it in passing. Yes, Steve was seriously wrapped up in whatever Lovell was pointed at right now.

'Wow, this is quite some place to work,' Jack said as he gave the giant radio dish an admiring glance.

'It really was; it once meant everything to me.'

'Another time, another life, hey?' Mike said.

'Exactly,' I replied as we approached the control room door.

I pressed the intercom button. 'Hey, any of you guys in there want to let your old mate, Lauren Stelleck, in?'

There was a moment's silence and then a muffled voice came through the speaker. 'Bloody hell, is that really you?' Steve said. 'I know you said you were going to swing by, but I didn't think you actually meant tonight.'

'No time like the present,' I said, raising my eyebrows at the others.

Less than five seconds later the door swung open and Steve himself was standing there. Not only that but he was also wearing the very faded *Millennium Falcon* T-shirt that I had given him all those years ago.

He stood almost gawping at me, barely giving Jack and Mike a second glance.

'I can't believe it's really you, Lauren,' he said. He slightly rocked on his feet, obviously not quite sure how to greet me, the guy who'd had a bit of a thing for me back in the day. Then his hand was rising for a handshake.

'Oh don't be daft,' I said, stepping towards him and pulling him into a hug. 'It's been far too long, you.' I felt him relax at once into my arms.

'It really has — and not so much as a Christmas card to say how you've been doing.'

'Yeah, sorry about that, but things have been a bit crazy.' I stepped back and gestured to the others. 'Anyway, before you give me another lecture that I totally deserve, I'd like to introduce some very good friends of mine. This is Mike Palmer and Jack Harper, two of the best guys you could ever hope to meet.'

Both guys shook Steve's hand, but I noticed that Jack held onto Steve's hand a fraction too long as he peered into the other man's eyes. Even though I hadn't said anything about Steve once being a bit infatuated with me, I had the distinct impression that Jack's cogs were spinning and he was trying to work out whether he was shaking the hand of a former boyfriend or not. But thankfully, rather than crush the other guy's hand, Jack just shot Steve one of his best winning smiles.

Steve withdrew his hand intact. 'Any friend of Lauren is a friend of mine. You guys have arrived during exciting times.'

'So I gather,' Mike said. 'Something about two near Earth asteroids?'

'Yes, but not just any old asteroids. It appears that they travelled across space to enter our solar system. Some are already talking about it in the same tone as they did about that famous Oumuamua asteroid in 2020 that passed through our solar system and got everyone so worked up.' He turned towards me. 'Look, would you like to grab a look at the data we've been capturing before you get me up to speed with why you're here?'

'God, I'd love to, Steve. But then we need to get straight to our meeting because it really is that important.'

Steve gave me a long look. 'Please tell me this hasn't anything to do with the murky world of UFOs that you were investigating the last time we spoke? The whole team is in there and you can imagine the reaction you'll get if you start talking about flying saucers and the like.'

I resisted the urge to radio Erin to ask her to unstealth *Ariel* and make a low pass over Jodrell Bank to make a point, but I fought back the temptation.

'If I said this has everything to do with Earth Song and reminded you that Jodrell Bank is now part of a secret global effort for research, then would you be interested?' I said.

Steve gawped at me. 'Bloody hell, keep your voice down. You do realise that's still classified information, right?'

I tipped my head to one side. 'Classified information that in no way whatsoever I learnt from you?'

He grimaced and then his eyes travelled to Jack and Mike. 'And I take it that you guys know about this too?'

'It's been part of our lives for the last four years,' Mike said with a shrug.

'Right...okay, then you better all come in and we'll talk. But first — that asteroid data, Lauren. Then we'll get into it.'

I nodded. Soon, Steve was ushering us into the control room.

The first thing that struck me as we entered was that for what would normally have been a graveyard shift with just a couple of people monitoring Lovell, the control room was heaving with people and was humming with conversation. About half the faces I recognised from the old days, who all gave me surprised looks. But many I didn't know and looked to be a fresh crop of astronomy university students that had been recruited in...just as I had been many years ago in that *other life*.

The control room had barely changed from exactly how I

remembered it, with its 1950s-retro-styling very much still in vogue by the looks of things. The monitors were currently the centre of all the attention and were filled with scrolling bar charts. Every time a big peak rolled past, the team frantically tapped calculations into their laptops and the conversation became muted as they concentrated on their work.

Mike whistled. 'Oh now this is very cool indeed. No wonder you loved working here, Lauren.'

'You said that?' Steve asked, turning towards me.

'Do you really need to ask?' I replied.

Steve smiled and shook his head. 'Just know that job offer still stands if you ever want to come back to us.'

'I'll keep that in mind,' I replied. But in reality, despite my agreement with Jack I knew that there was no way that was going to happen any time soon. Even if we did end up defeating the Kimprak, too much had happened to the old Lauren to ever work here again. And at that thought I felt a pulse of sadness inside.

'So those look like radio ranging charts?' I said, gesturing to one of the monitors, desperate to change the topic.

'Correct, you've obviously not forgotten anything.'

'And what's radio ranging when it's at home?' Jack asked.

'What it says on the tin. We're currently using Lovell to send out a radio ping to those two asteroids and wait for the echo. We time how long it takes the reflection to return to Lovell and from that we can deduce the distance to the asteroids. In other words, we're using radar, which is actually an acronym for Radio Detection and Ranging.'

'You could have said radar in the first place and we would all have immediately understood,' Jack replied.

'But where would the fun be in that be?' Steve replied with a grin.

'Yep, same old over-complicated Steve, who will use fifty words rather than one to answer a science question,' I said.

'If a job's worth doing, it's worth doing properly,' Steve said, his smile growing wider.

'So is the ranging data showing anything significant?' Mike asked.

'Well the first thing is the astonishing speed at nearly quarter the tenth the speed of light.'

'You're kidding me — no asteroid moves that fast,' I replied.

'None detected until now,' Steve said. 'But the team over at Green Bank Observatory are already putting a thesis together that Pollux and Caster may actually be the remnants of a planet or moon ripped apart during a supernova and flung out into space at incredible speeds. From what we've been able to deduce so far from the radio wave profiling, they are each about three hundred metres across. But the strange thing is that there's no variance to indicate the usual tumbling of an asteroid. We're checking through the data now just to make sure our initial readings are correct.'

It was the last bit that triggered an alert message in my brain. 'Hang on, any idea based on the trajectory of the possible origin of Pollux and Castor?'

'We currently have no way of knowing that, as working the numbers back based on their current trajectory, they appeared to have grazed Jupiter's atmosphere on the way into our solar system.'

'So there's no way they could have originated from Alpha Centauri then?'

Both Mike and Jack stared at me.

'That's unlikely as from what we can tell, they seem to have flown in from the ecliptic, so came from a totally different part of night sky to that star's position. But why ask about that specific system? If that had gone supernova we would definitely have known about it long before now.' Steve gave me a piercing look.

'But I'm getting the distinct impression that we need to have that meeting sooner rather than later.'

'I think that's a really good idea,' I replied.

Steve sucked the air over his teeth. 'Okay, then let's get the coffee on — something tells me we'll need a lot of it.'

'You better believe it,' Jack said with a smile.

CHAPTER SIXTEEN

HAVING DEPOSITED Jack and Mike in the meeting room, I'd joined Steve in the kitchen to help him make the drinks. He had just put the coffee on as I headed straight to the medicine cabinet and dug out a sealed bag of ground coffee.

'Hey, that's my secret stash,' Steve said as he turned to see the coffee bag in my hand.

'Well you should find somewhere new if you don't want me to raid it when I'm in town.'

'So you might be here a while then?'

I couldn't help but notice the puppy dog look that Steve gave me.

'I'm afraid we'll only stay as long as we need to and then we'll be heading off again,' I said.

'You sound like a busy group of people with places to be?'

'Like you wouldn't believe. Anyway, how have you been, Steve?'

'Pretty much the same old, although I've got a ton more paperwork to deal with since they made me Director General after Graham took early retirement.'

'Graham's retired? Seriously? I thought he said he was wedded to this place and he only ever planned to leave in a box.'

Steve sighed. 'He was never the same after the night that the Sentinel signal was captured by Lovell...' His words trailed away.

I didn't need to be a mind reader to know that he was thinking back to *that night*. Steve and I had been in this very control centre when we first captured a fast radio burst, an FRB that had contained a huge amount of data. Like a virus, it had hacked into Jodrell Bank's computers and compiled itself into another Angelus AI called Sentinel, who even Lucy hadn't heard from since. That night had been my first brutal introduction to Colonel Alvarez and his bunch of mercs. That encounter left lingering scars on the people who had witnessed it.

Before I realised what I was doing, I was reaching out to touch Steve's hand. 'But how are you doing really, Steve? That was one hell of thing that we all lived through together that night.'

'I couldn't sleep for shit for several months and even when I did drop off, I'd wake up drenched in a cold sweat. But as the months rolled past, the memory started to fade into the background, although even today I still get the odd flashback. Apart from that, I'm generally okay now for all sorts of reasons. But it hit Graham even harder. He kept a good pretence up at work of holding it together, but he confided in me that he was having regular trauma counselling.'

I let go of his hand and nodded. 'Nothing wrong in that and I wish I'd had some myself.'

'Which leads me to my next question. How are *you* coping after all this time and with whatever you've had to deal with since, Lauren?'

I was completely disarmed by his direct question. I had an immediate urge to spill my heart out and tell him everything about how the woman that he knew was long gone and had now turned into a battle-hardened soldier. It certainly took a consider-able mental effort not to do exactly that.

So instead I just raised my shoulders a fraction and did that whole British understated thing. 'You know, the same old.'

'As in the same old chasing UFO sightings around the world, you mean?'

I nodded. 'Pretty much. But that's the crazy world that I rock in these days.'

Steve gave me a slightly strange look. 'So, still single?' he asked.

At once every single alarm in my head went off. Steve was *still* into me.

I shook my head. 'Actually, no.'

A small smile filled his face. 'Don't tell me. It's that big blond American guy that looks like an extra out of that *Vikings* series?'

'Yes, but how did you guess?'

Steve blew the air out of his mouth with a popping sound. 'Oh that was easy, I could tell by the way you were looking at each other. Which, before you ask, wasn't all lovey-dovey. It was more that there was a real tenderness there.'

'God, you still know me way too well, Steve. But what about you? Has Lady Love made a house call yet?'

Steve chuckled. 'Actually, she did two years ago during one of our astronomy open days. And Bridgette is her name. She's a single mum who brought her son to the event — he's crazy about anything to do with space. We hit it off immediately and have been pretty much inseparable ever since. She has been my rock.'

I gave him a gentle punch on the shoulder. 'Wow, will you look at you, the family man now.'

He scraped his hand through his hair. 'I know and I've never been happier, even if there are a few things that I can never share with my partner.'

'I think most people have a few shadows they can never really share with anyone else.'

Steve gave me a sad smile. 'Exactly, although some shadows are way darker than others, hey?'

'I so know. But before we totally kill the mood of this reunion, let's get this coffee sorted out so we can get this meeting underway.'

Steve breathed out and nodded. 'Let's do that.'

A short while later we'd deposited four steaming mugs of coffee on the meeting room table, although Mike had barely looked up from the laptop he'd been busily coding the broadcast sim on. Steve had even raided his store of Jammie Dodger biscuits, which immediately elevated us to the highest level of VIP guests.

Jack gave the biscuits an approving look. 'These are damned fine cookies and with a jelly filling, although the heart-shaped hole is a bit weird.'

Mike shook his head at Steve. 'Please forgive my friend, but he is an American with no true appreciation of the merits of our finest English biscuits.'

Steve snorted. 'Don't worry, I'm not going to turn this into an international incident.'

'Always good to know,' I replied. I missed this sort of banter from the old days; there'd always been plenty of it when we used to work together.

I rested my elbows on the table and gave Steve my best attempt at a winning smile. 'So there's something we really need your help with, Steve and it has everything to do with Earth Song.'

'Okay, how so exactly?'

I gave him a straight *I'm really not messing around* look. 'We need to alter it.'

Steve almost spat out the coffee he'd just sipped. 'You have to be bloody joking, Lauren? How do you change the radio signature of a planet?'

Jack shrugged. 'It's been done before, several times in fact.'

Steve's eyes widened to circles. 'How the hell do you know about that? That's so classified that literally only a handful of people within the team here know about it.'

'Let's just say we have firsthand knowledge of what caused those events,' Mike said.

Now Steve was sitting up straighter. 'If you do then you have to tell me, because we've been pulling out our hair trying to work out what the hell is going on with that signal.'

I grimaced. 'I would if we could, Steve, but I'm afraid the less you know, the safer you'll be. This knowledge is extremely dangerous and we both know what that looks like from experience.'

'You mean as in the same military organisation who attacked us here at Jodrell Bank?'

'Exactly. So trust me when I say you really don't want to know.'

Steve held up his hands. 'Okay, if anyone could convince me about this, it's you, Lauren. But can you at least let me know why you need to try and change it, even if that does sound like the most stark raving bonkers plan that I've ever heard?'

I traded glances with the others. We needed to tell Steve enough to help him understand the situation, but not so much that it would endanger his life, and that was a fine balancing act to pull off.

'Okay, here goes, deep breath time,' I said. 'The Earth Song should have already been changed by now, but something went wrong and that's why it hasn't been altered.'

'So you're telling me there's an actual reason for this Earth Song broadcast?'

'In a word, yes,' Mike said.

'Then putting two and two together, is this something to do with that alien AI, Sentinel?'

'No, but not a million miles away either,' I replied.

'And even if you somehow manage to pull this off, what will happen when the Earth Song is changed?'

Jack shrugged. 'There we have no idea, other than we really need it to happen like yesterday.'

Steve blew out his cheeks. 'Then how do you propose to pull off this crazy stunt of yours?'

'We'd like to make use of the Merlin radio telescope array,' I said.

'To do what exactly?'

'To transmit the missing part of the Earth Song coded sequence,' I replied.

Steve's eyebrows crept up his forehead. 'Coded like the code we accidentally downloaded for Sentinel with Lovell that night, Lauren?'

'Not exactly, although it's based on the same technology. But as far as we're aware this isn't the code for another alien AI. Anyway, that really is as much as we can tell you. Mike here has the coded sequences that need to be transmitted.'

'Transmitted how, exactly?' Steve asked.

'By using an FRB transmission to transmit this data packet. We also need you to persuade every other radio telescope facility on the planet that you can to take part in a global experiment to attempt to alter Earth Song.'

Steve grimaced and was already shaking his head. 'I'm afraid that's not going to work, Lauren.'

'The convincing the other teams part?' I asked, trying to read his expression.

'Yes, that's a huge part of it, but the bigger problem is the transmission,' Steve replied. 'According to the specialist teams that have been researching this signal, the good news is that it is just like any normal sort of radio signal. The bad news is that it seems to be coming from our planet itself, based on some of the readings that the specialists who have been researching Earth Song discovered. It's almost like some sort of low vibration running through our world and no one has any idea what could be causing that. We've even had vulcanologists looking into it, but they've ruled out any seismic activity being responsible. Mind you, they did all get very excited nearly a year ago when a major tremor around Cuba seemed to coincide with a major shift in the Earth Song sequence.'

Even though I made sure I didn't look anywhere near Mike or Jack, there must have something in my expression because Steve's eyes immediately narrowed on me.

'But you already know all about that event, don't you?' he asked.

'We do and it's yet another thing we can't talk to you about, so moving quickly on.' I gave him an apologetic look. 'You mean that this signal isn't a normal radio signal?'

Steve nodded. 'Not in the strictest sense it isn't. The Earth Song signal that we can pick up is more like the back scatter of a transmission, which is originating beneath the surface of the planet.'

Jack grimaced. 'That does sound like bad news for any plan to use the radio telescopes to transmit the missing data packets, then. As far as I'm aware, radio waves can't penetrate solid rock.'

'Exactly,' Steve replied. 'Even if I wanted to help you — and for the record, I do — I'm afraid it simply wouldn't work.'

But Mike was already on his feet, heading for the white board. 'Actually I might have an idea. Do you mind if I scribble on your board, Steve?'

'No problem, I'd love to see what you crazy kids are thinking.' Steve took a large bite of his Jammie Dodger and leant back in his chair.

Mike set to work with a black marker pen and drew a large circle.

Jack put his hand half way up. 'Is that meant to be the Earth?'

'Yes, but this isn't high school class, so no need to put your hand up.'

'Right...' Jack winked at me.

Mike ignored him and drew wavy lines radiating out around our planet into space. 'Okay, these are the Earth Song radio signals that we've been able to pick up so far. And you've already worked out that Earth itself seems to be vibrating and generating the signal. That happens to fit in with something we already know about how Earth Song operates.'

This time it was my turn to sit up straighter. 'Of course, you mean what we learned in Cuba...' My voice trailed away as Jack gave me a straight look and jutted his chin towards Steve, who was now staring at me. 'Pretend you didn't hear that, Steve.'

'Already forgotten,' he said, shaking his head at me.

'So our challenge is that we need to change the harmonic vibration of our whole world,' Mike continued.

Steve rolled his eyes. 'And how do you propose we do that? Set off a perfectly choreographed series of explosions around the entire world?'

'No, we use VLF, like they use in mines to vibrate solid rock so they can use a receiver to pick up a voice or data signal,' Mike replied.

'And what's VLF when it's at home?' Jack asked.

'It stands for very low frequency,' I replied. 'Traditional radio uses frequencies above five-hundred kilohertz, but VLF, like the name suggests, operates at far lower frequencies than that.' I gazed at Mike. 'Using a VLF signal must be what Lucy meant about aiming a transmission towards the Earth's core.'

'Lucy? Is she some sort of science specialist on your team?' Steve asked.

'In a way, yes,' I replied. 'Anyway, we could easily fit a VLF transmitter into the focus box on Lovell.'

'But how can you aim that huge great dish at the ground?' Jack asked. 'The last time I looked that thing outside was designed to point up towards the sky not towards the dirt.'

'Well actually there is a way,' I said. 'Most dishes, including Lovell, can be inverted for regular maintenance work, so aiming it straight down won't actually be a problem.'

'But don't you need a receiver to pick up your proposed VLF signal?' Steve asked.

'There is one, we just don't know quite what it is yet,' I replied.

Steve blew his cheeks out. 'Oh god, so we're talking about some sort of alien technology again, aren't we?'

None of us said a thing, especially me, who couldn't quite meet his searchlight stare.

Steve sighed. 'Then I'll take that as a yes.'

Mike jumped in. 'Let's move things on...' He started to draw lots of small dishes all around the Earth, all pointing down. Then he started radiating overlapping cones projected towards the core of the planet.

I was already nodding as I could see exactly where he was headed with this.

'Hitting the Earth with a VLF signal simultaneously from multiple locations will mean that we set up an overlapping harmonic wave,' I said, with a growing sense of excitement. 'They will merge together and if powerful enough, should vibrate the entire mantle of the planet.'

'You nailed it, Lauren,' Mike said, beaming at me.

Steve put his hands on top of his head. 'That is one of the most out there things that I've ever seen in my life. But...' A slow smile filled his face. 'I do love big, out there science projects.'

'You mean you're actually prepared to help us?' I asked.

'Yes, but there is still that other major problem — trying to persuade the other teams to help us.'

'Aha, but I've already come up with a plan,' I replied. This was the moment when my conversation with Alice on the flight over here was hopefully about to pay serious dividends. 'I take it funding is as tight as it usually is across all the global teams?'

'Do bears shit in the woods?' Steve asked with a wry smile.

'Thought so, money was always an issue when I was here. So how about this for an idea? I happen to personally know the president of Sky Dreamer Corp and they are prepared to offer a one-hundred million dollar research fund. It can be distributed across all the radio telescope sites in any way you think is fit, with no strings or red tape involved.'

Steve gawped at me. 'Now I know you're taking the piss.'

'No, she really isn't,' Jack replied. 'If Lauren says the funds are there, they are.'

I nodded. 'This is the real deal, Steve, enough money to pursue all your pet projects. So what do you think — is that enough of an incentive to motivate the teams to take part so we can attempt this crazy science project of ours?'

A slow smile filled his face. 'Hell yes. Why should the guys at CERN have all the fun? Let's do this thing.'

I leant across the meeting room table and grabbed his hands. 'Thank you so much, Steve, I knew I could rely on you.'

'Yes, as always, just putty in your hands.'

'Yeah, I so know that feeling,' Jack said, shaking his head.

Steve snorted. 'Okay, if we're really going to do this, it's going to take a while to coordinate with the other groups and persuade them that the research money is real. Also, there is going to be merry hell around here to break off tracking of Pollux and Castor for even a moment. So, to avoid a mutiny we'll need to attempt this when the Earth is rotated away from the asteroids during the day, when it couldn't capture the data anyway. How long will we need to transmit this broadcast for?'

My mind immediately flitted back to Cuba, when we'd activated the Resonancy Generator. 'Actually, based on experience it shouldn't take too long. Maybe five minutes tops?'

Steve's eyes widened on me again. 'Don't ask, right?'

'Exactly. Sorry, but our lives have been out there like you wouldn't believe.'

'Like the truth, hey?' A slow grin filled his face.

'Oh right, *X-Files*,' Jack said. 'I'm beginning to really like this guy.'

'Yeah, he's not too bad with the right handling,' I replied, grinning at Steve.

But Mike was frowning now as he looked at the whiteboard. 'Ah guys, I may have found a problem with our highly inventive plan. To make sure the harmonic signal is radiated right round the Earth, we're going to have to make sure that every geographical region is covered. That won't be an issue where there are radio telescopes prepared to help, but apart from anything else, not every region will have coverage. Also, to point out the more obvious issues the Earth is seventy percent ocean and some of the ideal transmission points will need to be at the bottom of it.'

Steve sucked the air in through his teeth. 'Okay, that's a serious problem —the logistical challenges of getting a VLF transmitter down to some of the deeper parts of the ocean.'

Jack turned towards me. 'Is there any reason we couldn't put one of these VLF transmitters on one of our craft, Lauren?'

I began to think it through. 'To generate enough power it will have to be quite a large system... But we could link it into the existing array of a Pangolin... It could certainly easily fit in even with a large parabolic reflector. You know, that might just actually work, Jack.'

Mike was already nodding, his expression lighting up. 'I'll

need to update the numbers in my broadcast sim to accommodate this new plan. But who's going to tell Jodie that we need to adapt more ships for underwater use? I can tell you now it's going to be one hell of a lot of work to adapt enough of them, probably a hundred to play it on the safe side. And if anyone is going to walk into that particular firing line...if you ask me, that sounds like a job for a Commander.' He gave me a straight look.

'And as Commander, it's my job to delegate and I think it would be best coming from her boyfriend, don't you?' I said, grinning back at him.

Mike groaned. 'I so knew you were going to say that.'

Steve had spent the last part of the conversation just looking between us, his mouth hanging ever lower. 'Pangolins...hundred ships...Commander? But once again, don't ask — right, Lauren?'

I laughed. 'You are so catching on, Steve.'

CHAPTER SEVENTEEN

It had been several frantic days of work for everyone involved in our little project to literally shake up the whole world. The team at Jodrell Bank, with some unsolicited help from me, had installed a new VLF transmitter alongside the existing equipment. We'd even been able to get it finished in time for the team monitoring the asteroid swarm to begin their night shift again without being interrupted by our work.

And that same effort had played out with every radio telescope after they'd all jumped at a chance to share in the research fund. Of course, unlike Steve — who at least knew some of the real truth — they were being told it was a cutting edge science research project into planetary harmonic resonancy. Mike had worked with Steve on the project proposal to make it convincing enough to sound like the real reason. They had obviously done a good job because all the radio telescope teams that we had reached out to had been more than intrigued.

But the far greater challenge had been refitting a hundred of our Pangolins, not just with the VLF transmitters, but also enough

Pangolins for underwater use. Jodie, after quizzing us on the plan, had actually been really helpful. She had headed back from Antarctica to Eden to work with her Forge team to pull the usual miracle out of the hat that she was able to conjure up in these situations. All sixty ships needed for underwater use had been outfitted in less than a few days and were now moving into position around the world.

Me, Jack and Mike, along with Erin — who'd been desperate to see the interior of Jodrell Bank after being camped outside it for three days in *Ariel* — sat in the control room with Steve. Ruby, who didn't seem remotely interested, had remained onboard to keep guard just in case Alvarez got wind of us being here and decided to make a return appearance. But if he did it would go so badly for him and his mercs this time round; I would personally make sure of it.

On a table were several boxes from my all-time favourite pizza restaurant in the whole world, namely the famous *Mario's*. The pepperoni with extra anchovies was just as good as I remembered it to be as I sunk my teeth into the final slice.

'Damn, you weren't kidding, this is good,' Jack said, finishing his own identical pizza that I'd recommended he try.

'I did tell you that *Mario's* is one of the best pizza restaurants in the whole world,' I said, as I peeled a string of mozzarella off my chin.

'It seems you weren't wrong, and I say that as an American Italian who knows her way around a good pizza,' Erin said.

Steve nodded. 'I'll make sure I pass your praise onto the great man himself.'

'Just please tell me he's still dancing on customers' tables whenever he gets the chance?' I asked.

'With very little encouragement whenever the vino is flowing,' Steve said.

I chuckled. 'God, I've missed this life.'

Steve pushed his pizza box away. 'As I said before, you're always welcome to stay on, Lauren.'

'I'm afraid I'll have to take a rain check on that for now, but it's good to see the old place is in great hands with you at the helm.'

'Wow, you almost said that with a straight face.'

I snorted and soft punched him in the arm.

Jack looked between us with a slightly unreadable expression, the tiniest of smiles at the corner of his mouth. I was so going to ask him what that was all about later on.

It was at that moment that my Sky Wire warbled. Immediately a groan came from the team watching the data feed from the asteroid swarm as the data glitched out. And then every single one of them turned an accusing glare towards me as I grabbed my handset and quickly took the call from Jodie.

'Make it fast because I'm about to be lynched by the mob for interrupting a data capturing session with my Sky Wire,' I said.

'Okay, just to let you know I checked in with the team at Eden and everything is now in position for the Earth Song broadcast at two hundred hours GMT, in about ten minutes from now,' she replied.

'That's great news, I'll let the others know,' I said. I quickly ended the call and placed my Sky Wire on the table, then held up both hands like someone who'd just put their firearm down. 'Apologies everyone, but that was a very important call.'

There was a considerable amount of muttering as the team returned their attention to the monitors.

Steve was shaking his head at me with an amused look on his face. 'Have you forgotten about the signs everywhere about turning your mobile off so it doesn't interrupt a radio capture session, Lauren?'

'No, but I had to keep my phone on and take that call. Anyway, before you get going with another lecture aimed my way, it appears that everything is in place to begin the transmission in ten minutes. If the team hate me now for interrupting their work, they are really going to hate me when we take Lovell offline for the next hour to run our little science experiment.'

'Then here's an idea,' Steve replied. 'If your funding can also stretch to buying them all a *Mario's* pizza, I think your misdemeanours will be quickly forgiven.'

I grinned at him. 'Oh now that's a plan I can sink my teeth into.'

Jack and Mike both groaned in unison.

We sat at the control room window looking out as Lovell's giant dish slowly finished rotating into position, pointing straight downwards.

'That looks so wrong for a radio telescope,' Jack said, shaking his head.

'Yes, it's not a position that the public often get to see Lovell in. But apart from the routine maintenance that I mentioned before, we often put Lovell into that position during heavy snowstorms so that it doesn't collect in the bowl and overweight the structure.'

'Like a giant snow cone?' Jack asked.

'That's quite the analogy, but basically, yes,' Steve replied, shooting him an amused look.

The two had slowly but surely been hitting it off. In another world I was certain they'd be good mates.

I glanced over to the wall clock to see that it was only a minute away from 2am. 'Okay, if everything has gone to plan this scene should be being replicated at hundreds of sites around the world.'

'Well, it's certainly going to be an interesting experiment, whether it works or not,' Steve said.

'For all our sakes it has to work,' Mike replied, drumming his foot on the floor as he watched the clock count down to the last ten seconds.

I glanced at the screen to see a blinking icon that indicated our part of the Earth Song data patch transmission was queued up and ready to run automatically on Lovell's newly installed VLF transmitter at the designated time. Similar automations had been set up at every broadcasting station, including our Pangolins, all round the world.

We all watched the second hand sweep towards the top of the dial. When it reached it, a haunting howl began to rapidly rise and fall over the control room speakers. Immediately all eyes turned towards me to see how I was reacting to the signal that was now being aimed straight down at the core of our planet. It seemed the reputation of the former radio telescope operator who could *see* signals with her synaesthesia had preceded her.

As I hoped it would be, this occasion was similar to my previous experience when Sentinel had taken over the systems here. Now, superimposed over my view of Lovell I could see an aura shimmering round the entire structure of the giant dish. But that wasn't even the main attraction. A cone of light from what should have been invisible low frequency radio waves was blazing out from the giant dish and heading downwards, energy patterns shimmering outwards from where it was striking the ground. But here, unlike over in E8, no one could share this incredible spectacle.

Right on cue, Jack gently touched the back of my shoulder. 'Can you see anything, Lauren?'

I gave him a wide-eyed nod. 'Absolutely.' I gazed at it, trying to take in the details so I could describe what I was seeing to everyone gathered there. 'There's a large cone of blue light pouring out from Lovell's dish and where it's hitting the ground, energy patterns in reds and yellows are starting to ripple outwards and are racing away across the ground.'

Steve pointed towards the ripples in his coffee cup. 'Which would probably explain why those just appeared in my mug and suggests the harmonic effect you were hoping to achieve is already working.'

Mike, who'd been staring at a laptop screen, nodded. 'It is, according to those seismic probes that I've set up round Jodrell Bank; I'm seeing a slow moving monowave quake building.'

'Bloody hell, you're saying we're creating an earthquake here?' Steve asked.

Mike held his fingertips a fraction apart. 'A very small one, but basically yes.'

Steve shook his head. 'Ok, this is very cool as long as you don't damage anything. If you break it, you pay for it. Agreed?'

'Agreed, but don't worry, because I'm sure it's going to be okay,' I replied. 'But what about the other sites, Mike? How are they getting on?'

He peered at a data window that was scrolling down his screen. 'Yes, they are all seeing similar results, but things should start to get interesting when the harmonic waves that we're all transmitting start to merge together in the Earth's mantle.'

I picked up my Sky Wire and connected it to the live satellite feeds that we were monitoring for the Earth Song broadcast. A moment later the familiar warble and clicks of our world's radio signature was playing through its speaker.

Immediately the control room became filled with a kaleidoscope of geometric patterns. What with that and what was currently happening round Lovell, it was quite the head rush and almost made me feel dizzy.

'Are you okay, Lauren?' Jack asked, peering at me.

'Yes, but it's quite the light show right now.'

'Your gift never ceases to amaze me,' Steve said. 'It really does sound like random noise even to my radio astronomer's ear.'

Mike pointed towards his screen. 'The next lot of signals being transmitted over in Europe should be reaching us any second—'

His words were drowned out as the volume of Lovell's broadcast was suddenly amplified by a factor of ten.

Along with everyone else I instinctively clamped my hands over my ears as the whole control room began to shake.

Steve was already reaching towards a kill switch that would stop the transmission instantly, but I grabbed his hand.

'Not yet, Steve,' I shouted over the roar. I glanced at the clock. 'Just another minute to go.'

Mike was nodding. 'The harmonic effect is obviously working and each broadcast station is amplifying the effect of its neighbour. But we just need to keep it going a bit longer so it can penetrate deeper into the Earth's crust.'

'Only if it doesn't start tearing Jodrell Bank apart,' Steve replied.

'This must already be a magnitude two quake,' Jack said.

'Three actually, according to my sensors,' Mike replied. 'But the good news is that it isn't getting any worse either, so I think, touching wood—' his fingers brushed the desk, '—that this will be as bad as it gets. Anyway, for a clearer understanding, my simulator will show what's happening.'

Mike pulled up a fresh screen with a simple graphic of the Earth cut in half. A swarm of points were marked around the circumference, lines radiating down and outwards, all of which were overlapping and had penetrated about a third of the way towards the core of our planet.

'What are we looking at here?' Jack asked, leaning in for a closer look.

'This is a real-time simulation based on the data streaming in from all the sites round the world,' Mike replied. 'My programme is calculating just how deep the signal has currently penetrated and as you can see it is now about halfway towards the core of planet. Once we get there we can kill the signal immediately and keep our fingers crossed that this crazy science experiment of ours has actually worked.'

The shuddering increased and a crack suddenly spidered across the control room window. I glanced round to see quite a few people had taken to cowering under their desks.

Mike grimaced. 'Okay, the harmonic quake has reached 3.1 on the Richter scale, but that's still relatively mild.'

'Says the man who said it wouldn't get any worse,' Steve replied with a scowl as he stared at the crack running through the window. 'Tell me why we shouldn't stop this immediately?'

I put my hands together. 'Because we can't, Steve, literally the fate of our whole world depends on this. And as far as any damage incurred, Sky Dreamer will cover the cost of repairing that and any damage to the other sites too.'

He gave me the longest look and then just groaned. 'Just please tell me that the whole world hasn't been hit by this level of quake.'

Mike was already shaking his head. 'No, the epicentre of each of these mini-quakes will be relatively small around the focal points of the VLF broadcasting sites, and will extend out just a few kilometres from each one. Further out than that and you wouldn't even notice a thing.'

'Thank god for that,' Steve replied. 'But I'd better get on the landline to the other radio telescope sites who agreed to help. They are probably feeling less than thrilled by the results so far and will be getting ready to pull the plug.'

'Do what you can — I'm really sorry for putting you in the hot seat for doing this, but it really is critical that we finish this,' I said.

'So you keep telling me,' Steve replied with a frown. He headed over to a landline phone, picked it up and began dialling. The furrows on his forehead only grew deeper as whoever picked up at the other end laid into him.

I glanced back at Mike's simulation to see that it had now reached at least two-thirds of the way towards the centre of the Earth.

'Come on, you little beauty,' Mike said, watching it intently.

Outside, Lovell was visibly vibrating, with creaks and groans coming from its steel structure. That wasn't good — I knew that among all the other fallout that Steve would have on his hands, he'd also have to deal with the wrath of the maintenance team, who would insist on fully checking over Lovell before it resumed use. At best that would mean a delay of a day, more if any of the telescope's complex systems had been damaged. And that would mean the asteroid team would miss valuable data as they passed the Earth. We so weren't going to be popular round here when people started to realise the full implications of our *science project*.

But apart from the structural impact of what we were doing, I could actually see for myself that something was clearly working, thanks to my synaesthesia. Colourful rainbow fractal patterns were now cascading out across the ground from where the VLF beam was striking it. It looked purposeful and intended, suggesting that even if we didn't really know what we were doing, that we were very much on the right track with our slightly random, pushing button approach. If only Lucy had been here to reassure us.

'Come on, come on,' Mike said, as the signal crept the last full millimetres towards the core of our world.

The three of us watched as at last the radiating signals of all the transmitter stations reached the core within seconds of each other.

Immediately the broadcast stopped dead and a few seconds later the light show faded away.

'That's it, the code patch transmission has ended,' Mike said, slumping back into his seat.'

'So why is the world still shaking?' Steve asked, glaring at him as he cupped his hand over the phone.

'Because the harmonic vibration will take a few minutes to subside,' Mike replied. He glanced at one of the readouts on his screen. 'But the good news is that it's already dropped to two-point-five on the Richter scale.'

Steve nodded with a slightly relieved expression and resumed his phone call.

Over the next few minutes, the shaking gradually started to fade away. It was only then people began to clamber out from under their desks as they became more confident that the ceiling wasn't going to come down on their heads. A few minutes after that, just as Mike had promised, the quake dropped away to nothing.

'That's it, it's really over?' Jack asked.

Mike spun round in his chair to look at us. 'Yes, the harmonic resonance wave has subsided right around the world. The first indicator to show that we've been successful is detecting a change in Earth Song.'

I nodded and cranked the speaker back up, and the usual whistle and clicks filled the room. Steve was already pulling up comparison graphs on one of the computers.

He frowned at the screen. 'I'm afraid that after all that effort, everything looks almost identical to the previous signal.'

'Give it a moment to kick in and if I'm right, even those of us without synaesthesia will notice a change,' Mike replied.

Everyone fell quiet as we all listened in.

Then a slow, deep modulating tone began to rise in the back-ground. Immediately the air in front of me was filled with origami-like three dimensional shapes folding into one another in endless patterns and combinations.

I put my hands on top of my head as I gazed at them. 'Um, guys, something has definitely changed — I'm now seeing all these mathematical shapes in front of me.'

Steve nodded. 'Yep, the before and after comparative analysis of Earth Song is radically different too.'

'Even I can hear it's no longer a random bunch of noise,' Jack said,

Mike clenched his fist. 'Result! It's actually bloody worked.'

'So what happens now?' Steve asked.

Exactly on cue, my Sky Wire warbled and Jodie's name appeared on the screen. I picked it up and took the call.

'Hi Lauren, you and the team might want to get yourself down to the Antarctica base as fast as possible,' Jodie said.

'Why's that?' I asked.

'Because the sky has just exploded with Aurora Borealis and Mike's sensor network is picking up major increases in that magnetic anomaly activity beneath the surface.'

'Okay, we're on our way.'

I turned to Steve. 'We just received the call that I was hoping we'd get. It looks like it really has worked — we couldn't have done it without your help.'

'Thank god for that, although my team may have a different opinion right now,' Steve replied.

'Yes, please apologise to them on my behalf and tell them we'll pay their pizza budget for as much they can eat for the next year.'

Steve chuckled. 'That will definitely help. But I just wish I knew what you were guys are really up to; it sounds seriously intriguing.' He held my gaze.

I was about to bat his question away with the usual excuse when a thought struck me. Steve had really put his neck on the line and deserved to know something, just even a little bit of the bigger picture. I knew exactly what I could do that would make this geek's day, month and year.

'Steve — fancy taking a quick walk with us back to our lift? I think with your love of sci-fi you will get a real kick out of it.'

Jack and Mike were both staring at me.

'Are you sure that's wise, Lauren?' Jack said.

'Actually I do. As long as Steve promises to keep it to himself and tell absolutely no one... right Steve?'

He crossed his hands over his heart. 'You can always trust me to be the very word of discretion.'

I beamed at him. 'Then follow me.'

Steve had his hands on top of his head as he gawped at *Ariel*, which I'd just ordered Erin to briefly uncloak.

'Holy shit, no fucking way!' he said. 'A real, *I'm not out of my mind on meds*, flying bloody saucer?'

Jack laughed. 'It's the real deal, buddy.'

Steve started walking around our ship, waving his arms around. 'And now I suppose you're going to hit me with the punchline that a little green alien is your chauffeur and you're best mates?'

In a moment of perfect timing the ramp lowered, followed by the sound of footsteps descending it.

My old friend froze and went pale as he stared at whatever horror was about to emerge. Then he visibly relaxed when Erin appeared and gave him a wave.

She turned towards me. 'Fusion reactor is running hot and we're ready to depart when you are, Lauren.'

Steve's mouth literally dropped open. 'You're telling me you have a working fusion reactor inside that thing?'

'Yes and it's about the size of a small fridge, albeit a round one,' Mike replied.

'Yeah right, good one mate. The next thing you'll be telling me is that you have a working anti-grav propulsion system too.'

I gave him a straight look.

He stared back at me. 'No fucking way!' he shouted.

'Shhh, keep your voice down, but yes fucking way,' I replied, laughing.

Steve whooped and then shot me a guilty look. 'Sorry, but you know it's not every day that every sci-fi fantasy I've ever had comes true. So did one of your friendly aliens lend you this ride?'

'No actually, we built it ourselves,' Mike said.

Steve's already wide eyes grew even wider. 'Oh my god, I know I'm seeing it, but I still can't quite believe it's actually there. Is there time to take me for a quick joy ride, Lauren?'

'We would if we could, but we're on the clock here and need to head out,' I said.

'You do know I'm so going to hold you to that?' Steve replied.

'Do — it would be great to see you again.' I turned and gestured to Jack and Mike. 'You head in and I'll be along in a moment.'

They both nodded, shook Steve's hand and headed towards the ramp, Jack taking just long enough to give me a wink.

I stood before my old friend. 'There is so much more I'd love to tell you about what we've been up to, but I really can't, Steve. But you know that job you offered me? The same goes for you. There is an incredible job of your dreams waiting for you if you ever want it. We need brilliant minds like yours.'

'Now that's the most tempting offer I've ever had, but I've set down roots here now; I have Bridgette and her son in my life.'

'Of course, but there's no expiration date on that offer should you ever change your mind.'

'Got it,' Steve replied with a smile. He narrowed his eyes a fraction on me. 'You look like you were born for whatever this is the tip of?'

'It's more a case of having to quickly learn to swim or drown. As you can probably already guess, it's certainly been a big adjustment.'

Steve flapped a hand towards *Ariel*. 'I can. And Jack seems like a really great guy.'

'He's one of the best, Steve. We're just so good for each other.'

'I can tell that too.' He hitched his finger back over his shoulder towards Jodrell Bank. 'I better go back and face the music in there. But it's been so good seeing you, Lauren, really good, even if it's only for a short time.'

'You too,' I replied. I leant in and kissed him on the cheek. 'You take care and look after yourself.'

He gave me a goofy grin. 'I'll do my best.'

'I'd better get going too, but when you get Lovell back online, let me know. I feel more than a little bit guilty about interrupting the asteroid team's work.'

'Will do but that pizza budget will help. And good luck with whatever this is.'

'Thank you and hopefully I'll see you again one day soon.'

'Yeah...' A wide smile filled his face.

I held up my hand and resisted the urge to give him a Spock sign, although Steve would so have loved that. Then I turned and headed up the ramp into a ship that had once been the stuff of my own sci-fi dreams too.

CHAPTER EIGHTEEN

I'd seen the Aurora Borealis a few times in my life, but they were like absolutely nothing in comparison to the extraordinary display over the Antarctica site, which we were now all witnessing on *Ariel's* virtual cockpit. Alice had christened it the Shackleton Base in honour of the great man himself, who apparently was a distant relative. It seems he'd mounted an expedition to Antarctica back in 1914, which had turned into a mission of survival when their ship had become trapped in the ice. But I wondered to myself if the great explorer had ever witnessed anything this incredible in his lifetime.

Vast ribbons of green light were rippling in slow motion right across the sky from horizon to horizon. Breathtaking didn't even come close. The high-energy particles from the Sun were entering the Earth's atmosphere to create a display that had a distinct three-dimensional shape, the curtains reaching high up in the atmosphere towards the edge of space.

'Holy crap, I've never seen a display this intense before,' Jack said.

'I don't think any of us have,' I replied.

Ruby glanced up from her CIC display. 'Do you think it could be linked to what you guys did back at Jodrell Bank?'

'I'd bet good money on it,' Mike said. 'And I think it's further evidence that we managed to find the on switch for whatever this secret Angelus device is.'

'My money is still on it being some sort of vast forcefield,' Jack said.

'It could be and hopefully when Lucy wakes up she'll be able to do the big reveal of whatever it is that we just did,' I replied.

'Well, we should know soon enough because we're just a few minutes out,' Erin said.

I looked ahead to see a wide, snow-filled plateau opening up. Within it a green diamond box with a metadata label for Shackleton Base was displayed. The white camo net was obviously still doing an excellent job at hiding what we were up to down there because apart from the HUD marker, there was absolutely no other sign of Lucy's merged micro mind ship down on the surface.

'Is everything still clear on our sensors, Ruby?' I asked.

'Yes, just our own ships standing guard in the skies overhead, nothing else out there apart from that.' She sucked the air over her teeth.

'So why don't you look particularly happy about it?' Jack said.

'Because I'm not. The longer we don't see the Overseers sticking their noses into our business, the more paranoid I get. Why haven't they attacked yet?'

'Maybe they just don't know we're here?' Mike said.

'Could be and I'd love it to be that,' Ruby replied. 'But as your Weapons Officer, I can't afford to assume that's the answer. *Always be prepared for the worst-case scenario* is a motto I've got tattooed on my butt.'

'Which is why we now have the hundred plus ships to help to

defend this site,' I said. 'Surely that should be more than enough to cope if and when the Overseers eventually attack?'

'Yeah, I know, but something still feels off.' She frowned and returned her attention to her radar screens.

If I was honest, Ruby wasn't the only one that was getting more than a little bit nervous about the lack of attention. The Overseers had harried us at every opportunity they got when we'd been retrieving micro minds over the last year. So why such a stifling silence this time? As much as I would love to believe that Alvarez had thrown in the towel, I strongly doubted it.

Erin began to rapidly slow *Ariel* as she brought her in for landing. A very dim glow was just visible through the cracks in the camo netting, presumably coming from the tent erected over the micro minds, but so faint that you would need to be almost on top of it to notice. The only other clue that there was any activity at this site was in the snow immediately around the impact crater — it was churned up with footprints and vehicle tracks. But apart from that, you really wouldn't know that anything unusual was going on, especially that Niki's ship, *Thor* was already parked next to it in full stealth invisible mode, only revealed by our virtual cockpit.

With a swirl of snow Erin settled *Ariel* down right next to the other ship. As we started to pull our arctic combat gear on, Niki's voice came over the comm. 'Good to see you guys back here. Jodie's been itching to get back over to E8; she hasn't stopped nagging me since you left.'

'Oh god, I bet. I know what she can be like on a new project,' Mike said.

'Hey, I heard that,' Jodie said over the comm. 'Anyway, I don't see why me and the team couldn't stay over there in the hall?'

'Because I didn't want to risk you getting stranded in E8 with no way to get back, if we were delayed,' I replied.

'Yeah, yeah, yeah. But in my opinion we're wasting time here when we could have been doing good science over in E8. Mind you, apart from monitoring the magnetic anomaly data, the science and me have kept ourselves busy, keeping an eye on Lucy's quasicrystal down in the crater.'

'Any changes to report there?' Jack asked.

'Apart from the neutrino pulses stopping, just a faint green pulse that passed through the merged micro minds when you managed to alter the Earth Song signal. The next thing we knew, this incredible aurora display burst into life over our heads.'

'So you're saying this display isn't linked to any solar activity?' Mike said.

'Not according to the space weather satellites, it isn't. We've already sent a Pangolin into the upper atmosphere and have been reading a lot of increased electrical activity across every frequency that corresponds with this new supercharged version of Earth Song that is now broadcasting out into space.'

Jack pulled his combat jacket on and turned his head towards the speaker. 'Could this all be the Angelus equivalent of an SOS for something out there to come and help us?' He gestured towards the stars in the virtual cockpit over our head.

'We have no way of knowing until it happens, or at least until we get back to E8,' I replied.

'Then the sooner we get back there the better,' Jodie said over the link.

The hall shimmered into existence around us as we crossed over to E8 with Jodie and the science team. At once our ears were greeted with beautiful, whale-like song that filled the space like some sort of celestial choir.

But my gaze immediately swept towards Lucy and my heart

leapt as I saw her — her eyes, and the eyes of every other avatar were now open.

'Oh thank god, you're awake, Lucy,' I said, heading straight towards her.

But Lucy didn't so much as blink as I neared her. I tried waving my hand in front of her face but there wasn't a flicker in my friend's expression.

The others were trying the same with the other avatars, but getting similar results.

'Okay, that's more than a bit disappointing,' Jack said. 'I was expecting Lucy to be back to her usual sassy self.'

'Me too, but at least now her eyes are staying open, which is progress of sorts,' I replied. I reached out to touch her hand and this time also felt the softness of flesh under my fingertips. 'And she no longer feels like a statue, either.'

The triangular panels that had been surrounding the Earth hologram around the merged micro minds were gone; instead, at the dead centre of our world, a glowing blue sphere now hung, slightly larger than the merged micro minds. Circular, pond-like ripples were radiating from it and travelling out through the Earth, into the space around it.

'What is that thing the hologram is indicating at the middle of our world?' Jodie asked, peering at it.

'My guess is that it's something directly linked to the Earth Song transmission,' I said.

'Hang on, are you saying there's some sort of alien device in the solid iron core of this planet?' Jack asked.

'Well, based on this hologram there could be something down there, but the pressure must be immense?'

'With the whole weight of the planet and the atmosphere pressing down on it, you bet it is,' Mike replied. 'To give you an idea of just how immense it is, if we compare it to the surface it's about three point six million times greater at the core of our planet. And if that isn't enough, the temperature also runs at a toasty six thousand degrees Celsius, as hot as the surface of the sun and more than enough to give you a good tan.'

'So what the hell can survive those kind of conditions if we're talking some sort of Angelus artefact?' Jack asked.

Mike raised his shoulders. 'We're talking Angelus tech here, so who knows? But if there really is something there, how the hell did it get there in the first place?'

Jodie chewed her lip as she gazed at it. 'That's a good question. Even if the Angelus had the technology to sink a shaft anywhere as deep as that, as soon as you passed through the Earth's mantle you'd hit lava pretty quickly. Do that and it would be a bit like suddenly releasing the valve on a pressure cooker.'

'So a dirty great big eruption, in other words?' I said.

'Exactly,' Jodie replied. 'Certainly whatever it is, the Angelus made it basically impossible for humans to reach it, at least with our current level of technology.'

'But that doesn't sound right,' Mike said. 'The Angelus wouldn't have placed all the micro minds on our planet if they didn't want us ever to use whatever it is.'

'Maybe someone has to issue a final, *let's do this* command,' Jack said, his eyes on me.

My eyes widened as I realised what he was driving at and I raised the Empyrean Key to see a new, vortex-shaped icon had appeared. 'Okay, you might be onto something there, Jack,' I said, pointing towards the new icon.

Everyone peered at the icon floating over the stone orb, then peered at me.

I met their expectant gazes. 'Maybe we should just take a moment here,' I said. 'Just because we can do this, are we all definitely still sure we *should* do this?'

'I think we are so far past the point of should that it's become a bit academic now,' Jack said.

Mike nodded. 'Yeah and it's not as though we have any choice anyway with the Kimprak just six months out from our solar system. Even with all the X-craft ships that we've built, I still wouldn't bet on us winning a war with the Kimprak without whatever tech the Angelus left to help us.'

I looked at Jodie. 'And what do you think?'

'Look, if someone puts the equivalent of a big red button in front of me, who am I not to press it?'

I smiled at her. 'Okay. My own feeling is that there is no reason not to trust the Angelus based on how Lucy has been with us so far; to be frank, I would trust her with my life.'

Jack slowly nodded. 'It sounds like we're doing this thing.'

'It does doesn't it?' I held up the stone orb in front of me and — heart fluttering — rotated the icon into the selection window. 'Hang onto your hats, people.' I flicked my wrist forward.

The change in the hologram around the micro minds was instantaneous. The globe spun round, reorienting itself so that Antarctica was now facing us. Then the globe began to expand out beyond the walls of the domed hall as the view closed in on the continent. In a headlong rush the land mass filled the view, then the view was racing down towards the surface with over a hundred disc-shaped objects hovering in the sky.

'Holy crap, tell me that isn't a live view of our stealthed fleet over the Shackleton Base?' Jack said as one of the saucer-shaped craft sped past us and the view continued to zoom in.

I nodded. 'It looks like whatever else this is, it's some sort of live feed of what's happening on our world.'

The others nodded as the view continued to speed downwards towards the ground. Then just when I thought we were going to pass straight through the surface, towards whatever was sitting at the core of our planet, the view pivoted upwards like a plane coming out of a steep dive, before coming to a dead stop.

Within the circular balcony was now a hologram of Lucy's

merged micro mind craft sitting within its crater, with *Ariel* and *Thor* parked next to it. I could even see a live render of the Tin Heads patrolling the perimeter.

Out in the distance a number of pulsating markers had appeared. The view began to rotate to show the pulsing points of light were along the entire horizon, surrounding the site in an oval shape.

'Okay, that's more than a bit intriguing — what the heck is it?' Jodie asked.

'I have no idea, but my vote is that we should pop back home and find out,' I replied.

'Actually, it's probably a good idea if someone remains here so we can monitor any changes from this side,' Mike said.

'I can stay here and do that if you want to check the readings on Earth,' Jodie said.

'And if it's all the same to you, I'd like to get on with my archaeological work here,' Jack said.

I nodded. 'Then it sounds like you're with me, Mike. We shouldn't be long, guys.'

'We'll see you soon, but my instinct tells me that we're definitely on track to cross the finish line now,' Jack replied with a smile.

'Yes, me too.' I gave his arm a little squeeze as I lowered the visor on my helmet.

Mike and I stepped away from the others as I raised the Empyrean Key again. I selected the dot constellation icon that would return me to the particle reality of our world. As I flicked my wrist and the E8 hall started to disappear around us, I noticed that the points dotted around the horizon in the hologram were pulsating more quickly. But before I had a chance to take in any more detail, the tent had materialised back around us with Lucy's quasicrystal sitting in the middle of it. But now pulses of light were rapidly racing out through its conduit root system and into the solid rock below. There was no sign of the science team that should have been monitoring it.

Then with a huge groan the ground shook violently beneath my feet, toppling several racks of equipment over to crash into the ground. I staggered outside with Mike to see the last of the Tin Heads being hoisted by wires up into the belly of *Thor,* which had its cargo bay doors open.

'Oh bloody hell, this isn't good,' Mike said.

The ground bucked again and we sprawled to the ground.

'You think?' I said, picking myself up and holding out a hand to help Mike haul himself up.

The speakers in my helmet burst into life. 'Lauren, Mike — those seismic sensors you placed started going mad about a minute ago,' Ruby said. 'It looks like a big quake is on the way. Niki has already pulled everyone else out as a safety measure and you need to get back onboard *Ariel* pronto for the same reason.'

'Just give me a sec and I'll hop back and get the others from E8.'

'Okay, but don't be long. According to the science team there's less than two minutes until the main quake hits and it's going to be a big one.'

'Got it.' I turned to Mike. You head back to *Ariel* and I'll join you in a moment.'

'Okay, but be as fast as you can,' he replied.

'Oh don't worry, I intend to be.'

He nodded and headed over to one of the abandoned Taiga snowmobiles and started it up.

I turned round and rushed back into the tent, the Empyrean Key already raised in my hand to activate it. 'Delphi, activate carrier tone.'

'Transmitting carrier tone,' she replied.

The tone hummed out, but a feeling of utter dread flooded

my gut when no icons appeared. I tried reinitiating it, but once again nothing appeared.

'Shit, the Empyrean Key isn't working, Ruby, and I seem to be locked out,' I said into my helmet's mic.

At that moment the ground began to shake even more violently beneath me and I could hear the sound of splintering rock echoing all around.

'Then get back here before it's too late.'

'But I can't leave the team stuck in E8!'

'You have to, Lauren,' Ruby replied.

Mike's voice cut in over the channel. 'They can ride the quake out in safety in E8, unlike you who will be very much dead if a crevasse opens up beneath you and you fall into it.'

I knew he was right and in a split second my decision was made, because if I died Jack and Jodie would be permanently stuck in the higher reality, and that was the worst possible outcome.

'Okay, I'm on my way — be ready for immediate lift-off,' I replied.

'I already am,' Erin replied over the channel as I raced back out of the tent towards the solitary snowmobile.

I leapt onto it, pressed the start button and twisted the throttle right back. With an explosion of torque the snowmobile leapt forward, hurtling up the slope just as cracks began to open up in the crater around me.

Raw, brutal acceleration slammed into my body as I crested the rim and the Taiga took off from the slope and crashed hard on its shocks before the snowmobile's tracks dug in and the vehicle gained traction again. Just ahead of me, less than a hundred metres away, was the open ramp of *Ariel* where Mike was waiting.

I gunned the accelerator and sped straight towards *Ariel* as the ground roared and giant rips started to open up in the snow plain around the ship.

I skidded to a stop and leapt from the Taiga before it had even stopped moving, sprinting towards *Ariel* as Mike beckoned towards me frantically from the ramp. I had just put my foot on the bottom step, when a huge shudder came from the ground directly beneath *Ariel*. Then with the sound of dozens of cannon-balls being fired, the ice started to split apart around the crater's edge, tilting down into it and causing a mini avalanche that ripped away the camo net to reveal Lucy's merged micro mind ship, now strobing with the orange light.

Mike grabbed onto my arm as *Ariel* started to buck; the quake began to intensify and he hauled me inside. Even before we'd cleared the airlock, Erin was already lifting our ship up from the surface in a swirl of snow.

As we raced back into the cabin, Ruby was staring at her CIC screen.

'Crap, the seismic probes are reading a Richter level five earthquake and it's rising rapidly up the scale,' she said.

'Then get us to a safe height, Erin, to watch this play out,' I said, dropping into my seat.

'Punching it now —hang on, guys,' Erin replied.

Mike and I just had time to grab our seat arms as the crushing G-force overwhelmed *Ariel's* gravity dampeners and pinned me down with limbs the weight of lead. The next moment, the view on the virtual cockpit was transformed and we were suddenly at a couple of thousand feet according to the altimeter.

I looked straight down towards the site. 'Enhance the view of Lucy's micro mind ship, Ruby, I need to see what's happening down there.'

'On it, Commander,' she replied.

A large window appeared on the virtual cockpit. Massive fissures were opening up around the crater. Fountains of snow and rock were shooting up like geyser explosions from the surface all around the Shackleton site.

'Bloody hell, the quake has reached level seven now,' Mike said, staring at his own screen.

Then on the video feed, large holes suddenly started to appear dotted around the crater, each billowing smoke and fire.

Mike was staring at his screen. 'Shit, according to my sensor array the ground temperature down there is shooting up through the roof.'

I gawped at him. 'You're saying that this is an eruption, not just a quake?'

'It certainly looks like it's headed that way,' he replied.

'But what about Lucy — if she is destroyed by this?'

He gave me a helpless look as the ground immediately around Lucy's ship began to completely craze, then dropped away like a cracking eggshell, revealing lines of glowing red. We suddenly saw the source of the red light as the slabs of ice and rock fell into it. A pool of molten lava, easily a hundred metres wide, was bubbling up from just beneath the surface. The only thing that remained of Shackleton Base was Lucy's quasicrystal, which was still supported on her network of glowing blue crystal roots. She hung there like a spider as the bowl filled with lava beneath her.

'Lucy!' I shouted. 'Erin, we've got to get down there to save—' I never even got a chance to finish my sentence.

A huge spurt of molten rock exploded upwards and engulfed Lucy in a split-second.

'No!' I screamed, as the column of fire, rock and smoke carried on hurtling straight upwards at incredible speed to where we were hovering in the sky.

Erin, grim-faced, manoeuvred *Ariel* backwards away from the cloud of expanding black smoke rising from where Lucy had been just a moment ago. The column of ash rose like a gigantic writhing snake into the sky, shedding huge lumps of blazing rocks that tumbled away towards the ground.

Mike remained mute, his face twisted with the same horror that was flooding through me. Erin and Ruby were both talking at once, but I didn't hear a word they said as I stared at the spot where a moment before my friend had been before being wiped off the surface of the Earth.

Then the awful punchline hit me. With Lucy and the other micro minds destroyed, there would be no one to maintain the bubble of reality in E8 where we'd left Jack and Jodie. I put my hands over my mouth and stared down in sheer horror at the growing devastation. By leaving them behind, I'd condemned them both to death. And as that thought struck me, any fantasy of a battle-hardened commander was swept away in an instant as raw grief slammed into me and the tears began to flow.

CHAPTER NINETEEN

No one said a word as we stared down at the mounting destruction that had killed Jack and Jodie, and wiped out Lucy in the blink of an eye.

The one strange fact that my brain was able to register, even as a vast chasm opened up in the centre of my being, was that rather than the classic cone shape of a typical volcano — where what had been the Shackleton Base was just a moment ago — was actually an expanding bowl scooped out of the ground.

Every so often the pool of bubbling magma at the bottom of it sent up a huge gout of steam as fresh, snow-covered ground collapsed into it to feed this molten furnace's insatiable appetite. Over it, like a grave marker for Lucy and the others, was a large, continuing column of smoke and ash rising up past *Ariel*, where Erin had brought us to a hover to bear witness to this catastrophic event.

I was too numb to process what was happening as we watched the ash cloud grow to a mile wide and flatten out on the upper atmosphere into a smeared anvil that would be easily visible from orbit. Lightning crackled every so often inside the column, casting deep ruby glows throughout it.

Mike just stared at the screen as tears rolled down his cheeks. Just like me, he'd lost his soulmate in E8.

It was Erin who finally broke the terrible silence in the cockpit. 'I know how bleak this looks and I may be going out on a limb here, but is there any way that Lucy could have survived being dropped into that magma with her expertise with gravity shielding?'

At last Mike spoke, his voice monotone. 'Even if Lucy had been able to keep the magma at bay, she wouldn't have been able to do anything about the temperature. We're talking about sixteen hundred Celsius here — that's hot enough to melt even crystal.'

I clenched my hands into fists in my laps. 'But this doesn't make any sort of sense, Mike. Why would the Angelus set something up that would wipe out Lucy and the other micro minds? Not to mention strand anyone who was trapped in that E8 hall to die—' My voice caught and I tried again, even as my heart was splintering. 'I mean, how the fuck is that going to help us defend the world now?'

'Maybe this wasn't the Angelus's plan at all?' Mike said in a quiet voice.

Immediately, our eyes were on him.

'What do you mean?' I said, but I already had an awful feeling about where he was headed with this.

'Maybe we were wrong to even try activating it with what was pretty much a hack,' he replied. 'After all, we never recovered all the micro minds; what if Lucy didn't have enough available to her to pull off whatever this final step was? That's why the boot up sequence kept failing. But like idiots we found a way round it and what we set in motion with our hack, quite literally blew up in our faces.'

My blood iced as I stared at him. 'You mean when *I* activated it with the Empyrean Key?'

Ruby jumped in and held up both hands. 'Woah there, Lauren, don't go there. This isn't on you.'

Mike nodded too. 'Ruby's right. We all agreed it was the right call, including Jack and Jodie. This was a team decision, not just yours.'

I gestured towards the volcano on the screen. 'No, as Commander this is on me. I should have paused to think for a moment rather than act like a toddler randomly pushing buttons at a nuclear power plant. Basically, I didn't know what the fuck I was doing and now I've murdered Lucy and two people who meant everything to us, Mike.'

He smeared away his tears with his arm. 'No, you're still bloody wrong.'

Erin gave me a gentle look. 'Lauren, you made a call based on what information you had. And it's not like you're psychic. How could anyone, let alone you, know how this would play out? So will you please stop beating yourself up?' She tilted her head to one side and crossed her arms as she held my gaze with an expression that challenged me to disagree.

Ruby was now scowling at me too. 'Yeah, you're so far off the mark that it isn't funny, Lauren. And to be absolutely blunt, right now you need to suck it up.'

I wanted to scream at them about how I could never forgive myself — it felt like I'd murdered my friends. But then I caught Ruby giving me the gentlest smile. She *knew*. Despite our shock, everyone here knew and they understood.

I wiped away the angry tears and took a deep breath. Then I looked down at my hands in my lap as *I got ready to suck it up.*

'Lauren, I'm afraid we have Niki on the comm,' Ruby said.

I raised my panicked gaze back to meet hers. 'Oh bloody hell — I need to tell him that he just lost his daughter.'

Erin nodded. 'Look, I know your instinct is to probably tell him straight away, but don't, at least not yet. If Niki is anything like my dad, it will break him to hear this and now so isn't that moment, trust me.'

Mike dipped his chin. 'As much as it breaks me not to tell him, Erin is absolutely right, Lauren.'

'Oh god, really?' I replied.

The three people in the cockpit on this awful, emotional journey with me, all nodded.

I took a shaky breath. 'Okay, but when it's the right moment it needs to be me who tells him. I owe him and Jodie that.' I closed my eyes and took a moment to try and centre myself in the storm of grief spinning through me. Then I opened my eyes again and looked at Ruby. 'Okay, put him through.'

'Roger that, Commander,' Ruby said, the gentleness in her expression of just a moment ago gone.

It wasn't lost on me, her using that title rather than my name. This was a mission and I needed to put aside the grieving woman that I was right now and play the role of the commander that everyone needed me to be in this darkest of hours.

The comm crackled into life. 'About time, I've being trying to contact you for the last ten minutes,' Niki said. 'But thank god you made it out okay.'

I dropped my gaze, fighting every instinct to spill everything out. 'Yes, but Lucy didn't...'

'We saw that on our sensors,' Niki replied. 'And apart from what that means for our whole world, I'm so sorry for your loss, Lauren.'

I had to drive the fingernails hard into my palms to stop myself falling apart. And of all people it was Ruby who then got out of her seat, headed over, and wrapped me up in a hug.

Oblivious to the heartbreak playing out in our cockpit, Niki continued. 'One of the evacuated science team just flagged something to me that if you haven't detected already, you are really going to want to know. I'm afraid it looks like things are about to get a lot worse round here.'

Ruby pulled away and looked into my eyes.

I took a shaky breath and nodded.

She squeezed my shoulders and, seemingly satisfied that I wasn't going to fall apart, let go of me. She also patted Mike on the shoulder as she headed back to her seat.

I tried to gather my thoughts. 'In what way, Niki?'

'We obviously just lost all the sensors around the Shackleton Base, but we've been continuing to monitor an outer ring of the probes that are still active. I'm afraid they have been detecting secondary level-four Richter tremors about fifteen klicks out from what was the Shackleton Base.'

'That sounds like secondary shocks,' Mike replied, his voice becoming steadier. 'That's not exactly unusual in an eruption of this magnitude.'

'It is when you see the arrangement of them, Mike,' Niki said. 'The science team is transferring a data package over now that will make things clearer.'

'And we've got it,' Ruby replied. Then her eyes widened as she stared at her CIC screen. 'Oh crap.' She selected an icon and immediately a large, three-dimensional map appeared in a window on our virtual cockpit.

The large, lava-filled bowl was clearly visible in the middle. But around the oval radius a long way out from the eruption site, was a line of pulsating dots, lines rippling out and fading from every one of them.

'As you can probably see for yourselves, there looks to be nothing natural about this ring of secondary quakes. They are far too regularly spaced and in a symmetrical oval. Also, there are exactly twelve of them.'

'Like we saw in the hologram in E8, Lauren,' Mike said. 'And looking at this data, apart from the obvious symmetry, these are low frequency earthquakes, locked in precisely at one point forty-five hertz with absolutely no variation whatsoever.'

My thoughts began to focus within the storm of grief swirling through me. 'Are you sure that this isn't natural?'

'No more so than an eruption suddenly kicking off in, as you said, a highly geologically stable area,' Mike replied.

I felt a tiny flicker of hope ignite inside me that there could still be a small piece of good news hidden within this. 'You mean this could all still be part of the Angelus boot up process after all?'

'It could be, and the only way we'll know for sure is by going and investigating one of these sites for ourselves.'

I clung onto the thought, that maybe, just maybe we could salvage something from this disaster.

'Okay, we'd better go and have a look,' I said. 'Niki, you and the science team onboard *Thor* accompany.'

'Roger that,' he replied.

A fresh look of determination had appeared on Mike's face too. 'Let's go and science the shit out of whatever the hell is really going on here.'

I pushed down the storm of pain and locked it away as best I could in some recess of my brain. Apart from anything, it would be exactly what Jack would be telling me to do right now if he were still here. And I intended to honour his, Jodie and Lucy's memories in any way I could right now whilst there might still be a chance to save our world.

CHAPTER TWENTY

As RUBY and I stood before the closed ramp door, fully kitted out in arctic gear, I was doing my best to hold it together and not plummet into the black hole of grief currently flooding my soul. The thing I kept telling myself was *what would Jack want you to do* and that was this, following through on what we'd started — saving the world. Our heartbreaking grief was secondary to our mission's prime objective.

Niki's voice came over the group comm channel. 'Okay, everyone, make sure your respirators are working properly and that your face masks have a good seal before you step outside. According to our medics, if you breathe that ash in it will cause silicosis, which might permanently scar your lungs. Breathe too much in and you'll die a very painful death.'

Time for me to follow Niki's lead and start acting like the commander I was meant to be.

I activated my mic on the same channel. 'It's Lauren Stelleck here. To add to what Niki has just said, your responsibility whilst we're out on the surface will be to buddy up with someone and look out for each other. If you receive the order to evacuate you must abandon whatever you are doing and head straight back to your ship.'

Lots of *affirmatives* and *yes ma'ams*, came back over the comm channel.

I checked my mask for the third time and Mike did the same. Then I pressed the switch to open the door and *Ariel's* ramp lowered into something that resembled an end of the world movie.

We'd landed over fifteen klicks away, where the Shackleton Base had been and was now marked by the funeral pyre of smoke rising up from it, high into the sky. And to make sure there wasn't any doubt that an active eruption was underway, fine dust was falling everywhere and had already turned the white snow grey. Also — according to one of the science team who'd briefed us on what to expect — lava bombs were raining like mortar rounds in the distance. Just to underline how dangerous this was, just as the ramp fully opened, a lava bomb arced down from the sky and slammed into the ground less than a klick away with an explosion of fire and steam.

Mike and I traded tight frowns through our masks as we stepped off the ramp.

Through the swirling ash, I was just able to make out the science team led by Niki, according to the metadata tag on my HUD. The group was emerging from the *Thor,* which had parked about two hundred metres away from *Ariel.* Also descending from the other ship's hold were six Tin Heads, all suitably armed. Of course, Niki was following protocol to the letter and was going to guard us, although I wasn't sure from exactly what in the middle of this apocalypse.

The science team were all carrying silver flight cases, just like the one that Mike had in his hand which contained a ground sensor.

'Okay, remember this isn't the time or the place to mention

Jodie, so let me deal with it,' I said over a private comm channel to Mike.

'Yes, but it's going to be so tough not to,' he replied.

'I know, but we have to do it.'

I toggled my radio back to the open channel as we reached Niki and the others.

'Hey, where's Jodie?' Niki immediately asked. 'I expected to see her out here taking readings with you guys.'

I jumped in as Mike dropped his gaze. 'She's onboard *Ariel* monitoring the feed from the rest of the sensor network.' The lie felt bitter in my mouth. I was certainly grateful for the tinted visor so Niki wouldn't be able to see my face clearly.

Mike appeared to gather himself as he stood slightly taller and turned towards the science team, avoiding eye contact with Niki. 'We need you to place your sensors at regular intervals over this entire area. That will give us a more precise understanding of what's happening beneath our feet.'

I joined in, making sure we kept the conversation down this new route to keep both of us focused on work. 'Talking of earthquakes, I was expecting to see the ground bucking beneath us, when we landed after what happened at Shackleton.'

Mike glanced at me and shook his head. 'Thankfully, there's no chance of that; for now, the major quake appears to be very localised. But can you feel what's happening through the soles of your feet, Lauren?'

I'd been so caught up with my internal emotional trauma, not to mention the apocalyptic conditions, that I hadn't. But as soon as Mike mentioned it, I realised there was a slight vibration passing through the ground where we were all standing.

'Yes, I feel it now, a faint tremor,' Niki said. 'But isn't there a danger that things are about to get a lot more serious around here like they did at Shackleton?'

'I'm not sure and that's why we desperately need more data

about what's happening at this and the eleven other locations that ring what was the Shackleton site,' Mike replied. 'All we know right now is that each of them is experiencing a low level VLF quake, the epicentre of which is nearby.' He turned to the science team and clapped his hands together. 'Okay, let's get these probes placed pronto, people.'

Soon I was heading off with Mike into the growing ash gloom, towards what his initial readings suggested was the focal point of the vibration running through the ground.

I pulled up a map in the top right of my HUD. There were pulsing green blips for everyone currently out on the snow and two much larger ones for *Ariel* and *Thor*. Further out were the square green markers for Tin Heads. But a few hundred metres directly ahead of us was a blue diamond box, which we were heading directly towards.

Not surprisingly Mike wasn't exactly in a chatty mood and I wasn't either, both too busy processing the loss of the others. But left alone with my thoughts, my mind kept skating to the scenario where I had to break the news to Niki that his daughter had died. After I did that and when this day was done, I wasn't sure I would be able to continue my role at Eden. Too many memories would haunt that place and break me wide open. But rather than listen to the churn of my own despair, I tried instead to concentrate on what was happening around me.

In the arctic conditions the warmth of the ash settling on my combat suit was significant and the heating system was automatically dialling itself right back to compensate. The landscape that we were trekking through was distinctly eerie, the ash sucking the brightness out of everything. There had already been enough soot falling to create a striking resemblance to the bottom of the ocean that I'd seen off Cuba, during the deep sea dive in the submersible. Down there, silt had softened the seabed into a clay-covered world. Something similar was happening here and what this was all doing to the fragile ecosystem of Antarctica, I shuddered to even think about.

The falling ash was growing thicker quickly and we'd probably only headed out fifty metres or so when I glanced back to see that *Ariel* and *Thor* were no longer visible. Suddenly, I was very grateful for the HUD map that would help guide us back to them, as it would have been a serious challenge otherwise.

As we steadily closed on the blue diamond marker, the vibration running through the ground was growing noticeably more pronounced as we neared our destination. Then dead ahead, I saw a strange mound about two metres tall and half a metre wide.

'What's that?' I asked over the comm.

'Not sure, but whatever it is, it's bang in the centre of the VLF quake in this area, so maybe its connected somehow?' Mike replied.

As we reached it, he was the first to reach out a hand to touch the mound and instantly yanked it away, shaking his fingers. 'Fuck!'

I stepped closer to him and looked up into his face through his visor. 'Are you okay?'

'Yes, just caught out by a massive static shock, but look...'

I turned back to see that his hand had left a clear imprint in the ash covering the mound, revealing a glowing blue crystal surface beneath.

'Tell me that's not Angelus tech?' Mike said.

I felt that tiny flicker of hope growing stronger inside me that this was more evidence to show this was all part of the Angelus plan after all. Maybe even Lucy sacrificing herself was part of it too? But it would be a small consolation when the cost of losing Jack, Jodie and her, had been so high.

'Let's find out for sure and see what else is under this mound,' I said, reaching out towards it.

Mike grabbed my hand before I could touch it. 'Are you crazy? You saw what just happened to me.'

'Yes, but you've already earthed the static charge that built up in it. I used to have a treadmill that shocked me all the time until I finally put it on a rubber mat. Anyway, if I'm right, whatever this is shouldn't give me a shock now.'

Before he could stop me again, I reached out and placed my hand firmly on the mound with not so much as a tiny tickle of a static shock. But I could feel it vibrating beneath my fingers.

'You see,' I said, turning back towards him.

'Yeah, I do, but let's see what we're dealing with here,' Mike replied, placing his hand on it too.

Together we began wiping the ash away, slowly exposing more of the crystal surface until finally a curved, pointed claw-like structure was revealed.

'What the hell is that meant to be?' Mike asked, staring at the strange structure.

But already my instinct was kicking in. I squatted by the base and began excavating the ash and slushy snow around it. Within moments I'd cleared enough to realise that the curved claw was actually the tip of a taller structure. Then at last, with some help from Mike digging, we finally hit solid rock. But if anything, the crystal claw structure seemed to have passed through it, splintering the solid rock apart as it had pushed through.

'This reminds me of the Angelus runes growing from the rock that we've encountered before,' I said. 'But the obvious difference here is that there is no runic symbol to be seen on this thing; it's also a completely different shape.'

'Whatever it is or does, is there any chance you can connect to it with your Empyrean Key?' Mike asked.

'Only one way to find that out,' I replied. I fished the stone orb out of my rucksack.

In a few more seconds the carrier tone was being transmitted in my helmet.

'Well?' Mike asked, peering through my visor.

'Sorry, I'm seeing absolutely nothing here.'

Mike sighed. 'So much for that bright idea then.'

I looked at the claw structure and its curved tip. It was only then that I realised that the tip was directly orientated towards the volcanic plume rising into the sky.

'Hang on, it seems to be pointed towards the Shackleton site, could that be significant, Mike?'

'It's unlikely to be a simple coincidence, knowing what we do of Angelus technology,' he replied. 'Everything they do always seems to have some sort of serious intent behind it.'

I was about to gesture to the ash cloud and ask him – *this too?* – when a grinding sound came from the structure. Before either of us could move, the claw slid up from the ground, the base of its column growing wider as it did so. Within moments it was at least ten metres high and towering over us, as we started to back away.

'What the hell is happening?' Mike asked as it continued to push up through the ground.

'Whatever it is, I think that whatever we unleashed in E8 is far from over,' I replied.

It was at that same moment that we heard the unmistakable crack of automatic weapon fire from the distance.

'We're coming under ground assault from a large number of troops,' Niki shouted over the comm.

'What the hell? We didn't pick up any threats before now with our sensors?' I asked.

'I'm afraid they managed to sneak in under the cover of the ash cloud,' Niki replied. 'We need to evacuate immediately; I've already started pulling the rest of the science team out.'

'Okay, we're on our way,' I confirmed.

Mike and I started to run back towards the marker on my

HUD for *Ariel*. The ground shuddered and began to slope beneath us, back up towards the emerging monolith that was continuing to push up through the surface. It had already grown so tall that the top of it had become lost in the ash cloud.

'Lauren, we're receiving multiple reports rolling in from the teams who went to investigate the other sites and are witnessing similar monoliths to the one here, rising up from the ground,' Ruby said over the comm. 'Some of the teams are also coming under ground assault, although the Tin Heads are engaging the enemy now.'

'Can't we just use an air attack to push them back?' Mike asked.

'Negative to that,' Erin said. 'The ash cloud has made anything on the ground invisible to our ship's sensors.'

'Then it sounds like it's time for our Tin Heads to really earn their keep,' I said as we raced back. My heart was thundering in my chest by the time that *Ariel* and *Thor* came into view. But just as they did, a missile came barrelling out of the gloom straight towards our ship. Tracer fire lanced up from several of the Tin Heads, detonating the incoming missile with a loud boom and the remnants of it broke apart, corkscrewing sideways and crashing into the ground.

Without even pausing, Mike and I sprinted into the airlock and both slammed the button together to close the ramp.

'We're onboard — go, go, go, Erin!' I yelled into my mic.

'Roger that, hang on.'

As the air scrubbers started up in the airlock, clearing the ash that we'd managed to bring in with us, a punch of G-force pinned us to the floor, making us both groan. But then just as fast as it started, the excess gravity fell away. Then I was tearing my mask off and breathing in the sweet, oxygen-rich air of our ship as the inner airlock door opened. We raced through it and strapped ourselves in to our flight seats.

On the virtual cockpit, Ruby already had up a number of feeds from the Tin Heads that had been left behind and were trading fire with the unseen attackers from the ash cloud.

'What are your orders, Commander?' Ruby asked.

I looked across at Jack's empty seat for that petal of wisdom that he would have thrown towards me at a moment like this. I swallowed hard and forced myself to focus.

'For now we'll leave our Tin Heads to defend this monolith at all costs and deploy the others to protect the rest. The one thing we can be pretty sure of is that the ground assault is just the opening act to test our defences by what has to be an Overseer scouting force. Tell the ships at the far edge of our fleet to keep a sharp look out with any sensors that won't be affected by this ash cloud for any fast incoming contacts, and to be ready to take hostile defensive action.'

'You think the Overseers are going to attack us with a TR-3B fleet then?' Erin asked.

'I think you can pretty much guarantee it now that they've tracked us to this location.' I said. 'As far as they are aware, they probably think that Lucy is still alive, so will go all-out with a major offensive.'

'And what about those monoliths, what's their purpose in all of this craziness?' Erin asked.

'They must have appeared for a reason, so we just need to wait to find out what exactly,' Mike said.

My mind was also whirling, trying to mentally process the multiple options that were opening up. What I needed was a tactical overview of a situation that was already running away from us.

I tilted my head slightly towards the speaker in the ceiling. 'Delphi, initiate Battle Command centre.'

'Initiating Battle Command centre,' she repeated with exactly the unflappable calm that I needed to hear right now.

The virtual cockpit reorganised itself as the tactical options were displayed. On the left hand, the 3D map lit up with the reassuring sight of a hundred and twenty-three X-craft.

'Let the Overseers bloody try,' I muttered to myself as I glanced across at the list of tactical options that Delphi had already prepared for me.

CHAPTER TWENTY-ONE

BACK ONBOARD *ARIEL,* we climbed up with *Thor* alongside us, both craft no longer invisible as so much of the falling ash had landed on their hulls. Meanwhile, I was studying tactical options for defence patterns of our fleet on the virtual cockpit. So far, the green square dots denoting the position of our Tin Heads had been more than able to repel multiple ground attacks and for now the Angelus crystal monoliths were safe. How long we could keep it that way, I wasn't so sure.

Erin had pulled up some diagnostics for *Ariel* on a screen in front of her seat and was pursing her lips.

'Problem?' I asked.

'No, thankfully. I was just checking the performance of the multimode manoeuvring rockets to check they weren't getting clogged by that ash cloud.'

I shot her a sharp look. 'And are they?'

'Not according to my readouts they're not and we can thank Jodie for that,' Erin said. 'We learnt all about the modification because of how you guys crash-landed in a sandstorm back at the Richat Structure. After that, she made sure the Forge team fitted a modification to prevent a dirt ingress into the rockets. Now when the rockets are idling, there is less danger of them turning sand — or ash particles for that matter — into glass within them. She told me that was exactly what happened to *Ariel* last time, when you had to make that forced landing in the desert.'

That brought an immediate lump to my throat. Even though Jodie was dead, the care and attention to detail she applied to everything that she did was still protecting us.

Ruby was nodding. 'Yeah, that woman always had our backs.'

'Yes, she most certainly did,' Mike replied, not able to meet her eyes.

Not surprisingly, conversation fell away after that as Erin swept *Ariel* ever higher up into the sky, finally rising completely clear of the dust cloud into sudden, startling blue sunlit skies.

'Now that's better,' she said, settling us into a hover, a manoeuvre that was replicated by *Thor* flying in formation alongside us.

'Woah, what's that about?' Ruby said, pointing down towards the bottom of the virtual cockpit.

A bright blue flash of light had burst into life far beneath us on the surface.

Ruby was already scanning her curved CIC screen, opening up new windows with her fingertips. 'I'm overlaying radar data now over the main view, so we can hopefully get some sort of idea of what is actually going on down there.'

A new overlaid layer shimmered into view on the central cockpit. Thousands of green dots swirled and danced across it.

Erin pulled a face. 'If anything, that makes things worse.'

'I'm afraid it's the back scatter caused by the ash cloud,' I said. 'We used to see a similar degradation in Lovell's signal when intense thunderstorms passed overhead, thanks to all the water vapour in the air.'

Mike nodded. 'Then let's see if Delphi can help clear up the image a bit with the new algorithm Jodie had the Forge team upload to the fleet last week. Delphi, please run the radar sensor enhancement program.'

'Initiating radar sensor enhance program,' Delphi replied.

At once the blurring green dots started to organise themselves. Now, although the image was still hard to make out, green dots had clustered around the oval ring of crystal towers. The central bowl-shaped caldera that Lucy had dropped into was also visible and had grown significantly to about a klick wide.

'Lauren, we've got Alice on the comm for you,' Ruby said.

A sick feeling swirled through my stomach. I could avoid telling the truth to Niki when he couldn't see my face through my visor, but Alice was another matter. She was endlessly brilliant at reading people — probably one of the many reasons she'd risen to the heights that she had.

I took a deep breath. 'Okay, put her through.'

Ruby nodded and activated the comm.

'Are you reading me, *Ariel*, over?' Alice's voice said.

'Yes, we're here, Alice,' I said.

'Thank god, Lauren. I've been watching the reports rolling and I just wanted to hear your voice to know that you were okay. Anyway, I know you're in the thick of it, so I'll keep this brief. We've just received some data that you need to be aware of. The TREENO network is seeing significant neutrino activity at what was Shackleton Base. I can only begin to imagine what you're feeling about losing Lucy, which is why I knew you would want to hear this next piece of news straight away.'

A fluttery feeling started in my stomach. 'Go on...'

'The team here have just finished running an analysis of this new neutrino pulse event and we think it could be very significant. This latest activity bares the neutrino signature of every single micro mind that we've ever detected.'

I cupped my hands over my mouth. 'You're saying Lucy is still alive?'

'Well, *something* Angelus is down at that location where she used to be, and everything points towards it being Lucy's merged micro mind ship.'

I gasped, blinking back fresh tears as Mike shook his head, eyes wide in wonder.

'This could change everything, Lauren,' he said.

I nodded. 'Alice, thank you so much — that's great news to hear when everything was starting to look so bleak around here.'

'Then I'm glad to lighten your day. We're keeping everything crossed here for you, Lauren. Good luck and over and out for now.' The comm channel light turned off.

I turned to the others. 'Thoughts people? Obviously you're already thinking it too, right Mike?'

'That if Lucy has somehow survived being dunked in the lava, then the E8 hall is still intact...and we both know what that means?'

I covered my mouth with my hands, hardly daring to voice the thought in case I jinxed it. 'Jack and Jodie might still be alive...'

Suddenly everyone was whooping and clapping.

Ruby fist-pumped the air. 'Way to go, Lucy!'

'Okay, we may be getting ahead of ourselves, but for once I'm going to take this at face value as great news,' I said, half smiling, half crying as I scraped away my tears. 'But my next question is that if everything happening down on the surface is part of an Angelus plan, what could justify it creating a dirty great eruption in the middle of Antarctica?'

'Whatever it is, I don't think it's going to be much longer until we find out what it is,' Mike said. 'According to our sensors around the monoliths, the quake just hit ten on the Richter scale.'

'Bloody hell! At that level, they'll be feeling the vibrations on the other side of the planet,' I replied.

Then I spotted that the overlaid green radar dots that followed the contours of the lava-filled basin on the virtual cockpit had changed dramatically — they now dropped straight down, suggesting a huge shaft had opened up. Then, as if someone had switched off a massive vacuum cleaner, the billowing ash cloud started to spin around it.

Alarms warbled out as *Ariel* began to be drawn in by the growing maelstrom. But Erin had already responded and had increased the spin of our REV drive to compensate, settling us back into a hover. She glanced across her readouts.

'According to *Ariel's* sensors, there's a huge drop in pressures and a major wind vortex opening up directly over the centre of the original eruption,' Ruby said.

My comm light blinked on with *Thor's* name displayed on the panel and I pressed the button.

'Are you seeing this, Niki?' I said.

'Absolutely. We've just lost contact with all the Tin Heads on the ground as well as those attacking Overseer forces. I doubt anything could survive being down on the surface right now. So my question is whether our two ships are safe up here, or should we withdraw to a safe distance along with the rest of the fleet?' he replied.

I glanced over at Erin. 'Can *Ariel* hold her own in whatever this is that's happening?'

Our pilot gave me a sharp nod. 'Absolutely no question, Lauren. I can hover us here safely as long as you like. A conventional aircraft would be another matter, but that's not an issue for our X-craft.'

'Okay, you heard Erin, Niki. For now *Ariel* is going to hold position so we can see how this plays out. But the moment it looks like it might be getting too serious for us, we'll pull back. Meanwhile, I'd like you to join our main fleet to keep an eye out for any Overseer air attack headed our way.'

'But I'm quite happy to stay with you, Lauren,' Niki replied.

'No, we'll be fine, but I'm seriously worried about what the Overseers will do next and I need you to hold the fort for me.'

'No problem, I'll keep in contact.' The comm light blinked off as *Thor* began to pull away from us at high speed, heading towards the horizon.

'Holy hell, will you look at that?' Ruby said, pointing downwards.

On the virtual cockpit, so much of the ash cloud had cleared that we could finally see the oval ring of monoliths. I gasped out loud - where the lava-filled bowl had been, a shining gold spherical object was hovering just above the entrance to the shaft, as the ash cloud flowed past. It was Lucy.

If I'd had any more tears left to shed, they would have been tears of joy. Around me, a fresh wave of whoops and claps erupted as the others spotted Lucy.

A cone of blue plasma blazed straight down from her into the deep shaft like a vast blow torch.

'That confirms that Lucy is a-okay and looking very much intact despite her lava bath,' Ruby said, grinning at me.

I nodded. 'Can you zoom in on that for a better look at what exactly is going on here?'

Ruby nodded and a close-up view appeared in front of us on the main screen.

Through the rapidly thinning ash cloud it was possible to make out the walls of the shaft, pinpricked with truncated lava tubes where — strangely — the molten rock wasn't gushing out of them and appeared to be held back by some invisible force.

But Mike was frowning at his console.

'Is there a problem, Mike?' I asked.

'Actually, I think there might be. If Lucy keeps burrowing

through the Earth's mantle at the rate she's appears to be going, she's going hit the outer molten core of our planet. And if she does that, the release of pressure will be so immense that a Yellowstone super volcano eruption will look like a wet weekend at Barry Island.'

I gawped at him. 'You're saying that Lucy is about to release an extinction level event?'

'Based on what we're seeing, it's a strong possibility,' he replied.

Ruby's mouth dropped open. 'Hang on, you're not saying the Angelus's ultimate plan is a scorched earth strategy instead of letting the Kimprak capture it?'

'That doesn't make any sense,' I said. 'With all the technology available to the Angelus there must be a million easier ways for them to destroy a world, not least of which is a giant bloody bomb. Also, even if a nuclear winter severe enough to wipe out all life on Earth happens, that's actually doing the Kimprak's job for them, because any resources left that they want will be there for the asking, with no one left to try and stop them.'

'So why dig a bloody great hole right to the middle of our world like an overexcited gopher? Surely that's never going to end well for anyone?' Erin said.

'Well, we're about to find out,' Mike replied. 'At the rate she's going, I'm afraid we're probably about to witness that extinction within two minutes unless something happens to stop it.'

Ruby sucked the air between her teeth. 'Commander, I know this could be an impossible question...but are you sure enough about what you said not to take Lucy out with a railgun round before it's too late?'

My mouth literally fell open and I flapped it open and closed a few times before I was able to find any words. 'Ruby, you can't be serious?'

'Can't I? What we're witnessing is the possible beginning of an Armageddon level event that will wipe out all life on Earth. Can we really take the risk of just sitting here and doing nothing?'

My mind spun. 'But what if you're wrong? After all, hasn't that massive ash cloud already been scrubbed out of the atmosphere that could have done a lot of environmental damage? And do I even have to mention what the consequences for Jack and Jodie will be if we do that?'

'But what if this eruption was just an unexpected consequence of whatever is about to happen next?' Ruby continued, driving home her point. 'This is far from over and I know what I would be doing now if I was in command.'

So there it was, the nightmare decision landing squarely on my shoulders, damned if I did and possibly damned if I didn't. And having only just learnt that Jack and Jodie were almost certainly still alive, could I just sit there and throw their lives away based on what could easily turn out to be just paranoia?

I turned to Mike and Erin for moral support. 'What would you do if you were in my position?'

'I can see where Ruby is coming from but whatever you decide it's going to be a gamble,' Erin said.

I turned my beseeching gaze to Mike, like a drowning person spotting a life raft. 'And what about you?'

He was shaking his head at Ruby. 'No, I totally disagree. Even if at the end of the day Lucy is just a super advanced AI following her core programming, she is still someone I utterly trust, and so I trust the Angelus to not throw our species under the bus.'

Lucy's own words came surging through my mind. *'Always remember to trust me...'* Then I knew with utter certainty what I had to do.

'Ruby, we're going to see this thing through.'

'Are you absolutely sure, Lauren, because *Thor* is still in range to take the shot?' she replied.

I glanced at Jack's seat. 'Yes. Lucy told me to trust her and that's exactly what I intend to do.'

Ruby let out a long breath. 'Yeah ok, I get where you're coming from. I just hope you're right, Commander.'

As I returned my attention to what could be the beginning of the end of all life on our planet, my shoulders were practically hunched up to my ears. We all sat in silence to bear witness to what was about to happen. I was certainly never ever going to forget this moment, where sheer terror and hope roared through me in equal measure as I prayed I'd made the right call.

A few seconds ticked past, then a few seconds more. Those seconds quickly added up to a minute and still nothing had happened. Then, without warning, the plasma beam coming from Lucy shut down.

Immediately I turned towards Mike. 'And?'

His brow furrowed as he gazed at his screen, then a slow, glorious smile filled his face. 'I have absolutely no idea how, but all seismic activity has ceased around the area and there isn't any sign of any volcanic activity. But from what I can tell, looking at our readouts, Lucy stopped drilling because she has connected to an even deeper shaft that appears to have already been there. The good news is, according to our sensors there is absolutely no sign of the lava that should be rising up through it. It appears that we're in the clear.'

Instantly, Erin and Ruby high-fived each other.

'Oh thank the actual fuck for that,' I said, shaking my head. Both Erin and Ruby burst out laughing.

'Yeah, once again your instinct for these things is right on the money,' Ruby said.

'On this occasion it was all about trust. Anyway, we need to learn more about that shaft that Lucy seems to have uncovered and why it's there.'

Erin gave me a suspicious look. 'Before you ask, there is absolutely no way I'm going to endanger this ship and all your lives by taking *Ariel* down into that tunnel unless you are going to order me to do so, Lauren.'

I raised my palm to stop her protest. 'Don't panic, even as crazy as some of my plans have been, even I wouldn't be daft enough to risk that. No, my idea is simply to position us directly over that shaft so we can get a good look straight down it with our sensors and maybe discover why we're not seeing any sort of eruption yet. If possible, I'd also like to get us close enough to Lucy to see if we can make contact.'

'Okay, that sounds a lot less risky,' Erin said, visibly relaxing.

'Then take us in,' I replied.

With a nudge of controls Erin started to head down towards Lucy's micro mind ship, which was blazing like a freshly born star in a nebula of the remaining ash.

As we dived back, I eyeballed the crystal towers that had continued to grow to at least a thousand feet tall. For the first time, I realised that the curved tops that I'd likened to a claw were actually a hint of what had been below the surface. The curve that started at the top continued down throughout the monolith's length, giving a crescent shape to the columns radiating around the central axis like fins and the focal point, where Lucy was currently sitting.

'Tell me those things don't look like some sort of big machine?' Ruby said, following my gaze.

'Yes, this is starting to look like another Angelus megastructure — one that makes the Resonancy Chamber look minuscule by comparison,' Mike replied.

'Hey, maybe we're going to get a Death Star beam after all! If so, please put me in control of firing it, Commander,' Ruby said.

I snorted. 'We'll have to see about that.'

As we neared Lucy, who was hovering about five hundred feet above the shaft, we saw that wisps of smoke were rising from its edges as the rock began to cool down. The shaft's perfect symmetry was impossible to ignore. It walls were so smooth that it looked like it had been machined rather than blasted with a huge plasma torch. The other thing we couldn't ignore was that Lucy was beginning to glow a vivid green, which hinted that this wasn't a typical day at the office for her.

'Anything that even looks vaguely dangerous to us, Erin, you have my permission to make whatever violent manoeuvre you need to do to get us out of here,' I said.

'I'll make your noses bleed if I have to,' Erin replied, levelling *Ariel* off about a thousand feet up as we approached Lucy. As we cleared the lip of the tunnel for a direct look past her into the shaft, there was collective gasp of surprise as we all gazed down to see a dark tunnel, lit at the bottom by a distant pinprick of glowing light.

'So let's see if Lucy is in a talkative mood,' I said. 'Delphi, please broadcast the carrier tone.'

'Broadcasting carrier tone,' our ship's AI replied.

As the low tone hummed out, I grabbed the Empyrean Key from my bag. This time, an icon did appear over it but it wasn't the communication one or even the one for E8. Instead, a new vortex icon appeared, spinning. However, it was greyed out and that meant I couldn't currently access it.

I thinned my lips. 'Oh bloody hell, I'm still locked out and can't communicate with Lucy, although it does look like some sort of program is currently running.'

'It's just a shame we can't risk flying *Ariel* down for a closer look at where that shaft goes,' Ruby said, giving Erin a wide-eyed innocent look. Erin glared back at her.

But that gave me another idea. 'So...what about sacrificing

one of your WASPs by doing a reconnaissance mission instead, Ruby?'

Ruby tapped her finger on her lips and slowly nodded. 'I don't see why not, although with these temperatures, it'll be a one way trip for that WASP.'

'It will be worth it to gather some useful data,' Mike said.

'That could work, but we're going to have to boost the signal strength to stay in contact with it because that hole is over a hundred kilometres deep,' I replied.

'I've already had an idea about that,' he said. 'The WASPs generate their own mesh network and each drone is a node in it. Ruby, if you launch all of them and then stop them one at a time when they reach their maximum range, each one can act as a relay station to pass the signal along to the next one. It will give them some serious range.'

'Very nice,' she replied, nodding.

'Okay, get ready to launch, Ruby,' I said. 'Time to find out why an Angelus AI is so intent on boring that shaft straight down.'

CHAPTER TWENTY-TWO

THE THINNING ASH cloud billowed around our ship as Ruby took hold of the direct control joystick, ready to launch the WASP unit.

She met my gaze and answered the question that she had obviously seen in my eyes. 'I think I better take manual control — this is so far outside Delphi's mission experience that it isn't funny.'

'Good point, a trip down that shaft into the abyss isn't exactly something that the Forge team would have programmed into our drones,' I replied.

Mike gazed off into space. 'If you stare into the abyss, the abyss stares back at you.'

'Hey, what already?' Ruby asked.

'Sorry, it's a Nietzsche quote that an old student mate was heavily into — he wore way too much black with things like that written on his T-shirts,' he replied. 'Anyway, I can't quite shake the thought that there is something so dangerous down there that maybe it might have been better to leave it sleeping.'

'If you mean there's a dragon like Smaug at the bottom of that hole, I think it's probably a bit late for that,' I replied. 'We've already well and truly set off the alarm clock and I doubt there's a snooze button.'

A tiny smile crept across Mike's face as he gestured towards the ash cloud outside swirling across the virtual cockpit. 'You reckon?'

Ruby shook her head. 'Well, if you ladies have finished flirting, let's get on and do this.'

Yes, considering we might have just triggered an extinction level event and we still hadn't confirmed that the others stuck in E8 really were okay, the morale in the cockpit was a hell of a lot better than it had been ten minutes ago. But then again, maybe that was how we had all learnt to roll with the punches over the years, although until I saw Jack and Jodie again with my own eyes I wouldn't be able to fully relax.

Ruby toggled a few switches and a live video feed from the WASP — my old friend unit seven, according to the data tag display — appeared. He was currently in the hold with the other drones as the bay doors started to open beneath it, revealing a swirling maelstrom of fine ash.

'To point out one little drawback with this plan, isn't there a danger that the electric motors on that WASP will quickly clog up with all the crud floating around out there?' Erin asked.

'That's why I'm going to drop 007 and the other WASPs straight down into the shaft like bombs to start with,' Ruby replied.

'007 as in the spy?' Mike asked.

'Hey, naming my drones keeps me amused. I ran out of names after the seven dwarves, though. Anyway, as soon as they clear the ash cloud, I'll activate the motors, but only using them to steer the descent and using gravity to maximise the flight time range for the batteries. That's another reason to take over manual control of this — Delphi would throw a hissy fit if asked to do something this stupid.'

Erin gave Ruby a straight look. 'With all respect to your flying skills, maybe I should take over flying this drone, then?'

Ruby gave her a hard stare in return and I could tell she was gearing up a for a sarcastic comeback. But then a large grin filled her face.

'I love that in-your-face attitude, Erin. And there was me having you down as a bit wet behind the ears.'

I coughed. 'Sounds like the same attitude you had towards me when we first started working together.'

Ruby laughed. 'Yeah, it does, doesn't it? Anyway, Erin, you might have a point there, so I'm handing over control of 007 to you now.'

Erin gave her a nod, a small smile twitching her lips, and took hold of the auxiliary joystick next to her main flight one. 'Okay, little guys, let's do this.' She punched a button and the WASP drones dropped straight down through the ash cloud in a line towards the entrance of the shaft, with the metadata tags identifying 007 as the drone leading the swarm.

'Let's make this a drive-in movie experience, minus the popcorn,' Ruby said. She toggled an icon and 007's video feed was now superimposed in a 360-degree view round us.

I unbuckled my harness and crossed to the railing to look down at the bottom of the virtual cockpit. On the relayed view from 007, he and the other drones dropped through the remains of the ash cloud, rapidly gathering speed. The swarm had already hit sixty miles per hour as the mouth of the shaft came rushing up to meet them. Because the view was playing directly onto the virtual cockpit it almost felt like *Ariel* was actually doing the manoeuvre. My stomach did the whole rollercoaster rising to my mouth routine as 007 and the other drones plunged straight down into the tunnel towards the centre of the Earth.

Ruby started whistling the theme tune from *James Bond*, which raised a smile from the rest of us as the drones that had arranged themselves into a train line of carriages switched on their mini headlights to illuminate the shaft walls whipping past.

'Okay, we've hit terminal velocity, powering up motors now as the WASP swarm is well and truly clear of the ash and I need to start steering as I'm starting to see an increase in wind vortexes,' Erin said.

I glanced at the speed display and saw it had hit 118 miles per hour. Then I glanced at the altitude indicator, which was reading minus 11,000 feet.

'Good grief, just how deep does this shaft go?' Erin said.

'Radar pings basically aren't coming back, so I think this is the very definition of a bottomless pit,' Ruby replied.

'Well if this is the holy grail of Angelus tech, it's becoming increasingly obvious that they made it impossible for our species to stumble across it accidentally,' I replied.

'Or, for that matter, any other alien species that might attack our world,' Mike said. 'Whatever this ultimate defence is, the Angelus really weren't messing around when they hid it.'

I nodded as we continued to watch the rapid descent of 007 and the other WASPs.

'Okay, approaching the first relay point for the first drone,' Ruby said. 'It should automatically come into a hovering position any moment now.'

We all glanced up to see the last drone in the express line come to a stop, before quickly disappearing into the distance.

'Yep, signal strength is holding steady at eighty five percent,' Ruby said. 'I love it when a plan comes together.'

Without warning the surface of the tunnel suddenly changed

from polished rock to a metal wall ringed inwardly with large copper rings every hundred metres or so.

'What the heck is that all about?' Erin asked.

'I think we just passed the transition point between the shaft that Lucy just opened up and what was already here. Looking at it my guess is that those are electromagnetic coils for a mass accelerator.'

'You're saying this could be the barrel of some sort of massive Angelus gun?' I asked.

'Could be, but the obvious problem with that is that your target has to be in perfect alignment for it to be taken out and I doubt the Kimprak mothership will play ball unless the Angelus are planning to spin the whole world round to face it.'

'I strongly doubt it, the shift in gravity tidal forces alone would be enough to create havoc across the world,' I replied.

'So what is this then?' Erin asked.

'We're just going to have to wait and see what the WASPs discover at the bottom of wherever it is that this leads to.'

Time stretched on as we waited. One by one the other drones came to a hovering halt, the signal strength slowly decreasing with each one, but still very usable. We had just passed the eight minute mark when Ruby, who'd been resting her arms on the railing next to me to watch the show, shook her head and gestured to the altitude display that had now whipped past minus eighty thousand feet.

'Holy crap, 007 and Dopey are seriously deep now,' she said, as our penultimate drone came to a hovering stop. The signal strength display was now down to fifteen percent.

'And then there was one,' Erin said.

'Has anyone noticed that red light is starting to get much brighter?' Ruby said.

I had to peer hard to see it, but Ruby was right, there was a ruby glow at the bottom of the shaft and it was getting brighter.

'007 must be deep enough now to have almost reached the magma layer, so I reckon that explains the glow,' Mike said. 'But to be honest, I'm surprised he hasn't melted by now.'

'You're not the only one,' Erin said. 'But here's the thing — according to his instruments, the temperature is still holding steady at a very pleasant twenty Celsius.'

'Well at that rate and the way that light is glowing, it looks like the little guy won't last much longer. That has to be lava rushing up to meet him,' Ruby said.

'Okay, record all the data you can before 007 croaks his last, Ruby,' Mike said. 'We might still be able to find out something useful.'

'On it,' she replied, heading back to her CIC station.

I watched the glow intensify as 007 hurtled towards the growing pool of red light.

Then for the first time, I had a clear view of what was definitely lava. But there was something odd about it too, that my brain didn't have enough time to process as it rushed up to meet the drone.

'What the hell?' Mike just had time to say as 007 dropped from a shaft blasted through stone into another, where the walls were made of lava.

We all gawped at the relayed view on the virtual cockpit. Now we could see molten rock eddying and flowing around the tunnel that somehow had been driven straight through it. Apart from the invisible walls, all that was still visible as the drone sped past were the copper rings that lined the shaft.

I turned to Mike, spreading my hands wide. 'Just tell me how?'

'The only explanation I can think of is that it has to be some sort of giant gravity shield generated by whatever this leads to,' Mike replied. 'It would certainly explain the lack of an eruption. Also, maybe it wasn't Lucy who bored this tunnel, maybe she just did the first bit to open it up. That would also explain the magnetic anomaly on the surface.'

'Yes, that makes a lot of sense,' I replied. 'I just wish that Jack and Jodie were here to share this with us — they would have got such a kick out of it.'

'Well hopefully you can tell them all about it when we finally manage to head back to E8.'

I nodded and returned my attention to the last WASPs on their mesmerising journey.

'I can't believe 007 is still going,' Ruby said, shaking her head after another five minutes had passed.

'Well, the bad news is that I'm seeing a massive temperature build up according to 007's sensors, so there's no way he can last much longer,' Erin replied. 'Also, signal strength has dropped below ten percent.'

'Keep going, we need as much data as we can, even if it's just how deep 007 can get before he gets burned to a cinder,' I replied.

Erin nodded. The view of the virtual cockpit started to glitch out with static but still the little drone that wouldn't say die kept on rolling, continuing to relay the signal feed of its very surreal journey down through the flowing lava. But then finally, as we all knew it would, the view broke up completely with static and a moment later a black screen was displayed along with a *signal lost* message.

'Rest in peace, little guy,' Ruby said.

'That almost sounds sentimental,' Erin noted.

'Hey, that little drone more than proved itself. I'll be a raising a glass to its memory whenever it is that we get back to the Rock Garden. Anyway, restoring cockpit to standard viewing mode.'

As the view around *Ariel* replaced the blank screen, we could see Lucy was now smouldering with a deep red colour beneath us, the tips of the individual tetrahedron crystals glowing white hot.

'Okay, that has to be significant,' Mike said, peering at her.

'It almost looks like she's overheating. Could that be a thing, Mike?' Erin asked.

'It's certainly possible, the sheer amount of power she must be channelling through her from god knows where must be off the scale,' he replied.

I glanced down into the mouth of the dark shaft and had to resist an urge to order Erin to fly us down it. Whatever was down there, it wasn't worth risking the lives of my crew to find out, especially when our sensors could hopefully do as good a job at investigating.

Ruby stared at her CIC screen. 'You know how we were joking about waking something like a dragon at the bottom of that hole?'

'Yes?' I said.

'Well, I think we've just woken it up because according to our radar something is travelling up through that shaft at...holy shit balls...Mach 15.'

'Bloody hell, at that speed it will be here in about five minutes,' Mike said.

'Hang on, what happens if it runs straight into Lucy?' Erin asked.

'I think that whatever is about to happen, the Angelus would have thought of it and programmed Lucy accordingly,' Mike said.

'And if they didn't?' Ruby said.

'It'll be something like a good size nuke going off and there won't be a whole lot of anything left to worry about around here.'

'Then we're going to play this on the safe side,' I said. 'Erin, pull us right back to thirty klicks out. Let's just pray something isn't about to go catastrophically wrong and that this is all part of the game plan.'

Erin nodded and a moment later *Ariel* was hurtling through the deepening sunset towards the ring of crystal towers. Once again, my anxiety about Lucy, Jack and Mike took up residence in my stomach, twisting it into a knot as I stared at the screen, teeth clenched.

CHAPTER TWENTY-THREE

Ruby had toggled on a countdown timer that absolutely hadn't helped the sense of dread building inside me for the possible impact event by whatever was rising up that shaft. But my brain was doing its best to talk down the raw emotion churning through me. It was trying to use logic — that the Angelus just *wouldn't* crash whatever was rising from the depths of the planet straight into Lucy, destroying her and killing Jack and Jodie in the process. Unfortunately for me, the less rational side of my psyche was having a field day with a full blown paranoid parade, complete with marching band and cheering crowd. The executive summary was that I'd pretty much convinced myself that all our hopes were about to end with a nuke level catastrophe.

The broad shafts of one of the crystal towers, still glowing faintly blue, rushed past us as Erin slowed us to a stop and spun us back round. Slowly she began to raise *Ariel* until we had an uninterrupted view over the horizon towards Lucy, who was still hovering at ground zero over the shaft exit.

I realised that for all Mike's optimism that this was part of the grand plan, his jaw muscles were still cabling as the countdown reached the last few seconds. Witnessing that did absolutely nothing to help my own bleak internal narrative as to what was about to happen.

The counter raced to zero and a blinding pulse of light blazed from the shaft straight into Lucy. A few moments later a vibration rattled through *Ariel* as the light began to fade.

My hands gripped the arms of my flight seat hard as my nightmare scenario played out in front of us. 'Bloody hell, whatever it was has smashed into Lucy — that must have been a shock wave!'

But Erin was shaking her head, looking far too calm about what we'd just witnessed. 'Actually, I'm almost certain that was a sonic boom, probably caused by whatever just shot out of that shaft.'

Ruby was nodding. 'Definitely not a massive explosion, or we'd see some sort of fireball, or a mushroom cloud.'

'Yep, I agree,' Mike said, his face actually relaxing. 'My network of ground sensors are reading a huge spike across the entire radio spectrum from those monoliths. Each one of those things seems to be radiating out at least one gigawatt, which is basically the output of a typical power station.'

As my tension notched down a fraction from my emotional defcon one state, I returned my attention to the screen to see that the nearest crystal monolith tower was glowing even more strongly. Not only that, but the adjacent columns were lighting up like glow sticks at a rave.

Suddenly, a crack of thunder split the air outside our ship as a horizontal lightning bolt leapt straight out from the tower towards the glowing ball of light in the distance. And it wasn't alone. We could see ribbons of white hot plasma leaping out from the other towers, all lancing towards the same target.

'What the actual hell?' Ruby asked, staring at the pyrotechnic display blazing all around us.

'Hey, if that's not impressive enough for you guys, have you seen what's happening on the ground?' Erin asked.

We all looked at the bottom of the virtual cockpit to see large chunks of snow, earth and rock being scooped up by some invisible force and tumbling away through the air, drawn towards the light that had consumed Lucy. It was as though a vast, invisible fleet of diggers was beginning to surface mine the entire area to feed whatever had emerged from the shaft.

Before I could throw a question about what was bloody happening, a shudder passed through *Ariel* and she started to tip.

Erin grabbed the controls and stabilised us. 'We were just hit by major turbulence. It seems the wind speed outside just ramped up significantly from a gentle breeze to over four hundred miles per hour. The only reason that we're not more affected is because of *Ariel's* gravity bubble.'

'Commander, we have Niki on the line,' Ruby said.

'I'm not exactly surprised, put him through.'

Niki's voice came over the comm. 'What the hell is going on down there? I have a Pangolin in high orbit currently monitoring what's going on and from its vantage point it looks like a huge hurricane eye has just opened up over that shaft. I'm sending the feed through to you now so you can see it.'

At that exact moment, my Sky Wire warbled and I saw Steve's name on the display. This so wasn't the moment for a catch up chat with my old boss, so I ignored it.

'Putting the live feed from *Thor* up now,' Ruby said.

A satellite view of Antarctica appeared on the virtual cockpit with — exactly as Niki had said — a hurricane sitting in the middle of it. The remnants of the ash cloud that had spread out and smeared across the upper atmosphere were being slowly wound back in by the storm. But it was the blazing white point of light in the dead centre of the eye of the storm that caught my attention.

'Is that Lucy?' Erin asked.

'I'm zooming our optical camera array in so you can get a closer look,' Niki replied.

As a close-up appeared, the air caught in my throat. Over the pinprick of darkness that had to be the entrance to the shaft was what looked like a massive merged micro mind ship, surrounded by a glowing aura of light and a constellation of blue stars.

'Darn it, it looks like Lucy has been supersized to at least a hundred metres wide,' Erin said.

I peered harder at the orbiting points of light, as suspicion had already taken hold. 'Any chance you could clean up the image a bit more, Ruby?'

She nodded. 'I'll try running a sharpen filter through Delphi's systems and see if she can do anything with it.' She turned her attention to her screen and few taps later a much clearer image appeared. Now, not only could we see the lightning from the surrounding towers striking the glowing aura and making it pulse even brighter, but what had first looked like stars around the huge micro mind craft had now become individual tetrahedron crystals.

I stared at them. 'Are those individual micro minds, Mike?'

'I think so, suggesting Lucy has broken apart into her constituent AI parts,' he replied. 'But the big news is, that thing in the middle of them is what I'm pretty sure is an enormous quasicrystal.'

'Are you saying the Angelus hid a bloody giant crystal right in the core of our planet and it just rose up the shaft?' I asked.

'It certainly looks that way to me. If so, who knows how long that thing has been down there? Maybe the Angelus placed it there during an early part of the formation of our world?'

'What about all the material that is being mined out of the ground like a huge version of an open cast mine?' Erin asked.

'Ah, now that's where it gets interesting,' Mike said. 'You see, by definition a quasicrystal in theory can actually mould our reality into anything it wants it to be. You can almost think of it as advanced technical alchemy far beyond our current understanding of physics and even reality itself. But right now, based on what we're seeing happening down there, my guess would be that the quasicrystal is drawing all the material it needs to build whatever has been programmed into its matrix by its Angelus creators.'

'That Angelus super weapon that we've been hoping for?' Ruby asked.

'Now there's the billion-dollar question. But I'm afraid the only way we're going to find out the answer to that particular riddle is to wait and see,' Mike replied.

As the hours rolled past we'd watched the final wisps of the ash cloud being sucked into what Mike had started to refer to as some sort of Angelus production furnace. In fact, the air had cleared so much that we'd even risked taking *Ariel* closer in to one of the towers to take more sensor readings. Around the quasicrystal itself, the aura that initially surrounded it had expanded into a sort of glowing white fog that flowed up to the edges of the crystal towers, where it had stopped. Unfortunately, it also seemed impenetrable to our sensors, so for now we were unable to see what was happening within it, beyond the odd flash of light.

Meanwhile, in the distance the crystal towers had continued discharging plasma bursts into the fog towards the large quasicrystal.

'The sustained energy levels coming out of those monoliths is phenomenal, Lauren,' Mike said, gazing at the readouts on his screen. 'There is literally more than enough being generated by all these towers to power the US for a whole day.'

'So why does the quasicrystal need so much energy?' I asked.

'If I'm right and it *is* creating something using the crazy world of E8 physics, then I would guess that whatever it is building is something really huge.'

'I for one can't wait for the big reveal, especially if it's going to help us kick the Kimprak's asses,' Ruby said.

My Sky Wire warbled again and I saw Steve's name flash up on the screen. In all the excitement I'd completely forgotten his earlier call.

This time I pressed the *accept* button as I put the phone to my ear. 'Hey, it's good to hear from you,' I said.

'Oh thank god you've picked up at last, Lauren,' Steve said. 'I've been trying to get hold of you for ages.'

'Yes, sorry about that, a bit tied up with things here,' I said.

'I'm guessing that's a major understatement coming from you,' Steve replied.

I snorted. 'How did you guess? Anyway, I can tell that this isn't just a social call.'

'No, it really isn't – remember those near Earth asteroids, Pollux and Castor?'

'Yes, what about them?'

'They're not heading past Earth anymore. At the last moment, they made a course correction and are now hurtling straight *towards* our planet.'

I sat straight up in my seat. 'They did *what*? But asteroids don't suddenly change direction.' Now all eyes in the cockpit were locked onto me.

'Oh it gets scarier than that, Lauren. Because they are travelling at a tenth of the speed of light which means that they'll reach Earth in about eighty minutes. Governments all over the world have been alerted, but it's too late to organise a mass evacuation. The impact point is especially hard to predict as the asteroids keep changing direction — right now we have no way of knowing where they're going to hit. Of course, the leaders of our world are probably already heading for their bunkers, and the rest of the population be damned. Obviously it's too short a timeframe for any of the space agencies to come up with any credible plan to stop this. So I was wondering if a certain group of people with incredible technology at their disposal can do something about it?'

'You want us to intercept Pollux and Castor?' I asked.

'You're the only credible defence that I can think of,' Steve said.

I traded a look with the others, who were already nodding. 'Okay, leave it with us and we'll see what we can do.'

'Thank you and the very best of luck for all our sakes.'

'And to you too, Steve, I'll be touch.' I ended the call.

Mike scraped his hand back through his hair. 'So, two aster-oids have just behaved like spacecraft and are now hurtling straight towards our planet. You do know what that sounds like? Especially as the timing is so close to us having just released the Angelus quasicrystal from the core of our planet.'

'Yes, it sounds an awful lot like it might be something to do with the Kimprak,' I said.

'That's exactly what I was thinking too,' Ruby said. 'Some sort of small advanced force that arrived here first to check out any defences we might have. It makes a lot of sense from a tactical perspective.'

A sense of dread was building inside me as I nodded. 'It really does. And even if there is another explanation, we need to send out a force to intercept them. Even if they are just giant rocks they'll do a huge amount of damage if we let them crash into our planet. How long would it take ships from Eden to reach them?'

'Eighty minutes, which isn't exactly a lot of time to intercept them,' Ruby said.

'Hang on, a squadron departed Eden for a supply run out to Psyche 16 earlier today,' Erin said. 'They might be able to reach them in time.'

'Contact them and ask them to intercept if they are in range. Also, let Troy know what's happening — there might be more of those scout ships out there.'

'Okay, I'm on it,' she replied. 'Hang on, we have a message incoming from Niki marked urgent.'

'Put him through,' I replied.

The comm crackled into life. 'Lauren, we've just had reports from some of the X-craft patrolling the sea around Antarctica of multiple weapon contacts for at least a hundred cruise missiles. Analysis of their trajectories looks like they are targeting the crystal towers surrounding the Shackleton site.'

'Damn, those Overseer ground troops must have radioed back what they discovered,' Ruby said.

'But where did the cruise missiles come from? They don't just appear from nowhere. And they've got a relatively limited range,' I replied.

'From what we can tell they appear to have been launched by at least thirty subs around the Antarctica coastline,' Ruby said.

After all the raw emotion of the last few hours and the constantly worry about Jack, Jodie and Lucy, I now felt strangely calm. This sort of warfare was exactly what I'd been training for.

'Ruby, open a channel to the entire fleet, please.'

She nodded and a moment later my comm light blinked green. She gave me a thumbs up.

I took a centering breath before beginning. 'This is Lauren Stelleck. What we now know to be another Angelus megastructure is about to come under direct attack by Overseer forces. Prepare to engage all enemy contacts and protect the Angelus structure at all costs. Nothing must be allowed to get through. Good luck to us all.' I ended the transmission and shook my head. 'Bloody hell, this day just goes from bad to worse.'

'Then let's go and kick some serious Overseer butt. I'm reading multiple contacts heading in, Commander,' Ruby said.

I nodded. 'Delphi, initiate Battle Command centre.'

'Initiating Battle Command centre,' she replied.

The virtual cockpit was transformed as the left and right tactical display options appeared.

A dome of green triangles for our X-craft was centred over the Angelus megastructure and further out, a swarm of red triangles for the cruise missiles was travelling in over the ocean towards it.

'Get us back to our fleet and fast, Erin.'

She nodded and the world blurred around us as we raced towards the shoreline at maximum speed.

CHAPTER TWENTY-FOUR

THE BATTLE COMMAND system was already making a huge difference to my understanding of what was happening out there. The left hand 3D tactical map showed red triangles for each of the missiles filling the horizon and that alone would have been enough to overwhelm my mind. But with computerised ease, Delphi had begun identifying the incoming missiles. She'd already tagged them as a mixture of at least a hundred and twenty ACM and JASSM cruise missiles heading towards the megastructure.

Erin dived *Ariel* towards the surface so that we were skimming over it barely ten metres up, our gravity field throwing up a vortex of snow in our wake. We caught up with the rear wing of our fleet as they sped over the coastline and powered towards the approaching wave of missiles.

On the tactical display the red boxes started to turn to diamonds among the frontline of the cruise missiles.

Ruby cracked her knuckles and then her neck, which always freaked me out. 'The fleet has locks on at least thirty of those cruise missiles and they are waiting on your orders, Commander,' she said.

I looked across at the panel to see a single option — *Alpha* — was currently displayed for engaging all targets.

'Delphi, initiate *Alpha* command,' I said.

'Initiating *Alpha* command,' she replied.

Ruby pulled the trigger on her targeting joystick. 'Our AIM missiles away!'

A shudder passed through the craft as the missiles inheriting the incredible inertia that *Ariel* was already travelling at leapt forward, trailing vapour and speeding towards the lock boxes in the distance. The act was multiplied by a hundred ships in front of us as their AIM trails filled the skies and they streaked towards the cruise missiles.

At the same moment, distant screams of hypervelocity rounds filled the cockpit as our fleet's heavier Pangolin X104s also opened up with hypersonic railgun rounds.

Within moments, our weapons fire had vanished into the distance on the central visual display of the outside world, but on the Battle Command tactical map I watched the blinking green dots of our weapons speed out to meet the swarm of cruise missiles head on.

With bursts of fire and light flashes visible on the horizon, dozens of the cruise missiles started to wink out of existence on the 3D map.

Ruby scanned her instruments. 'That's at least thirty cruise missiles shot down, guys.'

Mike dipped his chin towards her. 'Nice shooting.'

She shrugged. 'We still have a long way to go yet.'

Ariel shuddered again as our AIM missiles joined the second wave already racing out towards the fast approaching contacts. A minute later we'd taken out at least half the remaining missiles and only thirty-five remained. Erin began to back off the throttle as the distance indicators raced down to less than three klicks.

'Spooling up miniguns,' Ruby said.

With a drum beat of large calibre rounds being fired, tracer rounds leapt forward from *Ariel* through the growing night, out over the waves towards the last remaining missiles as the rest of our fleet did the same. Ruby took out at least one before I caught a brief glimpse of another streaking past us.

'Not so fast!' Erin said.

With a deft twitch of the controls, she reversed *Ariel's* direction, the hard pull of gravity briefly pushing me forward in my seat, before we shot back the way we'd just come. This extreme manoeuvre would have killed us all outright in a conventional craft, but thankfully our REV drive's gravity bubble shielded us from the worst of it.

As we stabilised, the flight deck gyros whined and spun round to match the new flight orientation, and the staccato beat of the miniguns was already echoing through the cockpit as Ruby opened fire again.

My attention was split between the central video feed and the 3D tactical map that was really helping me to understand the bigger picture of what was going on.

Around us, the rest of the fleet were pulling similar manoeuvres to the one that we had just done. One by one we took out the remaining cruise missiles until *Thor*, who was now flying alongside us, took out the final missile with its four miniguns.

Mike whooped. 'Like shooting fish in a bloody barrel.'

But Ruby was shaking her head, pointing towards the tactical map. 'You spoke too soon, mate.'

Erin was already spinning us back round as red boxes seemed to appear all over the horizon at once.

'Crap, I'm seeing a second wave of cruise missiles from those damned subs,' Ruby said. 'Similar numbers to the first wave. We're going to need to take out those subs, Commander, otherwise the missiles will just keep on coming.'

Immediately my mind was back on the seas of Cuba, when we'd been forced to take out a Yasen-class Russian hunter killer submarine. It was on my command that all the souls onboard it had been wiped out, a decision that still haunted me. I avoided Ruby's gaze as my mind raced.

'Commander, you need to make a call and fast,' Ruby said, as another fresh round of our fleet's AIM missiles and hypersonic rounds began to pick off the cruise missiles.

As much as I hated this, I knew I didn't have any choice.

I finally met her gaze. 'Order a detachment of underwater-adapted X103s to hunt those damned subs down. Tell the flight crews to do whatever is necessary to stop them firing, which most importantly includes not to use lethal force if possible, but enough to put them out of this fight.'

She gave me a sharp nod and started pressing icons on her display whilst talking into her headset.

A few moments later at least twenty of X103s plunged straight down into the sea like diving birds, their gravity shields displacing the water around them with frothing plumes.

Once again the Battle Command system proved its worth as I was able to watch them speeding away on the tactical map towards our hidden enemy, as the fleet began to take out the second wave.

Mike rubbed his chin. 'Okay, there is something I don't get, Lauren. If this is an all-out attack by the Overseers, aren't they making it a bit easy for us?'

I flapped my hand towards the missiles streaking towards us. 'You think that this is *easy*?'

'I don't mean they're not dangerous, I mean that tactically it's relatively easy for us to defend against those missiles. Look, the Overseers know we have highly capable ships, so why try to use conventional weapons, which they know we'll be more than able to deal with?'

Ruby was slowly nodding. 'Mike's right — it's not like Alvarez to underestimate us in a firefight.'

'But why would they throw missiles away like this?' Erin said, spinning us round for another high speed strafing run on a missile that we were locked onto.

Then my blood iced as the truth hit me. 'Shit! Get us back to the Shackleton site as fast as possible. This is all a decoy to draw our attention away — this isn't the main attack at all!'

Ruby's eyes widened as she stared at her screen. 'Oh fucking hell, you're right. That Pangolin in high orbit has just reported two hundred new contacts heading straight down towards the Shackleton site. Confirmed sensor readings — they are all TR-3B craft.'

'Get us the hell back to there, Erin,' I said.

'Pedal to the metal right now,' she replied.

The world blurred as we sped away from the remaining missiles, quickly outpacing them. I could see a rainstorm of red boxes on the tactical display, heading down from the sky straight towards the site.

I thumped the comm button. 'Niki, Alvarez has played us. A large TR-3B attack force is heading straight from orbit towards Lucy and the quasicrystal.'

'Yes, already reading them on our sensors. Suggest we leave a handful of ships here to mop up these cruise missiles and the subs, and send the rest of the fleet to engage.'

'I absolutely agree,' I said, scanning down the tactical options that had changed from a few to at least a dozen, which include an *Echo* option for splitting our forces as I'd just discussed with

Niki. It seemed our ship's AI was already processing the battle and coming up with the same options.

'Delphi, initiate *Echo* command,' I said.

'Initiating *Echo* command,' she repeated.

Within moments at least twenty X103s were flying in formation behind us, followed by the slightly slower Pangolins.

'I don't care what you have to do to the REV drive — redline it all the way and get us between the TR-3Bs and Lucy and that quasicrystal, Erin,' I said.

'Maxing out engines now, but this is going to really overload our gravity shielding, so everyone get ready to pull some serious G,' Erin warned.

She pushed the throttle wide open and immediately lights started blinking on her console.

It felt like a wall of gravity slammed into my body as I saw our air speed spin up past Mach 10 all the way up to Mach 12. The cockpit vibrated, rattling us all hard as we hurtled upwards, pulling away from the rest of the fleet. My vision started to dim as my brain became starved of oxygen and I began to slip towards blacking out.

'If Lucy...could see...us now,' Mike ground out through his gritted teeth.

'As fast...as her,' I managed to reply.

Then just as the world threatened to go dark on me, Erin eased off of the REV drive.

That moment strongly reminded me of the ships in *Star Wars* dropping out of lightspeed, because as the G-forces let go of my pummelled body, the Mach 8 we were now travelling at almost felt like a crawl by comparison.

As I gulped in a lungful of air, I could see our tactical display was erupting with multiple fresh contacts for more TR-3Bs, which had grown to at least three hundred in number, nearly three times the size of our own fleet. Those three to one odds were also uncomfortably reminiscent of the battle sim that I'd done so badly in. I glanced down at the micro minds and the quasicrystal. So much depended on what happened in the next few minutes, including the lives of Jack, Jodie and Lucy.

'Commander, without pointing out the obvious, we're a sitting duck whilst the rest of the fleet plays catch up,' Ruby said.

'All part of the plan,' I replied. 'I'm going to try and stop this before we slide into an all- out pitch battle.' I glanced across at her. 'I want you to open a channel to the enemy fleet to see if we can talk them down off the ledge.'

She nodded. 'Worth a go I guess, but I doubt they'll listen.'

'Hopefully, someone up there will have some common sense, even if it is Colonel Alvarez,' Mike said.

'Let's keep everything crossed that they do,' I said, as my comm light blinked green.

After the physical breath of a moment ago, I took a mental one as I pressed the button. 'This is Commander Lauren Stelleck of the forces defending the Angelus megastructure that you're attempting to attack. Look, I'm doing the equivalent of waving a white flag here, so can someone please talk to me before this all gets out of hand? We should be working together to defend Earth, not bloody fighting each other.'

There was no response as a sequence of warbling alarms sounded.

'Enemy fleet has weapons lock on us,' Ruby said. 'Shall I return the favour, Commander?'

'Not yet, but make sure our gravity shielding is running at max just in case. Okay, let's try this again...'

'Alvarez, if you are up there, will you bloody listen to me? We have two asteroids hurtling towards Earth and I wouldn't be surprised if they are targeting the location below us. We believe that they may actually be Kimprak scout forces — some of our ships are doing their best to intercept them. But if they don't, the asteroids will cause a cataclysmic event that will almost certainly create a global nuclear winter severe enough to do most of the Kimprak's job for them. Both of our forces should be getting ready to intercept them, especially if they get past the squadron that we've already sent to engage them, out beyond the orbit of our moon.'

Pinpricks of black triangles appeared directly overhead as the TR-3Bs came into visual range just as our own fleet began to arrive around us, immediately taking up formation positions as dictated by the Battle Command system. A bead of sweat trickled down the back of my neck as I pressed our fleet comm button.

'No one is to engage unless you are ordered to do so by me,' I said.

'Talk about balls of steel,' Ruby said, shaking her head at me as she lightly gripped the weapons joystick for the targeting system.

'Or just utterly stupid and we're about to find out one way or another,' I replied.

'Well the good news is that they haven't opened fire on us,' Mike said.

'Yet,' Ruby replied with a scowl.

The black dots resolved themselves into black triangular craft as they plummeted towards us, then suddenly came to a dead stop.

A man's voice came over the comm. 'This is Commander Beltran of the USS Space First Flight Wing. You are to stand down and step aside or suffer the consequences for your alliance with the alien entities.'

'If you mean the Angelus AIs that are our best hope of defending this world, you can think again,' I replied. 'We will defend them to our last ship. Whether you realise it or not, yes they are our allies but they are also yours.'

'And are these the same allies who just unleashed a large volcanic eruption? The same allies who also created an ash cloud that threatened our world with a cataclysmic environmental change?'

'Which, if you haven't noticed, they are already in the middle of clearing up. Anyway, that eruption will be nothing compared to the devastation that the Kimprak asteroids will do if they strike our world,' I said calmly.

'I'm not about to get into a debate with you,' Beltran replied.

'Then put Colonel Alvarez on the line because even he will listen to sense when I explain it to him.'

'If you mean the military advisor who has been briefing us about your terrorist operations, he is not here. But unfortunately for you, he did fully brief me on the level of deception that you're capable of, Commander Stelleck.'

'So he told you all about me, did he?' I replied, rolling my eyes at the others. I knew *exactly* what that meant.

'Oh indeed he did. Not only did you steal one of his ships from a highly classified location, but you also then ambushed a further two that had been sent to intercept you. So forgive me, Commander Stelleck, because I'm far from convinced by anything you have said so far. Right now, based on evidence that I'm witnessing with my own two eyes, all I know is that some sort of major alien device appears to be being constructed on the surface of our planet. And unless you can prove to me otherwise, I have no reason to assume that it isn't a weapon that could be an even bigger threat to our world than the Kimprak.'

The others in the cockpit looked at me as I gathered my thoughts, trying to think of a line of reasoning that would make sense to the guy.

'Well, what's your explanation?' Commander Beltran asked, filling in my pause.

The only option I had was to give him the truth — I knew he would see through anything else straight away.

I sighed. 'We don't know for sure, Commander. But you, like me, have the lives of all those under your command to think of. Why endanger any of our people in a totally unnecessary fight when we should be sitting down and analysing what this is all about together?'

I heard the commander echoing my sigh at the other end of the line. 'So you're suggesting a truce whilst we thrash this through?'

'That makes so much more sense to me than lobbing missiles and hypersonic rounds at each other. So what do you say and like the old song says, give peace a chance?'

I already had a sense that whoever this guy was, he was nothing like the hothead Alvarez and maybe we could really do business with him. But this time, it was our turn to wait for his response as he obviously conferred with others on his ship.

The seconds stretched on and then at last Beltran spoke again.

'Okay, let's land and meet face to face, Commander Stelleck and—'

Beltran's words trailed away then stopped dead and for a moment, I thought we'd lost the comm link. But then Ruby was making a slicing motion across her throat as she pressed a button. 'Sorry, I had to kill the comm channel for a moment because we just had a report from one of our X103s that was trying to neutralise one of the US subs. A Spearfish missile was detonated too close to it and there was hull breach. All crew onboard are believed dead.'

I slammed my hand down onto my armrest. 'Shit! Shooting a

missile out of the air is one thing, but taking out a US sub is completely another.'

'This Commander Beltran may not know that yet?' Mike said. 'Maybe get an explanation in first before he finds out.'

I thought of just how furious I'd be if our positions were reversed. Would I listen to me after he learned that we'd just sunk one of their subs?'

'Okay, restore the comm channel, Ruby.' She nodded and the green LED blinked on the comm panel. 'Commander Beltran, I—'

'You damned bitch, you just sunk one of the navy's subs. Just like Alvarez warned me, you say one thing to my face whilst stabbing my back. We're done talking, Stelleck.'

The LED blinked off.

'Multiple launches detected from the TR-3B fleet,' Ruby said as the tactical map lit up with multiple fast moving contacts. Dozens of tactical options started to erupt down the right hand panel.

Erin hadn't waited for my order and was already reacting. *Ariel* zipped sideways as three railgun rounds roared past where we'd been a moment ago. At the same moment, dozens of lasers blazed down from the dozens of TR-3Bs that I could now see were the modified models with turrets at the bottom.

Even as my mind raced, I knew there was one option that still made sense despite this descent into madness.

'Delphi, initiate *Foxtrot* option.'

'Initiating Foxtrot command,' she replied.

Ruby gawped at me. 'The melee option? But you know how that ended up last time in the battle sim, right?'

'I do, but large scale tactics are off the table for the time being and this will be down to the individual skills of our crews until we have a chance to regroup.'

Ruby shook her head and bit back the obvious torrent she'd been about to unleash on me.

As our fleet responded to the Battle Command order, the skies erupted with weapons fire.

I might have initiated the order, but deep down I was wondering what the hell I had just done?

But as the world became a blur of ship to ship combat, Erin and Ruby proved themselves to be a formidable team in dog fighting. We ducked and weaved through the shafts of incoming railgun darts and missiles, our pilot doing her best to make sure no one got past us towards the Angelus megastructure as she spun *Ariel* through the sky, seemingly on every axis. I was certainly grateful for the stabilised deck that stopped me becoming totally disorientated, despite the extreme manoeuvres that Erin was putting our ship through.

And then, as I knew they would, the casualties reported by the Battle Command computer started to mount up on each side.

Then too late, I spotted that three TR-3Bs had aligned themselves for a simultaneous railgun shot directly down through our ranks, straight towards the glowing spec of the quasicrystal far below us that was Lucy and the other micro mind. They more than stood out as a target, as lightning was still pouring into it from the surrounding oval of crystal towers.

Jack! I found myself inwardly screaming.

But no tactical options presented themselves to prevent the disaster that was about to happen. Sheer panic rose through me as the hypersonic rounds sped straight towards the sitting duck of a target. The entire battle pivoted on the action of a single crew as they threw their X103 into the projectiles' path. Its gravity shield could easily have coped with one round, but unlike the more heavily armoured Pangolins, there was no way it could deflect three.

The hypersonic rounds ripped through the X103's hull, the

speed of the impact so great that the ship vapourised instantly, throwing burning debris out from the brutal explosion as the remains of the craft tumbled away, trailing smoke.

In a dreadful, ice-chilling heartbeat I absolutely knew there had been no time for the crew to safely eject. But I also knew that their incredible act of bravery had saved the quasicrystal.

The Battle Command system monitored every single ship in the aerial dance of death far faster than I could have kept up with it, keeping me informed that the fatalities weren't limited to our side. I spotted it for myself as two of our X103s opened the guts of one of the TR-3Bs. But at least on that occasion, I spotted the crew ejection spheres bursting from the craft as it careened down towards the ground, and I actually felt a sense of relief. But another TR-3B wasn't so lucky when it was sliced in half by a Pangolin railgun round. Yes, they might be the enemy, but for me it didn't really matter whose side the ships were on — I felt the loss of every single soul in this needless battle.

'This is absolute madness,' Mike said, shaking his head and echoing my thoughts precisely. 'We should be fighting on the same side. If only that sub hadn't been bloody sunk by one of ours.'

'Wars have been started over far less,' Ruby replied.

An immediate wave of guilt crashed over me, as that had been down to another of my orders.

But then Mike looked at me and shook his head as though he was reading my mind. Even though he hadn't said anything, I could tell that he knew that I would be feeling the responsibility for all of this, even if it wasn't technically my fault. At least, that's what my head kept telling me. My heart, however, was beating me up for engaging the subs in the first place. When exactly had I become so trigger happy?

'Oh fuck, now they are targeting the towers,' Ruby said.

Despite how dire the situation was becoming, I was starting

to feel a begrudging respect for my opposite number. Commander Beltran seemed to have far more of a battle plan that I had, which was little more than a reactive one so far.

Railgun rounds were already streaking from them and racing towards the nearest towers. My heart rose into my mouth as I waited for them to explode into a million pieces of crystals. But then suddenly, a glimmer in the air briefly revealed a gigantic transparent dome over the entire sixty-kilometre-wide site. The hypersonic rounds smashed into it and veered away, crashing into the surrounding plateau with explosions of rock and snow.

'Oh you little beauties,' Mike said, staring at his screen. 'The Angelus have some sort of massive gravity shield system to protect the megastructure from attack. And looking at where it appeared, I suspect that those crystal towers are helping to generate it.'

I felt part of me relax — Lucy, and whatever she was helping the quasicrystal to build, would be safe. And just as importantly, Jack and Jodie, too. I fought down the tears of relief I was so desperate to cry, because that so wasn't the right moment.

But then on the 3D tactical map, I spotted at least half of the ships coming in to land about a klick out from the edge of the shield. Before I could ask what they were up to, Ruby had already pulled up a zoomed-in window of one craft taking off into the air, leaving a shipping container behind. The next moment the doors flew open and six snowmobiles ridden by soldiers in white combat uniforms burst from them, followed by more soldiers on foot.

'Crap, more ground assault squads — you can bet they'll be bringing a shitload of C4 with them to try and take out those towers,' Ruby said.

'But they won't be able to get through the gravity shield, will they?' I asked.

'Don't be so sure about that,' Mike replied. 'Apart from

anything, we must have flown through it when the towers first powered up, and we didn't get squished like a bug on a windshield. My guess is that the automated defence systems that are clearly running the show, are stopping any ships on an obvious attack run, the rest they let through. But as to how it deals with people on the ground, your guess is as good as mine.'

'Do you want me to order part of the fleet to disengage from air combat and take them out?' Ruby asked, as that exact thing appeared on the tactical options list.

At last my spin of thoughts started to slow, as I began to see a pattern in our opponent's move. 'No, we'll be spreading ourselves too thin, something that Beltran is probably banking on.' I toggled the comm channel, selecting ship to ship with *Thor*. 'Niki, we've got a situation rapidly developing on the ground and we need to take action to stop them. Just tell me how many Tin Heads are in the holds of the Pangolins caught up in this fight?'

'About a hundred, give or take, plus a couple still in our own hold.'

'Then it's time to deploy them. You probably also spotted the gravity shield dome over the whole megastructure, like we just did. It's best to have the Pangolins drop them as near as they can get to the perimeter, so they can defend the towers. They may be our only chance of coming out on top of this fight.'

'Roger that, but we could do with an escort. These bloody TR-3Bs are like particularly annoying mosquitoes that have tasted blood.'

'Then we'll escort you in,' I replied, watching the video feed showing the first batch of snowmobiles racing towards the edge of the gravity shield. I knew in that moment that how the next few minutes played out would almost certainly dictate the outcome of the whole battle. Get this wrong and any real hope for our planet would be snuffed out in an instant.

On the virtual cockpit view, *Thor* — identified with a metadata label on the main screen — started to drop away from the rest of the fleet with another nine Pangolins close behind him. Erin moved us into formation in their slipstream as they sped towards the crystal tower that the enemy troops were heading straight towards. If this went the way I suspected it would, our Tin Heads would almost certainly be the only thing standing between the destruction of the quasicrystal and Lucy and the other micro minds right along with it, not to mention people who meant everything to me.

CHAPTER TWENTY-FIVE

THE ENEMY SNOWMOBILES were closing far too fast on the perimeter of the shield beyond the crystal tower for my liking but worse still, it was obvious that someone above us had spotted the breakaway move by a number of our ships to deal with the ground forces. Instinct told me that it was probably my opposite number, Commander Beltran, based on the astuteness he'd already shown in this battle, and he was taking steps to protect his forces. It was probably also him that was responsible for ordering a couple of TR-3Bs on a near kamikaze run through the ranks of the air battle to chase after us.

A green laser beam lanced past us and struck *Thor,* making the ship's ablative armour shielding glow as it started to heat up with the sustained blast. The gravity shield might be able to deflect conventional weapons, but an energy weapon it couldn't.

Ruby already had it covered, spinning up our minigun's targeting reticle towards the craft that had just opened fire. Twin streams of tracer rounds raced out from *Ariel,* peppering one of the glowing engine ports of the TR-3B, which erupted with a shower of sparks before bursting into a flames. A moment later the craft was corkscrewing away, smoke trailing behind it.

The air shockwave erupted around the second TR-3B as it fired and a moment later, railgun rounds ricocheted off one of our Pangolins to the right of our squad. As Ruby attempted to return fire it swooped, spun and dived through the sky like a whirling dervish.

'Damn it, that pilot is way too good, Ruby said as she fought to lock on with one of our AIM missiles.

I glanced down to see that *Thor* and the rest of the Pangolins were slowing, ready to deposit their precious loads of Tin Heads onto the surface.

'Erin, do whatever you can to keep us between that TR-3B and the Pangolins as they unload. We can use our gravity shielding to absorb a number of shots if we need to.'

'On it, Lauren,' Erin replied.

She jinked us sideways, straight into the path of a railgun round. A violent shudder went through us as the incoming round glanced off the gravity bubble enveloping the ship and tumbled away.

But even as the vibration faded away in the cockpit, I was already feeling a wave of relief as the Pangolins dropped the Tin Heads from a twenty-metre height straight down onto the surface with explosions of settled ash and snow, the next moment they were rushing off on their caterpillar drive systems, Barrett M82s clasped in their clawed hands. They headed out, forming a battle line to face the oncoming snowmobiles head-on, firing their weapons as they raced forward. The closing force immediately slowed to a stop as their riders were forced to take up defensive positions, using their snowmobiles as cover to return fire.

I had to grit my teeth as Erin briefly maxed out our REV drive to intercept another railgun round intended for one of the final Pangolins dropping towards the surface.

'Will you please do something about that frigging enemy craft, Ruby?' Erin said.

'Doing my best here, but that pilot is flying that thing like greased lightning,' she replied. The target lock button that had briefly flashed into a diamond reverted back to a square as the other pilot danced away from it with a swooping dive.

I pressed the ship to chip channel. 'Niki, we need to deal with a persistent enemy pilot. Are you okay to help deal with the ground assault with the other Pangolins?'

'No problem, leave it to me. Good luck,' Niki replied.

'You too.' I killed the channel. 'Okay, Erin, you are free to engage that bloody TR-3B in whatever way, shape or form you need to.'

'Yeah, time to show them who's the boss, lady,' Ruby said.

With a grin, Erin swooped *Ariel* round until we were heading straight towards the other craft. 'Okay, I'll go for a close fly by, then you shoot the rivets off that thing as we pass it, Ruby,' she said.

'Oh I'm all over this,' Ruby replied, stretching her fingers and then gripping her joystick.

We raced towards the other ship, Erin having rotated *Ariel* on her axis to avoid an incoming hypersonic round fired by the other craft, making the deck's gyros whine with effort as they fought to keep the flight deck level as our ship spun around us.

But the other pilot was also reading our every move and somehow managing to keep jumping out of position for Ruby to get a clear shot, almost like they were telepathic.

'Will you stay still already and allow yourselves to get damned well shot!' Ruby said through clenched teeth.

I had already started to work out just how good Erin was, but her next move was beyond anything I could have imagined.

She swooped down hard, overwhelming *Ariel's* gravity bubble and crushing us against our harnesses as we all experienced negative Gs. Then she flicked us sideways and straight back up in a box shape with a manoeuvre that I suddenly realised was her square dancing one from the battle sim. It seemed like the other pilot had never seen anything like it either because the next moment, Ruby had a clear shot at the TR-3B's belly. Our weapons officer was swinging the minigun's reticle to lock on for a strafing run to split open the enemy's hull, when I spotted a discoloured panel in its belly not quite matching the matt black of the rest of the ship.

Instantly a memory surged from the back of my mind. 'Hold fire!' I screamed.

Ruby shot me a startled look. 'You're joking, right?'

'No, I'm bloody not. Delphi, can you initiate ship to ship comms with the TR-3B in close proximity?'

'Yes, I can transmit a multi-frequency, unencrypted, low-powered radio transmission that only it will be able to hear,' our AI replied.

'Then do it!' I said as we skimmed past the other craft.

'Channel is now open,' Delphi replied.

A warbling alarm came from Ruby's console. 'Fuck, they've locked onto us now!'

'Let me handle this,' I said.

Erin had started to throw *Ariel* round the sky at ever crazier angles, to the point that Mike was groaning and looking decidedly green.

I activated my comm. 'Don, is that you and Zack on that other TR-3B that we're currently dog fighting with?'

'Yes, but how the heck do you know our names?'

'Because I'm Lauren Stelleck, the woman you ran into when we stole one of your TR-3Bs back at Area 51.'

'Lauren, seriously, is that really you?' Don's voice replied.

'Yes and someone on our two sides needs to start talking and stop this madness before we all wipe each other out. Unfortunately, I seemed to have well and truly pissed off your Commander Beltran.'

'Sinking a US subs tends to have that effect on him,' a voice I recognised as Zack, the navigator, said.

'Yes and if I were in his place I'd be feeling the same, but that was an accident, guys. The torpedo was only meant to flush the sub to the surface, but it detonated too close to it. And now because of that mistake our two forces are in a pitch battle against each other when we should both be defending the Angelus megastructure on the surface. The Kimprak are the real threat here and the Angelus are our allies, but no one seems capable of comprehending that fact on your side of this battle.'

'Even if that's true, there is a chain of command here, Lauren, so what exactly do you expect me to do about it? I'm only a captain,' Don said.

Ruby gestured towards me as both our craft pulled into level flight and then slowed to a hover. 'As ex-military, let me talk to them.'

I nodded. 'Go ahead.'

Ruby's nostrils flared. 'Hi mates, this is Ruby Jones here, former special forces sniper. Look, you don't know me and I don't know you, but I do know the situation that you're in. It wouldn't be the first time in military history that a hot head in the senior chain of command made a bad call that ended up with a lot of unnecessary deaths.'

There was a sigh at the other end. 'We hear you, Ruby,' Don said. 'But once again, we're one flight crew, so what can we do?'

'Talk some sense into your Commander,' I said. 'Get him to see that he's got this back to front. And then get him to question where the order to make this attack came from. Because I can tell you this for free — there are people in the shadows manipulating governments and their military around the world to their own ends. Your squadron is a pawn in this, even if your commander doesn't realise it yet.'

'Yeah, someone needs to blow the whistle on this, mate, even a grunt like you,' Ruby added.

Even as the battle raged on above and below us, Don and Zack laughed over the comm.

'We hear you, but here's the thing,' Don replied. 'Even if we manage to get through to Beltran and he listens to us long enough to hear us out, how the hell is he going to take us seriously?'

'You need to convince Beltran and maybe this will help make him believe that it's a serious offer, because so much rests on it.' I glanced at my watch. 'Look, at 8pm I will broadcast a message on an open channel for our forces to get ready to stand down, if Beltran does the same. But also warn him that if one of our ships is fired on in that period I will then be ordering them to do whatever they have to do to defend themselves and the megastructure. So let's do what we can to open a window of opportunity here and stop all this totally unnecessary bloodshed.'

'Then leave it with us, Lauren, let's see what we can do to make that a reality,' Don replied. 'We'll be in touch and good luck to us all. Over and out for now.'

'Amen to that sentiment,' Erin said as my comm light blinked off. 'So what are your orders in the meantime, Lauren?'

'We defend the hell out of the megastructure. Talking of which, can we take a quick fly over to see what's happening with Lucy and that quasicrystal? The sooner she wraps this up, the better for all our sakes.'

'Okay, setting course now,' Erin said.

As we peeled away from Don and Zack's craft, which was already accelerating back up into the sky, I was far too aware of how much was riding on the shoulders of a flight crew that I barely even knew. But the one thing I prided myself on was being a good judge of character; I just hoped that both of them were exactly the sort of men that I thought they were.

We sped away over the gravity dome, which glimmered with blue energy as an incoming railgun round skipped off its shield.

'Hey, will you look at those laser bursts when they hit the gravity dome shield?' Mike said.

I glanced down to see three pulses that — even though they were penetrating through the shield — were being deflected off at angles to strike the ground wide of their targets.

For a moment I didn't understand what I was seeing, but then it came to me. 'Of course, this is like the sort of gravity lensing effect that astronomers see around distant galaxies. The gravity field generated by them is actually powerful enough to bend light to the point we can actually see what's behind them.'

'I think that's exactly it, Lauren, and the same thing is happening here to bend the laser fire away,' Mike replied. 'But to able to do that the gravity field being generated within that dome must be immense.'

'I'd love to know what's powering all of this,' I replied.

'Knowing the Angelus, it will be something a lot more esoteric that a massive fusion reactor,' Mike replied.

I nodded as we sped towards the centre of the lightning storm, the constant flashes illuminating the landscape beneath us.

'ETA, thirty seconds,' Erin called out.

On the virtual cockpit the aura of light around the quasicrystal had come into view again and within it the glimmering points of blue light from micro minds hung like a constellation of geo-stationary satellites. I saw a stream of fine black dots being drawn into the shimmering aura from the surrounding landscape.

'Zooming in before you ask me to,' Ruby said, correctly heading off my next request.

A close-up appeared in a window on the virtual cockpit.

Now it was possible to make out that the dots were actually the individual boulders that we'd seen being sucked up into the white aura, atomising to nothing as they passed through the boundary. Not only that, streams of ash were being hoovered up by it too, everything moving into it in a slow dance of destruction.

'If that thing wasn't white, I'd say it was a black hole,' Erin said.

'Nothing like,' Mike replied. 'If it was a singularity, everything and I mean everything, would be sucked into it and at high speed. No, this is something else.'

'An E8 flavour of something else?' I asked.

'We certainly could be looking at some sort of very advanced form of physics in action,' Mike replied.

'So above your pay grade in other words?' Ruby said.

'I hate to admit it, but pretty much yes. So the summary is that I don't know what the hell is going on down there.'

'Whatever it is, it's getting bigger,' Erin said. 'Since we first arrived, it has expanded by at least a hundred metres and it's still covered by that white fog stuff. Right now, it's a couple of klicks wide and growing fast. But if you look hard you can see it's not actually a sphere, but more of an oval shape.'

I nodded. 'In other words the same shape as the arrangement of the crystal towers around it and I doubt that's a coincidence—'

The rest of my sentence was drowned out by our radio bursting into life. 'This is Troy Armstrong. Are you reading me, Lauren? Over.'

I punched the comm button. 'Yes, loud and clear. What's the problem?'

'We just received a message from the Peregrine squadron that you sent to intercept those asteroids and it's bad, very bad. When they first approached Pollux and Castor it all looked straightforward, just two large lumps of space rock about a few hundred metres wide. But as they closed on them, their sensors picked up micro detonations beneath the surface. The next thing they knew, things that resembled ball bearings about the size of a hand, erupted from both asteroids and rushed towards the three ships.'

An icy feeling trickled through my blood. 'You're telling me they are definitely not just asteroids?'

'Correct, especially given what happened next. Those ball bearing bastards latched onto all three of that squadron's hulls. One of the crews managed to send a last video through before we lost contact with them and I honestly don't have the words, so you'd better just see for yourselves.'

'Incoming video,' Ruby said.

A moment later we had Troy's footage playing on the screen.

Two X104s were tracking alongside the one filming the video as ball bearing objects slammed into all of them. But far from ripping through the hull like large calibre rounds, instead the chrome balls seemed to change shape, unfurling like woodlice into some sort of armoured insects that immediately began to consume the metalwork. And as they did so, the metallic creatures began to swell and then lay more of the chrome balls from the end of their abdomens, which then immediately unfurled into more of the creatures.

The pilots of the craft were desperately trying to shake the things off as large sections of the hull began to be eaten away by the robotic Kimprak creatures, whose numbers were quickly multiplying as they bored through the outer hull, exposing the inner cockpit shell. Then all the craft began corkscrewing away from each other and a moment later, two of the ships lit up with bright pulses of light as they detonated. Then the screen went black.

No one said a word as we exchanged shocked looks.

'I'm going to spare you the radio feeds from both craft, as the crew who'd donned their spacesuits as the hull started to breach were literally eaten alive by those damned things,' Troy said. 'The last thing that all the captains managed to do was detonate their self-destruct sequences. And I'm afraid the news gets even worse, Lauren. The Peregrine squadron managed a last radar sweep before we lost contact with them. Not only did the asteroids set a crash course for your location in Antarctica, but both of those lumps of rock seem to be filled with hundreds of pockets of metal. Our best guess is that they are stuffed to the gills with those ball bearing critters. Whatever you do, you have to stop them. If they reach Earth there'll be no stopping those bastards multiplying like a plague of cockroaches.'

My blood chilled at thoughts of hordes of them spilling out from whatever was left of Antarctica. 'Understood. We'll do everything we can.'

'Then may god protect you and all of us,' Troy said as the line went dead.

Ruby shook her head. 'Well this more than confirms our worst fears — it's a Kimprak scouting force.'

'A scouting force that we now know is heading straight for the Angelus megastructure,' I replied. I took a deep breath. 'Time to go and kick some sense into Commander Beltran before it is too late. Erin, get us back up into that air battle as fast as you can for that 8pm deadline.'

'Affirmative,' she replied.

A moment later we were soaring up into the sky, leaving the glowing oval of light and whatever the Angelus's last best hope for our world was, far below us.

CHAPTER TWENTY-SIX

My heart was filled with heaviness as explosions and shrapnel detonated all round us. We headed back up into the battle still raging in the skies over the megastructure. On the ground, it wasn't much better — rising columns of smoke indicated the crash sites of multiple craft. According to the Battle Centre display, at least a dozen TR-3Bs and half the amount again of our X-craft, had been shot down, losses that neither side could afford to lose. And already in my mind I could see the Eden crew's names added to the memorial wall, those who hadn't been able to eject in time.

'This is just so wrong,' Mike said, gazing out at the battle as Erin ducked and wove us through the melee. 'It says everything about our species when we are too busy fighting each other to deal with the real threat about to land on our heads.'

'Same old,' Ruby said, shaking her head.

'Well I'm going to knock heads together if I have to, so let's just hope Don and Zack have been able to argue some sense into Beltran,' I replied. 'Have we got a fix on their transponder, Ruby?'

'Yes, sitting out on the edge of the battle zone and trying their best not to shoot any of our craft down by the looks of things.'

'Open up a direct channel, let's find out how they got on.'

'Channel open,' Ruby said.

I pressed the comm button. 'Don, it's Lauren here. Are we up for that proposed ceasefire?'

'I tried, Lauren, I really tried,' he replied in a flat tone. 'But that knucklehead is as paranoid as they come. He's convinced it's a bluff and that the moment he orders the fleet to stand down you'll launch a sneak attack to wipe out all of our ships.'

Part of me wasn't surprised by what I was hearing. 'But please tell me that at least you and Zack know that is so not the case?' I said.

'I realise that we don't exactly really know each other, but for what it's worth, we do both believe you,' Don replied. 'But I have no idea how we are going to get our superiors to share that trust, particularly as they know that you're the same woman who stole one of our ships.'

'That was an act of necessity, but I take your point. But there has to be some way of convincing them.'

'What about showing them the video that Troy just sent us about the Kimprak attacking our ships?' Erin said. 'If anything might get through Beltran's thick skull, a much more immediate threat like that incoming invasion force could bring him to his senses.'

Don's voice cut in. 'Incoming invasion force, what damned invasion force?'

'We have two asteroids travelling in at high velocity, not only fast enough to create a significant impact event, but which are also carrying robotic Kimprak passengers within them that will begin strip mining our world the moment they crash land here,' I replied.

'Hang on, we were briefed that the alien invasion asteroid isn't due to reach our world for around a year yet,' Don replied.

'That's because this isn't the mothership invasion that we've all been preparing for,' I said. 'The two asteroids known as Pollux and Castor look like some sort of stealth mission sent ahead to help clear the way with a tactical first strike that will seriously soften our ability to defend ourselves.'

'And if that wasn't enough the bonus prize for the Kimprak is that they will also wipe out whatever that Angelus device is that is being constructed down there to defend us,' Mike added.

'Damn it, then we *have* to stop this battle and we have to stop it now,' Don said. 'And you say you have video proof of these Kimprak on their way here?'

'We do. If we transmit it to you, can you relay it to Commander Beltran...and...' I took a deep breath, 'Tell him that to show just how serious we are, I'm still going to order our fleet to stand down first.'

Ruby gawped at me. 'You can't be serious, Commander. That will leave our ships wide open to attack.'

'I'm deadly serious,' I replied. 'We're all going to be wiped out anyway unless we start working together and it's time to extend the olive branch before it's too late. So, transmit the video to Don's ship and let's get this thing done. I also want you to transmit a frequency for Commander Beltran to talk to me on a private channel.'

Ruby narrowed her eyes, then frowned as she began pressing icons on her display. 'Okay, Commander, message sent.'

'The data package is received,' Don replied. 'Relaying the video to Commander Beltran's flagship now.'

'Tell him that I'll be waiting for his call,' I said.

'Roger that.' The comm light blinked off.

I turned to the others. 'Look, I know you all probably think I'm being beyond reckless here, but if we carry this fight on like we are, we won't be left with anything left to defend. Someone has to break this deadlock and if it has to be, it's going to be me.'

My friends all looked at me and then one by one they all nodded, even Ruby.

'Yeah, sorry, I didn't mean to bust your balls, but lowering your weapon during a battle sort of goes against every instinct of a soldier,' Ruby said. 'But this is big picture stuff that you get paid the big bucks to decide about.'

'Hey, I get paid for this?'

Ruby snorted and shook her head.

Mike was looking at me with real admiration in his gaze. 'You are so much the commander that we need right now. And without making you blub, Tom would be so damned proud of you if he could see how you're handling all of this madness.'

Immediately, tears filled my eyes. 'Now see what you've made me bloody do.'

Mike chuckled. 'Just think of it as part of my job description of keeping it real for you.'

Erin was smiling at me too. 'However this pans out, Lauren, just know that we all believe in you and this is so the right call.'

'Yeah, hopefully your decision is about to save a lot of lives, not to mention rescuing Jack and Jodie from E8,' Ruby added.

I smiled at her, wiping my eyes and nodding. But at least now the ball of tension that I'd been carrying around inside since the start of this battle had disappeared. I already knew in my heart that this decision was the right one. And however this played out, at least I could live with the fact that I'd tried my best for as long as our world had left.

Ruby eyes widened as she looked at her screen. 'It appears that we have an incoming transmission from Commander Beltran no less.'

'Patch him through,' I replied. I breathed through my nose,

my hands clammy, then hit my comm button. 'I'm guessing that you've had time to look at that video, Commander Beltran?'

'I have...although I still suspect it's a deception on your part, because frankly I wouldn't trust you further than I could spit, right now. But Captain Don Jacobs said something about you standing your forces down to prove that your intentions are serious?'

'I will and that's a promise,' I said. 'But the caveat to that is that you need to stand yours down too when we've done exactly that. But let's get one thing clear, one shot by any of your ships against us, let alone against the Angelus megastructure, and it will make any truce null and void.'

'Okay, time to put your word to the test because I still don't trust you at all. But issue a ceasefire for sixty seconds time and if you do, I will think about following your lead. Then if by some miracle the truce holds and you don't try to stab us in the back, we'll really talk about what we can do about these Kimprak scout ships heading straight towards our world.'

'Understood, then we'll talk again in a moment.' I punched the comm button and the green LED blinked off. 'Okay, time to do this. Ruby, open up a fleet-wide, open channel. I want everyone to hear this, Beltran too.'

She toggled a few switches and then nodded at me.

I imagined the crews of our ships as I began to speak, all the lives we were hopefully about to save, and it helped me focus on what really mattered like nothing else could.

'This is your commander speaking. I have just started negotiations with Commander Beltran of the USSF force that we are currently engaged in fighting and...' I glanced at the clock. 'You are all to cease fire and halt all hostilities in fifteen seconds time. I realise that tactically this is a high risk gamble that many of you will already be questioning, but this is one that we have to take because it's become imperative that our two forces work together to take on an imminent Kimprak threat. Cease all hostilities in three, two, one...'

Outside, the barrage of weapons fire fell silent. And not just from our X-craft, but also from every single one of the TR-3Bs. I held my breath for a few seconds and then let out a long gasp as the others in the cockpit sagged back into their chairs.

'Way to go, Lauren,' Mike said, nodding towards me.

'Yeah, you really do deserve to sit in the big chair,' Ruby said, winking at me. 'And this is new...we seem to have a live video feed being sent through by Commander Beltran. Do you want me to display it on the virtual cockpit, Star Trek style, Commander?'

'Make it so,' I replied, grinning.

A large video window appeared and a rather imposing guy with light blue eyes, roughly in his mid-fifties with a neatly trimmed grey beard and a hawkish nose gazed out. 'Commander Stelleck, I presume?'

'In the flesh and it looks like our ceasefire is holding, Commander Beltran.'

'Yes, although I don't like this, don't like this at all.'

'Neither of us do, but we have to deal with the cards that we get dealt. But as much as I would like to chat, we have an imminent threat to deal with. I'm going to send our heavier X104s ahead into space to intercept the asteroids with their railguns similar to your own.'

His eyebrows arched over his forehead. 'Yes, and I wonder exactly where you reverse engineered that design from?'

I allowed myself a wry smile. 'Needs must and a discussion for another time. But I suggest that you do the same with your own railgun-equipped craft, then combine forces and throw as much firepower as possible into those asteroids before they get anywhere near the Earth.'

'That sounds like a reasonable strategy if I were talking to a fellow officer in the USSF. But I'm not, I talking to the commander of a rogue force. Tell me one good reason that I should even begin to trust you?'

'Because you have no choice, Beltran,' I replied. 'If we take them on as a divided force then we won't be able to put up half as good a defence against them, and if they get past then the consequences for our world will be severe. Do you really want to have that on your conscience for being a stubborn old warhorse who wouldn't listen to reason when the world needed you too?'

Beltran's eyebrows arched. 'I would have you court marshalled for talking to me like that if you were serving in the USSF forces, but as you're not...' He sighed. 'Okay, let's say we send our railgun-armed ships to the frontline. What role will they play in this coming battle?'

'Our X103s, including my own craft, will aim to destroy any of those Kimprak ball bearing robots that the asteroid attempts to shed. I suggest your laser-turreted variants help us in that mop-up role — we don't want a single one of those bloody things to make it past our blockade.'

'So they will form the quarterbacks of our combined defence force,' Beltran said, scratching his beard. 'Yes, that makes sense and after watching the video that you sent through, assuming it's not a fake, then we are obviously dealing with a formidable foe. If these Kimprak manage to make contact with any of our ships, it is obvious they will simply turn them into resources to multiply their own forces with.'

'Exactly and no, the video isn't any sort of fake. So can I have your word that you will make no further attempt to attack the megastructure below us?'

'You have, begrudgingly, but only as that's something of a moot point right now as we can't seem to penetrate that damned shield over the entire site. But just tell me how you can trust these Angelus? What proof do you have that they don't mean us harm?'

'Definitive proof I don't have, but what I can tell you is that I absolutely trust the integrity of the Angelus AIs involved in creating whatever this is. Besides, as I'm sure you can see from their level of technology that was able to bore down to the core of our planet without releasing a mass eruption, if they wanted to wipe our species out they would have already.'

'There you actually make a good point, one that even an old *war horse* like me can understand.' The corner of his mouth curled up the tiniest fraction. 'Then it seems that we have an alliance, Commander Stelleck, for now at least, but do nothing that will make me regret that decision as you *will* pay for it. So, whilst this truce holds for now, I will issue the necessary orders to our fleet and I suggest you do the same.'

'Hopefully by the end of this you'll know that I am someone you really can trust. In the meantime, let's throw this Kimprak scouting force a reception committee that they are never, ever going to forget.'

The Earth was growing smaller behind us as we headed out towards the radar lock target currently indicating Pollux and Castor at a distance of three hundred klicks, just out beyond the orbit of our moon. But what was more worrying was that the speed indicator showed that they were still travelling at a thousand kilometres a second. At that rate, they would hit Antarctica with the power of a hundred nukes in about thirty minutes time, and that timeframe didn't exactly feel like a lot of time to try and stop them.

On the positive side and much to my relieved surprise, the alliance had held. Around us the virtual cockpit was filled with views of the large combined flotilla of saucer and triangular-shaped craft, just shy of a couple of hundred craft, a credible Earth defence force to meet the Kimprak head on.

'I never thought I'd see the day that we were flying in formation with a TR-3B fleet to take on our mutual enemy,' Mike said.

Ruby raised her eyebrows. 'Yeah, we're going to have to add *miracle worker* to Lauren's job description.'

'Hey, it takes two to tango,' I replied. 'This Commander Beltran might describe himself as an old war horse, but at least he's a war horse that listens to reason.'

'That may be true, but I also think we have a lot to thank Captain Don for,' Erin said. 'I suspect he had to do a lot of mediating to get the commander onboard, albeit very reluctantly.'

'Yeah, but what I want to know is, what the hell has happened to Alvarez?' Ruby said. 'Not that I'm not grateful, but if he had been commanding that fleet of ships, you can guarantee we'd still be in an all-out pitch fight against each other.'

'Well, as Don himself made the point to me back at Area 51, they are US military and as far he was concerned, at least Alvarez was just an advisor.'

'An advisor and the people he works for who were still able to pull the military's strings,' Mike said.

'So why isn't he here still doing exactly that?' I replied. 'It seems more than a little bit out of character for Alvarez not to have his nose in the middle of such an important battle.'

'Nothing good, you can be sure of that,' Mike said.

'Perhaps his diary was double booked?' Erin said with an almost straight face.

'Hey, not only can this one really fly, she also has a sense of humour too,' Ruby said.

'Oh lord help you, that sounds like you have our illustrious Weapons Officer's seal of approval,' Mike said.

The smile that had been threatening the corners of Erin's

mouth turned into a wide one. 'And I'll take it. She's not bad herself. I think my old co-pilot Daryl would even approve...'

Her smile faded away along with her words. It was obvious that she was still mourning the loss of her friend in the depths of the sea off Cuba, just like I was with Tom. I prayed that by the time we were finished here, we weren't going to add to that heartache by losing anyone else close to us like Jack, Jodie or Lucy.

'We have a transmission coming in from our new military buddy, Commander Beltran,' Ruby said.

'Put him on screen. I'm so never going to get tired of saying that,' I replied.

'Damned Trekkies,' Ruby muttered, but she was smiling as she transferred the video feed to the virtual cockpit.

Commander Beltran's face appeared in a window. In the background we could see military personnel strapped into their flight seats as they operated their control screens.

'We need to discuss strategy and quickly, Commander Stelleck. Because of the high speed of the asteroids, we need to look at forming up that blockade now with the layered defence approach. And as you suggested, we'll put our railgun ships to the fore and our laser vessels with your smaller vessels to the aft to mop up anything that gets through.'

'I think that will work well, but we should also look at beginning to fire railgun rounds at them sooner rather than later, if you agree? I realise that back on Earth a range of two hundred klicks is quite long, but out here in space without the gravity well of our planet to slow them down, they will have limitless range. Also, whatever else those Kimprak scout ships are, the one thing that they aren't is very manoeuvrable.'

'You're saying they are basically a sitting duck?' Beltran asked.

'That's certainly hoping so, so let's get our ships into position.

Then when we've done that, we can open fire with a coordinated barrage and we'll find out one way or another.'

'I may not entirely trust you, Commander Stelleck, but I do approve of tactical thinking. The sooner we reduce those space rocks to rubble, the happier I'll be.'

'Then let's get this thing done,' I replied.

The commander nodded and the screen went dark.

Mike slowly nodded. 'I'm starting to warm to this guy.'

'Yeah, me too. Just such a shame that it took a bloody battle to get both sides finally talking.'

'Let's just hope it's the start of a real alliance that will survive this encounter and will hold until the mothership finally gets here,' Mike said.

'If we were just talking about Commander Beltran, I think that might be an actual possibility, especially when he's seen for himself that the Angelus are very much on our side. The problem is, Colonel Alvarez and whatever the Overseer agenda is in all of this. It all feels like we're pieces on a chess board being manoeuvred.'

Mike sighed. 'Yeah, isn't that the truth.'

I looked out at the stars and the crescent moon hanging in space, as our combined fleet slid into position and we got ready to fire the opening shots in the war with the Kimprak. Hopefully, it would be over before it had begun when the railgun rounds annihilated the asteroids. The problem was, I already had a sense of premonition that it would be anything but that easy.

CHAPTER TWENTY-SEVEN

WHAT WASN'T LOST on me while looking at the combined fleet on the 3D tactical map was that Beltran had kept most of his fleet at a safe distance from our own, rather than intersperse our X-craft among his TR-3Bs. Instinct told me that was probably down to his ongoing but healthy paranoia that we might double-cross him at any moment, as our ships — with their impressive mini-guns — could do an awful lot of damage at relatively close range. Of course, that background of underlying mistrust stretched both ways. We'd been forced into an alliance of convenience against a mutual enemy. I could only hope that things didn't go south however this worked out, because this really was an alliance that we could do with keeping in place until the mothership got here in eleven months. The more humanity fought amongst itself, the more we would degrade our ability to fight the true enemy that was heading our way from the cosmos.

With a few taps on my console, I repositioned the markers of our X104s slightly further to starboard of Beltran's fleet, increasing the distance between them. Yes, that healthy paranoia *definitely* swung both ways.

Our ships began their choreographed moves as Delphi relayed the order to the AIs on each of our ships. During actual combat, our human pilots would be in full control, although preset battle group movements would be under my control via the Battle Command Centre.

But as I watched the small rectangular markers for the X-craft moving gracefully into their positions whilst keeping in formation, it wasn't lost on me that the lives of every single person on those ships was reduced to a simple graphic on the map. After the disastrous experience of the sim, I intended to keep reminding myself of that fact rather than just thinking of them as resources that I could just throw into a battle with a casually issued command to Delphi.

'You look thoughtful,' Ruby said, looking over at me from the railing she'd been leaning on to watch the fleet on the virtual cockpit.

'Yes, just feeling the weight of responsibility pressing down on my shoulders right now.'

She nodded. 'I'm not surprised, but a word to the wise.'

I turned towards her. 'Any advice gratefully received.'

'I can guarantee that every single person in our squadron will be feeling that it's their responsibility to win this fight single-handedly. Of course, that's not actually true, even for you. Yes, you may be the person in charge, but an army fights as a unit. Every single person has their individual roles to play in winning a battle. I've known so many senior serving officers and often the higher the rank, the lonelier they feel. But you're not alone in this, Lauren — we're all with you every step of the way.'

'Wow, that's quite a speech for you, Ruby.'

'Yeah, not normally my thing, but it's that sort of moment, so sue me already.'

I laughed. 'Thank you, seriously, because I needed to hear that pep talk right now.'

'Just keeping it real for you whilst Jack's not around to kick your ass. Anyway, better get back to it.' She nodded at me and headed back to her CIC console.

I felt a surge of affection for my weapons officer. Yes, at some point we'd become good friends.

I returned my attention to the tactical map, which showed that the last of our ships had finally moved into position. The time had almost arrived to get this show on the road.

Ruby looked over as I sat down. 'Okay, we have a firing solution agreed with Commander Beltran. We're going to try going for a combined kill shot with our railguns, concentrating our fire in a narrow cone. The theory is that if enough hypersonic rounds hit, it should vaporise the targets, especially factoring in the incredible speed they are currently travelling at.'

'So when do we light them up?' Erin asked.

'We have an automated countdown to coordinate our attack with Beltran's ships, literally any moment now,' Ruby replied. 'Putting timer up on the virtual cockpit.'

It appeared and I watched the counter ticking down, the anticipation rising inside me as each second passed. Then at last it reached zero — jets of fire appeared from every single Pangolin and TR-3B not equipped with a laser turret.

The dart-like projectiles sped away too fast to track with the human eye, but already the green boxes were tracking them, speeding out on the 3D map.

'How long till they hit the target?' Mike asked.

'That's the thing about space combat, it operates at a whole different scale. Results are rarely instantaneous,' Ruby replied. 'Even though our hypersonic rounds are travelling at a speed off the scale, we're still going to be waiting about fifteen minutes before they hit those incoming asteroids.'

For the first time the practicalities of operating a battle at incredibly long range started to really hit home. 'But doesn't that mean that they are going to easily see them coming and take evasive action?'

'That's why this is going to be a two-punch strike,' Ruby replied. 'The second continual volley that's about to be begin will be fired in a wider random pattern that radiates out around the asteroids' current trajectory. Hopefully, even if they are able to adjust their flight paths, they will run into one of the thousands of further hypersonic rounds that we're about to launch.'

'That sounds like something straight out of the playbook for battleship fights in those old movies,' Mike said. 'Lob as much ordnance as you can in the general direction of your enemy, in the hope that eventually a few of your shells hit home.'

'That's actually a pretty good analogy,' I replied. 'Niki had me reading some famous navy battle books, everything from the Battle of Trafalgar to the sinking of the Bismarck, and our rail-guns are pretty much the equivalent of their cannons and unguided shell fire, albeit with a much longer range.'

'But what about our AIM missiles, can't we use them too, even though they aren't designed to work in space?' Erin asked.

'Actually they do work up to a point,' Mike replied. 'Their rocket motors will obviously work fine, but their fins won't as there's no air resistance for them to be able to steer themselves. That's why we so urgently need the next generation of space missiles that Jodie has the Forge team currently developing. If only we had them now.'

'We've all been caught on the back foot here, but of course that was exactly the Kimprak's intention with this sneak early attack,' I replied. 'Anyway, we're going to work with what we've got to play with. Ruby, did you discuss using our AIM missiles with Beltran's people as I requested?'

'Yeah, all part of the battle plan now. We're going to fire them all off in a volley just before the asteroids come into point defence range of our miniguns and lasers,' Ruby said.

'Let's just hope it doesn't come to that — we saw what happened to Troy's patrol on that video when their ships and crew were literally devoured by the Kimprak,' Mike said.

I nodded. 'We're the final line of Earth's defence and we can't let them get past us, for obvious reasons.'

'A last Hail Mary in other words,' Erin said.

'Pretty much,' I replied.

'Well it won't be much longer before we know whether it's going to come down to that, because the next sustained barrage is about to begin,' Ruby said.

Once again we watched the countdown tick down to zero, but this time the jet pulses from the railguns kept going as they continued to fire. A duration timer had also appeared on the Battle Command Centre and was ticking upwards. In a mesmerising display, pops of light rippled back and forth across the fleet as the ship's weapons were fired, casting light across the hulls of TR-3Bs and the X104s.

'That battleship analogy is a really good one for what we're seeing now,' Mike said.

'You're right, although a silent bombardment — thanks to the vacuum of space — doesn't have quite the same drama,' I replied. 'Of course, this particular battle is most probably going to be the most important one in human history, at least until we take on the mothership when it arrives. But I doubt anyone will get to write any stories about it like they did about the great naval battles from the past. Hopefully, if everything goes to plan, I doubt the general public will never know what we did out here.'

'Maybe they will one day, at least if history books are still being written,' Mike said.

'Can we please have a bit more of an upbeat tone round here?' Erin said. 'We haven't lost yet, guys.'

'Sorry, just me talking without engaging my brain filter first,' Mike replied.

I nodded. 'I think we're just all worried deep down because we know exactly what's at stake. But I believe in our ability to take those Kimprak ships down and so should all of you.'

I hoped my forced tone of belief sounded convincing, because the truth was I so wasn't feeling it inside yet. I was actually so tightly wound now that waves of nausea were fluttering in my stomach. I certainly wasn't feeling any of my normal battle calm, which I usually did when I was in the thick of it. Too much time to anticipate what might be about to happen had a lot to do with that, but so did the knowledge that I was carrying the lives of so many flight crews on my shoulders.

We watched as the duration time climbed towards five minutes and then in perfect unison every single Pangolin and railgun-equipped TR-3B stopped firing.

The comm light for ship to ship radio lit up on my chair's arm.

'Commander Beltran is on the line, patching him through,' Ruby said.

His face appeared on the video feed. 'As you've probably just seen, we've just finished our barrage, so keep everything crossed that enough of those rounds hit those things to vapourise them.'

'We'll be watching the telemetry and will be doing exactly that,' I replied. 'It's probably time to pull your frontline ships and our X104s back to our main force so together we can stop anything getting past that survives the initial bombardments.'

'I agree, but let's hope there's nothing left of the Kimprak scout ships left to mop up,' Beltran replied. 'But we should probably fire off a third and final round whilst we still have the opportunity to use our longer range weapons when they get closer, if they manage to survive.'

'That sounds like a good way to increase the odds in our favour.'

'We need to do everything that we can to make sure we win a

decisive victory here today,' Beltran replied. 'The time to start praying for exactly that outcome has begun. Over and out.' The video feed blinked off.

I turned my attention back to the tactical display as the first volley of hypersonic rounds headed straight towards the two asteroids, which still hadn't deviated in the slightest.

'Oh this looks like we might be shooting fish in a barrel after all,' Erin said.

Ruby nodded. 'We'll know for sure in three, two, one...'

The display filled with hundreds of detonations and the red triangles for the two asteroids disappeared.

I leant forward in my seat. 'Is that it? Did we do it?'

'Hang on, waiting for confirmation from the Pangolins — they're doing radar imaging of the impact zone,' Ruby said. 'Data is just coming through now.'

I drummed my fingers on the arm of my chair as we waited.

'Okay, data packet received. Putting it onto the virtual cockpit and sharing what we have with Commander Beltran.'

A grainy, radar-created, pixelated video appeared of two distinct asteroid shapes rotating as they sped through space. An impact timer raced down towards zero and then the asteroids began to move sideways away from each other. Little puffs of vapour were visible as they began to drift apart.

My stomach muscles tightened as the impact timer reached zero and then started ticking up as the asteroids continued out of the way of the incoming railgun fire. The radar video then pulled back for a wider field of shot to keep both asteroids in sight.

'Crap, they literally dodged a bullet — or I should say, bullets,' Ruby said.

I saw the same crushing sense of disappointment that I was feeling inside on the faces of those around me, and no doubt across our combined fleet's crews.

'Okay, we mustn't lose hope just yet,' I said. 'That was just the open hypersonic salvos round. Don't forget we fired a second wide dispersal pattern of hypersonic rounds in case the first wave didn't hit anything. Hopefully, we'll get lucky with a direct hit.'

Everyone nodded and we all waited until at last, the second wave countdown timer ticked down.

'Okay, keep everything crossed people, here we go again...' Ruby said.

But as the timer hit zero, the two asteroids remained very much in view.

I held up my hand. 'Before anyone says anything, that's was a five-minute barrage. There's plenty of time for it—'

My words died in my throat as the left hand asteroid vapourised and vanished from the radar feed.

Mike thumped the air as everyone clapped and whooped. I felt some of my tension fall away.

'Take that, sucker!' Ruby said.

Elation surged through me, but I clamped it down. 'Let's not celebrate just yet — have you got sensor confirmation that it really is destroyed?' I said.

Our weapons officer nodded, gazing at her screen. Then a broad grin filled her face. 'Yep, radar scan confirms target lost.'

I sagged into myself a fraction as relief flooded through me. 'Okay, let's just hope we get as lucky with the second asteroid before the second barrage finishes.'

Now we all watched the duration ticking up, the grainy view of the asteroid slowly tumbling as it kept coming, slowly growing bigger.

'This is getting a bit tight for comfort,' Ruby said. 'That remaining asteroid — Castor — has just passed the moon's orbit.'

I stared at the timer, which only had thirty seconds left until the second barrage of hypersonic rounds finished. My heart had risen to my throat when — with just five seconds to go — the asteroid seemed to shudder, before shattering into several smaller chunks.

I immediately turned towards Ruby. 'Okay, another direct hit, but has it been neutralised?'

Ruby scowled as she peered at her CIC screen. 'Not completely. Those remaining lumps of space rock are still on a collision course with the Angelus megastructure site. And now, not surprisingly, we have Commander Beltran on the line.'

'Put him up on the main screen,' I replied.

A moment later Beltran's supersized face was looking at us from the virtual cockpit. 'It looks like it's going to come down to the line after all, Commander Stelleck. I'm about to order my fleet to fire at will as the asteroid remnants close and I suggest you do the same. By our estimates, each of those fragments are still large enough to throw enough debris into the air if they strike the ground to create a nuclear winter for at least three months for our entire world.'

'I agree and we can't let a single one of those Kimprak ball bearing creatures reach the Earth either. We've already seen how they multiply like cockroaches...'

'Maybe one day, long after this is all over and the dust has settled, we'll have a drink sometime to celebrate our victory today,' he said.

'Then the drinks will be on me,' I replied with a small smile that Beltran actually returned. A moment later his screen blinked out.

I toggled on the fleet-wide channel for our ships. 'Okay, as I'm sure you're already aware, we've had partial success neutralising one of the asteroids. But the fragments of the other one are still hurtling towards the Angelus megastructure on Earth. So you are to do whatever it takes to stop a single piece of that asteroid from reaching the ground. Pangolins, you are to recommence firing railguns immediately to try to whittle what's left of those lumps of rock down to size. Then when they are within minigun range, open up with everything you have, including your AIM missiles. We are the line in the sand that we can't allow the Kimprak to cross. Good luck to us all.' I toggled the comm off.

'Wait until you see the whites of their eyes in other words,' Mike said, his expression drawn.

'Pretty much,' I replied.

'You do realise at the speed those rocks are hurtling in at, we will have literally a fraction of a second to stop them?' Ruby said.

'I never said this was going to be easy,' I said. I took a deep breath before continuing. 'And that's why our ships are going to have to rely on handing over weapon controls entirely to Delphi. We are going to be looking for a millisecond window of target opportunity for close combat, and that will be beyond even the speed of your reflexes.'

'Not sure I'm entirely happy handing over the fate of our world to an AI,' Ruby replied.

'Haven't we all pretty much done that already with Lucy?' I said.

Ruby nodded. 'True and yes, deep down I know you're right, but it still goes against all my training.'

'Trust in the tech,' Erin said, casting her a smile.

Ruby sighed. 'Yeah, I guess I'll have to.'

'Then let's put together a battle engagement plan with Delphi and relay it to the rest of the fleet,' I replied.

I returned my attention to the multiple asteroid locks on my tactical display, which were hurtling towards us at a nausea-inducing speed. This was going to be impossibly tight. Maybe we'd got lucky when we'd taken out one of the asteroids, but twice? In a very literal sense, this was going to come right down to the line in space, in this case, one formed by human ships.

CHAPTER TWENTY-EIGHT

THE FINAL BARRAGE of hypersonic rounds fired by our Pangolins and the TR-3Bs was speeding towards the patch of space that the Castor asteroid remnants were currently heading away from, straight towards our fleet and the Antarctica site far below. On the radar feed that Delphi was using, highly pixelated images tracked each of the four remaining boulders, each of which was at least fifty metres across, according to the data tag next to it. Then suddenly, one of them exploded, then winked out of existence. But any whooping had stopped now — we were all too focused on the fact that every single one of them needed to be taken out.

'And that just leaves three,' Ruby said, gazing at her CIC screen. 'Targets within range of our AIM missiles. We've set them up with a time detonation and a wide dispersal targeting pattern in case those fragments are still able to dodge them. Launching now...'

From every single X-craft, including our own, missiles burst out. Then a second later, like a thousand candles being lit all at once against the inky black of space, their rockets burst into life and they sped away towards the remaining targets.

We watched then fly away from the fleet in silence, the pensive mood visible in everyone's expressions. I suspected this mood was identical in every other cockpit in our combined fleet. Certainly, if I hadn't been about to endure high speed manoeuvres rather than being strapped into my flight seat, I would probably have been pacing up and down the flight deck, wearing a groove into the floor.

Ruby's nostrils flared. 'Time to impact, in three, two, one...'

Like distant supernovas flaring into existence before dying again, the missiles detonated. The radar view of the fragments hurtling towards us was filled with static. It took several seconds for it to clear, but when it finally did I saw that two of the lumps of rock had vanished.

'And then there was one,' Ruby said with a wide smile.

'Oh thank god for that,' I replied, allowing myself to enjoy a moment of relief from my churning gut.

Mike was looking thoughtfully at the screen. 'Interesting thing is — they didn't attempt to move this time, which suggests their manoeuvring system was taken out by the railgun strike,' he said.

'That sounds like great news, but the bad news is that our fleet is all out of missiles,' Ruby replied.

'Then it will be down to our miniguns and the adapted TR-3Bs and their lasers to take that last one down,' I said. 'Time to hand over weapon control to Delphi across the fleet.' I scanned the list of tactical options currently available on the Battle Computer. 'Delphi, initiate *Kilo* command.'

'Initiating *Kilo* command,' Delphi said. 'I now have weapon control of all X-craft weapons and flight systems. Intercept parameters have been calculated.'

Erin withdrew her hands from the flight controls.

'Target is thirty seconds out,' Ruby said, her tone noticeably strained as she let go of her targeting joystick.

I knew instantly that this was going be hard for both of them — to sit on their hands during a fight, trusting an AI to finish the battle for us. Erin's foot was drumming on the floor as she chewed her lip. I was far from immune to this either. I needed coffee — a lot of it — to take my mind off the increasing spin of anxiety in my gut.

'Target in range,' Ruby said, her tone even tighter.

Absolutely on cue, the whir of our miniguns echoed through the hull. Then, with a clatter as the large calibre, armour-piercing rounds were discharged, they started to fire. Despite the acoustic shielding the cockpit was lined with, and even though I should have been used to it by now, the sound was still deafening. It reminded me of when I'd taken shelter in a cowshed in Somerset during a walk with an old boyfriend. A sudden thunderstorm had dumped huge hailstones straight down onto the tin roof. That had been loud, but this was ear-numbingly louder — or maybe because of my heightened state of anxiety I was just more tuned into it.

Around us, the armour-piercing rounds streaked away, leaving burning tracer trails through space. And lancing out between them, hurtling into space, were green laser beams — everything that our combined fleet was firing, all heading towards a single target.

'Come on, come on,' Erin said, chewing her lip.

The tactical 3D map showed the last fragment of the asteroid race into the path of our outgoing fire. Then for the first time, in the middle of the Battle Command Centre display, we saw sparks of light flashing off a distant pinprick of rock that was blurring towards us fast.

'Enhanced visual image of target now displayed,' Delphi announced over the din of the minigun rounds.

A far clearer telescope image replaced the radar one. We could see countless ricochet bursts all over the surface of the asteroid as our minigun rounds splintered off large sections of what remained of Castor. The TR-3B's lasers were also doing their job, vapourising sections of rock that had broken free.

Multiple alarms warbled out as the distance indicator raced down past five thousand klicks. The details on the asteroid also became pin sharp in *Ariel's* telescope sensors as the rock raced towards our combined fleet. I just had enough time to make out all the Kimprak ball bearings peppered across the surface like thousands of silver pimples. I could now see that they weren't just restricted to the exterior surface, but were visible in the open cross-sections of the rock where the Kimprak had eaten their way into the asteroid's core like metallic maggots.

Round after round blazed, atomising great slabs of rock and destroying the Kimprak buried in them. Meanwhile, the laser fire converged on a single section of the asteroid and it started to grow red hot.

Then, much to my and even Ruby's obvious surprise, Delphi made an announcement.

'Valid targeting solution has been calculated for a final wave of remaining railgun rounds, firing now,' Delphi said.

The tactical display showed markers of fifty railgun rounds from every single Pangolin, as the distance between us and the asteroid raced down past a hundred klicks. The rounds hurtled towards the rock, but the closing speed was too fast for even our AI to fully allow for all the variables. The vast bulk of the rounds missed the target by a wide margin, shooting off into empty space. But then I saw a single round head directly towards the asteroid.

'Fifty clicks,' Ruby said as her hand strayed towards the targeting joystick and our mini-guns kept up their hammer-on-metal soundtrack.

And then my heart leapt as we saw a blinding pulse come

from the final fragment of the asteroid. One moment it was there — the next it was gone.

'Booyah!' Ruby shouted.

But Erin was frowning, leaning forward to look at her display. 'Lauren, I don't think it's over.'

The brief sense of elation that had started to take hold was swept away instantly as the light faded. Indeed, the rock *had* been vapourised, but now a glinting silver cloud of shrapnel was racing towards our ships. Immediately, lock icons appeared all over the cloud as Delphi sorted out last second targeting solutions. Ruby zoomed the view into the cloud to reveal it was made up of a vast swarm of individual Kimprak trilobites, curled up in their armoured ball bearing configuration.

'Shit, those metallic bastards are still coming straight at us,' Mike said.

The Battle Computer targeting options blinked off. Delphi was completely overwhelmed by the number of Kimprak zooming towards the fleet.

But then I was thumping my finger onto the ship-wide comm button. 'Take over manual control and take immediate evasive action now, everyone. Try to take out as many of those damned Kimprak trilobites as you can.'

Our fleet immediately began to scatter as the silver cloud of death raced towards us. The TR-3Bs were moving too, their automated laser cannons still doing a good job of thinning out the ranks of the fast approaching robot craft, but nothing like fast enough.

As Erin sped us sideways out of the impact zone, Ruby began pouring fire into the swarm. The problem was that not all of the flight crews' reactions were quite as fast.

The Kimprak slammed straight into a dozen of our craft and twice as many of the TR-3Bs. On the video feed, the ball bearing robot creatures began to unfurl into their trilobite forms and started burying their way into the hulls. And that wasn't all. A second large cluster was already unfurling, linking to form vast chains.

Even as Ruby's lightning fast responses blazed our minigun rounds into the enemy, along with many other ships to blast that chain apart, new chains were already forming in the approaching silver cloud. Like a woven metal net, they hit and snagged many of the craft in our combined fleet, wrapping around the ships, quickly enveloping them.

The sheer horror of what was happening slammed into my mind as I saw TR-3Bs and X-craft alike being eaten into by the trilobites. And in every place where a section of hull was devoured, a new trilobite emerged like a maggot from the devoured metal. Even as Erin dived us around the swarm along with the rest of the unaffected ships, taking out as many of the Kimprak machines as we could, their numbers were multiplying far faster than our ability to keep on top of them.

'I have Commander Beltran on the comm,' Ruby said, blazing a burst of minigun rounds through one of the long robot chains that had begun wrapping itself around a laser-turreted TR-3B.

I pressed my green button and Beltran's face appeared on my screen. He had a space helmet on and behind him I could see the crew of his ship firing sidearms at the trilobites that had penetrated the cockpit.

'Shit, get yourself out of there, Commander!' I shouted.

'Too late — our escape pods are already offline. I'm going to issue the order to our compromised ships, including our own, to initiate their self-destruct sequences.'

I stared at him as a sense of horror buried its claws into me. 'But you can't throw your lives away like this!'

'We have to, Commander Stelleck,' Beltran replied in a quiet voice. 'And as much as it will grieve you to do so, you need to issue a similar order to your own ships.'

I stared at him. 'But I can't!'

He gave me a sad look. 'I know far too well the pain of what you're about to do, to order people under your command to certain death. But you need to do it, because as you yourself once lectured me, the fate of everyone in our world is on the line right now. I am going to issue one final order to our remaining ships to assist you in any way that they can. Good luck, Lauren.'

Before I could reply the video link blinked off.

Raw shock flooded through me as a point of light blossomed — one of the TR-3Bs was detonating within the net of the swarm. It was followed by others in a cascade of annihilation, wiping out all of the Kimprak attached to their hulls with fireball explosions.

I could feel the others' eyes on me without even looking.

'What are you going to do, Lauren?' Mike said in a gentle voice.

'I just can't tell our people to kill themselves,' I whispered.

'I don't think you're going to have to — look,' Erin said, her face pale as she gestured to the virtual cockpit.

Pulses of strange yellow light were coming from our X-craft that I'd never seen before and a split second later they began to detonate, their hulls splitting apart as massive explosions ripped through them.

Ruby shook her head. 'They must have seen what was happening and decided to do the same,' she said, her voice husky.' Then she peered at her screen. 'I'm also seeing strange secondary contacts that keep blinking in and of existence faster than our sensors can keep up.'

'It's probably the expanding debris clouds confusing them,' Mike said, his eyes filling with tears.

If I thought my heart was about to break, I was tipped over the edge when my comm light blinked on and I flicked the button.

'Lauren, I'm afraid *Thor* has been badly compromised. We

have no choice but to initiate our self-destruct sequence like the other ships,' Niki said, his tone flat.

Immediately my hands were balled up into fists. 'But you can't!'

'No choice, Lauren. Better to die quickly and to make our deaths mean something, rather than waiting to be devoured by those damned robots. Just tell Jodie how proud I am of her and that I love her with my whole heart.'

'But Niki—'

He cut me off. 'No time for speeches, dear friend. Just make sure that you and the remaining ships finish this and live to fight another day. Goodbye and I want you to know that it was an absolute honour to fight under your command.'

The comm light blinked off. Before I could even attempt to order Ruby to get him back, a bright flash of light came from the middle of the maelstrom. I knew, just knew in that instant that he and his crew had just sacrificed their lives.

None of us said anything and I couldn't stop the tears that were now flowing down my face. Neither could Erin or Mike. Only Ruby was somehow holding it together out of the four of us.

All I wanted to do was drop to the floor and scream. But now I needed to be a commander. Exactly as what had happened when we'd lost Tom and I'd been on the verge of falling apart. Just like then, the time for grieving would have to come later.

Ruby stared harder at her CIC screen. 'Shit, now I'm detecting movement in one of the infected craft.'

'They are probably just trying to get away,' Mike said.

'No, I don't think so because I can't raise that particular X103 and it's now heading straight down towards Antarctica.'

Mike's eyes widened. 'The Kimprak must have somehow taken over its flight control systems.'

I began to thread my thoughts together, pushing through my

grief. 'You mean they're going to use them to attack the Angelus megastructure?'

Mike nodded. 'I think that's exactly what they're doing.'

'Then we need to order what's left of our combined fleets and take out that X103 before they can get anywhere near the surface.'

Ruby nodded and her fingers flew over her CIC screen as Erin barrelled us around the edge of the swarm that had begun hauling into the metallic net the dead ships that hadn't been able to self-destruct in time.

I smeared my tears away as we hurtled back down towards Earth, and the single red marker superimposed over the tactical display on the virtual cockpit. I was going to make the Kimprak pay for every single life that had just been lost.

Erin sped *Ariel* down through the atmosphere without the red glow and buffeting of a rocket re-entry thanks to our gravity bubble. Around us, nine X-craft and a single TR-3B had formed up, the small number of craft that was left of our two fleets. The loss of so many people was truly shocking, but I couldn't afford to give into the anguish that was churning in the centre of my being.

Ahead of us the remnants of the heavily Kimprak infected X103 was trailing flames, its drive system obviously heavily compromised. The hull had been peppered with hundreds of holes as the trilobites continued to consume their host ship. And every so often a new ball bearing machine created from the repurposed metal was born from their ongoing carnage.

The crippled ship spiralled and rolled in a random pattern as the Kimprak intelligence piloting it did everything it could to try and avoid the weapons fire pouring into it from the remnants of the combined fleet.

My comm light blinked on.

'It's Don,' Ruby said, flicking the minigun sight around and trying to get a lock on a frantically manoeuvring ship ahead of us.

A metadata tag appeared overlaid on the display next to a TR-3B that had pulled up alongside us.

I pressed the comm button. 'Thank god you guys are okay.'

'You too, Lauren,' Don said. 'This battle has been as bad as they come, but it isn't over yet.'

'We have to make sure that the sacrifices of the others aren't in vain.'

'Amen to that,' Zack said in background.

'Then we'll see you on the other side of this fight,' Don said.

'I certainly hope so,' I replied. 'Over and out.'

I returned my attention to the towering tops of the storm clouds that we were racing towards.

'That storm seems to have seriously strengthened, which has to be everything to do with the Angelus megastructure,' I said.

'Yeah, according to the weather station data at the various Antarctic bases, that mother of a snow blizzard seemed to form out of nowhere,' Mike said. 'It's certainly going to play hazard with our sensors when we enter it.'

'Then whatever you do, don't lose visual contact with that infected ship,' I said.

'Don't worry, Lauren, I have absolutely no intention of letting that happen,' Erin replied.

Our small flotilla of ships poured red tracer and laser fire towards the crippled TR-3B as it plummeted into the snow-filled clouds.

'That craft will impact the Angelus megastructure in thirty seconds at that speed,' Erin called out.

'Then do whatever it takes to blow it out of the sky,' I said as we plunged headlong into the clouds in close pursuit.

'Working on it,' Ruby said, gritting her teeth as she poured another blast of minigun rounds towards the target, a few shots striking the ship and ricocheting away. 'Crap, that ship's shield is still strong enough to deflect our rounds.'

'Haven't we got *any* way to stop it?' I asked.

Before Ruby could reply, Don and Zack's TR-3B surged ahead of us through the billowing snowstorm with an impossible turn of speed.

I opened the comm channel. 'What the hell are you doing, Don?'

'We're overloading our engines to max and are going to eject a fraction of a second before we ram straight into that ship. That should bring its damned shield down long enough for you to be able to take it down.'

'But you could be killed!'

'Better to die a hero than watch this play out.'

'Damned right, bro,' Zack said.

Their TR-3B raced down, Don matching the wild gyrations of the infected craft move for move. As I became convinced that they weren't going to eject in time, my mouth went bone dry. But then two spheres burst from the cockpit and arced away.

Their ship crashed straight into the Kimprak-infected X103, which instantly blossomed into a fireball.

'Hit that bastard with everything we've got!' I shouted over the open channel.

Minigun and laser fire sped down towards the expanding fireball and a second detonation lit up the snowstorm with an orange pulse, shrapnel exploding out from it and plummeting downwards.

Then, almost played out in slow motion in my mind, I saw a section of the broken X-craft hull spiralling straight into one of the ejected spheres from Don and Zack's ship. The sphere was ripped apart instantly and the escape pod next to it was peppered by the shrapnel blast, tearing two of its three parachutes to ribbons. Immediately it began to spiral faster down towards the ground.

I had no time to even think about what had just happened to

Don and Zack, as I could see the specks of ball bearing Kimprak hurtling down from the wreckage of the ship.

'Pull up, pull up,' Delphi announced, just as the snowstorm thinned enough to see a vast wall of light a thousand feet below us. I knew that the vast Angelus gravity dome was just waiting for us to crash into it.

Erin did the equivalent of standing on the brakes, vectoring all our multimode manoeuvring rockets straight down and red-lining our REV drive, which whined as our whole cockpit shook. We came to an impossible dead stop, G-forces completely overwhelming our REV drive field and slamming us all bone-achingly hard into our seats.

But below us, the ball bearing machines that could do nothing to change their velocity struck the gravity field with the impact of hypersonic rounds hitting solid steel.

As I sucked in large lungfuls of air, Ruby opened up a zoomed-in video window so we could see the Kimprak machines. It was then that I saw that rather than being spread out into metal pancakes, each of the spheres had somehow maintained its shape. Now, supported by the giant gravity field beneath them, they had begun to unfurl into their trilobite forms, quickly linking together into a structure that resembled a chain link fence.

'Darn it, we have more incoming!' Erin said, staring at her screens. She put a second screen up showing more damaged wrecks from our former fleet plummeting down through the blizzard, straight towards us.

'They must have started to take over the ships that didn't manage to self-destruct in time,' Mike said.

I slammed my hand down on the fleet comm button. 'Take out as many of those infected ships as you can!' I shouted. But I already knew we'd lost, even as our combined weapons fire began to race up to meet the new arrivals. Too little, too late. Then suddenly our miniguns fell silent and that silence was shocking.

Ruby threw up her hands. 'And just to add to this real fun day, now we're completely out of ammo.'

Erin and the others sped our ships sideways out of the way of the plummeting craft as they raced past us into the top of the gravity shield and exploded into fireballs.

'Surely that has to be enough to punch through that thing?' Erin said as the multiple explosions began to thin.

But somehow the gravity shield was still glimmering with a vast oval bank of white light fog beneath it that easily had to be thirty klicks long. Spread across the shield was the burning wreckage from multiple craft and more significantly, countless thousands of the Kimprak. Already, the robotic creatures had begun to link up with each other and as they did so the trilobite chain link structure became denser and deeper.

'What the hell are they doing?' Ruby asked.

'Nothing good, you can be sure of that,' Mike replied.

The words were barely out of his mouth when the chain link structure seemed to sag, pressing downwards in a bowl shape into the shield over the shimmering fog beneath it. And even as we watched, freshly created Kimprak machines were emerging from the wreckage of the crashed ships and were scuttling across the shield to join the other trilobites. And as they did so the chain link structure grew deeper and deeper, only slowed slightly by the spray of sporadic fire from our remaining ships who still had ammo.

Everyone turned to me and I answered the unasked question in their eyes. 'I don't know what we can do, short of throwing rocks at those damned things.'

It was then that my comm light blinked on.

'What the hell? Something just hacked into our systems,' Ruby said, staring at her CIC screen.

Before I could ask her whether it could be the Kimprak, a video window appeared on the virtual cockpit and suddenly Jack was sitting there looking out at us, a large bank of strange displays behind him.

'Look, there's no time to explain the situation, Lauren, but you and the other ships need to fall back as fast as possible,' he said.

I stared at him in total confusion — apart from anything else, how could I be talking to him at all? 'But what about the Kimprak that are attacking the Angelus gravity shield?'

'Leave them to us,' Jodie said, appearing behind Jack in the feed. 'We literally have a few seconds to open fire on them before it's too late, but you've got to get out of here.'

I ignored the million questions that were instantly crowding my mind as I thumped the fleet comm channel. 'This is a direct order, everyone fall back immediately!'

Erin had already spooled up our REV drive and once again I was pressed hard back into my seat as all of our ships hurtled away as the Kimprak pressed further down into the shield.

In that single second everything seemed to happen at once; the Kimprak chain link structure burst downwards when they'd suddenly broken through; thousands of lances of blue light blazed up from the glowing fog to meet the Kimprak swarm, which was instantly vapourised; the destruction rippling through it like a scythe.

Ariel and the other surviving ships now several klicks clear of the megastructure, had begun to slow just as a vast pulse of light raced up from the glowing fog into the sky, blasting away the snowstorm in an instant.

Then like some omnipotent being upstairs had just thrown the light switch, clear blue sky broke through the thinning cloud. But it was what was happening down on the ground that stole all of our attention.

Where there had been a vast bank of glowing light there was

nothing but a snow-filled plain. Even the crystal towers had grown dark and were now dissolving back into the ground.

'Can someone please tell me what the heck just happened?' Erin asked with a bewildered expression on her face.

I stared back at her. 'To coin a phrase, I think something wonderful, although I have no bloody idea what flavour of wonderful.'

Then Jack's face appeared on the screen again. 'Thank god you made it, guys, but that was cutting it seriously close before we were able to take out those Kimprak.'

I gawped at him. 'You guys did that?'

'With some significant help. But there is too much to explain and you just need to see this for yourselves. Bring *Ariel* into land at the coordinates we're sending over to you now.'

'Yep, got them,' Ruby said, holding up a thumb.

'But how can you and Jodie even be back from E8?' Mike asked, shaking his head with a wide-eyed expression.

Jodie appeared again behind Jack, beaming at Mike. 'Like Jack said, there is so much to tell you guys and I promise we will when you get here. But for now, let's just put it this way — the Angelus secret plan to defend our world? Well, boy have they over delivered!'

'Then we're on our way,' I replied, my curiosity now on fire as I nodded towards Erin to take us back in.

A lot more slowly that we'd just left the Angelus megastructure behind, Erin began to manoeuvre *Ariel* back towards the coordinates that Jack had just given us, which seemed to be right on top of what had been Shackleton Base.

CHAPTER TWENTY-NINE

ON THE VIRTUAL COCKPIT, I wasn't sure if I was seeing things because in the middle of the Antarctica wilderness of featureless snow, there was a woman gazing up at the ship and waving both arms at us as we came in to land at the coordinates. And that woman, impossibly, was somehow Lucy, who was wearing jeans and a crop top in the middle of the freezing plain.

'You both are seeing Lucy standing there, right?' Mike said, his voice wobbling.

Erin nodded, her eyes wide as she brought *Ariel* in to land. 'And quite the choice of outfit for the conditions.'

'Good, because I was starting to wonder whether I'd lost the plot too,' I said. 'But then the obvious next question is — how can she be standing here in our world?'

'Maybe some sort of holographic projection like she uses in the Cage to talk to us?' Mike said.

'That makes sense, but if so, what's projecting it?'

Mike shrugged. 'We'll just add that to the long list of questions we're going to be asking.'

With a gentle shudder, Erin settled *Ariel* down onto the

surface. But rather than the soft crump of snow coming from outside, there was a distinct metal clang.

'Probably just solid rock beneath the snow,' Erin said, preempting my question.

'Yeah, whatever else that megastructure did, it obviously filled in that massive hole that it scooped out of the ground when it was done,' Mike said.

Ruby pulled a face. 'Their moms would be proud of them, tidying up like that after themselves.'

But I barely even registered what she was saying because I was already out of my flight seat and was pulling on my Arctic combat gear as fast I could. The others followed my lead.

As we changed, the magnitude of what had happened started to sink in. We might have won the battle and even now I wasn't quite sure how, but at what cost? I didn't have enough tears inside me for all the grief that was building up for Niki and all those other lives. Don and Zack—

A sudden thought rushed into my mind. 'Delphi, please relay my order to the remaining ships to begin searching for any survivors in escape pods that might have landed by now.'

'Order relayed,' Delphi replied.

'Do you really think anyone could have survived that battle, Lauren?' Mike asked as we all headed for the exit.

'I know it's a long shot, but we have to hang onto what little hope there is,' I replied as I pressed the button for the ramp.

The ramp started to lower and there was Lucy waiting for us with not so much as a hint of frost on her exposed tummy.

'Yeah, definitely a hologram otherwise she'd be freezing to death by now,' Mike said through my helmet's speakers.

Even though I had a full face mask on, Lucy's gaze immediately tightened on mine. Then she was striding towards me, her holographic feet somehow making very metallic clunks on the snow, her arms outstretched. And then things got really confusing as she pulled me into a tight hug, with real hands gripping my back.

'Oh my little sunflower, I'm so sorry about what happened in that battle. It was awful to watch it happening whilst we tried desperately to power up our systems to help you.'

Before I could ask her what systems, she had let go of me and had then hugged Mike, Erin, and even Ruby, who looked totally surprised, not just by Lucy's sudden physicality, but most of all by her show of affection.

I flapped a hand towards her. 'How can you be here, in our world? I know you can't be a hologram because we can physically touch you.'

Lucy did a little pirouette and gestured to herself. 'Oh you mean this little old thing that I'm wearing?' A wide grin split her face. 'This, my dears, is an Angelus android, mark fifteen body with a psionic brain that my brain has been downloaded into. And it's fully functional, if you catch my drift,' she said, winking at Mike, who snorted.

'Okay, how...?' I shook my head. 'No, let's cut straight to the chase. Not that I'm not grateful about you and the guys destroying the rest of the Kimprak swarm, but how the hell did you manage to do it?'

She gave me an even wider grin. 'I think this calls for the orientation tour, because seeing it with your own eyes will probably save several billion words trying to explain it. So if you would like to follow me.' She turned on her trainer heel and started to head away from *Ariel* into the snow.

'Lauren, maybe I should stay behind on the ship to make sure that none of those Kimprak are left over and make it down from space,' Ruby said,

'No need,' Lucy replied over her shoulder. 'We have it all taken care of and you have done more than enough work for one day. Besides, aren't you out of ammo according to what Delphi told me when I had her debrief me just now?'

I shrugged. 'You heard the lady, Ruby. Looks like no one is going to be able to duck out of this tour of the Antarctica winter wasteland.'

'I promise you that none of you are going to want to miss this,' Lucy said, making a clicking sound with her fingers.

Suddenly, in what had been a solid expanse of snow, a large metal hatch ten metres wide appeared in the ground. It silently slid open to reveal a metal ramp sloping down into a well-lit tunnel leading away towards a second door.

'What the actual fuck?' Ruby said, staring at it like we'd just discovered the entrance to Narnia.

'Okay, I get it, this is some sort of Angelus hidden underground base like our very own Eden, isn't it? And built by that quasicrystal?' Mike said.

'So very close and almost right, but not quite,' Lucy replied. 'But as I said before, let the tour do the talking rather than you all stand out here in the cold whilst I try to explain everything. I mean, it's alright for me as my android body is pumping heating fluid through my capillaries, but even with your combat suits on, it's not going to be exactly pleasant for you guys out here.'

I gestured towards the tunnel. 'Then lead the way.'

As we followed Lucy down the slope, the outer hatch slid closed behind us. At once I felt the warmth of the air. A quick check with my HUD confirmed the outside ambient temperature was a very pleasant twenty-one Celsius.

As I took off my helmet, the second door slid open. Then Jack and Jodie were standing before us, just the other side of it, both grinning like fools. I rushed towards Jack as Mike raced for Jodie, both of us throwing our arms around them and them us. I hung onto Jack, not quite daring to let go in case this was all some sort of incredible illusion.

'Yeah, I missed you too,' he said, holding onto me just as hard.

I finally pulled away from him, 'I thought we'd left you stranded in E8 forever.'

'You should be so lucky,' Jodie said, smiling at me from her place wrapped up in Mike's arms.

And then almost in unison both her and Jack's faces fell.

'Jesus, that battle, Lauren,' Jack said. 'We saw the tail end of it when our sensors came online. That was when we found out about those two Kimprak asteroids that you'd been battling.'

I grimaced. 'I haven't got the head space to even think about it, in fact I may never have.' My eyes skated away from Jodie. How could I tell her that her dad had just died? No, I needed to catch my mental breath first. I vowed to myself that I would tell her after that.

Jack took my hands in his. 'Whatever you need and whenever you need it, I'm here for you.'

I nodded, but had to force back down the sudden lump that had filled my throat. 'Okay, but right now I need distracting from my own head, so what is it exactly that you guys have got lined up for us?'

A wide smile filled Jack's face. 'Oh I think we have something here that may help do exactly that.'

He turned, taking my hand in his. 'Lucy, I think it's best if we start at the beginning, where it started for us. That will probably make the most sense to them.'

Lucy nodded. 'Okay, let this magical mystery tour begin, although to get there we will have to pass through the sanctuary.'

'The what?' Erin asked.

'Just wait until you see it,' Jodie said, beaming at her.

I immediately felt awful for not telling her straight away and I could tell Mike did too, because he just nodded and quickly looked away, not quite meeting her eyes.

We began to follow Lucy along a corridor that seem to be

constructed from a slightly iridescent form of metal that cast rainbow refractions as the light caught it.

'What sort of material is this ?' Erin asked.

'The Angelus called it krine, a crystal metal alloy with extraordinary qualities that include exceptional strength,' Jodie said. 'I was all over it like a rash when I first saw it. And that's just a tiny hint of the incredible things to come.'

'Then I'm looking forward even more to seeing this,' Erin replied.

We followed Lucy though a door with a glowing sign above it filled with Angelus geometric symbols and stepped into an oval room. It was lined with seats and had transparent curved walls that led seamlessly up, flowing into a transparent domed roof. Outside there appeared to be a shaft made of more of the krine metal, lit with horizontal yellow crystal light strips, glowing softly.

'If you'd like to take your seats, the gravity dampeners in the room will protect you from the acceleration G-forces.'

'You mean this is some sort of vehicle?' I asked.

'Hell yes and it's just like something from the *Forbidden Planet* movie that you love so much, Lauren,' Jack replied, grinning.

I allowed myself to smile back at him and I took my seat along with the others. 'Oh, now you're talking my language.'

No sooner had we all sat down than the light strips started to whisk past as our ride began to plummet.

Just as I'd begun to get my head round how deep we seemed to be heading, with the sort of right angle shift of direction that *Ariel* was capable of, we were suddenly shooting sideways towards a growing pool of light at the end of the tunnel.

Mike, Erin, Ruby and I let out a collective gasp as we emerged into an enormous chamber that had to be at least five kilometres long and almost as wide again, our ride now transformed into a flying car speeding towards the other end of the vast chamber.

Overhead, large, glowing yellow dome structures in the curving ceiling gave the chamber the feel of being bathed in sunlight.

But it was what was in the distance that immediately drew the eye. A cityscape of krine metal towers stood towering up towards the top of the domed roof, most linked together by wide floating walkways. In the foreground a perfectly landscaped parkland that included forests, rivers and even a large lake stretched away before us.

Ruby whistled. 'Holy hell, this is one mother of an alien base.'

Jack and Jodie exchanged wry smiles.

'What?' I asked, looking between them.

'Let's just say that this is the tip of the metaphorical iceberg,' Jack said. 'There's dozens of other chambers just as big as this one. The others include industrial zones, a lab section like you wouldn't believe and a medical block that is beyond mind-bending, plus a whole lot more. There's also a huge complex of agricultural biodomes for food production. How big did you say this place was again, Lucy?'

'Thirty kilometres long by about fifteen wide. The bulk of what you can't access are the engineering zones that help to make all this magic possible.'

'Wow, a sort of supersized Eden, in other words,' Erin said.

'Once again, even that analogy doesn't begin to do this place justice,' Jodie said. 'Think Eden, but on a much grander scale and with a serious trick up its sleeve.'

After everything we'd already been through, I was feeling more than a little overwhelmed by the minute as we reached the city and began to speed through it. But unlike a normal city, this place was so completely empty that tumbleweed blowing through it wouldn't have looked out of place. Now we were up close to the towers I could see they were exquisite pieces of architecture made from flowing shapes and organic curves that resembled giant sculptures more than buildings. And each of them was dotted with countless thousands of large, round portholes, many tinted to give the effect of vast stained glass windows lit from within.

As we cleared the city the curved wall reared up before us as we sped towards an exit tunnel. Another minute later we sped out into a second chamber that literally made my jaw drop. There, hanging in the middle of the chamber was what appeared to be a blue dwarf star and it made everything else, even the towering buildings of the last zone, look tiny in comparison. It reached all the way to the ceiling and floor that was as deep again and curved round it. Ribbons of energy flowed from the star into a vast array of giant spherical-shaped electrodes mounted around it. More of the boulevard walkways also ringed the structure in dozens of layers.

I turned to Lucy, eyes wide as I pointed towards it. 'Are you powering this place with a bloody star?'

'Oh it's much more powerful than that,' she said, winking at Jack and Mike.

'Will you all please tell us what the heck this place is already?' Erin said.

'Patience,' Jack said, 'Because you are about to see for yourself.' He nodded towards the blue dwarf star that we were racing towards. As we neared it I could see the surface was rippling like water, as if the light was coming from somewhere beneath the surface of a very opaque swimming pool.

'Okay, get ready because we're about to pass though the event horizon and you'll experience a brief tingling sensation,' Lucy said.

'Event horizon, please tell me that's not actually some sort of singularity?' Mike said.

'So close, but you're still not quite there yet,' Jodie said, holding her thumb and forefinger a fraction apart and grinning at him.

Our transport pod swept towards it and as we passed through it I felt a brief feeling of static not just passing over my skin, but actually through my entire body. For a moment it was like we were passing through thick, viscous water that was now flowing over our transparent canopy, distorting the view of the chamber outside with a series of dancing refracted patterns. Then we were through what had to be some sort of membrane into a star-filled space of an inky black night sky.

And then the next moment we weren't.

Literally appearing out of nowhere, our transport pod was suddenly slowing as it approached a curved tunnel made from crystal. Our ride entered it and a moment later was pulling up to somewhere that was like an alien version of a Tube station but one that was also made from crystal.

As our ride slowed to a stop next to a doorway, I realised that as weird as this all was, suddenly it felt like a very familiar form of weird.

I stared at Lucy as the door from the pod opened. 'We're in E8 aren't we?'

She beamed at me. 'You see, I knew you'd work it out. Yes, it absolutely is E8, or to be more precise, a sphere of it contained within your spacetime that we just crossed over from to enter it.'

'So this is like a portal straight to E8?' Mike asked.

'Better to think of it as a bubble of the higher reality that exists within our universe,' Jodie said.

It literally felt like my brain was starting to melt and was in danger of dribbling out of my ears.

I shook my head. 'I'm not sure I can quite get my head around all of this, let alone the implications.'

'That's why we wanted you to see this for yourself,' Jack replied. 'We've both had brain ache since we first arrived here.'

'Talking of which, how did you guys get here?' I asked.

'If you'd like to follow me it will all become a lot clearer, I promise,' Jodie said as we stepped out of the pod.

We followed her and Jack to the closed door that looked fused to the walls. But of course this was E8, where anything was possible, so as we approached the door it simply dissolved. And through it was a familiar round hall filled with avatars, who all looked at us as we entered like we were VIP guests at our very own surprise party.

Mike gaped. 'So the E8 hall is actually here?'

'If you mean the hall where you left us in E8, then yes it is,' Jack said. 'One moment we were trapped in there and the next...' He pointed to the ceiling.

I looked up to what had been a tessellated ceiling, but where now sat what had to be all the micro minds glowing softly, sitting in the recesses in the dome like some sort of crystal-jewelled planetarium, dancing slowly with soft, multicoloured lights. That also explained the lack of the quasicrystal in the middle of the room, suggesting the micro minds had broken apart to take up their individual places in the recesses that I now realised had been designed for them.

Lucy gestured towards herself and all the other avatars, including Poseidon, all with warm smiles on their faces. 'Welcome to the consciousness that was designed to run this—'

Jack made a coughing sound and shook his head. 'Not yet, Lucy. Let's show them like you did us because it will make more of an impact.'

'Yes, definitely more show and less tell,' Jodie added.

Lucy nodded. 'In that case, if you would like to follow me, guys?'

She skirted around the edge of the hall, the other avatars

parting for us as we passed among them and headed towards the door opposite that we had tried but failed to open. But like the first door, it dissolved away to reveal another, much larger elongated oval room with control consoles at least a hundred metres long. Towards the far end of it was a flat, glowing disc mounted into the floor. Like the vehicle that we'd ridden in to get here the walls were made from glass, but much thicker and with what appeared to be closed metal shutters beyond them.

But as I stepped through I felt the tingle of static pass through my body again.

'We just stepped out of that E8 sphere didn't we?' I said.

Lucy nodded. 'Correct. And as your spacetime is a fairly fluid concept when it comes to E8, that doorway actually just led us to an area towards the front of this...' She caught Jack shaking his head at her. 'Um, facility,' she continued.

'So this is obviously some sort of control centre based on all the screens that we saw in the video link,' Mike said. 'Presumably, this is where the weapons systems are operated from that you just used to take out that Kimprak swarm.'

'Correct,' Jodie said. 'And the controls are like nothing you have ever experienced — they can even link directly into your mind.'

'Yeah, that was quite the rush when I first tried it,' Jack said.

'So we were right,' Ruby said. 'This is some sort of Angelus super weapon that we can attack the Kimprak mothership with.'

Jack and Mike exchanged a long look with Lucy.

'I think it's time to put them out of their misery, don't you?' Lucy said, smiling.

She swung her hands round in a pantomime gesture of waving a wand and lights lit up on a number of pillars as they began to scroll downwards. At the same time the walls beyond the glass began to slide down past the room.

'Citadel activated,' Delphi's voice announced.

'Going up, first stop ladies underwear,' Lucy said, grinning at us.

I stared at her. 'You installed Delphi in here?'

'I thought it might help you in terms of an interface with the systems of this place for you guys and as I had all the source code for her, it was a doddle to do.'

'Okay, so presumably the Citadel is what it sounds like and is some sort of fortified control bunker?' Ruby asked.

Jodie immediately caught Lucy's eye before she could answer. 'Show not tell, remember,' she said, rubbing the side of her nose.

Lucy grinned as the lights on the pillars slowed to a stop and the Citadel approached a metal-domed room.

Jack exchanged a look with Jodie, then cleared his throat. 'Delphi, please lower blast shutters.'

'Lowering blast shutters,' the AI replied.

With the sound of a heavy locking mechanism being released, the krine panels beyond the glass walls began to slide away to reveal a view of the Antarctic landscape with a bright blue sky overhead.

'Wow, very cool, but I don't remember seeing that structure on the surface when we landed,' Erin said.

'That's because there wasn't anything there,' Lucy replied. 'This whole room known as the Citadel, has just been raised to the surface.'

'But there was absolutely no sensation of movement,' Mike said.

'That's because there are inertia dampeners built into the Citadel,' Lucy replied.

I narrowed my eyes. 'Okay, why would you need something to reduce G-forces in an underground base?'

Mike and Jodie's grins grew annoyingly, *we know something you don't,* wide.

'I think it's time for the big reveal, Lucy,' Jack said.

Lucy nodded. 'Delphi, please lower the MPP shield.'

'MPP?' Ruby asked.

'The Massive Photonic Projector,' she replied.

'I'm sorry I asked,' Ruby said, shaking her head.

'Think of it as a hologram that you can touch,' Jodie said.

'Seriously?' I asked, staring at her.

'There is so much that we need to tell you, including how this whole place was flat-packed into that quasicrystal at the middle of our world. You probably saw that how it was able to build was stored inside it by transforming the material it mined from the surface?'

'We certainly did,' Mike replied, nodding.

'And that is one conversation that I'm so looking forward to having with you guys later to fully brief you,' Lucy said. 'But it's time for that big reveal now.'

'Get ready to have your minds well and truly blown,' Jack said as he indicated that we should look out of the glass walls towards the far end of the room.

I honestly thought there was nothing left that could leave me with an even greater sense of awe than I'd experienced already as I gazed out at the snowy plain.

I was wrong.

With a shimmer, what had been a flat, featureless expanse vanished. Now instead, I saw a two-klicks long nose section of what could only be a spaceship.

Erin, Ruby and I pretty much all gasped in unison.

'What the bloody hell?' I finally asked when I'd found the ability to speak again.

Jack grinned at me. 'Oh you haven't seen anything yet, Lauren.' He took me gently by the shoulders and turned me round to stare at what had been behind us, which Erin and Ruby were already staring slack-jawed at.

Then I let out a small *oooh* as I took in what was before me.

On the far side of the glass wall, stretching away in the opposite direction was indeed a spaceship but also one that was totally off the scale. A massive central hull stretched away in a dart shape growing wider towards the horizon. In the distance an oval elliptical wing section encircled what was obviously the rear hull. Also towards the rear of the ship were two huge, angular, nacelles jet-style engines that stretched forward from the elliptical wing section on either side of the vast ship, curved spiky panels sticking up and down from them. But out of all those wonders what immediately caught my eye was the massive dome section poking out of the hull at its widest point.

I immediately pointed towards it. 'That dome shape, is that anything to do with that E8 sphere by any chance?'

'In one,' Lucy said, beaming at me. 'And those conduits that you saw drawing energy from it are what powers this entire starship. As you can probably imagine, the electricity bill for something this big and the E8 field is more than enough to power it all.'

Erin turned a full three-sixty, waving her hands at the spectacle around us. 'And you're telling us that this behemoth of a ship can actually fly?'

'It will when its systems are fully powered up, which will unfortunately take some considerable time,' Lucy said. 'You see, with a starship of this nature it's not a case of just flicking the on switch, especially as some of the key engineering zones are still being reconstructed.'

'But at least it will be on time to take on the Kimprak asteroid mothership?,' Ruby said.

Lucy thinned her lips. 'Yes, but there is a caveat. Among the micro minds that the Overseers managed to destroy was one in particular that should have built the main weapons systems. Those would easily have been powerful enough to take out that entire asteroid ship with one strike. So, very unfortunately for us they are missing from this starship.'

'But what about all those energy beam blasts that you vaporised the Kimprak with? They were utterly incredible,' Ruby asked.

'That was actually this ship's point defence system,' Jack said. 'Still damned impressive, but not powerful enough to deliver the killer blow to the Kimprak mothership.'

Lucy nodded. 'That's why you're still going to need your X-craft fleet. The good news is this ship has massive hangars, certainly enough to handle a few thousand craft, so easily big enough. You can load all of the X-craft fleet onboard if you want to and then once this ship is flight ready we can head out to intercept the Kimprak.'

'You mean with some sort of warp drive to tackle them before they have even entered the solar system?' Erin asked.

'Actually this ship does have a jump drive system using the E8 field to completely fold space between two points in the universe.'

I stared at her. 'You mean we now have a starship capable of instantly travelling anywhere in the universe we want to go?'

'Normally, yes. But even with an E8 field powering the jump drive, for longer range destinations it needs to do it in a number of smaller hops, with the system having to recharge between jumps.'

'Just like *Battlestar Galactica* in other words?' I asked.

'Precisely,' Lucy replied, smiling.

'Hang on I heard the word *normally* in there that this ship can use a jump drive?,' Mike said.

'That's the problem, because guess what another one of the micro minds that the Overseers managed to destroy was meant to build?' Jack said.

'The jump drive by any chance?' Erin said.

'In one and although this starship is almost fully capable,

there are a few critical systems that are going to remain offline for the final battle,' Lucy said.

'But still,' I said, gesturing round me. 'This beast is incredible. But you keep calling it a starship, surely something this impressive has a name?'

'It does, but in Angelus it sounds like someone clearing their nose after a heavy cold, so I suggest you put your heads together and come up with a name more sympathetic to the human ear.'

'Oh I'm sure we can think of something,' I replied, smiling at her. But then my eyes strayed to the blue sky visible through the windows above the ship and my smile faded. 'I just wish that the cost hadn't been so high to retrieve this ship. We lost so many people.'

This time I steeled myself and looked directly at Jodie. I couldn't delay telling her any longer.

'Look, there's no easy way to tell you this, but I'm afraid Niki and his crew didn't make it.'

Her hands flew to her mouth. 'No, no, no!'

Mike was immediately by her side, his arms wrapped round her.

Jack stared at me, his face pale. 'What exactly happened up there before our sensors came online, Lauren?'

'It was the bravest thing I ever witnessed in my life, that's what. Niki and many of our fleet, including the TR-3B crews, all activated their self-destructs to try and take out all the Kimprak that had infected their ships rather than let them make it to the ground.'

Jodie's eyes blossomed with tears. 'But Dad can't be gone.'

My heart was breaking along with everyone else's in that room as we watched Jodie fall apart. Suddenly, despite everything it felt like a very hollow victory against the Kimprak.

But then Lucy, who'd been battling back tears too, was

suddenly alert. 'Hang on, I've just received an incoming transmission, Lauren, and it's intended for you.'

The circle in the floor at the front of the citadel glowed into life and suddenly the hologram of a Grey alien was standing in the room. Immediately it turned towards me and pain briefly filled my head before the sensation faded away again.

'*Lauren Stelleck it is good to see you again,*' the Grey said directly into my mind.

'You know who I am?' I replied as the others stared at me, obviously unable to hear the telepathic transmission.

'*Indeed. You encountered one of our hive minds that been captured and was being held at a facility that I believe your species refer to as Area 51.*'

'But he died? So how could you know about that?'

'*Because we are all linked via a hive consciousness and we are one. And you did our brother a great service by ending his life that day, something for which we will always be indebted. And it is that debt we hope to repay to you now.*'

'How exactly?' I asked as the others continued to watch me.

But Lucy held up her hand. 'Hang on, just adjusting the mind control interface so the others can listen in on this conversation.' One of the consoles lit up. 'Okay, please continue.'

The Grey nodded. 'By the time we knew that the Kimprak had sent a scouting force we were too late to take direct action,' he said. Everyone's eyes widened as they heard him too for the first time. 'However, we were in time to be able to beam many of the survival capsules that the crews had taken shelter in before their self-destruct sequences detonated. Unfortunately, we didn't arrive in time to rescue the crews of the craft you refer to as TR-3Bs. However, many of the humans in what you refer to as X-craft, we were able to teleport onboard to our own craft just before your ships exploded.'

Erin snapped her fingers. 'Those pulses of light that we saw just before the reactors blew?'

'Yes, indeed they are the signature of a teleport jump,' the Grey said. 'And we can transfer them back to you if you could provide us coordinates?'

'And does this include the human known as Niki Lindén?' Mike asked, holding tight onto Jodie.

'Yes, he is among the survivors of the battle.'

Jodie partly collapsed and Mike just had time to catch her and keep her upright, as tears of relief filled my own eyes.

I stared at the Grey's hologram, unable to speak as a wave of a hundred emotions crashed through me all at once. There were survivors — lots of them — and this changed everything. Thankfully, Lucy stepped in as I stared at the alien, barely able to think, let alone speak.

'Yes, I will transmit a homing beacon for you to home in on so you can land in one of the hangar bays,' she said.

The Grey appeared to look at the bridge round us. 'Do I take that to mean that you have successfully activated the quasicrystal seeded at the heart of the Earth?'

'Yes, but only because of the extraordinary men and women that I'm here with,' Lucy said.

The Grey's gaze swept over everyone standing in the room and then he nodded. 'Then this has been a good day for our universe. One last thing before we end this transmission, the human you just asked about, Niki Lindén, is very keen to talk to you.'

Then before I could respond his hologram appeared and he was looking out at us. 'Well this is novel.'

Jodie burst into laughter. 'Oh god, you don't know how good it is to see you, Dad. We thought...' she flapped a hand towards him.

'Yes, I can guess what you thought. So I take it we won, Lauren?'

I finally found my words as I smiled through my tears. 'We did, but it was feeling like a hollow victory until just now when we heard that you were all safe.'

Niki's face fell. 'Some but not all. And none of those brave pilots of the TR-3Bs, who self-destructed their ships ahead of us.'

A thought came surging from the back of my mind. 'Don and Zack! Their escape pods ejected and we sent the rest of our remaining ships to search for them.' I spun round to Lucy. 'You need to contact our ships to find out if they survived.'

Lucy gave a sharp nod. 'On it now.' She tilted her head to one side as though she was listening to something, before looking at me again. 'I'm afraid that Zack was killed outright on impact. Don is alive and has just been recovered by a Pangolin, but he's badly injured and needs urgent medical attention.'

I spun round to look at Jack. 'Can you help him?'

He nodded. 'Time to put that state of the art medical facility to the test, Lucy.'

She nodded. 'We can put him in a stasis pod whilst we attend to his injuries, along with the other survivors who need treatment.'

'Then bring them all here as fast as possible,' I said. 'But Jack, this will be too much for you alone.'

He nodded. 'Yeah, I could really do with some help. Could you contact Eden to transport over as many medics as possible, Lucy?'

'Of course. Also, myself and the other avatars will assist you in the meantime,' Lucy replied.

Suddenly I felt lightheaded and didn't so much sit as almost collapse into a chair.

Jack was immediately by my side. 'Are you okay, Lauren?'

'I will be now, but like we are fond of saying, it's just been one hell of a day at the office.'

He took my hands in his and nodded. 'Hasn't it just.' Then he turned to Lucy. 'I don't suppose this starship does good strong coffee? I suspect our commander could do with a large cup of it.'

'Of course. I can synthesise the finest roasts of any roast you can care to imagine.'

But I held up a hand. 'If it's all the same to you, a Lapsang Souchong would so hit the spot now. It's always been my favourite brew for shock, even the good kind.'

'And that too,' Lucy replied, smiling.

'I would have thought a stiff whiskey after everything we've been through,' Ruby said.

'Oh I intend to have one of those too later,' I replied.

I sat back in the chair, staring out at the vast ship around us and just beginning my long mental journey to fully process what had actually just happened and how it changed everything.

CHAPTER THIRTY

JACK and I sat having a picnic on the embankment of the lake near Alice's log cabin at Eden on a perfectly simulated summer's day in the underground cavern. It was also the first time I'd seen him in weeks since the battle with the Kimprak.

I put down Tom's copy of *The Tempest* that I'd been reading and stretched out my toes on the picnic blanket. Then I sat up and took a sip of the blueberry and banana smoothie that Jack had conjured up for me in the kitchen. I felt a sense of contented stillness as I gazed at the ducks paddling their way through the reed beds looking for food.

Jack stretched out and looked up at me. 'So how are you doing there?'

'To be honest, much better for a bit of decompressing after spending the last few weeks in the Angelus starship. I know I've barely stopped trying to get my head around everything there and I know you certainly haven't.'

'Yes, but I've also been like a very happy pig in clover studying the ancient Angelus artefacts throughout that ship. I've been working with Poseidon, who has been the best guide that I could have asked for, especially now that his memory has been fully restored, reversing the damage that the Kimprak virus did. He even introduced me to an Angelus museum that turned out to be an absolute treasure trove for understanding their history and culture. There's several lifetimes' worth of material there alone for me to research. I've already asked Alice if I can have a team of assistants to help me start cataloguing everything.'

'You make it sound less like a spaceship and more like a regular city. And based on that report that you circulated, I'm beginning to understand why.'

'Yes, a multi-generation starship, designed to helped nurture life wherever the Angelus found it. To think that so many of the Angelus lived out their whole lives onboard it, followed by their descendants for twenty hundred thousand years is absolutely jaw-dropping.'

'And have you learnt anything more about where they all disappeared to? Even now, Lucy seems vague about it.'

'That's because she doesn't actually know,' Jack replied.

'But I thought the virus damage had been reversed?'

'Yes it has, but the memory archives that included the origin of the Angelus seem to have been deliberately wiped by her creators. The one reference I was able to discover in the museum was a sculpture called the *Day of Transmutation,* with figures floating up into the air. That was apparently commissioned to honour the day that the Angelus disappeared. Beyond that, the trail goes cold.'

'So the Angelus still have some secrets that they don't want anyone to discover just yet,' I replied.

'Indeed, although at least we now know about them visiting Earth at the dawn of our civilisation, which was when they left their generation starship behind for us to one day inherit.'

'Yes, in our hour of need,' I replied. 'It's like they anticipated the threat of something like the Kimprak arriving in the universe one day.'

'They had a whole science dedicated to a sort of future history called the Procession. According to Poseidon, they used quantum computers that ran simulations that were able to model the kind of threats that were likely to emerge in the universe. Part of that plan was sending out starships like that one to protect the flickering flame of life wherever they found it. This galaxy is apparently littered with Guardian micro minds, keeping an eye out for signs of anything bad. And it's one of those that alerted Lucy and the other micro minds here on Earth that a Kimprak force was headed our way. That message should have been the start of rolling out the big guns in the form of this ship that the Angelus had hidden at the core of the planet.'

I pulled a face. 'Just a shame that message also contained a Kimprak virus that also invaded their systems.'

'Yes, but at least finally that's behind us and we have our hands on the big prize that the Angelus intended us to have all along.'

'Without making it easy for us, it has to be said.'

'It was never meant to be that difficult. The plan was that the micro minds would alert us when the time came and then automatically boot up the ship from the quasicrystal from somewhere that no one would ever unintentionally discover, aka the core of our planet.'

'Did you hear what Mike was saying about that? He thinks the unique frequency that our planet sends out into the universe, Earth Song, has always been there, and to a certain extent is influenced by the quasicrystal sitting at the middle of our world and fine tuning it. For all these years since it was first placed there, our world has literally been singing its heart out into the cosmos.'

'There is more than a bit of poetry to that,' Jack replied with a smile. 'But the fact that the Angelus folded it away as a sort of multidimensional flatpack in E8 still blows my mind.'

'It blows everyone's minds,' I replied. 'And like the typical flatpack a few key pieces, like weapons and a jump drive are missing. And it's not like we can go back to the manufacturer to ask for spares.'

Jack snorted. 'Isn't that the truth.'

I reached over and took one of the sandwiches that Jack had prepared and took a large bite. I immediately pulled a face at him as my tastebuds processed what they were actually eating.

'Jam and peanut butter? Seriously?'

'Hey, a P&J is one of the great culinary sensations of the world.'

'Not in my head it isn't.' I put the sandwich back down with a slight shudder.

'Heads-up, we've got company,' Jack said, nodding towards the house.

I glanced over to see Alice and Lucy, the latter resplendent in her new android body, heading towards us.

Lucy had insisted on travelling back with us to Eden. We'd already been hearing on the grapevine about her wild, party girl antics in the Rock Garden. There was even a rumour that she had hooked up with one of the security guards, making full use of her anatomically complete, fully functional android body. Knowing that Lucy could run without a charge for a week at a time, I just hoped the poor guy could still walk this morning.

'I hope you won't mind us gatecrashing your picnic,' Alice said as she reached us in her wheelchair. 'We just wanted to get you up to speed with what's been happening since you left the Angelus starship.'

We both nodded as Lucy eyed our sandwiches. 'Do you mind?' she asked, practically licking her lips. 'I'm rather enjoying the fact I can properly discover food after all this time, thanks to this inbuilt molecular processing plant.'

'Knock yourself out,' Jack said.

She beamed at him. 'Great — I've so got the munchies this morning.'

'I wonder why?' Alice said, rising her eyebrows at us. She'd obviously heard the same rumours that we had.

Lucy's smile reached her ears as she grabbed a sandwich and tucked in. A blissed out expression immediately filled her face. 'God, these are *sooo* good.'

'At least someone enjoys my culinary skills,' Jack said, raising an eyebrow.

'Yeah, yeah, yeah,' I replied, dismissing him with my hand. 'Anyway, what's the news?'

'First off, Don is finally out of intensive care after his heart transplant and is making good progress.' Alice said. 'The prognosis from the team is that he should be able to make a full recovery from the injury that would have killed him if it hadn't have been for that extraordinary Angelus nano technology.'

'Yes, the ability to literally grow him a new heart was absolutely incredible,' Jack said. 'It was touch and go there for a moment, but their medical nanobots will utterly transform the whole field of medical research. Anyway, it's great to hear that he's pulled through.'

'It is,' Alice replied. 'He's also asked to join us, which is quite a surprise and something I wanted your opinion on, Lauren.'

'I'd be more than happy for him to join the team if that's what Don really wants. He's a good guy and we could certainly do with his skills.'

'We could and it will help us with opening up a line of permanent dialogue with the USSF, which is about time. We should never have been fighting between ourselves all this time, but we have a real opportunity now to change things, with his help.'

'This is all down to the Overseers,' I replied. 'But surely there must be a real threat that they will intercede again, playing sides off against each other for their own warped agenda?'

Alice shook her head. 'I wouldn't be so sure. According to all our agents there have been no active missions detected. Even Colonel Alvarez is nowhere to be seen.' She frowned.

'But that sounds like good news?' Jack said.

'It is, but I can't help but feel they are up to something,' Alice replied.

I shrugged. 'Does it really matter when we now have an Angelus starship at our disposal?'

'Maybe not, but I would never rule out the Overseers' ability to cause us serious headaches.'

Lucy, who'd been munching her way through the pile of sandwiches, nodded. 'We will need to be on the lookout. Anyway, I wanted to let you know that Troy arrived at Antarctica with the first squadron of one hundred X-craft, which have all been loaded onboard the starship and barely touched the sides of one of the six hangers.'

'So we are literally going to have our own equivalent of an aircraft carrier?' Jack said.

'Basically, yes,' Alice replied. 'We can now take the fight to the enemy with a serious amount of firepower to deploy whenever we need to.'

'So the billion dollar question is — will we be flight ready to take on the Kimprak mothership when it gets here, Lucy?' I asked.

'Everything is on track for that, so I'd say yes. But a more pertinent question is how hamstrung the starship is without its main weapon systems and will it be enough to take down the Kimprak?'

'I really wouldn't write off those incredible point defence systems in operation — they looked pretty deadly from what we witnessed,' I replied.

'Yes, with a small Kimprak scout swarm. But multiply that attack by millions and you'll get closer to the level of the considerable challenge that we'll be facing in a pitch battle with that asteroid mothership. If even a few of the Kimprak get through it could prove devastating. So it really is important that we have as many X-craft as possible to bring to the fight.'

Alice nodded. 'Thankfully our industrial 3D printers are running at maximum and we hope to be able to replace all the craft that were lost in the skirmish within four months. The next thing to do will be to reach out to the USSF forces to create a plan to combine our forces when the final battle comes. Hopefully, even the Overseers will see that tackling the Kimprak by themselves is a zero sum game when we work together. Our combined resources will create a major fighting force to take the enemy on.'

'Do we have any idea whether they know about our Angelus starship yet?'

'Not beyond the fact that there was a significant Angelus device in Antarctica, that to all intents and purposes appears to have disappeared. If Alvarez can play his cards close to his chest, so can we. I think we should reveal its presence only when we have to. I for one wouldn't trust him not to try and capture it for use by the Overseers.'

'Then that makes two of us,' I said. 'But surely they are bound to eventually send out expeditionary forces to the site just to check if they can find anything?'

'With the starship's Photonic Mass Projector, our hope is that they will just assume that the Kimprak succeeded in destroying it,' Alice replied.

'Yes, that's a narrative that even their military satellites support, thanks to a little help from yours truly,' Lucy said, 'I made a point of looking at what footage the satellites had already recorded and slightly doctoring it. Now all they will see is a bright pulse of light as the Kimprak destroyed whatever was sitting down there on the ground, before being taken out themselves by sustained weapons fire from what was left of our fleet.'

'So as far as Alvarez and his masters are concerned, there is no longer any credible threat to concern themselves with, especially as there has been no further unexplained neutrino activity at that location,' Alice said.

'If that's true, I still can't quite believe that we've managed to pull off hiding a starship of that size.'

Jack frowned. 'Look, I don't know about the rest of you, but I really think it's about time we came up with a name rather than just keep calling it starship.'

Alice nodded. 'I agree and I feel it's only fair that you and rest of the team have that honour.'

But Jack was shaking his head. 'Actually I've already discussed this with the others and we feel that it should be Lauren's call.'

'Really? But honestly if you guys have got any suggestions, I'd love to hear them.'

'You're telling me that all the pieces of paper I found screwed up in the bin in our room weren't you trying to come up with a name already?' He gave me a straight look.

I laughed. 'Okay, busted.'

'Then let's hear your top choice?' Lucy said.

I held up my hands. 'Okay, okay. First off, I need to explain my suggestion though. To start with, it's partly to honour Tom and his love of Shakespeare, a specific play in fact. It also fits in with the whole *Ariel* from *A Midsummer Night's Dream* vibe, although it is a different play. The other reason for choosing it is something you said, Jack, when I first saw the interior of the Angelus starship.'

'Which was?' he asked.

'You said it reminded you of my favourite old sci-fi film, *Forbidden Planet*. But do you know what story that film was based on?'

Jack eyes widened as he gazed down at the book I'd been reading. 'Of course, *The Tempest*.'

I smiled at him. 'It seems that my educating you about all things sci-fi has been paying off. So what do you think of it as a name for our starship?'

The others exchanged a look and then they all nodded.

'I absolutely love it,' Lucy said, clapping her hands together. 'And much better than the original Angelus name, which will leave you with spittle all over your clothes trying to pronounce it.'

'I think it's perfect,' Jack said.

'Oh it's more perfect than you realise, Lauren,' Alice said. 'You won't know this but it was actually Tom who suggested *Ariel* as the name for your ship, so I know he would get a huge kick out of this.'

That little nugget of information immediately filled my throat with a stone and all I could do was manage a nod.

'There's a line he sometimes used to quote, which I always loved. What was it?' Alice continued. She screwed her eyes up in thought. 'Ah yes, this is it...*we are such stuff as dreams are made on, and our little life is rounded with a sleep.*'

Now tears filled my eyes as I thought just what a fitting epitaph that line was for Tom.

Alice caught my expression and exchanged a look with Lucy. 'I think it's time for us to let these two enjoy their picnic in peace. Come on, I promised you a portion of my world famous gumbo and I'm even going to show you how to cook it.'

Lucy nodded, but reached out and touched my hand, her

gaze holding mine with real tenderness in her eyes. And then she was blinking back tears too as she turned away with Alice and headed back to the house. Yes, my AI friend more than understood how I felt right now.

'Are you okay?' Jack asked gently.

I gave him a sad smile. 'Yes, yes I am.' I let out a little sigh. 'Anyway, let me have another attempt at one of your P&J sandwiches. Maybe I need to give them a second try.'

'Now you're talking!' He went to hand me one and then we both saw that there were none left. 'Ah, I think Lucy has cleaned us out.'

I gave Jack a straight look. 'Oh what a shame.'

He burst out laughing and pulled me to him, and I felt the sadness of a moment ago melt away. Yes, maybe *Tempest* really was the perfect name in so many, many ways.

LINKS

Do please leave that all important review for ***Earth Scream***
here: https://geni.us/EarthScream
And are you ready to preorder the final page-turning instalment
in the series, **Earth Roar?**

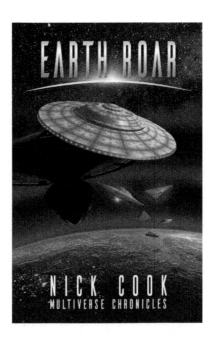

The final instalment of the **Earth Song** series heralds the arrival of the Kimprak asteroid ship in our solar system. With the Angelus starship Tempest almost ready to be deployed, the stage is set for an epic final confrontation where everything is on the line as the destiny of our species hangs in the balance. You can preorder **Earth Roar** here: https://geni.us/EarthRoar

Meanwhile, whilst you are waiting for the final book, you may want to consider reading the **Fractured Light** trilogy which is also part of the Multiverse Chronicles. This continues the story of the AI *Sentinel* six years after the events covered in **The Signal.** A secret hidden in human DNA is about to be unlocked, but can college students Jake and his underground hacker friend Chloe solve the mystery before reality itself starts to break down?

The **Fractured Light** trilogy is here: https://geni.us/
FracturedLightTrilogy

AUTHOR NOTES

And so the penultimate book in the Earth Song series has drawn to a close and I'm sure you can tell that I had an absolute blast writing it. It would be fair to say that I completely geeked out with this story, referencing among other things one of my all-time favourite sci-fi movies, *Forbidden Planet*. That film will always occupy a soft spot in my heart and I will never forget the impact that seeing it for the first time had on me as a teenager. For me it is the very definition of classic sci-fi, and the extraordinary Krell machine beneath the surface of the planet completely lit up my imagination.

In many ways the spark first lit by that extraordinary film burst into serious fire with Earth Scream. I think many sci-fi writers will tell you that there is a combination of books, movies and TV series that first got them hooked on the genre. So, yes, *Forbidden Planet* and *2001 - A Space Odyssey*, along with the *Dune* books and anything by Arthur C. Clarke and Isaac Asimov I would cite as responsible for setting me on the path that would one day lead to me writing my own sci-fi books. And in so many ways that lineage of inspiration can be found in the pages of this book.

As you will know by now, Earth Song is first and foremost a character-centred story. I for one find it hard to engage with a story if I don't really care about the characters and this is something I've strived to do in all of these books. Hopefully, by this point in the series you are completely invested in them, particularly Lauren's journey. However, it's the background story arc that has truly been revealed in this story with the discovery of *Tempest*. To say that I have been looking forward to this particular big reveal would be a serious understatement. As an author it's a bit like knowing a secret that you aren't allowed to tell anyone, but here we are at last, heading towards the finale.

I have actually been modelling the *Tempest* in a 3D package which will be used in the final cover for this book and also the series that comes next. The problem I have now is not tipping off readers new to Earth Song with a great big starship on the final book for the series, so I will need to come up with a subtle solution that doesn't give the game away, perhaps with just a hint of the vast starship lurking in the background and lit in a silhouette, as you can see for yourself on the previous page.

With the *Tempest*, Lauren and the team have finally got their hands on some serious Angelus technology. Even partly crippled with its jump drive and main weapons system offline, it is still the stuff of sci-fi dreams. And humanity will need every aspect of its advanced systems to take the fight to the Kimprak, if our planet has a chance of survival.

The coming battle is something I've been planning for years and now everything is in place to make it suitably epic, so keep an eye out for book seven and the grand finale.

In terms of locations, Angkor Wat is somewhere that I visited with my wife Karen when travel was still a thing pre-pandemic —

it is a truly extraordinary place. Admittedly, as far as I know it doesn't have a micro mind buried in the main temple, but if you ever get a chance do visit it because it's truly exceptional.

Of course in Earth Scream, Lauren finally gets to return to Jodrell Bank and see her old boss Steve again as featured in *The Signal*. I absolutely loved revisiting this site and discovering how Steve would react when he got an insight into what Lauren had been up to. That was just so enjoyable to write and to discover what happened when I brought old characters and new together, which even I wasn't sure until I wrote it how it would all play out.

The only location I haven't visited is Antarctica for much the same reason as Lauren, namely just how expensive it is to visit because of the considerable logistics involved. But it is absolutely on my bucket list and we plan to go there one day in a post-pandemic world.

Anyway, this is where I thank everyone involved. As always a huge thank you to my tirelessly working editors who help to make this all possible, namely Beverly Sanford and Catherine Coe, who once again bought that extra level of polish to my work and as always helped to really make it shine. I should also take this opportunity for a separate shout out to Chloe De Burgh, who is the actor bringing the audiobooks to life. If you haven't heard them, give them a listen because Chloe has done an amazing job and has made the characters feel real.

Also thank you so much for your support — it means everything and certainly motivates me to keep writing. I have so much planned for the Multiverse Chronicles that interweave each series into a far larger story. But for now this series is about to conclude in the next book and I hope to see you there for what comes next.

Right, time to get back to it and start planning for the final book in the series, *Earth Roar*.

I will hopefully see you again soon on a voyage into the imagination, where anything and everything is possible.

Nick Cook, June 2021